Praise for
The Immortals of Meluha

'Shiva rocks . . . a reader's delight . . . What really engages is the author's crafting of Shiva, with almost boy-worship joy.'
The Times of India

'Gripping and well paced. An essentially mythological story written in a modern style, the novel creates anticipation in the reader's mind and compels one to read with great curiosity till the end . . . leaves one thirsting for more.' **Business World**

'Amongst the top 5 books recommended by *Brunch* . . . the story is fascinating.' **Hindustan Times**

'Philosophy [is] its underlying theme, but [it] is racy enough to give its readers the adventure of a lifetime.' **The Hindu**

'A fast-paced story, you are bound to read it cover to cover in one sitting.' **Deccan Chronicle**

'Amish [has] created a delightful mix of mythology and history by making Lord Shiva the hero of his trilogy.'
The Indian Express

tHe
IMMORTALS
of
MELUHA

THE SHIVA TRILOGY: BOOK 1

AMISH

Jo Fletcher

BOOKS

First published in 2010 by Tara Press, India
First published in Great Britain in 2013 by

Jo Fletcher Books
an imprint of Quercus
55 Baker Street
7th Floor, South Block
London
W1U 8EW

A CIP catalogue record for this book is available
from the British Library

ISBN 978 1 78087 400 5 (PB)
ISBN 978 1 78087 402 9 (EBOOK)

10 9 8 7 6 5 4 3 2 1

Typeset by Ellipsis Digital Limited, Glasgow

Printed and bound in Great Britain by
Clays Ltd, St Ives plc

To Preeti & Neel . . .
You both are everything to me,
My words & their meaning,
My prayer & my blessing,
My moon & my sun,
My love & my life,
My soulmate & a part of my soul.

Om Namah Shivaiy.
The universe bows to Lord Shiva.
I bow to Lord Shiva.

CONTENTS

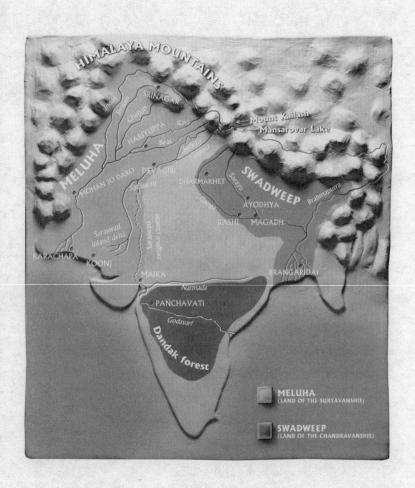

The Shiva Trilogy

Shiva! The Mahadev. The God of Gods. Destroyer of Evil. Passionate lover. Fierce warrior. Consummate dancer. Charismatic leader. All-powerful, yet incorruptible. Quick of wit – and of temper.

No foreigner who came to India – be they conqueror, merchant, scholar, ruler, traveller – believed that such a great man could ever exist in reality. They assumed he must have been a mythical god, a fantasy conjured in the realms of human imagination. And over time, sadly, this belief became our received wisdom.

But what if we are wrong? What if Lord Shiva was not simply a figment of a rich imagination but a flesh-and-blood person like you and me, a man who rose to become godlike because of his karma? That is the premise of the Shiva Trilogy, which interprets the rich mythological heritage of ancient India, blending fiction with historical fact.

This work is therefore a tribute to Lord Shiva and the lesson his life teaches us. A lesson lost in the depths of time and ignorance. A lesson that all of us can rise to be better people. A lesson that there exists a potential God in every single human being. All we have to do is listen to ourselves.

The Immortals of Meluha is the first book in a trilogy chronicling the journey of this extraordinary hero. Two more books are to follow: *The Secret of the Nagas* and *The Oath of the Vayuputras*.

CHAPTER ONE

He Has Come!

1900 BC, Mansarovar Lake (at the foot of Mount Kailash, Tibet)

Shiva gazed at the orange sky. The clouds hovering above Mansarovar had just parted to reveal the setting sun, the brilliant giver of life, drawing another day to a close. Shiva had seen a few sunrises in his twenty-one years, but sunset – he tried never to miss a sunset. On any other day, he would have relished the vista – the sun and the immense lake against the magnificent backdrop of the Himalayas stretching as far as the eye could see.

But not today.

As he squatted on a narrow ledge extending out over the lake, the shimmering light reflected off the waters picked out the numerous battle-scars that marked his muscular body. Shiva recalled his carefree childhood days, when he had perfected the art of skimming pebbles across the surface of the lake –

he still held the record in his tribe for the highest number of bounces: seventeen.

On a normal day, Shiva would have smiled at this memory from a cheerful past, but today he turned to look back towards his village without the merest hint of joy.

The slightly hump-backed Bhadra was alert, guarding the main entrance to the village. Shiva looked to Bhadra's side, and his tribesman turned to find his two back-up soldiers were dozing against the fence. He cursed and kicked them awake.

Shiva turned back towards the lake.

God bless Bhadra! At least he takes some responsibility.

He brought the chillum made of yak-bone to his lips and inhaled deeply. Any other day, the marijuana would have dulled his troubled mind and allowed him some moments of solace.

But not today.

He looked left, towards the edge of the lake where the soldiers accompanying the strange foreign visitor were being kept under guard. With the lake behind them and twenty of his own soldiers watching over them, it was impossible for them to mount any surprise attack.

They let themselves be disarmed so easily. They aren't like the blood-thirsty idiots in our land, always looking for any excuse to fight.

The foreigner's words came flooding back to Shiva: 'Come to our land, which lies beyond the great mountains. Others call it Meluha, but I call it Heaven. It is the richest and most powerful empire in India – perhaps in the whole world – and our government offers immigrants fertile land and resources for farming. Today the Gunas, your tribesmen, fight for survival in this rough, arid land. Meluha offers you a paradise beyond your wildest dreams – and we ask for nothing in return, save that you live in peace, pay your taxes and obey the laws of our land.'

Shiva had been musing on the stranger's offer, weighing the pros and cons. He would certainly not be a chief in this new land – but would he really miss that so much? His tribe would have to live by the foreigners' laws rather than their own. They would have to work every day for a living, but surely that would be better than fighting every day just to stay alive?

He took another puff and as the smoke cleared he turned to stare at the hut in the centre of his village, right next to his own, where the foreigner was housed. He had been told he would sleep more comfortably there, but in truth, Shiva wanted him close as a hostage. Just in case.

Almost every month we have to fight the Pakratis, just so we can keep our village on the shore of the Holy Lake – but they are growing stronger every year, forming new alliances with new tribes. We can beat the Pakratis, but not all the mountain tribes together. If we move to Meluha, we can escape this pointless violence, maybe even start to live in some comfort. What could possibly be wrong with that? Why shouldn't we take this deal? It sounds so good!

Shiva took one last drag, then knocked the ash from the chillum and rose quickly from his perch. Brushing a few specks of ash from his bare chest, he wiped his hands on his tigerskin skirt and strode rapidly to his village. Bhadra and his backup stood to attention as Shiva passed through the gates. Shiva frowned and gestured for Bhadra to ease up.

Why does he always treat me like this? Does he keep forgetting that he's been my closest friend since childhood? Me becoming chief hasn't really changed our relationship – he doesn't need to be so servile.

The huts in Shiva's village were luxurious compared to those of other tribes. Tall enough that a grown man could actually stand upright inside them, they were also strong enough to withstand the harsh mountain winds; they would last for three years before surrendering to the elements. Shiva flung the empty chillum into his own hut as he strode past it to the one next door where he found the visitor sleeping soundly.

Either he doesn't realise he's a hostage, or he genuinely believes that good behaviour begets good behaviour.

Shiva remembered what his uncle – and his guru – used to say: 'People do what their society rewards them for doing. If the society rewards trust, people will be trusting.'

Meluha must be a trusting society indeed if it teaches even its soldiers to expect the best of strangers.

Shiva scratched his shaggy beard as he stared hard at the visitor, who had given his name as Nandi. The Meluhan was huge, and he looked even bigger sprawled on the floor in a stupor, his immense belly jiggling with every breath. In spite of his obese appearance, his skin was taut and toned. His child-like face was even more innocent in sleep as he lay there with his mouth half-open.

My uncle used to talk of my great future – is this the man who will lead me to my destiny?

'Your destiny is much larger than these massive mountains,' his uncle had told him, 'but to make it come true, you will have to cross these very same massive mountains.'

Do I deserve a good destiny? My people must always come first – will they be happy in Meluha?

As Shiva contemplated the sleeping Nandi he heard the warning sound of a conch shell.

Pakratis!

'Positions,' screamed Shiva as he unsheathed his sword and headed for the door.

Nandi was up in an instant, drawing a hidden sword from beneath his fur coat, and together they sprinted to the village gates. Following standing instructions, the women were already rushing to the centre of the village carrying their children, while the men were running the other way, swords drawn.

'Bhadra – call our soldiers at the lake,' shouted Shiva as he reached the gates.

Bhadra relayed his chief's orders and the Guna soldiers were up and running towards the village before he'd finished shouting. They were as surprised as Shiva had been when the Meluhans drew hidden weapons from their coats and joined the Gunas as they took up defensive positions.

The Pakratis were upon them within moments, and their ambush was well planned. At dusk, the Guna soldiers customarily thanked their gods in prayer for a day without battle while the women finished their chores by the lakeside. If there was a time of weakness for the formidable Gunas, a time when they were not a fearsome martial clan but just another mountain tribe trying to survive in a tough, hostile land, this was it.

But fate was against the Pakratis this time: the foreigners in their midst had prompted Shiva to order his tribesmen to remain more alert than usual, so the Pakratis lost much of the element of surprise. The Meluhan presence was also decisive in the skirmish itself, quickly turning the tide of the short, brutal battle in the Gunas' favour. The Pakratis had no choice but to retreat.

Cut and bloodied, Shiva surveyed the damage at the end of the battle. Only two Guna soldiers had succumbed to their injuries, and they would be honoured as clan heroes. But the warning had come too late for at least ten Guna women and children, whose mutilated bodies were found next to the lake.

Bastards! They kill women and children when they can't beat us.

Livid, Shiva called the entire tribe to the centre of the village. His mind was made up. 'This land is fit only for barbarians,' he announced. 'We've fought countless pointless battles with no end in sight. You know my uncle tried to make peace, even offering the mountain tribes access to the lake shore, but they mistook our desire for peace as weakness. We all know what followed—'

Despite being accustomed to the brutality of regular battle, the Gunas had been utterly appalled by the viciousness of the attack on the helpless women and children.

'I keep no secrets from you,' Shiva went on. 'You are all aware of the invitation the foreigners have extended to us.' He pointed to Nandi and the Meluhans. 'They fought shoulder-to-shoulder with us today, and they've earned my trust. I want to go with them to Meluha. But this cannot be my decision alone.'

'You're our chief, Shiva,' said Bhadra firmly. 'Your decision is our decision. That's our tradition.'

'Not this time,' said Shiva. 'This will change our lives completely. I believe the change will be for the better – anything will be better than this endless, pointless violence. I've told you what I want to do, but the choice to stay or go is yours. Let the Gunas speak. This time, I follow you.'

The Gunas were clear on their tradition, but their respect for Shiva was based on his character as well as tribal convention. His genius and sheer personal bravery had led the tribe to their greatest military victories.

They spoke with one voice. 'Your decision is our decision.'

— ⁂𝕆𝕌⚓☸ —

Five days had passed since Shiva had uprooted his tribe, and now the caravan was camped in one of the great valleys along the route to Meluha. Shiva had organised the camp in three concentric circles. The yaks had been tied around the outer-most circle, to act as an alarm in case of intruders; the men were stationed in the intermediate ring, ready to fight if a battle broke out; and the women and children, the most vulnerable, were inside the innermost circle, gathered around the fire.

Shiva was prepared for the worst, convinced there would be an ambush — it was only a matter of time. The Pakratis should have been delighted to gain access to the prime lands along the lakeside, but Shiva knew that Yakhya, the Pakrati chief, would not allow the Gunas to leave peacefully. Yakhya would like nothing better than to become a legend by claiming he had defeated Shiva's Gunas and won their land for the Pakratis. Shiva detested this nonsensical tribal logic — in such an atmosphere, there was no hope for peace. While Shiva relished the call of battle and revelled in its arts, he also knew that, ultimately, the battles in his land were an exercise in futility.

He turned to study Nandi, who was sitting some distance away with his men. The twenty-five Meluhan soldiers were seated in an arc around a second camp circle.

Why did he pick the Gunas to invite to his homeland? Shiva wondered. *Why not the Pakratis?*

His thoughts were broken by the movement of a shadow in the distance. He stared hard in that direction but everything was still — sometimes the light played tricks. Shiva relaxed his stance — and then he saw the moving shadow again.

'To arms,' he cried, and the Gunas and Meluhans immediately drew their weapons and took up battle positions as fifty Pakratis charged recklessly towards the camp. The stupidity of rushing in without thinking cost them dearly when they encountered a wall of panicky yaks. The animals bucked and kicked uncontrollably, injuring many Pakratis before they could even begin their skirmish.

But a few slipped through, and weapons clashed.

A young Pakrati, obviously a novice, charged at Shiva, swinging his weapon wildly. Shiva stepped back, easily avoiding the strike, then brought his sword up in a smooth arc, inflicting a superficial cut across the Pakrati's chest. The young warrior cursed and swung back, opening his flank. That was all the invitation Shiva needed. He thrust his sword brutally into his enemy's gut, then as quickly pulled the blade out, twisting it as he did so, leaving the Pakrati to a slow, painful death. He turned, and finding a Pakrati about to strike a Guna he jumped high and swung from above, slicing neatly through the Pakrati's sword arm, severing it from his body.

Bhadra was as adept at the art of battle as Shiva; a sword in each hand, he was fighting two Pakratis simultaneously. His hump did not impede his movements as he transferred his weight easily, slashing the throat of the Pakrati on his left, then swinging with his right hand and cutting across the other soldier's face, carving one of his eyes out. As the soldier fell, Bhadra brought his left-hand sword down brutally, quickly ending this hapless enemy's suffering.

The battle at the Meluhan end of camp was very different. They were exceptionally well-trained soldiers, but they were not vicious, and they were following their own code, avoiding killing as far as possible.

The Pakratis were outnumbered and poorly led, and they were beaten in short order. Soon almost half of them lay dead, and the rest were on their knees, begging for mercy. One of them was Yakhya. A deep cut in his shoulder – inflicted by Nandi – was restricting the movement of his sword-arm.

Bhadra stood behind the Pakrati chief, his sword raised high, ready to strike. 'Shiva – quick and easy or slow and painful?'

'Sir,' intervened Nandi before Shiva could speak.

Shiva turned towards the Meluhan, surprised at the interjection.

'This is wrong! They're begging for mercy – killing them is against the rules of war.'

'You don't know the Pakratis,' said Shiva. 'They're brutal, and they'll keep attacking us even if there's nothing to gain. This has to end, once and for all.'

'It's already ending – you'll be living in Meluha soon.'

Shiva stood silent, considering Nandi's words.

'How you end this is up to you,' Nandi added. 'Will you choose more of the same, or something different?'

Bhadra looked at Shiva, waiting.

'You can show the Pakratis that you're better than them,' said Nandi.

Shiva turned towards the horizon and gazed at the massive Himalayas, remembering his uncle's prediction about his destiny lying beyond the great mountains.

Destiny? Or the chance of a better life?

He turned back to Bhadra. 'Disarm them, take all their provisions, then release them.'

Even if the Pakratis are mad enough to return to their village, rearm and come back, we'll be long gone.

Shocked, Bhadra stared at Shiva for a moment, then he started implementing the order without further question.

Nandi gazed at Shiva with hope in his heart and one thought reverberating through his mind: *Shiva has the heart. He has the potential. Please, let it be him. I pray to you, Lord Ram, let it be him.*

Shiva walked back to the young soldier he had stabbed in the gut. He lay writhing on the ground, his face contorted in pain as gore oozed slowly from the wound. For the first time in his life, Shiva felt pity for a Pakrati. He drew his sword and swiftly ended the young soldier's suffering.

— ⚶ ◍◐∪⚢◉ —

Four long weeks of marching brought the caravan to the crest of the final mountain and the outskirts of Srinagar, the capital of the valley of Kashmir. Nandi had talked so excitedly about the glories of his perfect land that Shiva was expecting to see incredible sights he could not even have imagined in his simple homeland. But nothing could have prepared him for the sheer spectacle of this paradise: *Meluha* – the land of pure life!

The mighty Jhelum River, a roaring tigress in the mountains, slowed to the plodding of a languorous cow as she entered the valley. Caressing the heavenly land of Kashmir, she meandered into the immense Dal Lake, eventually flowing out and away, continuing her long journey to the sea.

The vast valley was a lush green canvas for the masterpiece that was Kashmir. Row upon row of gloriously coloured flowers and soaring chinar trees offered the weary travellers a majestic yet warm Kashmiri welcome. The melodious singing of the birds was a relief to their ears after weeks surrounded by the howling of icy mountain winds.

'If this is the border province, how perfect must the rest of the country be?' whispered Shiva in awe.

Upon the western banks of the Dal Lake, alongside the Jhelum, lay the site of an ancient Meluhan army camp and the frontier town that had grown beyond its simple encampments into the grand Srinagar, literally, the 'respected city'.

Srinagar had been built upon a massive platform of earth almost two hundred and fifty acres in size and towering almost fifteen feet high. On top of the platform, twelve-foot-thick city walls soared another sixty feet high. The Gunas were astounded by the simplicity and brilliance of building an entire city on a platform. First and foremost it offered a strong protection against attacking enemies, who would have to fight up the steep sides of the platform before they even reached the city walls. The platform served another vital purpose: it raised the ground level of the city safely above the floodplains of the mighty Jhelum.

Inside the fort walls, a neat grid pattern of roads divided the city into blocks. There were specially constructed market areas, temples, gardens, meeting halls – every amenity necessary for sophisticated urban living. From the outside, all the houses looked the same: simple multi-storey block structures, and the only difference between a rich man's house and a poor man's was the size.

In contrast to the extravagant natural landscape of Kashmir, the city of Srinagar itself was painted in restrained greys, blues and whites, and the entire city was a picture of cleanliness, order and sobriety. Nearly twenty thousand souls called Srinagar their home. Shiva gazed at the two hundred Gunas who had just arrived from Mount Kailash and felt a lightness of being he hadn't experienced since that terrible day, many years ago . . .

I have escaped. I can make a new beginning. I can forget.

The caravan made its way to the immigrant camp, which was built on a separate platform on the southern side of Srinagar. Nandi led Shiva and his tribe to the Foreigners' Office, which was located next to the camp, and asked Shiva to wait outside while he fetched an official. The young man he returned with gave a practised smile and folded his hands in a formal namaste. 'Welcome to Meluha. I am Chitraangadh, and I will be your Orientation Executive. Think of me as your single point of contact for all issues whilst you are here. Would your leader Shiva make himself known, please?'

Shiva stepped forward. 'I'm Shiva.'

'Excellent,' said Chitraangadh. 'Would you be so kind as to

follow me to the registration desk, please? You will be designated the caretaker of your tribe, and any communications concerning them will go through you. As the designated leader, the implementation of all directives within your tribe will be your responsibility—'

Nandi cut into Chitraangadh's officious speech to tell Shiva, 'Sir, if you'll excuse me, I'll go to the immigrant camp and arrange the temporary living quarters for your tribe.'

Shiva noticed that Chitraangadh's ever-beaming face lost its smile for a fraction of a second when Nandi interrupted his flow. But he recovered quickly and the smile was soon back in place.

Turning to Nandi, Shiva said, 'Of course you may go, Nandi – you don't need my permission. But I would ask you to promise me something, my friend.'

'Anything, sir,' replied Nandi, bowing slightly.

'Call me Shiva, not sir.' Shiva grinned. 'I'm your friend, not your chief.'

A surprised Nandi looked up, bowed again and said, 'Yes, sir – I mean, yes, Shiva.'

Chitraangadh, whose smile looked more genuine to Shiva now, said, 'If you will follow me to the registration desk, we will complete the formalities quickly.'

— 𑀦 𑀰𑀉𑀢𑀑 —

The newly registered tribe arrived at the residential quarters in the immigration camp to find Nandi waiting near the main gates to lead them inside. The roads of the camp were laid out like those of Srinagar, in a neat north–south and east–west grid. The carefully paved footpaths contrasted sharply with the dirt tracks in Shiva's own land. He noticed something strange about the roads, though.

'Nandi, what are those differently coloured stones running along the centre of each road?' asked Shiva.

'They cover underground drains that take all the waste water out of the camp, ensuring that the camp remains clean and hygienic.'

Shiva marvelled at the Meluhans' almost obsessively meticulous planning.

When the Gunas saw the large building that had been assigned to them, for the umpteenth time they thanked their leader's wisdom in deciding to come to Meluha. The three-storey building had comfortable separate living quarters for each family. Every family room was luxuriously furnished, including a highly polished copper plate on one wall in which they could see their reflections. Clean linen bed sheets, towels and even some clothes were also provided.

Feeling the cloth, a bewildered Shiva asked, 'What's this material?'

'It's cotton, Shiva,' Chitraangadh replied enthusiastically. 'The plant is grown in our lands and fashioned into the cloth that you hold.'

Broad windows allowed the light and the warmth of the sun to enter, and notches on each wall supported metal rods from which lamps could be hung at night. Every family room had an attached bathroom with a sloping floor that allowed water to flow naturally to a drainage hole. On the floor at the right-hand end of each bathroom was a paved basin with a large hole at its centre, the purpose of which was a mystery to the tribe. The side walls incorporated some kind of device which, when turned, allowed water to flow through it.

'Magic,' whispered Mausi, Bhadra's mother.

Beside the main door of the building was a house from which a doctor and her nurses emerged to greet Shiva. The doctor, a petite wheat-skinned woman, was dressed in a simple white cloth tied around her waist and legs in a style the Meluhans called *dhoti*. A smaller white cloth was tied around her chest as a blouse, while another cloth called an *angvastram* was draped over her shoulders. The centre of her forehead bore a white dot. Her head had been shaved clean except for a braid at the back, called a *choti*. A loose string, a *janau*, ran from her left shoulder across her torso to her right side.

Nandi was genuinely startled to see her. With a reverential namaste, he said, 'Lady Ayurvati! I didn't expect to find a doctor of your stature here.'

Ayurvati smiled at Nandi and made a polite namaste. 'I'm a firm believer in the fieldwork experience programme, Captain. My team follows it strictly. Forgive me, though – I don't recognise you. Have we met before?'

'My name is Nandi, my lady,' he replied. 'We haven't met before, but who doesn't know you – the greatest doctor in the land?'

'Thank you, Captain Nandi,' said the doctor, visibly embarrassed, 'but I think you exaggerate. There are many far superior to me.' Turning quickly to Shiva, she continued, 'Welcome to Meluha. I'm Ayurvati, your designated doctor. My nurses and I will be at your service while you're in these quarters.'

Hearing no reaction from Shiva, Chitraangadh said in his most earnest voice, 'These are just temporary quarters, Shiva. The actual houses that will be allocated to your tribe will be much more comfortable. You only have to stay here for the period of quarantine, which will not last more than seven days.'

'Oh no, my friend,' Shiva replied, 'these quarters are more than comfortable – they're beyond anything we could have imagined. What say you, Mausi?' Shiva grinned mischievously at Bhadra's mother before turning back to Chitraangadh with a frown. 'But why the quarantine?'

Nandi cut in. 'The quarantine is merely a precaution, Shiva. We don't have many diseases in Meluha, and sometimes immigrants arrive with new ones. During this seven-day period, the doctor and her nurses will observe and cure you of any such ailments.'

Ayurvati added, 'And one of the guidelines you must follow to control diseases is to maintain strict hygiene standards.'

Shiva grimaced at Nandi and whispered, 'Hygiene standards?'

Nandi's forehead crinkled into an apologetic frown while his hands gently advised acquiescence. He mumbled, 'Please go along with it, Shiva. It's just one of those things we *have* to do in Meluha. As I said, Lady Ayurvati is considered to be the best doctor in the land.'

'If you're free right now,' Ayurvati said, 'I can give you your instructions.'

'I'm free right now,' said Shiva with a straight face, 'but I may have to charge you later.'

Bhadra giggled softly, while Ayurvati stared at Shiva with a blank face, clearly not amused by the pun.

'I don't understand what you're trying to say,' she said frostily. 'In any case, we'll begin in the bathroom.' With that, Ayurvati walked into the guest-house, muttering under her breath, 'These uncouth immigrants . . .'

Shiva raised his eyebrows towards Bhadra, grinning impishly.

— ⚕ ⚕ ⚕ ⚕ ⚕ —

Late in the evening, after a hearty meal, all the Gunas were served a medicinal drink in their rooms.

'Yuck!' Bhadra's face contorted in a grimace. 'This tastes like yak's piss!'

'How do you know what yak's piss tastes like?' asked Shiva, laughing as he slapped his friend hard on the back. 'Now go to your room. I need to sleep.'

'Have you seen the beds? I think this is going to be the best sleep of my life!'

'Of course I've seen the bed,' said Shiva, grinning. 'Now I want to experience it. Get out!'

Bhadra left Shiva's room, laughing loudly. He wasn't the only one excited by the unnaturally soft beds. The entire tribe had rushed to their rooms for what they anticipated would be the best sleep they'd ever had.

They were in for a surprise.

— ⚲ ◍Ʊ⚴✴ —

Shiva tossed and turned on his bed. His tigerskin skirt had been taken away to be washed, so he was wearing an orange-coloured *dhoti*. His cotton *angvastram* was lying on a low chair by the wall and a chillum smouldered forlornly on the side table.

This damn bed is too soft. Impossible to sleep on . . .

Shiva yanked the sheet off the mattress, tossed it on the floor and lay down on it. That was a little better. Sleep was stealthily creeping up on him, but not as quickly as at home. He missed the rough cold floor of his own hut. He missed the shrill winds of Mount Kailash that broke through the most determined efforts to ignore them. He missed the comforting stench of his tigerskin skirt. No doubt his current surroundings were excessively comfortable, but they were still alien.

As usual, his instincts revealed the truth: *It's not the room — it's you.*

Just as that realisation dawned, Shiva noticed that despite the cool breeze he was sweating profusely. The room was spinning, and he felt as if his body was being stretched out. His frostbitten right toe was on fire and his battle-scarred left knee was being distended, somehow. His tired, aching muscles felt as if a great hand was remoulding them. His shoulder joint, dislocated years ago and never completely healed, appeared to be ripping the surrounding muscles aside to re-engineer the joint, the muscles in turn giving way so that the bones could do their work.

Breathing was becoming an effort, so Shiva opened his mouth wide and tried to suck in as much air as he could. The curtains alongside the window rustled as a welcome breeze rushed in, and Shiva's body relaxed a little with the sudden gust of air. But all too quickly the battle to breathe began again. He focused and willed giant gasps of air into his hungry lungs.

Knock! Knock!

The light tapping on the door broke Shiva's concentration, disorientating him for a moment. Still struggling for breath, he mentally scanned his body. His shoulder was twitching, but the familiar pain was missing. He looked down at his knee – it didn't hurt any more either, and the scar had vanished. He glanced at his toe: it was whole and completely healed now. He tried to bend it and a cracking sound reverberated through the room as his toe made its first movement in years. There was also an unfamiliar tingling coldness in his neck.

Knock! Knock! The tapping was a little more insistent now.

A bewildered Shiva staggered to his feet, pulled the *angvastram* around his neck for warmth and opened the door.

The darkness veiled his visitor's face, but Shiva still recognised Bhadra even before he whispered in a panic-stricken voice, 'Shiva, I'm sorry to disturb you so late but my mother has a very high fever – what should I do?'

Shiva instinctively touched Bhadra's forehead. 'You have a fever too, Bhadra. Return to your room – I'll fetch the doctor.'

As Shiva raced along the corridor he encountered many more doors opening, and an increasingly familiar cry: 'Sudden fever – help!'

He sprinted down the steps to the attached building where the doctor was housed and knocked hard on the door. Ayurvati opened it immediately, almost as if she'd been expecting him.

He spoke calmly. 'Ayurvati, many of my tribe have suddenly fallen ill. Please come quickly – they need your help.'

'You're sweating – do you have a fever?'

Shiva shook his head to say no and Ayurvati frowned, surprised. She touched Shiva's forehead for confirmation, then turned and ordered her nurses, 'Come on – it's begun. Let's go.'

As Ayurvati and her nurses rushed into the building, Chitraangadh appeared out of nowhere. He asked what had happened, and Shiva said, 'I don't know. Practically everybody in my tribe has suddenly fallen ill.'

'You're sweating heavily yourself,' Chitraangadh pointed out.

'Indeed – but for some reason I don't have a fever. I'm going back inside – I need to see how my people are doing.'

Chitraangadh nodded, adding, 'I'll fetch Nandi.'

As Chitraangadh sped away in search of Nandi, Shiva ran back into the building. He was surprised to find every torch had been lit and the nurses were going methodically from room to room, administering medicines and talking to their scared patients, telling them what they should do. A scribe walked alongside each nurse, meticulously noting each patient's details in a palm-leaf booklet. The Meluhans were clearly prepared for this sort of eventuality. Ayurvati stood at the end of the corridor, hands on hips, like a general supervising superbly trained and efficient troops.

Shiva rushed up to her and asked, 'What about the second and third floors?'

Ayurvati answered without turning to him, 'There are nurses all over the building already. I'll go up to supervise once the situation on this floor has stabilised. We'll cover all the patients in the next half-hour.'

'I can see how incredibly efficient your people are, but I pray that everyone will be okay,' said a worried Shiva.

Ayurvati turned to look at him. Her eyebrows were raised slightly and a hint of a smile hovered on her serious face. 'Don't worry — we're Meluhans. We're capable of handling any situation. Everybody will be fine.'

'Is there anything I can do to help?'

'Yes — please go and take a bath.'

'What?'

'Please go and take a bath. Right now,' said Ayurvati as she turned back to address her team. 'Everybody, please remember that all children below the age of fifteen *must* be tonsured. Mastrak, go upstairs and start the secondary medicines, will you? I'll be there in five minutes.'

'Yes, my lady,' said the young man she had addressed. He hurried up the steps carrying a large cloth bag.

'You're still here?' asked Ayurvati when she noticed that Shiva hadn't left.

Shiva said softly, controlling his rising anger, 'What difference will my bathing make? My people are in trouble. I want to help them.'

'I don't have the time or the patience to argue with you. You will go and take a bath immediately,' said Ayurvati, clearly *not* trying to control her own temper.

Shiva glared at Ayurvati as he made a heroic effort to swallow the curses that wanted to leap out of his mouth. His clenched fists were eager to answer Ayurvati even more aggressively. But she was a woman.

Ayurvati glared right back at Shiva. She was used to being obeyed. She was a doctor. If she told a patient to do something, she expected it to be done without question. But in her long years of experience she had encountered a few patients like Shiva, especially amongst the nobility. Such patients had to be *reasoned with*, not *instructed* – yet this was no nobleman, just a simple immigrant.

Controlling herself with great effort, Ayurvati said, 'Shiva, you're sweating profusely. If you don't wash it off, it will kill you. Please trust me on this. You can't be of any help to your tribe if you're dead.'

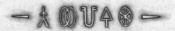

Chitraangadh banged loudly on the door and a bleary-eyed Nandi woke up cursing. Wrenching the door open, he growled, 'This had better be important!'

'Come quickly – Shiva's tribe has fallen ill.'

'Already? But this is only the first night,' exclaimed Nandi. Picking up his *angvastram* he said, 'Let's go!'

— ⋏ ⍟U⚲ ⊛ —

The bathroom felt like a strange place to take a bath. Shiva was used to splashing about in the chilly Mansarovar Lake for his bi-monthly ablutions, and the bathroom felt oddly constricting in comparison. He turned the magical device on the wall to increase the flow of water and used the strange cake-like substance the Meluhans called 'soap' to rub his body clean. Ayurvati had been very clear: the soap *had* to be used. Eventually he turned the water off and picked up a towel. As he rubbed himself vigorously, the mystifying physical developments he'd ignored for the past few hours came flooding back. His shoulder felt better than new. He looked down in awe at his knee. No pain, no scar. He stared in wonder at his completely healed toe. And then he realised that it wasn't just the injured parts that had been healed – his entire body felt rejuvenated and stronger than ever. His neck, though, still felt intolerably cold.

What the hell is going on?

He stepped out of the bathroom and quickly donned a clean *dhoti*. Ayurvati had given strict instructions that he was not to wear old clothes stained by his sweat. As he was draping the *angvastram* around his neck for some warmth, there was a knock on the door.

It was Ayurvati. 'Shiva, may I come in, please? I'd like to check how you're doing.'

Shiva opened the door. Ayurvati stepped in and took Shiva's temperature – it was normal. She nodded slightly and said, 'You appear to be healthy, and your tribe is also recovering quickly. The trouble has passed.'

Shiva smiled gratefully. 'Thanks to the skills and efficiency of your team. I'm truly sorry for arguing with you earlier – it was unnecessary. I know you meant well.'

Ayurvati looked up from her palm-leaf booklet with a slight smile and a raised eyebrow. 'Being polite now, are we?'

'I'm not that rude, you know.' Shiva grinned. 'You people are just so supercilious!'

Ayurvati suddenly stopped listening and stared at Shiva with a stunned expression on her face. How had she not noticed it before? She had never believed in the prophecy. Was she going to be the first one to see it come true? Pointing weakly, she mumbled, 'Why have you covered your neck?'

'It's very cold, for some reason. Is it something I should worry about?' asked Shiva as he pulled off the *angvastram*.

Ayurvati's cry resounded loudly through the silent room as she staggered back, her hands covering her mouth in shock while the palm-leaf booklet slipped from her nerveless fingers and scattered pages across the floor. Her knees were too weak to hold her up; she collapsed with her back against the wall, never once taking her tear-filled eyes off Shiva. She kept repeating, '*Om Brahmaye namah. Om Brahmaye namah.*'

'What's happened? Is it serious?' asked Shiva, beginning to get worried.

'You have come – my Lord, *you have come!*'

Before a bewildered Shiva could react to her strange behaviour, Nandi rushed in and saw Ayurvati on the ground, tears flowing down her face.

'What's happened, my lady?' he asked, sounding startled.

Ayurvati pointed wordlessly at Shiva's neck and Nandi looked up to see it glowing an eerie iridescent blue. With the cry of a long-caged prisoner just released from captivity, Nandi collapsed to his knees. 'My Lord – you have come! The Neelkanth has come!' He bowed low and brought his head down to touch Shiva's feet reverentially.

The object of his adoration stepped back, befuddled and perturbed. 'What the hell is going on here?' he asked agitatedly. Holding a hand to his freezing neck, he turned around to face the polished copper plate and stared in stunned astonishment at the reflection of his *neel kanth* – his *blue throat*.

Chitraangadh had just arrived. Now, holding the door frame for support, he stood and sobbed like a child. 'We're saved! We're saved! He has come!'

CHAPTER 2

Land of Pure Life

Chenardhwaj, the governor of Kashmir, wanted to broadcast to the entire world that the Neelkanth had appeared in his capital city – not in one of the other frontier towns like Takshashila, Karachapa or Lothal, but in *his* Srinagar! But the bird-courier had arrived almost immediately from Devagiri, the Meluhan capital, the 'abode of the gods', and the emperor's orders were crystal-clear. The news of the Neelkanth's arrival had to be kept secret until the emperor himself had seen Shiva. Chenardhwaj was instructed to send Shiva to Devagiri immediately, along with an escort. Most importantly, Shiva himself was not to be told about the prophecy. 'The emperor will advise the supposed Neelkanth in an appropriate manner,' were the exact words in the message.

Chenardhwaj had the privilege of informing Shiva about the journey. Shiva, however, was not in the most amenable of moods. He was utterly perplexed by the sudden devotion of every Meluhan around him. Since he'd been transferred to the gubernatorial residence where he lived in luxury, only the most important citizens of Srinagar had access to him.

'My Lord, we will be escorting you to Devagiri, our capital,' said Chenardhwaj as he struggled to bend his enormous muscular frame lower than he ever had before. 'It is a few weeks' journey from here.'

'I'm not going anywhere until somebody tells me what's happening! What the hell is this damned prophecy of the Neelkanth?' Shiva asked angrily.

'My Lord, please have faith in us. You will know the truth soon. The emperor himself will tell you when you reach Devagiri.'

'And what about my tribe?'

'They will be given lands right here in Kashmir, my Lord. All the resources they need to lead a comfortable life will be provided.'

'Are they being held hostage?'

'Oh no, my Lord,' said Chenardhwaj, visibly disturbed, 'they are *your* tribe, my Lord. If I had my way, they would live like nobility from this day forward. But our laws cannot be broken, my Lord, not even for you. We can only give them what has been promised. In time, my Lord, you may decide to change the laws as you feel necessary. Then we could certainly accommodate them anywhere.'

'I beg you, my Lord,' pleaded Nandi, 'have faith in us.

You can't imagine how important you are to Meluha. We've been waiting a very long time for you. We need your help.'

Please help me – please!

The memory of another desperate plea from a distraught woman years ago returned to haunt Shiva as he was stunned into silence.

— ⚲ ◍ U ⚕ ◉ —

'*Your destiny is much larger than these massive mountains.*' Shiva's uncle's words echoed in his mind.

Nonsense – I don't deserve any destiny. If these people knew my guilt, they'd stop this bullshit instantly!

'I don't know what to do, Bhadra.' Shiva was sitting in the royal gardens on the banks of the Dal Lake.

His friend sat at his side, carefully pressing some marijuana into a chillum. As Bhadra used a lit stick to bring the chillum to life, Shiva said impatiently, 'That's a cue for you to speak, you fool.'

'No. That's actually a cue for me to hand you the chillum, Shiva.'

'Why won't you counsel me?' asked Shiva in anguish. 'We're still the same friends who never made a move without consulting each other!'

Bhadra smiled to soften his words. 'No, we're not. You're the chief now. The tribe lives and dies by your decisions, and they must not be corrupted by any other person's influence. We're not like the Pakratis, whose chief has to listen to the loudest mouths on his council. The chief's wisdom is supreme amongst the Gunas. That's our tradition.'

Shiva rolled his eyes in exasperation. 'Some traditions are meant to be broken.'

Bhadra stubbornly remained silent. Shiva grabbed the chillum from him and took a deep drag, letting the marijuana permeate his body.

'I've only heard one thing about the prophecy of the Neelkanth,' said Bhadra. 'Apparently the Meluhans are in deep trouble and only the Neelkanth can save them.'

'But I can't see any trouble here – everything looks perfect. If they want to see real trouble we should take them to our land.'

Bhadra laughed, a little uneasily. 'But what is it about the blue throat that makes them believe you can save them?'

'Damned if I know – they're so much more advanced than us, and yet they worship me like I'm some god, just because of this blue throat.'

'I think their medicines are magical, though. Have you noticed that the hump on my back is a little smaller than it was?'

'So it is – their doctors are seriously gifted.'

'You know their doctors are called Brahmins?'

'Like Ayurvati?' asked Shiva, passing the chillum back to Bhadra.

'Yes. But the Brahmins don't just cure people. They're

also teachers, lawyers, priests – basically any intellectual profession.'

'Talented people.' Shiva sniffed.

'That's not all,' said Bhadra, pausing for a long draw on the pipe. 'They have a concept of specialisation that influences their entire society. So in addition to the Brahmins, they have a group called Kshatriyas, who are the warriors and rulers. Even women can be Kshatriyas.'

'Really? They allow women into their army?'

'Well, apparently there aren't too many female Kshatriyas, but yes, they're allowed into the army.'

'No wonder they're in trouble!'

The friends laughed loudly at the Meluhans' strange ways. Bhadra took another puff before continuing, 'And then they have Vaishyas, who are craftsmen, traders and businesspeople, and finally the Shudras, who are the farmers and workers. And one caste can't do another caste's job.'

'Hang on,' said Shiva. 'That means that since you're a warrior, you wouldn't be allowed to trade at the marketplace?'

'Yes.'

'Bloody stupid rule – how would you get me my marijuana? After all, that's the only thing you're useful for.'

Shiva leaned back to avoid Bhadra's playful blow. 'All right, all right. Take it easy,' he said, laughing. Stretching out, he grabbed the chillum from Bhadra and took another deep drag.

We're talking about everything except what we should be talking about.

Shiva became solemn again. 'But seriously, strange as they are, what should I do?'

'What are you thinking of doing?'

Shiva looked as if he were contemplating the roses in the far corner of the garden. 'I don't want to run away again.'

'What?' asked Bhadra, not hearing Shiva's tormented whisper clearly.

'I said,' repeated Shiva loudly, 'I can't bear the guilt of running away again.'

'That wasn't your fault—'

'Yes, it was.'

Bhadra fell silent. There was nothing more to be said.

Covering his eyes, Shiva sighed. 'Yes, it was . . .'

Bhadra put one hand on his friend's shoulder, grasping it gently, waiting for the terrible moment to pass.

Shiva turned his head to look at Bhadra. 'I'm asking for advice, my friend. If they need my help, I can't refuse, but how can I leave our tribe here all by themselves? What should I do?'

Bhadra continued to hold Shiva's shoulder. He breathed deeply. He could think of an answer: it might even be the correct answer, for Shiva, *his friend*. But was it the correct answer for Shiva, *his chief*? At last he said, 'You have to find that wisdom yourself, Shiva. That's the tradition.'

'Oh, the hell with you, and the hell with tradition.' Shiva threw the chillum back at Bhadra and stormed away.

A few days later, a minor caravan consisting of Shiva, Nandi and three soldiers was scheduled to leave Srinagar. The small size of the party would ensure that they moved quickly through the realm and reached Devagiri as soon as possible. Governor Chenardhwaj was anxious for Shiva to be recognised quickly by the empire as the true Neelkanth. He wanted to go down in history as the governor who had found the Lord.

Shiva had been made 'presentable' for the emperor. His hair had been oiled and smoothed, and his fair face had been scrubbed clean with special Ayurvedic herbs to remove years' worth of dead skin and ingrained dirt. Expensive clothes and attractive earrings, necklaces and other jewellery adorned his muscular frame. A cravat had been fabricated out of cotton to cover his glowing blue throat; it had been cleverly embroidered with beads to make it look like the traditional necklaces that Meluhan men wore on religious pilgrimages. The cravat felt warm against his still-cold throat.

'I'll be back soon,' said Shiva as he hugged Bhadra's mother. Amazingly the old woman's limp was a little less pronounced than before.

Their medicines are truly magical.

As Bhadra looked at him rather morosely, Shiva whispered, 'Take care of the tribe – you're in charge until I return.'

Bhadra stepped back, startled. 'Shiva, you don't have to do that just because I'm your friend.'

'I do have to do it, you fool – and the reason I have to do it is because you're more capable than me.'

Bhadra stepped up quickly and embraced Shiva, lest his friend notice the tears in his eyes. 'No, Shiva, I'm not. Not even in my dreams.'

'Shut up and listen to me carefully,' said Shiva as Bhadra smiled sadly. 'I don't think the Gunas are in any danger out here – at least, not as much as we were at Mount Kailash. But even so, if you feel you need help, ask Ayurvati. I saw her in action when the tribe was ill. She showed tremendous commitment to save us all. She's worth trusting.'

Bhadra nodded, hugged Shiva again and left the room.

$$-\lambda \, \text{ⓄU} \, \dagger \, \circledast -$$

Ayurvati knocked politely on the door. 'May I come in, my Lord?'

This was the first time she had visited him since that fateful moment seven days back. It felt like a lifetime ago to her. Though she appeared to be her usual confident self again, there was a slightly different look about her. She had the appearance of someone who had been touched by the divine.

'Come in, Ayurvati. And please, none of this "Lord" business – I'm still the same uncouth immigrant you met a few days ago.'

'I'm sorry about that comment, my Lord. It was wrong of me to say it and I'm willing to accept any punishment you may deem fit.'

'What's wrong with you? Why should I punish you for

speaking the truth? Why should this weird blue throat change anything?'

'You'll learn the reason soon, my Lord,' whispered Ayurvati with her head bowed. 'We've waited centuries for you.'

'Centuries! In the name of the Holy Lake, why? What can I do that none of you smart people can?'

'The emperor will tell you, my Lord, but after everything I've heard from your tribe, if there's one person worthy of being the Neelkanth, it's you.'

'Speaking of my tribe, I've told them that if they need any help, they should call on you. I hope that's all right.'

'It would be my honour to provide any assistance they might require, my Lord.' Saying this, she bent down to touch Shiva's feet in the traditional Indian manner of showing respect.

Shiva had resigned himself to accepting this gesture from most Meluhans, but he immediately stepped back as Ayurvati bent down. 'What the hell are you doing?' he asked, horrified. 'You're a doctor, a giver of life – please don't embarrass me by touching my feet.'

Ayurvati looked up at Shiva, her eyes shining with admiration and devotion. This was certainly a man worthy of being the Neelkanth.

— ☥ ⓦⓤ⚡⊛ —

Nandi entered Shiva's room carrying a saffron cloth with the word 'Ram' stamped across every inch of it. He asked Shiva to wrap it around his shoulders. As Shiva complied, Nandi muttered a short prayer for a safe journey to Devagiri, then he announced, 'Our horses are waiting outside, my Lord. We can leave whenever you're ready.'

'Nandi,' said an exasperated Shiva, 'how many times must I tell you? My name is Shiva. I'm your friend, not your Lord.'

'Oh no, my Lord,' gasped Nandi, 'you're the Neelkanth. You *are* the Lord. How can I speak your name?'

Shiva rolled his eyes and turned towards the door. 'I give up – can we leave now?'

'Of course, my Lord.'

They stepped outside to find three mounted soldiers waiting patiently. Tethered close to them were three more horses – one each for Shiva and Nandi, the third for carrying their supplies. The well-organised Meluhan Empire had rest-houses and stores spread along all major travel routes. Carrying provisions for just one day, a traveller with Meluhan coin could comfortably keep buying fresh food along the way to supply a journey of months.

Nandi's horse had been tethered next to a small platform with steps leading up to it on the side furthest from the horse – a convenient aid for obese riders who found mounting a horse a cumbersome business. Shiva looked at Nandi's enormous form, then at his unfortunate horse, and then back at Nandi.

'Aren't there any laws in Meluha against cruelty to animals?' asked Shiva with the most sincere of expressions.

'Oh yes, my Lord. Very strict laws. In Meluha *all* life is

precious. In fact, there are strict guidelines as to when and how animals can be slaughtered, and—'

Suddenly Nandi stopped speaking as Shiva's joke finally breached his slow wit. They both burst out laughing as Shiva slapped Nandi hard on his back.

— ⚐ ◍Ʊ♀✸ —

Shiva's entourage followed the course of the Jhelum, which had resumed its thunderous roar as it crashed down the lower Himalayas. When it reached the magnificent fertile plains, the turbulent river calmed once again and flowed smoothly on, smoothly enough for the group to board one of the many public transport barges and sail quickly down to the town of Brihateshpuram.

From there, they travelled east along a well-laid and clearly marked road through Punjab, the heart of the Meluhan Empire's northern reaches. Punjab literally means 'the land of the five rivers' – the land of the Indus, Jhelum, Chenab, Ravi and Beas. After convoluted journeys across the rich plains of Punjab, the four eastern rivers joined the grand Indus, which flowed furthest to the west. The Indus itself eventually found comfort and succour in the enormous, all-embracing ocean. The mystery of the ocean's final destination, though, was yet to be unravelled.

Standard Meluhan protocol required the three accompanying soldiers to ride at a polite distance behind Shiva and Nandi, far enough away not to overhear any conversation but close enough to move in quickly at the first sign of trouble.

'What's "Ram"?' enquired Shiva as he looked down at the word stamped all over his saffron cloth.

'Lord Ram was the emperor who established our way of life, my Lord,' replied Nandi. 'He lived around twelve hundred years ago and he created our systems, our rules, our ideologies, everything. His reign is known simply as "Ram Rajya" or "the rule of Ram". The Ram Rajya is considered to be the gold standard for how an empire ought to be administered, in order to create a perfect life for all its citizens. Meluha is still run according to his principles. *Jai Shri Ram.*'

'He must have been quite a man, for he truly created a paradise right here on Earth.'

Shiva was not just being polite when he said this. Meluha was a land of abundance, of almost ethereal perfection, an empire ruled by clearly codified and just laws to which every Meluhan was subordinated, including the emperor. The country supported a population of nearly eight million, which without exception looked to be well fed, healthy and wealthy. The average intellect was exceptionally high. They were a somewhat serious people, Shiva reflected, but unfailingly polite and civil. It appeared to be a flawless society in which everyone knew his role and played it perfectly. They were dedicated – nay, obsessive – when it came to their duties. The simple truth hit Shiva: if the entire society carried out its duties, nobody would need to fight for their individual rights since everybody's rights would automatically be taken care of by someone else's duties. Lord Ram was indeed a genius!

Shiva quietly repeated Nandi's cry: *'Jai Shri Ram'*, *Glory to Lord Ram.*

Leaving their tired mounts behind at a government-run crossing-house, they took a boat over the River Ravi close to the city of Hariyupa. Shiva lingered there a while, admiring the city, his soldiers waiting just beyond his shadow on fresh horses from the crossing-house on the other side of the Ravi. Hariyupa was a much larger city than Srinagar and looked grand from the outside. Next to Hariyupa, a new platform was being erected to accommodate the city's expanding population.

I'd love to know how they raise these magnificent platforms, thought Shiva, making a mental note to visit the construction site on his return journey. Tempted as he was to explore the city, it would only delay their journey to Devagiri.

A short way off, Jattaa, the captain of the crossing-house, was talking to Nandi as he prepared to climb the platform to mount his fresh horse.

'Avoid the road via Jratakgiri,' advised Jattaa. 'There was a terrorist attack there last night – all the Brahmins were killed and the village temple was destroyed. As usual, the terrorists escaped before any back-up soldiers arrived.'

'When in Lord Agni's name will we fight back? snarled Nandi angrily. 'We should attack their country!'

'I swear by Lord Indra, if I ever find one of these Chandravanshi terrorists, I'll cut his body into minute pieces and feed it to the dogs,' growled Jattaa, fists clenched tight.

'Jattaa! We are followers of the Suryavanshis. We mustn't even *think* of committing such barbaric acts,' said Nandi, scandalised that Jatta could think of defiling the dead in this hideous manner, even if the dead were terrorists.

'Do the terrorists follow the rules of war when they attack us?' Jattaa replied angrily. 'Don't they kill unarmed men?'

'That doesn't mean we can act the same way, Captain. We're Meluhans,' said Nandi firmly.

Jattaa didn't counter Nandi's statement. He was distracted by Shiva, who was still sitting on his horse at a distance, studying the city. 'Is he with you?' Jattaa asked.

'Yes.'

'He isn't wearing a caste amulet – is he a new immigrant?'

'Yes,' replied Nandi uneasily, growing uncomfortable answering questions about Shiva.

'And you're going to Devagiri?' asked Jattaa as he looked more curiously towards Shiva's throat. 'I've heard some rumours coming from Srinagar—'

'Thank you for your help, Captain Jattaa,' Nandi interrupted firmly, and before the captain could act on his suspicions, Nandi quickly climbed the platform, mounted his horse and rode towards Shiva. 'We should leave now, my Lord.'

Shiva wasn't listening; once again he was perplexed, as he saw the proud Captain Jattaa fall to his knees. Jattaa was looking directly at Shiva, his hands folded in a respectful namaste, and he appeared to be mumbling something very quickly. Shiva couldn't be sure from that distance, but it looked as if the captain was crying. He whispered, 'Why?'

'We should go, my Lord,' repeated Nandi, a little louder.

Shiva turned to him, still confused, but then he nodded and kicked his horse into motion.

As they travelled the straight and rather boring road, Shiva took the opportunity to study Nandi's jewellery, which he had begun to think might be more than merely ornamental. He wore two amulets on his thick right arm: the first was engraved with some symbolic lines, the meaning of which Shiva could not fathom. The second was etched with the likeness of an animal, probably a bull. Two pendants dangled from one of his gold chains. One was shaped like a perfectly circular sun with rays streaming outwards. The other was a brown, elliptical seed-like object with small serrations all over it.

'I'm curious about the significance of your jewellery – or is that another state secret?' teased Shiva.

'Of course not, my Lord,' replied Nandi earnestly. He pointed at the first amulet, which had been tied around his massive arm with a silky gold thread. 'This amulet represents my caste. The lines drawn on it symbolise the shoulders of the Parmatma, the Almighty. This indicates that I'm a Kshatriya.'

'And I'm sure there are clearly codified guidelines for representing the other castes as well.'

'Right you are, my Lord. You're exceptionally intelligent.'

'No, I'm not. You people are just exceptionally predictable.' Nandi smiled a little ruefully as Shiva continued, 'So what are the symbols for the Brahmins, Vaishyas and Shudras?'

'Lines drawn to represent the head of the Parmatma indicate that the wearer is a Brahmin, while the Vaishyas' symbol denotes the thighs of the Parmatma. An amulet engraved with the feet of the Parmatma would make the wearer a Shudra.'

'Interesting,' said Shiva with a slight frown. 'I imagine most Shudras are not too happy with their symbol.'

Shiva's comments surprised Nandi; why would a Shudra have a problem with this ancient symbolic order? But he kept his thoughts to himself, not wishing to disagree with his Lord.

'And the other amulet?' asked Shiva.

'This one depicts my chosen-tribe. Every Meluhan, guided by their parents' advice, applies for a chosen-tribe when they turn twenty-five years old. Brahmins choose from birds and Kshatriyas from animals. Flowers are allocated to Vaishyas, and fishes to Shudras. The Allocation Board oversees a rigorous examination process – you must qualify for a chosen-tribe that represents both your ambitions and skills. Choose a tribe that's too mighty and you'll embarrass yourself if your achievements don't measure up to the standards of that tribe. Choose a tribe too lowly and you'll not be doing justice to your own talents. As you can see, my chosen-tribe is represented by a bull.'

'Forgive me if this is an impolite question, but what does a bull mean in the hierarchy of Kshatriya chosen-tribes?'

'Well, it's not as high as a lion, tiger or elephant – but it's not a rat or a pig, either!'

'For my money, a bull can beat any lion or elephant.' Shiva smiled. 'And what about the pendants on your chain?'

'The brown seed is a representation of the last Mahadev, Lord Rudra. It symbolises the protection and regeneration of life. Even divine weapons cannot destroy the life it protects.'

'And the sun?'

'The sun shows that I am a follower of the Suryavanshi kings – the kings who are the descendants of the sun.'

'What? The sun came down and some queen—' teased an incredulous Shiva.

'Of course not, my Lord.' Nandi smiled, appreciating Shiva's humour. 'All it means is that we follow the solar calendar, so you could say instead that we're the followers of the "path of the sun". In practical terms it denotes that we're strong and steadfast. We honour our word and keep our promises, even at the cost of our lives. We never break the law. We deal honourably even with those who are dishonourable. Like the sun, we never take from anyone but always give to others. We sear our duties into our consciousness so that we may never forget them. Being a Suryavanshi means that we must always strive to be honest, brave and, above all, loyal to the truth.'

'A tall order. I assume Lord Ram was a Suryavanshi king?'

'Yes, of course,' replied Nandi, his chest puffed up with pride. 'He was *the* Suryavanshi king. *Jai Shri Ram.*'

'*Jai Shri Ram,*' echoed Shiva.

— ⚡ 𝕄𝕌 ⚥ ✳ —

Nandi and Shiva crossed the River Beas by boat, followed by their three soldiers, who waited to follow on the next craft. The Beas was the last river before the long, straight road to Devagiri. Unseasonal rain the previous night had made the crossing-house captain consider cancelling the day's sailings, but calm weather from first light had persuaded him to keep the service operational. Shiva and Nandi shared the boat with two other passengers in addition to the boatman who rowed them across.

They were a short distance from the opposite bank when a sudden storm blew up, bringing torrential rain and ferocious winds. The boatman made a valiant effort to row the remaining distance to the shore, but the boat tossed violently as it surrendered to the elements. Nandi leaned over to tell Shiva to stay low for safety, but he didn't do it gently enough. His considerable weight caused the boat to list dangerously, and he fell overboard.

The boatman struggled with the oars to steady the vessel and save the other passengers from the same fate. Meanwhile, the other two passengers exchanged uneasy glances, knowing they should jump overboard and try to save Nandi, but his massive build made them hesitate. They knew that if they tried to save him, they would most likely drown.

Shiva felt no such hesitation as he quickly tossed aside his *angvastram*, pulled off his shoes and dived into the turbulent river. Powerful strokes quickly brought him to the rapidly drowning Nandi. He had to use all his considerable strength to pull Nandi to the surface, for he weighed significantly more than any normal man, and Shiva was thankful for the extra vitality he'd been enjoying ever since the first night at the Srinagar immigration camp. He positioned himself behind Nandi and wrapped one arm around his chest, then used his other arm to propel them both to the bank. Nandi's weight made it exhausting work, but finally he was able to tow the Meluhan captain to the shore to meet the emergency staff now running towards them from the crossing-house. They dragged Nandi's limp body onto the bank, but he was unconscious.

The emergency staff then began a strange procedure: one of them started pressing Nandi's chest in a quick rhythmic motion, counting as he did so. At the count of five he stopped and another man covered Nandi's lips with his own and exhaled hard into his mouth. Then they repeated the procedure all over again. Shiva didn't understand what was going on, but he trusted the wisdom of the Meluhan medical personnel.

After several anxious moments Nandi suddenly coughed up a considerable amount of water and returned to consciousness with a start. At first he was disorientated but quickly regained his wits and turned abruptly towards Shiva, screeching, 'My Lord, why did you jump in after me? Your life is too precious – you must never risk it for me!'

Shiva, surprised, supported Nandi's back and whispered calmly, 'You need to relax, my friend.'

Agreeing with Shiva, the medical staff quickly placed Nandi on a stretcher to carry him into the rest-quarters attached to the crossing-house. Now that the immediate excitement was over, the other boat passengers were looking at Shiva with increasing curiosity. They knew that the fat man was a relatively senior Suryavanshi soldier, judging by his amulets, yet he called this fair, caste-unmarked man his 'Lord'. Strange. But the important thing was that the soldier was safe, and they soon dispersed after Shiva followed the medical staff into the rest-quarters.

CHAPTER 3

She Enters His Life

Nandi lay in a semi-conscious state for several hours while the medicines administered by the doctors worked on his body. Shiva sat by his side, repeatedly changing the damp cloth on his burning forehead to alleviate the fever. Nandi babbled incoherently as he tossed and turned in his sleep, making Shiva's task that much more difficult.

'I've been searching . . . long . . . so long . . . a hundred years . . . never thought I . . . find Neelkanth . . . *Jai Shri Ram* . . .'

Shiva tried to ignore Nandi's babble as he focused on keeping the fever down, but his ears latched on to something. *Did he just say he's been searching for a hundred years?* He frowned. *The fever's addled his brain – he doesn't look a day older than twenty.*

'I've been searching for a hundred years . . .' continued Nandi, delirious, '. . . I found . . . Neelkanth . . .'

Shiva paused for a moment and stared hard at the captain.

Then, shaking his head dismissively, he continued his ministrations.

Shiva had been walking on a paved, signposted road along the River Beas for the better part of an hour. He had left the rest-quarters to explore the area by himself, much against a rapidly recovering Nandi's advice. The captain was out of danger, but they would have to remain there for a few days until he was strong enough to travel. There was not much Shiva could do at the rest-quarters and he had begun to feel agitated, so he hoped a walk would calm him. When the three soldiers tried to shadow him, he had angrily dismissed them.

The rhythmic music of the gentle waters of the Beas soothed Shiva and a cool, refreshing breeze lightly teased his thick hair. He rested his hand on the hilt of his sword as his mind swirled with persistent questions.

Is Nandi really more than a hundred years old? Surely that's impossible? And what the hell do these crazy Meluhans need me for anyway? And why in the name of the Holy Lake is my throat still feeling so cold?

Lost in his thoughts, Shiva strayed off the road into a clearing, where he was surprised to discover the most beautiful building he had ever seen. It was built entirely of white and pink marble, with an imposing flight of stairs leading up to the top of a high platform surrounded by pillars. The ornate roof was topped by a vast triangular spire, like a giant namaste to the gods, and elaborate sculptures covered every available surface.

All the Meluhan buildings Shiva had seen so far had been functional and efficient, but this structure was oddly flamboyant. At the entrance, a sign announced *Temple of Lord Brahma*. Perhaps the Meluhans reserved their creativity for religious places?

A small crowd of hawkers surrounded a courtyard within the clearing. Some were selling flowers and food, and others were sellng assorted items required for *puja* – prayer. Leaving his shoes with a stallholder who offered to look after them while he visited the temple, Shiva walked up the steps and entered the main building, where he gazed in awe at the designs and sculptures, mesmerised by the magnificent architecture.

'What are you doing here?'

Shiva turned around to meet the quizzical stare of a pandit. His wizened face sported a flowing white beard matched in length by his silvery mane. Wearing a saffron *dhoti* and *angvastram*, he had the calm, gentle look of a man who had already attained *nirvana*, but who had chosen to remain on Earth to fulfil some heavenly duty. Shiva realised that the pandit was the first truly old person he had seen in Meluha.

'I'm sorry – am I not allowed in here?' asked Shiva politely.

'Of course you're allowed in here. Everyone is welcome in the house of the gods.'

Shiva smiled, but before he could respond, the pandit asked another question: 'But you don't believe in these gods, do you?'

Shiva's smile disappeared as quickly as it had come. *How the hell does he know that?*

The pandit answered the question in Shiva's eyes. 'Everyone who enters this place of worship looks only at the idol of Lord Brahma. Almost nobody notices the brilliant efforts of the architects who built this lovely temple. You, however, have eyes only for the architecture. You haven't even glanced towards the idol yet.'

Shiva grinned apologetically. 'You guessed right – I don't believe in symbolic gods. I believe that the real God exists all around us – in the flow of the river, in the rustle of the trees, in the whisper of the winds. He speaks to us all the time. All we need to do is listen. But I apologise if I've caused some offence by not showing proper respect for your god.'

'You don't need to apologise, my friend,' said the pandit with a smile. 'There is no "your god" or "my god". All godliness comes from the same source. Only the manifestations are different. But I have a feeling that one day you'll find a temple worth walking into for prayer, not simply to admire its beauty.'

'Really? Which temple might that be?'

'You'll find it when you're ready, my friend.'

Why do these Meluhans always talk in bizarre riddles?

Shiva nodded politely, his expression pretending an appreciation for the pandit's words that he didn't truly feel. He thought it wise to leave the temple before he truly outstayed his welcome.

'It's time I returned to my rest-quarters, Panditji, but I eagerly look forward to finding the temple of my destiny. It was a pleasure meeting you,' said Shiva as he bent down to touch the pandit's feet.

Placing his hand on Shiva's head, the pandit said softly, '*Jai Guru Vishwamitra. Jai Guru Vashishta.*'

Shiva rose and left the temple. The pandit observed him as he walked away, an admiring smile playing on his lips for he had recognised *a fellow traveller in karma*. When Shiva was clearly out of earshot, the pandit said, 'The pleasure was all mine, my *karmasaathi*.'

Shiva returned to the shoe stall and offered a coin which the shoe-keeper politely declined. 'Thank you, sir, but this is a service provided by the government of Meluha. There's no charge for it.'

Shiva smiled. 'Of course! You people have a system for everything. Thank you.'

The shoe-keeper returned his smile. 'We're simply doing our duty, sir.'

Shiva walked back to the temple steps. As he sat down, he breathed in deeply and let the tranquil atmosphere suffuse him with its serenity. And then it happened: that unforgettable moment every unrealised heart craves yet only a lucky few experience. The moment when *she* enters *his* life.

She rode into the clearing on a chariot, guiding the horses expertly into the courtyard, a lady companion by her side. Although her black hair was tied in an understated bun, a few wayward strands danced a spellbinding *kathak* in the wind. Her hypnotic blue eyes and bronzed skin would make a goddess jealous, and even though a long *angvastram* demurely covered her body, Shiva had no trouble imagining the lovely curves that surely lay beneath. Her flawless face was a picture of concentration as she manoeuvred the chariot skilfully to a halt, and she dismounted with an air of calm confidence that betrayed no hint of arrogance. Her walk was dignified, stately, her manner detached, but not cold. Shiva's gaze was that of parched earth mesmerised by a passing rain cloud.

Have mercy on me!

'My lady,' said her companion, 'I still don't feel it's wise to wander so far from the rest of your entourage.'

'Krittika, just because others don't know the law, that doesn't mean we can ignore it. Lord Ram clearly stated that once a year, a pious woman must visit Lord Brahma. I won't break that law, no matter how inconvenient it is for the body-guards!'

The lady noticed Shiva staring at her as she passed by him and her delicate eyebrows arched into a surprised and annoyed frown. Shiva made a valiant attempt to tear his gaze away, but found that his eyes were no longer under his control. Helplessly he watched her walk up the temple steps, followed by Krittika.

She looked back when she reached the top to see the caste-unmarked immigrant still staring at her unabashedly. Before entering the main temple, she muttered to Krittika, 'These uncouth immigrants – as if we'll find our saviour amongst these barbarians!'

It was only when she was out of sight that Shiva could breathe again. As he desperately tried to gather his wits, his overwhelmed and helpless mind made one obvious decision – there was no way he was leaving the temple before getting another look at her. He remained seated.

Undistracted by her presence, his breathing and heartbeat returned to normal and he began to notice something odd about his surroundings. He glanced along the road on the left from which she had emerged. She had ridden past the cucumber-seller standing near the banyan tree.

But why is the cucumber-seller not trying to hawk his wares? He's just staring at the temple. Odd . . . but none of my business, I suppose.

His gaze followed the path her chariot had taken as it swerved left around the fountain at the centre of the courtyard, then sharp right past the shepherd standing at the entrance of the garden.

But where are this shepherd's sheep?

Shiva continued tracking the route the chariot had taken into the parking area. Next to the chariot stood a man who had just walked into the temple complex but had not immediately entered the temple itself, as all the other visitors did upon their arrival. As Shiva watched he turned to the shepherd and nodded almost imperceptibly . . .

But before Shiva could piece together the information he had just gathered, he felt her presence again. He stood up and turned to watch her walking down the steps, Krittika following silently behind. Still finding this rude, caste-unmarked, obviously foreign man staring at her, she approached him and asked in a firm but polite voice, 'Excuse me, is there a problem?'

'No, no, there's no problem,' he replied, flustered. 'I just feel as if I've seen you somewhere before.'

The lady wasn't sure how to respond to this. It was obviously a lie, but the man looked sincere.

Before she could react, Krittika cut in rudely, 'Is that the best line you could come up with?'

Shiva's sharp retort died on his lips as a quick movement from the cucumber-seller caught his attention; he saw him drawing a sword as he tossed his shawl aside. The shepherd and the man next to the chariot were also now standing poised in traditional fighting stances with their own swords drawn.

Shiva immediately unsheathed his weapon and stretched out his left hand to pull the object of his fascination behind him. She, however, deftly sidestepped his protective gesture, reached into the folds of her *angvastram* and drew out her own sword.

Shiva glanced at her, surprised, and flashed her a quick admiring smile. Her eyes flashed right back, acknowledging their unexpected yet providential partnership.

She whispered under her breath to Krittika, 'Run back into the temple. Stay there till this is over.'

'But, my lady—' Krittika protested.

'Now,' she ordered, and Krittika turned and ran up the temple steps.

Shiva and the lady stood back to back in a standard defensive-partner position, covering all the directions from which a possible attack might come. The three assailants charged in as two more jumped out from behind the trees to join them. Shiva raised his sword defensively as the shepherd came up close. Shiva feigned a sideways movement to draw the shepherd into an aggressive attack, then suddenly dropped his sword low. The shepherd should have been tempted to move in for a kill-strike, and in response Shiva would have quickly raised his sword and thrust it deep into the shepherd's heart.

But the shepherd reacted unexpectedly. Instead of taking advantage of the obvious opening, he thrust his sword at Shiva's shoulder. Shiva quickly raised his right arm and swung viciously, inflicting a deep wound across the shepherd's torso. As the shepherd fell back, another attacker moved in from the right. He swung from a distance – not a smart move, for at best it would merely have inflicted a surface nick – and when Shiva stepped back to avoid the swing and brought his sword down with a smooth motion, he plunged it deep into the attacker's thigh. Screaming in agony, this man too fell back.

As another assailant joined the fight from the left, Shiva thought what a very strange assault this was. The attackers looked like good warriors who knew what they were doing, but they also appeared to be engaged in a bizarre dance of avoidance, as if they didn't want to kill, but merely injure.

Yet by holding themselves in check they were being beaten back easily. Shiva parried another attack from the left and pushed his sword viciously into the man's shoulder. The man screamed in agony as Shiva shoved him off the blade with his left hand. Slowly but surely, the attackers were flagging. They were suffering too many injuries to sustain the assault for long.

Suddenly a giant of a man carrying a sword in each hand ran into the courtyard from behind the trees. He was cloaked from head to toe in a black hooded robe, his face hidden behind a black mask. The only visible parts of his body were his large, impassive almond-shaped eyes and strong fleshy hands. He charged at Shiva and the lady as he barked an order to his men. He was too large to be agile in battle, but he was unusually skilled, which more than compensated for his slow pace. Shiva registered from the corner of his eye that the other attackers were picking up the injured and withdrawing. The hooded figure was fighting an efficient rearguard action as his men retreated.

Shiva realised that the man's hood would impair his lateral vision – a weakness that could be exploited. Moving to the left, he swung his sword ferociously, hoping to pin him back so that the lady could finish the job from the other side, but his opponent anticipated the move, stepping slightly back and deflecting Shiva's swing with a deft move of his right hand. Shiva noticed a leather band around the hooded figure's right wrist, decorated with a strange-looking symbol. Shiva swung his sword back but the hooded figure moved aside, effortlessly avoiding the blow and simultaneously deflecting a brutal flanking attack from the lady with his left hand. He was maintaining just enough distance to defend himself while still keeping them engaged in combat.

All of a sudden the hooded figure disengaged from the battle and stepped back. He began to move backwards more quickly, still pointing both his swords ahead, one at Shiva and the other at the lady. His men had all disappeared into the trees, and as soon as he reached a safe distance, he turned and ran after them. Shiva considered chasing him, but almost immediately decided against it: he might be rushing straight into an ambush.

Shiva turned to the lady warrior and enquired, 'Are you all right?'

'I am,' she said curtly before asking with a sombre expression, 'Are you injured?'

'Nothing serious. I'll survive.' He grinned.

Krittika came running down the temple steps and asked breathlessly, 'My lady – are you all right?'

'I am,' she repeated, 'thanks to this foreigner here.'

Krittika turned to Shiva and said, 'Thank you for your assistance – you've helped a very important woman.'

Shiva did not appear to be listening, though; he just continued to stare at Krittika's mistress as if he were possessed. Krittika struggled to conceal a smile.

The noblewoman averted her eyes in embarrassment, but said politely, 'I'm sorry, but I'm quite sure we haven't met before.'

'No, it's not that,' said Shiva, smiling, 'it's just that in our society, women don't fight. You wield your sword quite well for a woman.'

Oh hell! That came out all wrong.

'Excuse me?' she said, a slightly belligerent tone colouring her voice, clearly upset by that *for-a-woman* remark. 'You don't fight too badly yourself – for a barbarian.'

'Not too badly? I'm an exceptional sword-fighter! Do you want to try me?'

What the hell am I saying? I'm not going to impress her like this!

Her expression resumed its detached, supercilious look once again. 'I have no interest in duelling with you, foreigner.'

'No, no – I don't want to duel with you. I was just trying to tell you that I'm quite good at sword-fighting – I'm good at other things as well . . . but it came out all wrong. I like the fact that you fought for yourself. You're an accomplished swordsman – I mean swords*woman*. In fact, you're quite a woman . . .' bumbled Shiva, losing the filter of judgement at exactly the moment when he needed it the most.

Krittika, her head bowed, smiled gleefully at the increasingly amusing exchange.

Her mistress, on the other hand, wanted to chastise the foreigner for his highly inappropriate words – but he had undoubtedly saved her life, and she was bound by the Meluhan code of conduct. 'Thank you for your help, foreigner. I owe you my life and you'll not find me ungrateful. If you ever need my help, do call on me.'

'Can I call on you even if I don't need your help?'

Shit! What am I saying?

She glared at this caste-unmarked foreigner who clearly didn't know his place. With superhuman effort, she controlled herself, nodded politely and said, 'Namaste.'

With that, the aristocratic woman turned to leave. Krittika continued to stare at Shiva with admiring eyes, but seeing her mistress leaving, she too turned hurriedly to follow.

'At least tell me your name,' said Shiva, walking to keep pace with the noblewoman.

She stopped and stared even more gravely at Shiva.

'Look, how will I find you if I need your help?' he asked.

For a moment, she was out of words and glares. The request sounded reasonable. She turned towards Krittika and inclined her head.

'You can find us at Devagiri,' replied Krittika. 'Ask anyone in the city for Lady Sati.'

'Sati . . .' said Shiva, letting the name roll over his tongue. 'My name is Shiva.'

'Namaste, Shiva,' said the lady, Sati. 'And I promise you, I'll honour my word if you ever need my help.' With that, she turned and climbed into her chariot, followed by Krittika.

Expertly turning the chariot, Sati urged her horses into a smooth trot and sped away from the temple without a backward glance. Shiva's gaze never left the disappearing chariot. Once it was gone, he continued to stare jealously at the dust. It was fortunate enough to have touched her.

I think I'm going to like this country.

For the first time on this journey, Shiva actually found himself looking forward to reaching the Meluhans' capital city. He smiled and started back towards the rest-quarters.

CHAPTER 4

Abode of the Gods

'What? Who attacked you?' cried a concerned Nandi as he rushed towards Shiva to check his wounds.

'Relax, Nandi,' replied Shiva, 'you're in worse shape than I am after your adventure in the water. It's just a few superficial cuts, nothing serious, and the doctors have already dressed them. I'm fine.'

'I'm sorry, my Lord – this is all my fault – I should never have left you alone. It will never happen again. Please forgive me, my Lord.'

Pushing Nandi gently back onto the bed, Shiva said, 'There's nothing to forgive, my friend. How can this be your fault? Please calm down – getting worked up will only slow your recovery.'

Once Nandi had settled down, Shiva continued, 'In any case, I don't think they were trying to kill us. The whole thing was very strange.'

'Us?'

'Yes, there were two women involved.'

'But who could these attackers be?' mused Nandi. Then a disturbing thought dawned on him. 'Did the attackers wear pendants inscribed with a crescent moon?'

Shiva frowned. 'No, but one man was stranger than the rest – and he was the best swordsman of them all. He was covered from head to toe by a hooded robe and his face was concealed behind a mask. It looked like the mask you showed me at Brihateshpuram, the one that is worn at that colour festival – what's it called?'

'*Holi*, my Lord?'

'Yes, a *Holi* mask. In any case, I could only see his eyes and his hands. His only distinguishing feature was a leather bracelet with a strange symbol on it.'

'What symbol, my Lord?'

Picking up a palm-leaf booklet and a thin charcoal writing-stick from the side table, Shiva drew the symbol.

Nandi frowned. 'That's an ancient symbol for the word "Aum". But who would want to use this symbol now?'

'And what is "Aum"?' asked Shiva.

'My Lord, Aum is the holiest word in our religion, the primeval sound of nature, the hymn of the universe. For millennia, it was considered so holy that most people wouldn't even render it in written form.'

'Then how did this symbol come about?'

'It was devised by Lord Bharat, a great ruler who conquered practically all of India many thousands of years ago. He was a rare Chandravanshi worth respecting – he even married a Suryavanshi princess with the aim of ending the perpetual war between our peoples.'

'Who are these Chandravanshis?' asked Shiva.

'Think of them as the very antithesis of us, my Lord. They are the followers of the kings who are the descendants of the moon.'

'Meaning they follow the lunar calendar?'

'Yes, my Lord. They are a crooked, untrustworthy and lazy people with no laws, morals or honour. They are cowards who never attack like principled Kshatriyas. Even their kings are corrupt and selfish. The Chandravanshis are a disgrace to humanity!'

'But what does the Aum symbol have to do with them?'

'King Bharat devised it as a symbol of unity between the Suryavanshis and the Chandravanshis. The shaded top half represented the Chandravanshis.

'The bottom half represented the Suryavanshis.

'The shaded part in the bottom right represented the common path.

'The crescent moon and the sun above it to the right of the symbol represented the traditions of the Chandravanshis and Suryavanshis respectively.

'To signify that this was a pact blessed by the gods, Lord Bharat issued a mandate decreeing the pronunciation of this symbol as the holy word Aum.'

'And then what happened?'

'As expected, the pact died with the good king. Free of Lord Bharat's influence, the Chandravanshis returned to their old ways and the war began again. The symbol was forgotten, and "Aum" reverted to its original form of a word without a written representation.'

'The symbol on the masked man's bracelet was black. And the parts of the symbol didn't look like lines to me – they were more like a drawing of three serpents.'

'Naga,' exclaimed a shocked Nandi, before mumbling a soft prayer and touching his brown seed-like Rudra pendant for protection.

'And who the hell are the Nagas?' asked Shiva.

'They are cursed people, my Lord,' Nandi replied. 'They are born with hideous deformities, like extra hands or horribly misshapen faces, because of the sins of their previous births, but they also have tremendous strength and martial skills. The Naga name alone strikes terror into every Meluhan's heart. They are not even allowed to live in the Sapt Sindhu.'

'And the Sapt Sindhu would be—?'

'Our land, my Lord – the land of the seven rivers, of the Indus, Saraswati, Yamuna, Ganga, Sarayu, Brahmaputra and Narmada. This is where Lord Manu decreed that all of us, Suryavanshis and Chandravanshis alike, must live. The city of the Nagas is located south of the Narmada, beyond the border of our lands. It's bad luck even to speak of them, my Lord.'

'But why would a Naga attack me? Or any Meluhan, for that matter?'

Cursing under his breath, Nandi said, 'Because of the Chandravanshis! What depths have those two-faced people sunk to, using the demon Nagas in their attacks? In their hatred for us, they don't even realise how many sins they're inviting on their own souls.'

Shiva frowned. During the attack, it hadn't looked to him as if the soldiers were using the Naga — on the contrary — it had looked very much as if the Naga was the leader.

— 🏹 ꙮ U ✝ ☀ —

Another week's travel brought them at last to Devagiri. The Meluhans' capital city stood on the west bank of the Saraswati, which emerged at the confluence of the Sutlej and Yamuna Rivers. Nandi explained that the Saraswati's flow was severely reduced compared to her once mighty size, but even in her diminished state she was still an awe-inspiring sight.

Soaring Devagiri was a complete contrast to the mellow Saraswati. The vast city sprawled over three giant platforms, each covering more than eight hundred and seventy-five acres — significantly larger than those Shiva had seen in other cities. The platforms were nearly twenty-four feet high and bastioned with giant blocks of cut stone interspaced with baked bricks. Two of the platforms, named Tamra and Rajat — meaning Bronze and Silver — were inhabited by the general population, while the platform named Svarna — Gold — housed the royal citadel. Tall bridges made of stones and baked bricks connected the platforms, soaring high above the floodplains below.

Towering city walls enclosed each platform, surrounded in turn by ranks of giant spikes facing outwards. There were turrets at regular intervals along the walls from which soldiers could repel approaching enemies. This spectacle was beyond anything Shiva had ever seen – the construction of such a city must truly be man's greatest achievement.

Shiva's entourage rode up to the drawbridge that lay across the field of spikes surrounding the Tamra platform. The drawbridge had been reinforced with metal bars and roughened baked bricks were laid out on top so that horses and chariots would not slip. Something about the bricks intrigued him and turning to Nandi, he asked, 'Are these made using some standard process?'

'Yes, my Lord,' replied Nandi, surprised. 'All the bricks in Meluha are made according to the Chief Architect's specifications and guidelines. But how did you guess?'

'They're all exactly the same size and shape.'

Nandi beamed with pride at his empire's efficiency and his Lord's powers of observation.

Beyond the drawbridge, was an area that the Meluhans called the 'two walls'. It was an open area, with the drawbridge behind it and two steep fort walls to its left and right. This area was a valley of death for any enemy who dared to attack from here, since they could be easily attacked from the high walls to the sides. At the far end of the two-walls area, a road spiralled up to the summit of the platform on a continuous gentle curve, facilitating the passage of horses and chariots, while a broad flight of stairs led straight up the incline for pedestrians.

The city gates were made of a metal Shiva had never seen before. Nandi called it 'iron', a new metal that had just been discovered. It was the strongest of all the metals, but very expensive as the ore required to make it was not easily available. Above the city gates was etched the symbol of the Suryavanshis – a bright red circular sun with its rays blazing out in all directions. Below it was the motto they lived by: *Satya. Dharma. Maan – Truth. Duty. Honour.*

Seeing even this much of the city had left Shiva awestruck, but it was nothing compared with the wondrous sight that awaited him at the top of the platform. Breathtaking in both its efficiency and simplicity, the city was divided into a grid of square blocks by the paved streets. There were footpaths on the sides for pedestrians, lanes marked for traffic travelling in different directions, and covered drains along the centre of each street. All the buildings were two-storey block structures made of baked bricks with wooden extensions on top for increasing the buildings' height. Nandi told Shiva the layout of the buildings differed internally, depending on their specific purpose. Windows and doors were always on the side walls, never facing the main road.

The blank walls that faced the main roads bore striking black line drawings depicting various Suryavanshi legends set against sober backgrounds of grey, light blue, light green or white. The most common background colour appeared to be blue, which the Meluhans considered the holiest colour of all.

The most recurring illustrations on the walls featured the great emperor Lord Ram, lovingly depicting his victories over his enemies, his subjugation of the wicked Chandravanshis and other events that demonstrated his statesmanship and wisdom. Lord Ram was deeply revered, and Nandi explained to Shiva that many Meluhans had come to worship him like a god. They referred to him as Vishnu, an ancient title for the greatest of the gods meaning 'protector of the world and propagator of good'.

Shiva also learned that the city was divided into many districts, each consisting of four to eight blocks. Each district had its own markets, commercial and residential areas, temples and entertainment centres. Manufacturing and other polluting activities were conducted in separate areas away from these districts. The efficiency and smoothness with which Devagiri functioned belied the fact that it was the most populous city in the entire empire: at the last census, taken just two years earlier, the city's population stood at two hundred thousand.

Nandi led Shiva and the three soldiers to one of the city's numerous guest-houses, built for the many tourists who visited Devagiri for business and leisure. After tying up their horses in the designated area outside, the party entered to register and check into their rooms. The guest-house was laid out like the many others Shiva had seen during their journey, incorporating a central courtyard surrounded by residential units. The rooms were comfortably furnished and spacious.

'My Lord,' said Nandi, 'as it's almost dinner-time, I will speak with the housekeeper and have some food arranged. I recommend eating early and getting a good night's sleep as our appointment with the emperor is at the beginning of the second *prahar* tomorrow.' The day was divided into four *prahars* of six hours each, the first one beginning at midnight.

'Sounds like a good idea.'

'May I dismiss the soldiers and send them back to Srinagar?'

'That also sounds like a good idea,' said a smiling Shiva. 'Why, Nandi, sometimes you are a fount of brilliant ideas.'

Nandi laughed. 'I'll be back momentarily, my Lord.'

Shiva lay down on his bed and was quickly lost in the thoughts that really mattered to him.

I'll finish the meeting with the emperor as soon as humanly possible, give him whatever the hell he wants and then scour the city for Sati.

He had considered asking Nandi's help to locate Sati but had eventually decided against it. He was painfully aware that he had made a less than spectacular impression on her at their first meeting. If she didn't make it easy for him to find her, it would indicate that she wasn't terribly keen to see him again. He had no desire to compound the issue by speaking casually about her to others.

He smiled as the memory of her face filled his mind's eye and he replayed the magical moments when he had fought alongside her. Not the most romantic of sights for most men of his tribe, maybe, but for Shiva, it was divine. He sighed, recalling her soft, delicate body, which belied the brutal killer qualities she had displayed upon being attacked. The sensuous curves that had so captivated him had flowed smoothly as she transferred her weight to swing her sword, her demurely styled hair swaying sensuously with each thrust of her sword arm. He sighed again. *What a woman!*

— ⚚ 𝕄 𝖀 ⚜ ✹ —

Early the following morning, Shiva and Nandi crossed the bridge between the Tamra and Svarna platforms to reach the royal citadel. The bridge, another marvel of Meluhan engineering, was flanked by thick walls drilled with holes to allow soldiers to shoot arrows or pour hot oil on their enemies. The bridge was bisected by a massive gate, a final protection in case the other platform was lost to an enemy.

The Svarna platform took Shiva completely by surprise, not because of the grandeur of the royal citadel but rather the lack of opulence. Despite ruling over such a massive and wealthy empire, the nobility lived in a conspicuously simple manner. The royal citadel was laid out almost exactly like the other platforms, dominated by the same simple block structures found throughout Meluha, with no special variations for the aristocrats. The only elaborate structures were the Great Public Bath and a glorious wooden temple to Lord Indra with a cupola plated with solid gold. Recalling the temple to Lord Brahma, Shiva reflected once again that the Meluhans appeared to reserve special architecture for structures built for the gods, or those that served the common good.

Probably exactly what Lord Ram would have wanted.

Shiva and Nandi entered the royal private office to find Emperor Daksha sitting on a simple throne at the far end of the modestly furnished room, flanked by a man and a woman.

Greeting Shiva with a formal namaste, Daksha said, 'I hope your journey was comfortable.'

He looked too young to be emperor of such a large country. Though he was marginally shorter than Shiva, the major difference between them was in their physiques. Shiva was powerfully built, while Daksha's body had clearly not been honed by exercise – although he wasn't obese, just average. The same word could be used to describe his wheat-complexioned face, in which unremarkable dark eyes flanked a straight nose. He wore his hair long, like most Meluhans, and his head bore a majestic crown, the sun symbol of the Suryavanshis sparkling with gemstones at its centre. Daksha's homely appearance was offset by an elegant *dhoti* and an *angvastram* draped across his right shoulder, accompanied by a large amount of functional jewellery, including two amulets on his right arm. His only distinguishing feature was his smile – which appeared innocent and genuine. Emperor Daksha looked like a man who wore his royalty lightly.

'It was, your Majesty,' replied Shiva. 'Your empire's infrastructure is wonderful – a credit to an extraordinary emperor.'

'Thank you, but I only deserve reflected credit. The work is done by my people.'

'You're too modest, your Majesty.'

Smiling politely, Daksha asked, 'May I introduce my most important aides?' Without waiting for an answer, he pointed to the woman on his left. 'This is my prime minister, Kanakhala. She takes care of all administrative, revenue and protocol matters.'

Kanakhala offered Shiva a formal namaste. Her head was shaved except for a tuft of smooth hair at the back which had been tied in a knot. Like Ayurvati she wore a *janau* string across her torso, running from her left shoulder down to her right side. She looked young, like most Meluhans; there were folds of flesh peeping out between her white blouse and *dhoti*. Her complexion was dark and incredibly smooth, and like all her countrymen her jewellery was restrained and conservative. Shiva noticed that the second amulet on Kanakhala's arm showed a pigeon – not a particularly high chosen-tribe amongst the Brahmins. Shiva bent low and made a formal namaste in reply.

Pointing to his right, Daksha said, 'And this is my chief of the armed forces, General Parvateshwar. He's in charge of the army, navy, special forces, police, and so forth.'

Parvateshwar looked like a man Shiva would think twice about taking on in battle. He was taller than Shiva, and his immensely muscular physique dominated the space around him. His long curly hair had been fastidiously combed and fell neatly from beneath his crown. His smooth, swarthy skin was marked by the proud scars of many battles. His body was hairless, rare amongst the normally hirsute Kshatriya men who regarded body hair as a sign of masculinity. Perhaps to make up for this deficiency, Parvateshwar sported a long, thick moustache that curled upwards at the ends. His eyes reflected his uncompromisingly strong and righteous character. The second amulet on his arm bore a tiger, a very high chosen-tribe amongst the Kshatriyas. He nodded curtly at Shiva – no namaste, no elaborate bow of his proud head. Shiva, however, smiled warmly and greeted Parvateshwar with a formal namaste.

Glancing at Nandi, Parvateshwar said, 'Please wait outside, Captain.'

Before Nandi could respond, Shiva cut in, 'My apologies, but might Nandi stay here with me? He's been my constant companion since I left my homeland and has become a dear and trusted friend.'

'Of course he may,' replied Daksha.

'Your Majesty, it's not appropriate for a captain to attend this meeting,' said Parvateshwar. 'The service rules for his rank clearly state that he may escort a guest into the emperor's presence but not remain there while matters of state are discussed.'

'Oh, relax, Parvateshwar,' Daksha said. 'You take your service rules too seriously sometimes.' Turning to Shiva, the emperor continued, 'With your permission, may we see your neck now?'

Nandi slid behind Shiva to untie the cravat. Seeing the beads sewn on the cravat to convey the impression that the throat was covered for religious reasons, Daksha smiled and whispered, 'Good idea.'

As Nandi pulled the cravat off, Daksha and Kanakhala approached to inspect Shiva's throat more closely. Parvateshwar stayed where he was, but Shiva could see he was straining his neck slightly to get a better look. Daksha and Kanakhala were clearly stunned by what they saw.

The emperor gently touched Shiva's throat and whispered in awe, 'The colour comes from the inside. It's not a dye – it's true and genuine.'

Daksha and Kanakhala glanced at each other, tears glistening in their astounded eyes. Kanakhala folded her hands into a namaste and began mumbling a chant under her breath. Daksha looked up at Shiva's face, trying desperately to suppress the excitement that was coursing through him. With a controlled smile, the emperor of Meluha said, 'I hope we've not done anything to cause you any discomfort since your arrival in Meluha.'

Despite Daksha's controlled reaction, Shiva could tell that both the emperor and his prime minister were taken aback by his blue throat.

Just how important is this blue throat to the Meluhans?

'Umm, none at all, your Majesty,' replied Shiva as he tied the cravat back around his neck. 'In fact, my tribe and I have been delighted by the hospitality we've received here.'

'I'm glad of that.' Daksha smiled, bowing his head politely. 'You may want to rest a little now, then we'll talk in more detail tomorrow. Would you like to shift your residence to the royal citadel? I believe that the quarters here are a little more comfortable.'

'That's a very kind offer, your Majesty.'

Daksha turned to Nandi and asked, 'Captain, what did you say your name is?'

'Nandi, your Majesty.'

'You're also welcome to stay here. Please take good care of our honoured guest. Kanakhala, would you make all the arrangements?'

'Of course, your Majesty.'

Kanakhala rang a bell and summoned one of her aides, who escorted Shiva and Nandi out of the royal office.

As Shiva exited the room, Daksha went down on his knees with great ceremony and touched his head to the ground on which Shiva had just stood. He mumbled a prayer softly and stood up again to look at Kanakhala with tears in his eyes. Kanakhala's eyes, however, betrayed impatience and a touch of anger.

'I don't understand, your Majesty,' she said, glaring at Daksha. 'The blue mark is genuine. Why didn't you tell him?'

'What did you expect me to do?' exclaimed Daksha. 'This is only his second day in Devagiri. Did you honestly want me to tell him out of nowhere that he's the Neelkanth, our saviour? That he's been sent to solve all our problems?'

'Well, if he has a blue throat, then he's the Neelkanth, isn't he? And if he's the Neelkanth, he's our saviour. He has to accept his destiny.'

Exasperated, Parvateshwar interjected, 'I can't believe we're talking like this. We're Meluhans – we're the Suryavanshis and we've created the greatest civilisation ever known to man. And now some barbarian with no education, skills or merit is going to be our saviour? Just because he has a blue throat?'

'That's what the prophecy says, Parvateshwar,' countered Kanakhala.

Daksha interrupted both his ministers. 'Parvateshwar, I believe in the prophecy. My people believe in the prophecy. The Neelkanth has chosen my reign to appear. He will bring the Meluhan ideals to all of India – transforming it into a land of truth, duty and honour. With his leadership, we can end the Chandravanshi crisis once and for all. All the agonies they inflict upon us will be over – from the terrorist attacks to the shortage of *Somras* to the killing of the Saraswati.'

'Then why delay telling him, your Majesty?' asked Kanakhala. 'The more time we waste, the weaker our people's resolve becomes. You know there was another terrorist attack just two weeks back at a village not far from Hariyupa. As our reactions weaken, our enemies become bolder. We must inform the Lord of his destiny at once and announce his arrival far and wide. It will give us the strength to fight our cruel enemies.'

'I will tell him, but I'm trying to be more far-sighted than you. Until now, our empire has only faced the morale-sapping influence of fraudulent Neelkanths. Imagine the consequences if the people found out that the true Neelkanth has come but refuses to stand by us. First we must be sure that he's willing to accept his destiny. Only then will we announce him to our people. And I think the best way to convince him to help us is to share the whole truth with him. Once he sees the unfairness of the attacks we endure, he'll fight with us against our evil enemies. If that takes time, so be it. We've waited centuries for the Neelkanth. A few more weeks won't destroy us.'

CHAPTER 5

Tribe of Brahma

Shiva took himself for a walk in the royal guest-house's verdant gardens while Nandi helped Kanakhala's efficient aide to move the Neelkanth's possessions. At length he sat down on a comfortable bench overlooking a bed of red and white roses. A cool breeze brought a smile to his face. It was early afternoon and the garden was deserted. Shiva's thoughts kept returning to his conversation with the emperor that morning. Despite Daksha's controlled reaction, Shiva had come to realise his blue throat was of great significance to all Meluhans, including their emperor – which meant that the prophecy of the Neelkanth, whatever it was, was not restricted to some small sect in Kashmir. If the emperor himself took it so seriously, all of Meluha must need the Neelkanth's help.

But what can they possibly need help with? They're so much more advanced than us—

His thoughts were interrupted by the sounds of a *dhol*, a

percussion instrument, and some *ghungroos*, the anklets worn by dancers. Someone must be practising near the dance pavilion, which was separated from the rest of the garden by a hedge. Shiva, himself a passionate dancer, would normally have rushed to join in, but his mind was preoccupied. He listened distractedly to some conversation floating across from the dancers.

'No, my lady, you must let yourself go,' said a distinguished male voice. 'It's not a chore that you have to complete. Enjoy the dance. You're trying too hard to remember all the steps rather than allowing the emotion of the dance to flow through you.'

Then a female voice interjected, 'My lady, Guruji is right – you're dancing correctly but you're not enjoying it, and the concentration shows on your face. You have to relax a little.'

'Let me get the steps right first, then I can learn to enjoy them.'

The last voice made Shiva's hair stand on end. It was *her* – it was Sati. He rose quickly and followed the sound of the voices. Coming around the hedge, he saw Sati dancing on a small platform. She held her hands rigidly at her sides as she performed the various movements of the dance. She swayed her shapely hips to one side and placed her hands precisely on her waist in the manner required to convey the mood of the dance. He was mesmerised once again – but entranced though he was, Shiva had to agree with the Guruji: Sati's precise but mechanical movements lacked the uninhibited surrender characteristic of a natural dancer. She conveyed nothing of the bliss and anger of the story being told. She wasn't using the entire platform – her steps were small, which kept her movements constricted to the centre.

The dance teacher sat facing Sati, tapping out her beats on the *dhol*. Her companion, Krittika, sat to the right. It was the dance teacher who noticed Shiva first and immediately stood up. Sati and Krittika turned as he did so, and were astonished to find Shiva standing in front of them. Unlike Sati, Krittika could not control her surprise and blurted out, 'Shiva?'

Sati, as composed and restrained as at their first meeting, asked politely, 'Is everything all right, Shiva? Do you need my help with something?'

How have you been? I've missed you. Don't you ever smile?

He continued to stare at Sati, the words running through his mind but never making it to his lips. An amused Krittika glanced at Sati for her reaction.

An even more serious Sati repeated, very politely, 'Can I help you with something, Shiva?'

'No, no, I don't need any help,' replied Shiva when he regained the power of speech. 'I just happened to be in the area and heard your dancing . . . I mean your conversation – your dance steps were not so hard that I could hear them. You were dancing very accurately. Actually, technically it was all—'

Krittika interjected, 'You know a bit about dancing, do you?'

'Oh, just a little,' Shiva replied, smiling at Krittika before turning rapidly back to Sati. 'My apologies, Sati, but Guruji is right – you were being far too methodical. As they say in the land I come from, the steps were all technically correct, but the *bhav* – the emotion – was missing. And a dance without *bhav* is like a body without a soul. When a dancer's emotions direct her movements, she does not even need to remember the steps. The steps come on their own. The *bhav* is something you cannot learn. It comes to you if you can create the space for it in your heart.'

Sati listened patiently to Shiva without saying a word, although her eyebrows rose slightly as the barbarian spoke. How could he know more about dancing than a Suryavanshi? But she reminded herself that he had saved her life. She was duty-bound to honour him.

Krittika, however, took offence at this caste-unmarked foreigner pretending that he knew more about dancing than her mistress. She glowered at Shiva. 'You dare to think that you know more than one of the best dancers in the realm?'

Realising that he might have caused offence in spite of his best efforts not to, Shiva turned to Sati and said earnestly, 'I'm terribly sorry – I didn't mean to insult you in any way. Sometimes I just keep talking without realising what I'm saying.'

'No, no,' replied Sati, 'you didn't insult me. Perhaps you're right – I don't feel the essence of the dance as much as I should. But with Guruji's guidance, I hope to learn how to, in time.'

Seizing his chance to impress Sati, Shiva said, 'With your permission, may I perform the dance? I'm sure I won't be as technically correct as you, but perhaps the *bhav* will guide my steps.'

That was well put – surely she can't say no?

Sati looked surprised. This was unexpected. 'Um, okay,' she managed, and a delighted Shiva immediately moved to the centre of the stage.

He took off the *angvastram* covering his upper body and tossed it aside. Krittika's initial anger at the perceived insult to her mistress was quickly forgotten when she glimpsed Shiva's rippling physique, though Sati began to wonder how Shiva would bend such a muscular body into the contortions required by this style of dancing. Flexibility was usually sacrificed at the altar of strength.

Playing lightly on his *dhol*, the Guruji asked Shiva, 'Tell me the beat you're comfortable with, young man.'

Shiva folded his hands into a namaste, bent low and said, 'Guruji, could you give me a minute, please? I need to prepare for the dance.'

Dancing was something Shiva knew as well as warfare. Facing east, he closed his eyes and bowed his head slightly, then knelt down and touched the ground reverently with his head. Standing up again, he turned his right foot outwards. Then he raised his left leg off the floor in a graceful arching movement until his foot was above knee height, simultaneously bending his right knee slightly to balance himself. His left foot pointed exactly between the angle of his right foot and his face. Only a calm breeze broke the almost total silence that enveloped his audience as the Guruji, Sati and Krittika stared in amazement at Shiva. They didn't understand what he was doing but they could feel the energy emanating from Shiva's stance.

Shiva raised both his arms and moved them to the sides in an elegant circular movement, bringing them in line with his shoulders. He moulded his right hand as if it was holding an imaginary *dumru*, a small percussion instrument. His left hand was open with its palm facing upwards, almost as if it was receiving some divine energy. He held this pose for a few moments, his glowing face showing that he was withdrawing into his own world. Then his right hand moved effortlessly forwards, almost as if it had a mind of its own, its palm now open and facing the audience. Somehow the posture conveyed a feeling of protection. His left arm then circled slowly from its shoulder-height position, moving in front of him with the palm facing down, stopping when the hand was pointing almost directly at his left foot. Shiva held this pose for some time.

And then the dance began.

Sati watched in wonder. This Shiva was performing the same steps she had, yet it looked like a completely different dance. His hands and body moved effortlessly, almost magically. How could a physique this muscular be so flexible?

The Guruji tried to beat for Shiva with his *dhol*, but clearly he didn't need them; instead, Shiva's feet were leading the beat for the *dhol*.

The dance told the story of a woman's emotions: at the beginning her feelings of joy and lust as she cavorted with her husband, then her fury and pain over the wrongful death of her mate. Even with his muscular body, Shiva somehow managed to communicate the grieving woman's tender yet powerful emotions.

Shiva's eyes were open, but his audience soon realised he was oblivious to them; caught up in his own world. He didn't dance for the audience, or for the music, or for appreciation; he danced only for himself, almost as if guided by a celestial force. Sati realised Shiva was right. He had opened himself and the dance had come to him.

After the dance came to an end, Shiva closed his eyes. He held the final pose for many moments as the glow slowly left him, as if he were returning to this world from some celestial realm. He gradually opened his eyes to find Sati, Krittika and the Guruji gaping at him, awestruck.

The Guruji was the first to find his voice. 'Who *are* you?'

'I'm Shiva.'

'No, no, not the body – I meant who are *you*?'

Shiva crooked his brows together in a puzzled frown and repeated, 'I'm Shiva.'

'Guruji, may I ask a question?' At his nod, Sati turned to

Shiva and said, 'What was that thing you did before the dance? Was it some kind of preparatory step?'

'Yes – it's called the *Nataraj* pose, the pose of the Lord of Dance.'

'And what does this *Nataraj* pose do?'

'It aligns my energy with the universal energy so that I may become a channel for the dance.'

'I don't understand.'

'Think of it like this: my people believe that everything in the world – plants, animals, objects, our bodies – carries and transmits *shakti*, energy, and the biggest carrier of energy of all is Mother Earth herself – the ground we walk on.'

'What does that have to do with your dance?'

'Everything we do requires energy, and we must source this energy from the world around us – from people, from objects, from Mother Earth herself – and we have to ask for that energy respectfully.'

'So your *Nataraj* pose helps you to access energy from everything around you?' asked the Guruji with keen interest.

'Different poses access different kinds of energy. The *Nataraj* pose helps me to ask respectfully for energy to channel a dance that wants to flow through me. If I wanted to access energy for thinking, I would have to sit cross-legged and meditate.'

'The energy appears to favour you, young man,' said the Guruji. 'You are the *Nataraj*, the Lord of Dance.'

'Oh no,' exclaimed Shiva, 'I'm just a medium for the boundless *Nataraj* energy. Anyone can be the medium.'

'Then you're a particularly efficient medium, young man,' said the Guruji. Turning to Sati, he said, 'You don't need me if you have a friend like him, my child. If you want to be taught by Shiva, it would be my honour to excuse myself.'

Shiva looked at Sati expectantly. This had gone much better than he could have hoped.

Say yes, dammit!

Sati, however, withdrew into herself, and Shiva was startled to see the first signs of vulnerability in this woman. She bowed her head, an act at odds with her proud bearing, and whispered softly, 'I mean no disrespect to anyone, but perhaps I don't have the skills to receive training of this level.'

'But you do have the skill,' argued Shiva. 'You have the bearing. You have the heart. You can very easily reach that level.'

Sati looked up at Shiva, and the profound sadness her eyes conveyed made his mind reel.

What the hell is going on here?

'I am far beneath many levels, Shiva,' mumbled Sati.

As her mysterious statement echoed in Shiva's mind, she visibly summoned the strength to restore her composure, and her customary politely proud mask was soon back in place. 'It's time for my *puja*. With your permission, Guruji, I must leave.' She turned towards Shiva. 'It was a pleasure meeting you again, Shiva.'

Before Shiva could respond, Sati turned quickly and departed, followed by Krittika.

The Guruji continued to stare at the flummoxed Shiva until at length, he bent low in a formal namaste towards Shiva and said, 'It has been my life's honour to see you dance.' Then he too turned and left.

Shiva stood alone again, wondering at the inscrutable ways of the Meluhans.

— 🕉️ —

Late the following morning, Shiva and Nandi entered the private royal office to find Daksha, Parvateshwar and Kanakhala waiting for him. Shiva, surprised, said, 'I'm sorry, your Majesty – I thought we were to meet four hours into the second *prahar*. I hope I haven't kept you waiting.'

Daksha, who had risen with a formal namaste, bowed low and said, 'Not at all, my Lord – we came in early so that we wouldn't keep you waiting. It was our honour to wait for you.'

Parvateshwar rolled his eyes at the extreme subservience his emperor, the ruler of the greatest civilisation ever established, was showing towards this barbarian. Shiva, hiding his surprise at being referred to as 'Lord' by the emperor, bowed low towards Daksha with a namaste and sat down.

'My Lord, before I begin to recount the prophecy of the Neelkanth, do you have any questions?' enquired Daksha.

The most obvious question came to Shiva's mind first: *Why in the Holy Lake's name is my blue throat so important to you people?* But his instincts told him that although this might be the most obvious question, it could not be answered to his satisfaction until he understood more about Meluhan society. Instead he said, 'It may sound like an unusual question, your Majesty, but might I ask your age?'

Daksha looked in surprise at Kanakhala. Then, turning back towards Shiva with an awed smile, he said, 'You're exceptionally intelligent, my Lord. You've asked the most pertinent question first.' Crinkling his face into a conspiratorial grin, Daksha continued, 'Last month I turned one hundred and eighty-four.'

Shiva was stunned. Daksha did not look a day older than thirty. In fact, nobody in Meluha looked old, except for the pandit Shiva had met at the Brahma temple.

So Nandi is more than a hundred years old after all.

'How can this be, your Majesty?' he asked, trying not to sound as flabbergasted as he felt. 'What sorcery makes this possible?'

'There's no sorcery,' the emperor explained. 'Our talented scientists make a potion called the *Somras*, the 'drink of the gods'. Taking the *Somras* at prescribed times postpones death and allows us to live our entire lives in the prime of our youth, both mentally and physically.'

'But what is this *Somras*? Where does it come from? Who invented it?'

'So many questions.' Daksha smiled indulgently. 'I'll try my best to answer them all. The *Somras* was invented many thousands of years ago by one of the greatest Indian scientists who ever lived. His name was Lord Brahma.'

'I think I visited a temple dedicated to him on the way to Devagiri. At a place named Meru?'

'Yes, that's where he's said to have lived and worked. Lord Brahma was a prolific inventor, but he never profited personally from his inventions. His primary concern was ensuring that his innovations were used for the good of mankind. He realised soon after discovering the *Somras* that a potion so powerful could be misused by evil men, so he imposed restrictions on its usage.'

'What kind of restrictions?'

'He didn't give the *Somras* freely to everyone,' continued Daksha. 'After conducting a rigorous countrywide survey, he selected a group of adolescent boys of impeccable character, one from each of the seven regions of ancient India. He chose young boys who would live with him as his *gurukul*, the family of the Guru, so that he could mould them into selfless helpers of society. The *Somras* was administered only to these boys, and because the *Somras* gave them practically an additional lifespan, they came to be known as the *dwija* or twice-born. With the strength of the *Somras*, Lord Brahma's training and the numerous other inventions they collectively produced, this group became more powerful than any other in history. They honed their minds to achieve almost superhuman intelligence. The ancient Indian title for men of knowledge was *Rishi*. Since Lord Brahma's chosen were seven in number, they came to be known as the *Saptrishis*.'

'And these *Saptrishis* used their skills for the good of society?' Shiva asked.

'Yes, Lord Brahma instituted strict rules of conduct for the *Saptrishis*. They were not allowed to rule, or to practise any trade – essentially, they were forbidden from doing anything that would have resulted in personal gain. They had to dedicate their skills to professions that would help society, so they became priests, teachers, doctors and so on. They were not allowed to charge for their services; they had to live on alms and donations.'

'Tough service rules,' joked Shiva, winking mischievously at Parvateshwar.

Parvateshwar did not deign to respond, but the others appreciated his humour. Shiva glanced at the *prahar* lamp by the window – it was almost the third *prahar* – the time when Sati would probably come out to dance. He turned his attention back to the emperor as he continued his story.

'Tough rules indeed, but nevertheless they followed their code of conduct strictly. Over time, as their responsibilities grew, the *Saptrishis* selected many more people to join their tribe. Their followers swore to live by the *Saptrishis'* code and were also administered the *Somras*. They devoted their lives to the pursuit of knowledge and to the wellbeing of society without asking for any material gain in return. For this reason, society accorded these people almost devotional respect. Over the ages the *Saptrishis* and their followers came to be known as the Tribe of Brahma, or simply the Brahmins.'

Shiva said thoughtfully, 'But as usually happens with all good systems over long periods of time, some people stopped following the Brahmin code, right?'

'Absolutely, my Lord,' answered Daksha, shaking his head at the all-too-familiar human frailty. 'As the millennia passed, some of the Brahmins forgot the strict code instituted by Lord Brahma and honoured by the *Saptrishis*. They started misusing the awesome powers that the *Somras* gave them for their own personal gain. Some Brahmins used their influence over large numbers of people to conquer kingdoms and become rulers. Some misused other *Saptrishi* inventions to accumulate fabulous wealth for themselves.'

'And some of the Brahmins,' interjected Kanakhala, her tone horrified, 'even rebelled against the *Saptrishi Uttradhikaris*.'

'And they were—?' enquired Shiva.

'The successors to the *Saptrishis*,' clarified Kanakhala. 'When a *Saptrishi* realised that he was coming to the end of his mortal life, he would appoint a man from his *gurukul* as his successor. This successor was then treated for all practical purposes like the *Saptrishi* himself.'

'So rebelling against the *Saptrishi Uttradhikaris* was like rebelling against the *Saptrishis* themselves?'

'Yes, my Lord. And the most disturbing aspect of this corruption was that the higher chosen-tribe Brahmins – the eagles, peacocks and swans – were the first to rebel,' she said sadly. 'These higher-status chosen-tribes were not even allowed to work under the Kshatriyas and Vaishyas lest they became enticed by the lure of the material world. Yet they succumbed first to the temptations of evil.'

'And chosen-tribes like yours, the pigeons, remained loyal to the old code despite working for the Kshatriyas?' asked Shiva.

'Yes, my Lord,' replied Kanakhala, her chest puffed up with pride.

The town bell rang loudly, indicating the beginning of the third *prahar*. Everyone, including Shiva – who was learning some of the Meluhans' ways – said a short prayer welcoming the next part of the day. A Shudra entered to reset the *prahar* lamp and left as quietly as he had come. Any time now, thought Shiva, Sati would start her dance in the garden.

'So am I right in thinking that the Brahmins' betrayal of the *Saptrishi* code led to some kind of revolution?' Shiva asked, turning to the emperor. 'You, Parvateshwar and Nandi are Kshatriyas, and yet clearly you have taken the *Somras*. In fact, I've seen people of all four castes in your empire who look youthful and healthy, which suggests that the *Somras* is now given to everybody. This change must have been the result of a revolution, right?'

'Yes – and the revolution was known as Lord Ram, the greatest emperor who ever lived – *Jai Shri Ram!*'

'*Jai Shri Ram*,' repeated everyone in the room.

'His ideas and leadership dramatically transformed Indian society,' he continued, 'and radically altered the course of history itself. But before I continue with Lord Ram's tale, may I make a suggestion?'

'Of course, your Majesty.'

'As it's now the third *prahar*, shall we move to the dining room and partake of some lunch before continuing with this story?'

'An excellent idea, your Majesty,' said Shiva, 'but may I be excused for a while? I have another pressing engagement to attend to. Could we continue our conversation tomorrow?'

Kanakhala's expression fell immediately while Parvateshwar's lips curled into a contemptuous grin.

Daksha, however, kept a smile on his face. 'Of course we can meet tomorrow, my Lord. Will the beginning of the second hour of the second *prahar* work for you?'

'Absolutely, your Majesty. My apologies for this inconvenience.'

'Not at all, my Lord,' said the still-smiling Daksha. 'Can one of my chariots take you to your destination?'

'That's very kind of you, but I prefer to make my own way there. My apologies once again.'

With a hasty namaste to everyone in the room, Shiva quickly made his exit, closely followed by Nandi.

When the door had closed behind them, Kanakhala looked accusingly at Daksha. The emperor gestured for calm. 'It's all right. We're meeting again tomorrow, aren't we?'

'My Lord, we're running out of time,' said Kanakhala. 'The Neelkanth needs to accept his responsibilities immediately—'

'Give him time, Kanakhala. We've waited for so long – a few more days won't make much difference.'

Parvateshwar rose suddenly, bowed low towards Daksha and said, 'With your permission, your Majesty, may I be excused? More important things than educating a barbarian require my attention.'

'You will speak of him with respect, Parvateshwar,' growled Kanakhala. 'He's the Neelkanth.'

'I will speak of him with respect when he has earned it,' snarled Parvateshwar. 'I respect achievements, nothing else. That's Lord Ram's fundamental rule – only your karma is important, not your birth, not your sex – and certainly not the colour of your throat. Our entire society is based on merit – or have you forgotten that?'

'Enough,' exclaimed Daksha. 'I respect the Neelkanth – and so will everybody else!'

CHAPTER 6

Vikarma, the Carriers of Bad Fate

Nandi waited at a distance in the garden as instructed while Shiva went behind the hedge to the dance area. Looking at the silent stage, Nandi had the feeling that his Lord was about to be disappointed, but Shiva was filled with hope and waited expectantly for Sati. After the better part of an hour had passed, however, he realised there would be no dance practice today. Deeply disappointed, he walked silently back to Nandi.

'Can I help you find somebody, my Lord?' asked Nandi earnestly.

'No, Nandi. Forget it.'

In an attempt to change the topic and cheer him up, Nandi said, 'My Lord, you must be hungry – shall we return to the guest-house and eat?'

'I think I'd rather see a little more of the city,' said Shiva, hoping that fate would be kind to him and he would run into

Sati in the town. 'How about one of the restaurants on the Rajat platform?'

'That would be wonderful.' Nandi smiled, glad of the respite from the simple, bland Brahmin-influenced vegetarian food served at the royal guest-house. He missed the spicy meats served in rough Kshatriya restaurants.

— ⅄ ⓪Ｕ⇕⊛ —

'What do you want, Parvateshwar?' asked Daksha.

'My Lord, my apologies for requesting a meeting so suddenly, but I just received some disturbing news that we must discuss in private.'

'Out with it, then.'

'Shiva is already causing trouble.'

'What have you got against the Neelkanth?' groaned Daksha, rolling his eyes to the ceiling in disapproval. 'Why can't you believe that the Neelkanth has come to save us?'

'This has nothing to do with my opinion of Shiva, my Lord, as will become clear if you hear me out. Chenardhwaj saw Shiva in the gardens yesterday.'

'Chenardhwaj is here already?'

'Yes, your Majesty — his taxation review with you is scheduled for the day after tomorrow.'

'Good, good. So what did Chenardhwaj see?'

'You should know that he's also sickeningly taken in by the Neelkanth, so I think we can safely assume he doesn't have any malicious intent.'

'Good to know. So what did he see the Neelkanth do?'

'He saw Shiva dancing in the gardens,' replied Parvateshwar.

'So what? Is there some law banning dance that I'm not aware of?'

'Please let me continue, your Majesty. He was dancing while Sati watched, spellbound.'

Parvateshwar suddenly had Daksha's full attention, and he leaned forward to ask, 'What happened next?'

'Sati behaved correctly and took her leave the moment Shiva tried to get too familiar. But Chenardhwaj heard Shiva whisper something when Sati had left.'

'And what was that?'

'He whispered: *Holy Lake, help me get her. I won't ask for anything else from you ever again.*'

Daksha couldn't contain his delight. 'You mean the Neelkanth might actually be in love with my daughter?'

'Your Majesty, you can't forget the laws of the land,' Parvateshwar exclaimed, horrified. 'You know Sati can't marry.'

'If the Neelkanth decides to marry Sati, no law on Earth can stop him.'

'Your Majesty, forgive me, but our civilisation's most basic tenet is that *nobody* is above the law. That's what makes us who we are, what makes us better than the Chandravanshis and the Nagas. Not even Lord Ram was above the law – so how can this barbarian possibly be so important?'

'Don't you want Sati to be happy?' asked Daksha. 'Don't you want her to find joy again?'

'I love Sati like the daughter I never had, your Majesty,' said Parvateshwar, his eyes alight with a rare display of emotion. 'I'd do anything for her. Except break the law.'

'That's the difference between you and me, Parvateshwar. For Sati's sake, I'd break any law. She's my daughter, my flesh and blood. She's suffered enough already. If I can find some way to make her happy, I'll do it, no matter what the consequences!'

— ⚶ ⓂⓊ✝ ☸ —

Shiva and Nandi tethered their horses in the designated area next to the main Rajat platform market, and Nandi guided Shiva towards one of his favourite restaurants. The inviting aroma of freshly cooked meat stirred a hunger in Nandi that had not been satisfied in the past two days at the royal guest-house. The owner, however, stopped Shiva at the door.

'What's the matter, brother?' asked Nandi.

'I'm deeply sorry, brothers,' said the restaurant owner politely, 'but I too am subject to religious vows at this time.' He pointed to the beads around his throat. 'And as you know, those vows forbid me from serving meat to fellow vow-keepers.'

'But who's taken religious—?' Nandi started, then quickly fell silent when he saw Shiva flick his eyes downwards at the bead-covered cravat around his throat. Nandi nodded and followed Shiva out of the restaurant.

'This is the time of year for religious vows, my Lord, being close to the summer solstice,' explained Nandi. 'Why don't you wait here for a moment? There are some good places along the lane to the right – let me check if there's a restaurant owner who has not yet taken his vows.'

Shiva nodded and leaned against a wall to take in the street scene as Nandi hurried off. It was a busy market area split between restaurants and shops, but despite the crowds and volume of commerce being conducted, the street was not bursting with noise. None of the shopkeepers were out screaming to advertise their wares, and the customers spoke softly and in an unfailingly polite manner, even when they were bargaining.

These well-mannered idiots wouldn't get any business done in our boisterous mountain market, he thought.

Lost in his thoughts about the Meluhans' strange practices, he did not hear the town crier until he was almost right behind him.

He cried, 'Procession of *vikarma* women approaching – please move aside!' and Shiva turned around to find a tall Meluhan Kshatriya looking down at him. 'Would you like to move aside, sir? A procession of *vikarma* women needs to pass for their prayers.'

The crier's tone and demeanour were unquestionably courteous, but Shiva was under no illusions. The Kshatriya was not *asking* Shiva to move; he was *telling* him. Shiva stepped back to let the procession pass just as Nandi touched him gently on his arm.

'I've found a good restaurant, my Lord,' he said with a grin. 'It's one of my favourites, and the kitchen will be open for at least an hour – there'll be plenty of food to stuff ourselves with.'

Shiva laughed out loud. 'It's a wonder that just one restaurant can actually make enough food to satisfy your hunger!'

Nandi laughed along good-naturedly as Shiva patted his friend on the back.

As they turned into the lane, Shiva asked, 'Who are those *vikarma* women?'

Nandi sighed deeply, his gentle face troubled. '*Vikarma* are men and women who are being punished in this birth for the sins of their previous birth. The only way they can wipe their karma clean is to live this life with dignity and tolerate their present sufferings with grace. Men and women have their own orders of penance. For example, every month, *vikarma* women must offer a special *puja* to Lord Agni, the purifying fire god, to ask his forgiveness. They're not allowed to marry, because they might poison others with their bad karma, nor are they allowed to touch any person not related to them, or anyone they encounter outside their normal duties. There are many other conditions I'm not familiar with – if you're interested, there are pandits at the Agni Temple who'd be happy to tell you all about *vikarma* people—'

'Not right now,' said Shiva with a smile. 'I'm not really in the mood for confusing and abstruse philosophies. But tell me one thing – who decides that the *vikarma* people had committed sins in their previous births?'

'Their own karma, my Lord,' said Nandi, surprised that

Shiva had to ask about something so obvious. 'For example, if a woman gives birth to a stillborn child, why would she be punished thus unless she had committed some terrible sin in her previous birth? Or if a man is suddenly paralysed by an incurable disease, why would that happen to him unless the universe was penalising him for the sins of his previous life?'

'That sounds pretty ridiculous to me. A woman could give birth to a stillborn child simply because she didn't take proper care during her pregnancy, or because of a disease. How can anyone say that she's being punished for the sins of her previous birth?'

Shocked by Shiva's words, Nandi struggled to find a polite response. He was a Meluhan, and sincerely believed in the concept of karma being carried over many births. He mumbled softly, 'It's the law, my Lord—'

'Frankly, that sounds like a rather unfair law to me.'

Nandi's crestfallen face showed his profound disappoint-ment that Shiva did not understand such a fundamental Meluhan concept, but he kept his own counsel. After all, Shiva was the Neelkanth.

Seeing how dejected Nandi was, Shiva patted him gently on the back. 'Nandi, that's just my opinion. If this law works for your people, I'm sure there must be some logic to it. Your society might be a little strange to me at times, but it has some of the most honest and decent people I've ever met.'

As a relieved smile lit Nandi's face, his whole being was

overcome by a more immediate problem – his debilitating hunger – and he entered the restaurant like a man on a mission, with Shiva chuckling softly behind.

A short distance away, the procession of *vikarma* women walked silently along the main road, all of them draped with long *angvastrams* dyed blue, the holy colour. Their heads were bowed low in penitence, their *puja thalis* or prayer plates full of offerings to Lord Agni. The low-level noise of the market street faded to deathly silence as the pitiful women lumbered by. At the centre of the procession, unseen by Shiva and covered from head to toe with her blue *angvastram*, her face a picture of resigned dignity and her head bowed low, trudged the forlorn figure of Sati.

— ⸱⸱⸱ —

'So where were we, my Lord?' asked Daksha as Shiva and Nandi settled down in his private office the next morning.

'You were about to tell me how Lord Ram defeated the renegade Brahmins,' answered Shiva.

'Ah, that's right,' said the emperor. 'Lord Ram did indeed defeat the renegade Brahmins, but in his view, the problem went much deeper than some Brahmins not following the code. The real problem was the conflict between a person's natural karma and what society forced him to do.'

'I don't understand, your Majesty.'

'If you think about it, what was the essential problem with the renegade Brahmins? Some of them wanted to be Kshatriyas and rule, while others wanted to be Vaishyas, make money and live a life of luxury, though their birth meant they had no choice but to be Brahmins.'

'But I thought people became Brahmins through a rigorous selection process, not by birth,' said Shiva, confused.

'That was true originally, but over time Lord Brahma's selection process lost its fairness. Children of Brahmins became Brahmins, children of Kshatriyas became Kshatriyas and so on. The formal system of selection soon ceased to exist. A father would ensure that his children got all the resources needed to grow up to become a member of his own caste, and so the caste system became rigid.'

'So a child born to Shudra parents who was talented enough to be a Brahmin would no longer get the opportunity to become a Brahmin?' asked Shiva.

'Exactly, Shiva,' said Parvateshwar, addressing him directly for the first time – although without any fawning, Shiva noticed. 'In Lord Ram's opinion, any societal hierarchy not based on merit was doomed to fail. His view was that a person's caste should be decided only by that person's karma, not his family of birth or his sex.'

'That's nice in theory, Parvateshwar,' argued Shiva, 'but how do you enforce it in practice? A child born into a Brahmin family would automatically have access to an upbringing and resources unavailable to a child born into a Shudra family. Consequently this Brahmin-born child would grow up to be a Brahmin even if he were less talented than the Shudra child.

Isn't this unfair to the child born into the Shudra family? Where's the "merit" in such a system?'

'That was the genius of Lord Ram, Shiva,' replied Parvateshwar. 'He was a brave general, a brilliant administrator and a fair judge, but his greatest legacy is the system he created to ensure that a person's karma is determined by his abilities alone. That system has made Meluha the greatest nation in history.'

'The *Somras* has also played an important role, Parvateshwar,' said Daksha. 'Lord Ram's most revolutionary act was to give the *Somras* to everyone. This elixir has given us the ability to create our remarkable and near-perfect society.'

'Begging your pardon, your Majesty,' said Shiva, 'but I'd like to hear more from Parvateshwar about this system Lord Ram set up.'

'It's actually a remarkably simple system,' said Parvateshwar, 'and Meluhans start it at birth. Every child born in Meluha is compulsorily adopted by the empire, and to make sure no children fall through the cracks, all pregnant women are required to give birth in a great hospital city called Maika, built specially for this purpose in the south, just north of the Narmanda River. Only pregnant women are allowed into the city.'

'Nobody else? What about their husbands, their parents?' asked Shiva.

'One exception to this rule was voted in around three hundred years ago, allowing the husbands and parents of women of noble families to enter Maika.' Parvateshwar's grave expression clearly showed his disapproval of this corruption of Lord Ram's system.

'So who takes care of all the pregnant women in Maika?'

'The well-trained hospital staff,' replied Parvateshwar. 'Once the child is born, he or she is kept in Maika for a few weeks for health checks, and the mother travels back to her own city.'

'Without her child?' asked Shiva, astonished.

'Of course,' replied Parvateshwar, frowning slightly at Shiva's failure to grasp the obvious. 'The child is then put into the Meluha Gurukul, the school near Maika. Every single child receives the benefit of exactly the same education system and enjoys all the empire's resources.'

'Do they maintain records linking parents with their birth-children?'

'Of course – but they're archived with the utmost secrecy by the record-keeper of Maika.'

'So no one in the Gurukul or the rest of the empire knows who the child's birth-parents are?' said Shiva, thinking through the implications of what he was hearing. 'So every child, whether born to a Brahmin or a Shudra, gets exactly the same treatment at the Gurukul?'

'Exactly.' Parvateshwar smiled, clearly proud of the system. 'When the children enter adolescence, they're all given the *Somras*, and every child has exactly the same opportunity to succeed. At the age of fifteen, when they have reached adult-hood, all the children take a comprehensive examination, the results of which determine which *varna* or caste the child will be allocated to – Brahmin, Kshatriya, Vaishya or Shudra.'

Kanakhala cut in, 'And then the children are given one more year of caste-specific training. They wear their *varna* colour bands – white for Brahmins, red for Kshatriyas, green for Vaishyas and black for Shudras – and complete their education in their respective caste schools.'

'So that's why your caste system is called the *varna* system,' said Shiva. '*Varna* means "colour", right?'

'Yes, my Lord,' said Kanakhala, smiling warmly at Shiva. 'You're very observant.'

Aiming a withering look at Kanakhala, Parvateshwar added sarcastically, 'Yes, that was a very difficult conclusion to draw.'

Ignoring the barb, Shiva asked Parvateshwar, 'So what happens after that?'

'When the children turn sixteen, they're allocated to applicant parents from their caste. These adoptive parents then raise the child as their own.'

'That's a remarkably elegant system,' said Shiva. 'Each person is given a place in society based on only his abilities, regardless of any other factor.'

'Over time, my Lord,' said Daksha, 'we found the percentage of children entering higher castes actually increasing across the population – which proves that any child with ability can excel and succeed, given a fair chance.'

'The lower castes must have loved Lord Ram for offering them this opportunity,' said Shiva.

'Indeed they did,' answered Parvateshwar. 'They were his most loyal followers. *Jai Shri Ram!*'

'But I don't suppose many mothers would have been happy with this. I can't imagine a woman willingly giving up her child as soon as he's born with no chance of ever meeting him again.'

'But it's for the greater good,' said Parvateshwar, scowling at Shiva's lack of understanding. 'Plus every mother who wants a child can apply and be allocated one who suits her position and dreams. Nothing can be worse for a mother than having a child who doesn't measure up to her expectations.'

Shiva frowned at Parvateshwar's explanation, but let it pass. 'So were the upper castes like the Brahmins unhappy with Lord Ram for taking away their stranglehold on power?'

'Many in the upper castes did oppose Lord Ram's reforms,' Daksha said, 'not just Brahmins, but even some Kshatriyas and Vaishyas. Lord Ram fought a great battle to defeat them, and those of the vanquished who survived became the fore-bears of the Chandravanshis.'

'So your differences go that far back?'

'Indeed,' said Daksha. 'Some of us believe that Lord Ram was too kind, that he should have completely destroyed them, but he forgave them and let them live. Sadly the Chandravanshis are a corrupt and disgusting people – no morals, no ethics. They are the source of all our problems. We even have to endure the mortification of seeing the Chandravanshis rule over Ayodhya, Lord Ram's birthplace.'

Before Shiva could react to this information, the bell of the new *prahar* was rung. After the quick welcoming prayer, he immediately looked towards the window, an expectant expression appearing on his face.

Daksha smiled as he observed this. 'We could break for lunch now, and return to the story afterwards – or, if you have another engagement you would like to attend, we could continue tomorrow.'

Parvateshwar glared at Daksha disapprovingly. He knew exactly what the emperor was trying to do.

'That would be perfect, your Majesty.' Shiva smiled, albeit a little ruefully. 'Is my face that transparent?'

'It is, my Lord, but that's a gift – nothing is prized more than honesty in Meluha. Why don't we convene here again tomorrow morning?'

Thanking the emperor profusely, he left the room with Nandi in tow.

Shiva approached the hedge with excitement and trepidation. The moment he heard the sound of the *dhol*, he despatched Nandi to have lunch at the guest-house. He wanted to be alone. He crept behind the hedge and let out a deep sigh of ecstasy as he found Sati practising under the watchful eye of the Guruji and Krittika.

'So good to see you again, Shiva,' said the Guruji as he stood up with a formal namaste.

'The pleasure is all mine, Guruji,' replied Shiva as he bent down to respectfully touch the Guruji's feet.

Sati watched silently from a distance.

Krittika said enthusiastically, 'I just couldn't get your dance out of my mind!'

He blushed at the compliment. 'Oh, it wasn't that good.'

'Now you're fishing for compliments,' she teased.

Turning towards Sati, Shiva said, 'I was wondering if we could start where we left off last time. I don't think I have to be your teacher or anything like that – I just want to see you dance.'

Sati felt her strange discomfort returning again. What was it about this man that made her feel as if she was breaking the law just by speaking with him? She was allowed to talk to men as long as she kept a respectable distance, so why should she feel guilty?

'I'll try my best,' she said formally. 'It would be enriching to hear your views on how I can improve myself. I really do respect you for your dancing skills.'

Respect – why respect? Why not love? He smiled politely but remained silent. Something inside told him that saying anything just then would spoil the moment.

Sati took a deep breath, girded her *angvastram* around her waist and committed herself to the *Nataraj* pose. Shiva smiled as he felt Mother Earth project her *shakti*, her energy, into Sati.

Energised by the earth beneath her feet, Sati began her dance. And she really had improved. Already technically accomplished, the passion now coursing through her elevated her dance to the next level. Her lithe body radiated a magnetic hold on her audience as she moved through the steps, and Shiva felt a dreamy sense of unreality overcome him as he imagined he was the man Sati was longing for in her dance. When she finally came to a stop, her audience spontaneously applauded.

'That was the best I've ever seen you dance,' said the Guruji with pride.

'Thank you, Guruji,' said Sati as she bowed. Then she looked expectantly at Shiva.

'It was fantastic,' exclaimed Shiva, 'absolutely fabulous. I knew you could do it.'

'I don't think I got the attacking sequence quite right,' said Sati critically.

'You're being too hard on yourself,' he said consolingly. 'That was just a slight error – you missed one angle with your elbow, which made your next move a little awkward.' Rising swiftly to his feet, he continued, 'Here, I'll show you.'

He walked quickly towards Sati and touched her elbow to move it to the correct angle – and realised instantly he'd done something terrible as she recoiled in horror and the Guruji and Krittika gasped out loud.

'I'm sorry,' he said, regret written over his face, 'I was just trying to show you where your elbow should be.'

Sati continued to stare at Shiva, stunned into immobility. The Guruji was the first to recover his wits and realised that Shiva must undergo the purification ceremony. 'Go to your pandit, Shiva. Tell him you need a *shudhikaran*. Go before the day is over.'

'What's a *shudhikaran* – and why do I need one?'

'Please go for a *shudhikaran*, Shiva,' said Sati, tears filling her eyes. 'If something were to happen to you because of me, I'd never be able to forgive myself.'

'Nothing's going to happen to me – look, I'm really sorry if I've broken some rule by touching you – I won't do it again. Let's not make a big deal out of this.'

'But it is a big deal!' she shouted.

Her vehemence threw Shiva off-balance. *Why the hell is she blowing such a simple thing out of all proportion?* he wondered.

Krittika came close to Sati, being careful not to touch her, and whispered, 'We should return home, my lady.'

'No – no, please stay,' pleaded Shiva. 'I won't touch you again, I promise.'

With a look of hopeless despair, Sati turned to leave, followed by Krittika and the Guruji. At the edge of the hedge, she turned around and beseeched Shiva once again, 'Please go for your *shudhikaran* before nightfall. *Please*.'

Seeing the look of uncomprehending mutiny on Shiva's face, the Guruji advised, 'Listen to her, Shiva. She speaks for your own good.'

'What ridiculous nonsense,' yelled Shiva, still unable to justify or understand the events of the afternoon. He was in his bedroom at the royal guest-house. He hadn't undergone the *shudhikaran* – he hadn't even bothered to find out what the ceremony entailed, or why it was required.

Why would I need to be purified for touching Sati? I want to spend all my remaining years touching her in every possible way. Will I have to undergo a shudhikaran *every day? Ridiculous!*

And then another troubling thought entered Shiva's mind. *Am I the impure one? Am I not allowed to touch her because I'm an inferior barbarian, caste-unmarked?*

'No. That can't be true,' he whispered to himself. 'Sati surely doesn't think like that. She's a good woman.'

But what if it is true? Maybe everything will change once she knows I'm the Neelkanth . . .

CHAPTER 7

Lord Ram's Unfinished Task

'You look a bit distracted this morning, my Lord. Are you all right?' asked Daksha, sounding concerned.

'Hmm?' said Shiva as he looked up. 'I'm sorry, your Majesty. I am a little out of sorts.'

The emperor cast a worried expression at Kanakhala. He'd seen a similar look of despair on Sati's face at dinner the previous evening, but she'd refused to say anything about it. 'Do you want to meet later?' he asked.

'Of course not, your Majesty,' said Shiva. 'I'm fine, really. My apologies – please continue.'

A little reluctantly, Daksha began, 'We were talking about the changes Lord Ram brought about in our society.'

'We were indeed,' said Shiva, shaking his head slightly in an effort to dislodge the disturbing image of Sati's last plea from his mind.

'The Maika system worked fantastically well, and our society boomed. Meluha has always been one of the wealthiest lands on Earth, but in the last twelve hundred years we've become the richest and most powerful country in the world by far. Our citizens lead ideal lives, doing what they are best suited for rather than something forced on them by an unfair social order. There's no crime. We don't force or fight unprovoked wars with any other country. It's a perfect society.'

'I don't personally believe that absolute perfection can ever be achieved,' Shiva replied, slowly shifting his thoughts from Sati to the conversation. 'Progress is more of a journey than a destination. But yours is certainly a near-perfect society.'

'What makes you think we're not perfect?' snapped Parvateshwar, instantly aggressive in response to the perceived criticism.

'Do you truly think your society's perfect, Parvateshwar?' asked Shiva politely. 'Does everything in Meluha go exactly as Lord Ram would have mandated?'

Parvateshwar reluctantly fell silent. Shiva had a point, even if he didn't like to admit it.

'The Lord is right, Parvateshwar,' said Daksha. 'There are always things to improve on.'

'That said, your Majesty,' replied Shiva, 'your society is indeed wonderful and well organised. What doesn't make sense to me, though, is why you and your people are so concerned about the future. What's the problem? Why is a Neelkanth required? I don't see anything so obviously wrong that disaster might be a mere breath away. Meluha is so different from my homeland, where there are so many problems you wouldn't know where to begin.'

'My Lord, we need a Neelkanth because we're faced with challenges we don't know how to meet. For generations we've kept to ourselves and left other countries in peace. We trade with other societies but never interfere with them, and we don't allow uninvited foreigners into Meluha beyond the frontier towns. So we think it's only fair that other societies should leave us alone to lead our lives the way we want to.'

'And presumably they don't, your Majesty?'

'No, they don't.'

'Why not?'

'One simple word: jealousy. They hate our superior ways. Our efficient family system offends them. The fact that we take care of everyone in our country makes them unhappy because they can't take care of themselves. They lead sorry lives, but rather than improving themselves, they want to pull us down to their level.'

'I understand. My tribe encountered a lot of jealousy at Mount Kailash because we controlled the shore of the Mansarovar Lake and hence the best land in the region. But sometimes I wonder whether we could have avoided blood-shed if we'd shared our good fortune more willingly.'

'But we do share our good fortune with those who wish it, my Lord – and yet jealousy still blinds our enemies. The Chandravanshis have worked out that it's the *Somras* that

guarantees our superiority. They even know how to manufacture it, but they haven't learned to mass-produce it like
we do, so they haven't reaped all the benefits it has to offer.'

He stopped the emperor, apologising, and asked, 'Where
is the *Somras* produced?'

'The *Somras* powder is manufactured at a secret location
called Mount Mandar and then distributed throughout the
empire. At designated temples across Meluha, trained Brahmins
mix it with water and other ingredients and administer it to
the population.

'They haven't enough *Somras*, so the Chandravanshis can't
become as powerful as us. Consumed by their jealousy, they've
contrived a devious plan to destroy the *Somras* and our way
of life. One of the key ingredients in the *Somras* is the water
of the Saraswati – water from any other source does not work.'

'Really? Why not?'

'We don't know, my Lord – the scientists can't explain it.
But only the waters of the Saraswati will do. Which is why
the Chandravanshis have tried to kill the Saraswati.'

'Kill the *river*?' asked Shiva incredulously.

Daksha's eyes flashed angrily at the thought of the
Chandravanshi perfidy. 'The Saraswati emerges from the
confluence of two mighty rivers in the north – the Sutlej and
the Yamuna. The Sutlej and Yamuna used to be in neutral
territory, and both Suryavanshis and Chandravanshis visited
the land to draw waters for the *Somras*.'

'But how did they try to kill the Saraswati?'

'They diverted the course of the Yamuna so that instead of flowing south, it started flowing east to meet their main river, the Ganga.'

'You can do that?' asked Shiva in amazement. 'Change the course of a river?'

'Of course,' answered Parvateshwar.

'We were livid,' interjected Daksha, 'but we still gave them a chance to make amends for their duplicity.'

'And what happened?'

'What can you expect from the Chandravanshis?' said Daksha in disgust. 'They denied any knowledge of this, claiming that the dramatic change in the river's course was due to some minor earthquake. And even worse, they claimed that since the river had changed course of its own accord, we Meluhans would simply have to accept what was essentially God's will!'

'We refused to do that, of course,' Parvateshwar continued. 'Under the leadership of Emperor Brahmanayak, his Majesty's father, we attacked Swadweep.'

'Is that the land of the Chandravanshis?' asked Shiva.

'It is,' said Parvateshwar, 'and it was a resounding victory. The Chandravanshi army was routed. Emperor Brahmanayak magnanimously allowed them to keep their lands and their system of governance. Nor did he demand any war reparations or yearly tribute. The only term of the surrender treaty was the restoration of the Yamuna to its original course.'

'You fought in that war, Parvateshwar?'

'Yes,' said Parvateshwar, his chest puffed up with pride, 'I was a mere soldier then, but I did fight in that war.'

Turning to Daksha, Shiva asked, 'Then what's the problem now, your Majesty? You defeated your enemy, so why is the Saraswati still dying?'

'We believe the Chandravanshis have devised another plot against us, but we're not sure what it is yet. After their defeat, the area between our two countries was designated a no-man's-land and the jungle has reclaimed it, including the early course of the Yamuna. We've honoured our part of the bargain and never disturbed that region. It appears they haven't been so honourable.'

'Are you sure of that, your Majesty? Has the area been reconnoitred? Have you discussed your suspicions with the Chandravanshis' ambassador in your empire?'

'Are you accusing us of lying?' countered Parvateshwar indignantly. 'True Suryavanshis don't lie!'

'Parvateshwar,' scolded Daksha angrily, 'the Lord was not implying any such thing—'

'Hear me out, Parvateshwar,' said Shiva politely. 'If I've learned anything from the pointless battles fought in my land, it's that war should always be the last resort. If another solution is possible, there's no shame in saving some young soldier's life. A mother somewhere would bless us for it.'

'Let's not fight? Wonderful! What a great saviour we have here,' Parvateshwar muttered under his breath.

'You have something to say, Parvateshwar?' barked

Kanakhala. 'I've told you before – you will not insult the Neelkanth in my presence!'

'I don't take orders from you,' growled Parvateshwar.

'Enough,' ordered Daksha, and turning to Shiva, he said, 'I'm sorry, you're right – we shouldn't just declare war without being sure of the situation – which is why I've avoided it until now. But look at the facts of the case: the flow of the Saraswati has been slowly depleting for the last fifty years.'

'And the last few years have been horrible,' said Kanakhala, struggling to control her tears at the thought of the slow death of the sacred river the Meluhans regarded as a mother. 'The Saraswati doesn't even reach the sea now – it ends in an inland delta just south of Rajasthan.'

'That alone is evidence that the Chandravanshis haven't kept their part of the bargain,' said Daksha darkly.

'What does the Swadweepan ambassador have to say about that?'

'We have no diplomatic relations with Swadweep, my Lord,' said Daksha.

'Really? I thought having diplomats of other countries here was one of your innovative systems. It gives you the opportunity to better understand them – and maybe avoid jumping into an unnecessary war. Did I hear right: that a diplomatic mission from Mesopotamia arrived here two days ago? So why not extend the same invitation to Swadweep?'

'You don't know them – they're untrustworthy people. No

Suryavanshi will dirty his soul by willingly speaking to a Chandravanshi.'

Shiva frowned, but he didn't say anything as Kanakhala said in disgust, 'You don't know the depths they have sunk to, my Lord. During the last few years they've even started using the cursed Nagas in their terrorist attacks on us!'

'Terrorist attacks?'

'Our overwhelming defeat of their army kept them quiet for many decades,' said the emperor. 'It led them to believe that they couldn't overpower us in an open confrontation. Consequently they've resorted to terrorism – a form of assault only countenanced by the most repulsive people.'

'I don't understand – what exactly do they do?'

'They send small bands of assassins who launch surprise assaults on non-military public places – they attack noncombatants, Brahmins, Vaishyas or Shudras, and try to destroy places like temples, public baths – places where there aren't soldiers to fight back, but whose destruction will wreck morale and spread terror throughout the empire.'

'That's disgusting,' said Shiva.

'These Chandravanshis don't fight like men,' Parvateshwar snarled. 'They fight like cowards.'

'So why don't you attack them and finish this once and for all?'

'We'd like to, but I'm not sure we can defeat them,' Daksha admitted.

Shiva observed Parvateshwar seething silently at the

perceived insult to his army before turning to Daksha. 'Why not, your Majesty? By all accounts you have a well-trained and efficient military force. I'm sure your army could defeat them.'

'Two reasons: firstly, we're outnumbered – we were outnumbered even a hundred years ago, though not by a very significant margin. But today, we estimate that they have a population of more than eighty million compared to our eight million, so they can throw a much larger army at us – their sheer numbers will cancel out our technological superiority.'

'But why should your population be less? You have people older than two hundred years – surely your population should be higher?'

'Sociological causes,' said Daksha. 'Our country is rich, and children are a matter of choice rather than a duty or a necessity, and fewer and fewer mothers are giving birth at Maika. Parents prefer to adopt children from the Maika, maybe one or two, so they can devote more attention to their upbringing. In Swadweep, the poor use their children as bonded labour to supplement the family income – the more children they have, the less poor the family, and as a result, Swadweep has a far larger population.'

'And the second reason for avoiding war?'

'The second reason is ethical: we have "rules of war"; the Chandravanshis have nothing like that. I fear that this is a weakness in us that our ruthless enemies can and will exploit.'

'What sort of rules?' asked Shiva, curiously.

'Well, for example, an armed soldier will not attack an unarmed man. A superior armed person – a cavalry man, say – will not attack someone with inferior arms, like a spear-wielding foot-soldier. A swordsman will never attack below the waist, because we believe that to be unethical. The Chandravanshis care nothing for such niceties; they'll attack whomsoever and however they think expedient to ensure victory.'

'Begging your pardon, your Majesty,' interrupted Parvateshwar, 'but it is that very difference that makes us who we are. Lord Ram said a person's ethics and character are not tested in good times. It is only in bad times that a person shows how steadfast he is to his *dharma*.'

'But Parvateshwar,' Daksha replied, sighing, 'we're not under attack by people who are as ethical and decent as us. Our very way of life is threatened. If we don't fight back any way we can, we'll lose everything.'

'My apologies once again, your Majesty,' said Parvateshwar, 'but I've never said that we shouldn't fight back. I'm *eager* to attack. I've been asking repeatedly for permission to declare war on the Chandravanshis. But if we fight without our rules, our codes, our ethics, then our "way of life" is already as good as destroyed, and the Chandravanshis will have won without even lifting a sword!'

The town's *prahar* bell momentarily halted the conversation, and as everyone said the customary prayer Shiva turned towards the window, wondering if Sati would be dancing today.

Daksha turned to Shiva expectantly. 'Do you need to leave, my Lord?'

'No, your Majesty,' said Shiva, hiding the confusion he felt inside. 'I don't believe I'm expected anywhere at this time.'

At these words, the smile on Daksha's face disappeared, along with his hopes.

Shiva continued, 'If it's all right with you, your Majesty, may we continue our conversation? Perhaps we can have our lunch a little later.'

'Of course, my Lord,' said Daksha, pulling himself together.

'I can understand your reasons for not wanting to attack right now, but you clearly have a plan — and one in which my blue throat has some strange role to play.'

'We do have a plan, my Lord. I do not feel that giving in unthinkingly to the anger — however righteous — of some of our people will solve our problem. I don't believe that the people of Swadweep themselves are evil. It's their Chandravanshi rulers and their way of life that have made them evil. The only way forward for us is to save the Swadweepans themselves.'

'Save the Swadweepans?' Shiva repeated, genuinely surprised.

'Yes, my Lord: we need to save them from the evil philosophy that is infecting their souls. We need to save them from their treacherous rulers and from their sorry, meaningless existence. And we can do this by giving them the benefits of the superior Suryavanshi way of life. Once they become like us, there will be no reason to fight — we will live like brothers.

This is my father's unfinished task. In fact, it is the unfinished task of Lord Ram.'

'That is indeed a noble task,' said Shiva, 'but it's also a daunting one. You'll need soldiers to defeat their army and missionaries to convert them to your beliefs. It's not going to be easy.'

'I agree. There are many in my empire who are concerned about even attacking Swadweep – and here I am, giving them a much bigger challenge: to reform the whole country. That is why I did not want to launch this without the Neelkanth, my Lord.'

Shiva remembered his uncle's words, spoken many years ago in what felt like another life: *Your destiny lies beyond the mountains. Whether you fulfil it or run away again is up to you.*

With those words ringing in his mind, Shiva refocused his attention on Daksha.

'The problems we're facing were prophesied,' the emperor continued. 'Lord Ram himself said that any philosophy, no matter how perfect, works only for a finite period. That is the law of nature, and it can't be avoided. But what the prophecy also tells us is that when the problems become insurmountable for ordinary men, the Neelkanth will appear to destroy the evil Chandravanshis and restore the forces of good. My Lord, you're the Neelkanth. You can save us. You can complete Lord Ram's unfinished task. You must lead us, help us defeat the Chandravanshis, then rally the Swadweepans to the side of good. Otherwise I fear that this beautiful country, this near-perfect Meluhan society, will be destroyed by years of endless war. Will you help us, my Lord? Will you lead us?'

Shiva was confused. 'But I don't understand – what exactly would I do?'

'I don't know,' he admitted. 'We only know our destination, and that you will be our leader. The path we take is up to you.'

They want me to destroy the entire way of life of eighty million people by myself! Are they mad? He spoke carefully. 'I empathise with your people and their hardships, your Majesty, but I don't really understand how one man can make any real difference.'

'If you are that man,' said Daksha, his eyes moist with devotion and faith, 'you can change the entire universe.'

'But how will my presence make such a difference?' said Shiva with a weak smile. 'I'm no miracle worker. I can't snap my fingers and cause bolts of lightning to strike down the Chandravanshis.'

'It's your presence itself that will make the difference. I invite you to travel through the empire, see the effect your blue throat has on the people. Once my people believe they can do it, they'll be *able* to do it!'

'You are the Neelkanth, my Lord,' added Kanakhala. 'The people have faith in the prophecy of the blue throat – they'll have faith in you. Will you help us, my Lord?'

Or will you run away once again?

'But how are you so sure that I am the genuine Neelkanth?' asked Shiva. 'For all you know, there might be many Meluhans with blue throats just waiting to be discovered—'

'It can't be a Meluhan, or a person from the Sapt Sindhu. The prophecy says that the Neelkanth will be a foreigner, and that he will get a blue throat when he drinks the *Somras*.'

Shiva was stunned speechless as the truth suddenly dawned upon him. *Srinagar. The first night. Somras. That's how my body was repaired. That's why I'm feeling stronger than ever.*

Daksha and Kanakhala looked at Shiva, breathlessly waiting for his decision. Praying for him to make the *right* decision.

But why only me? All the Gunas were given the Somras. Was my uncle right, after all? Do I really have a special destiny?

Parvateshwar stared at Shiva with narrowed eyes, carefully observing his reactions.

I don't deserve any special destiny – but maybe this is my chance to redeem myself.

But first . . .

With controlled politeness, Shiva said, 'Your Majesty, before I answer, may I ask you a question?'

'Of course, my Lord.'

'Do you agree that honesty is required to make any friendship work, even if you know the truth will deeply offend your friend?'

'Yes, of course,' replied Daksha, wondering where Shiva was going with this.

'Complete honesty isn't just the bedrock of an individual

relationship, but of any stable society,' interjected Parvateshwar.

'I couldn't agree more,' said Shiva. 'And yet Meluha wasn't honest with me.'

Nobody said a word.

Shiva continued in a courteous but firm tone, 'When my tribe was invited to come to Meluha, we were given the impression you wanted immigrants because you needed workers. And I was happy to escape my benighted land. But now I realise you were systematically searching for your Neelkanth.'

Turning to Nandi, Shiva continued, 'We weren't told that a medicine called the *Somras* would be administered to us as soon as we arrived. We weren't told that the medicine would have such effects on us.'

Nandi looked down guiltily. Shiva had every right to be angry with him.

Turning to Daksha, Shiva continued, 'Your Majesty, you know that the *Somras* was administered to me on my first night in Kashmir, without my knowledge or consent.'

'I'm truly sorry about that dishonesty, my Lord,' said Daksha, his hands clasped in a penitent namaste. 'It's something I'll always be ashamed of. But the stakes were too high for us to take the risk that you wouldn't drink it. In any case, the *Somras* has considerable positive effects on the body. It doesn't harm you in any way.'

'Of course, and I'm not exactly upset about having to live a long and healthy life,' said Shiva wryly. 'But do you know that my tribe fell seriously ill the night they were given the *Somras* – I assume as a result of the elixir?'

'They were at no risk, my Lord,' said Kanakhala apologetically. 'Some people are predisposed towards certain diseases. When the *Somras* enters the body, it triggers the immediate occurrence of these diseases, but once they're cured, they never recur, so the body remains healthy until death. Your tribe is actually much healthier now.'

'No doubt they are,' said Shiva, 'but the point isn't about the effects of the *Somras*; there's no doubt both my tribe and I are better for it. But from what I understand of Meluha, getting somebody to do something without telling him all the facts beforehand would not have been Lord Ram's way. You should have told us the whole truth at Mount Kailash. Then you should have let *us* make an informed choice, rather than *you* making that choice for us. We'd probably still have come to Meluha, but then it would have been *our* decision.'

'Please forgive us the deception, my Lord,' said Daksha, his voice full of guilty regret. 'It truly is not our way to be deceitful, even by omission – we pride ourselves on our honesty – but in this instance we really felt we had no choice. The situation is *desperate*, and we need the Neelkanth to act now if our way of life is to survive. We're truly sorry, my Lord – but your people are well taken care of. They are healthier than ever. They will live long, productive lives.'

Parvateshwar finally broke his silence, speaking what had been in his heart since the search began, many decades ago.

'Shiva, we are truly sorry for what has been done. You have every right to be angry. Lying is not our way. I think what was done is appalling, and you are right: Lord Ram would have never have condoned this. No matter how serious our troubles, we have no right to deceive someone into helping us. I am deeply sorry.'

Shiva raised his eyebrows. He was genuinely surprised.

Parvateshwar is the only one apologising without making excuses. He's a true follower of the great Lord Ram's way.

He couldn't help smiling at the gruff military man, and Daksha let out an audible sigh of relief.

Shiva turned towards the emperor. 'I do appreciate your honesty – belated though it is – so let's try to put this episode behind us. Like I said, there are some things about your nation that could be improved. No doubt about that. But it is among the best that I have seen, and it *is* worth fighting for. But I have a few conditions.'

'Anything, my Lord,' said Daksha, eager to please.

'I have no idea whether I'm capable of performing the tasks you've set before me, but you have my word that I will try my best. In order to work out how I can best help you, I need to know everything there is to know about your society. I'm assuming that from this point forward nothing will be hidden from me, and that I won't be lied to.'

'On that you have my word, my Lord,' said Daksha.

'Secondly, you still need immigrants to expand your population, but you shouldn't mislead them. I think you should tell them the whole truth about Meluha and let them make an informed decision about whether or not they want to come here – or you don't invite them at all. Is that fair?'

'Of course it is, my Lord,' said Daksha, nodding briefly towards Kanakhala. 'We'll implement that policy immediately.'

'Furthermore, it's clear I'm not going back to Kashmir any time soon. Can my tribe be brought to Devagiri? I'd like them to be with me.'

'Of course,' he repeated, with another quick glance at Kanakhala. 'Instructions will be sent today to bring them here.'

'Also, I'd like to visit the location where you manufacture the *Somras*. I'd like to know more about this drink of the gods. Something tells me this is important.'

'Of course you may,' said Daksha, his face finally breaking into a nervous smile. 'Kanakhala will take you there tomorrow itself. In fact, my family will be visiting the Brahma temple there for a *puja* the day after tomorrow. P-perhaps we could meet there?'

'I'd like that,' said Shiva, returning the smile. Then, taking a deep breath, he added, 'And last but not least, I imagine you're anxious to announce the Neelkanth's arrival to your people.'

Daksha and Kanakhala nodded hesitantly.

'I'd ask that you don't do it just yet.'

Their faces fell immediately.

Nandi's eyes were glued to the floor. He'd stopped listening to the conversation. The enormity of his prevarication towards Shiva and the other immigrants was tearing him apart.

'I have a terrible feeling that as soon as people know I'm the Neelkanth, my every action and word will be overinterpreted and overanalysed,' Shiva explained. 'I'm afraid I don't know enough about your society or my task to be able to handle that just yet.'

'I understand,' said Daksha, willing a smile back on his face. 'You have my word – only my immediate staff, my family and the people you allow will know of the Neelkanth's arrival. Nobody else.'

'Thank you, your Majesty. But I'll say it again: I'm a simple tribal man who just happened to get a blue throat because of some exotic medicine. I still don't know what one man can achieve in the face of such overwhelming odds.'

'And I'll say something again, my Lord,' said Daksha, smiling with ardent faith. 'If you are that man, you can change the entire universe!'

CHAPTER 8

Drink of the Gods

As they were walking back to the royal guest-house, Shiva told Nandi that he wanted to eat lunch alone. Nandi, head bowed in self-recrimination, was a few steps behind. 'My Lord, I'm so sorry,' he murmured, and Shiva stopped, turned and looked at Nandi until he raised his eyes to meet Shiva's steady gaze.

'You're right, my Lord,' the captain continued, 'we were so lost in our own troubles and caught up in the search for the Neelkanth that we didn't stop to think how unfair our actions have been to the people we've invited into our land. I misled you, my Lord. I lied to you.'

Shiva continued to stare intently into Nandi's eyes.

'I'm so sorry, my Lord. I've failed you. I'll accept whatever punishment you deem fit,' he finished.

Shiva's lips twitched with a very faint smile and he patted Nandi gently on his shoulder, the smile and touch clearly signalling he had forgiven him, but his eyes delivered a clear message. 'Never lie to me again, my friend,' he said.

Nandi nodded and whispered, 'Never, my Lord. I'm so sorry.'

'Forget it, Nandi,' said Shiva, his smile a little broader now. 'It's in the past.'

They turned and continued walking, side by side this time. Suddenly Shiva shook his head and chuckled, 'Strange people!'

'What do you mean?' asked Nandi.

'Oh, I was just contemplating some of the more . . . interesting features of your society.'

'Interesting in what way?' Nandi was feeling a little more confident now that Shiva was speaking to him again.

'Well, some of your countrymen believe that the mere presence of my blue throat can help you achieve impossible tasks. Some people actually think that my name has suddenly become so holy that they can't even speak it. On the other hand, there are those who find my touch so polluting that I need to get a *shudhikaran* done, whatever that is.'

'A *shudhikaran*?' asked Nandi, his brow furrowed with concern. 'Why would you need that, my Lord?'

'Yesterday I touched someone, and afterwards I was told I would need to undergo a *shudhikaran*.'

'What? Who did you touch — was it a *vikarma* person?' Nandi sounded troubled. 'Only the touch of a *vikarma* person would require you to get a *shudhikaran*.'

Shiva's face abruptly went white as a veil lifted from his

eyes. He suddenly understood the significance of the previous day's events – her hasty withdrawal when he touched her, and the shocked reactions from the Guruji and Krittika.

'Go back to the guest-house, Nandi. I'll see you there,' said Shiva as he turned towards the guest-house garden.

'My Lord, what happened?' asked Nandi, trying to keep pace with Shiva. 'Did you get the *shudhikaran* done or not?'

'Go to the guest-house, Nandi,' Shiva repeated firmly, walking rapidly away. 'I'll see you there.'

— ⚜ ⵔ Ʋ ⵟ ⊕ —

Shiva waited for the better part of an hour, but he waited in vain, for Sati did not make an appearance. He sat alone on the bench, cursing himself for being such an idiot.

How could I ever have thought that Sati would find my touch polluting? I'm such a fool!

In his mind, he replayed and analysed every second of that fateful encounter.

If something were to happen to you because of me, I'd never be able to forgive myself – what did she mean by that? Does she have feelings for me? Or is she just an honourable woman who can't bear to be the cause of someone else's misfortune? And why should she think of herself as inferior? This entire concept of the vikarma is so utterly ridiculous!

Realising that she wasn't going to come, Shiva stood. He kicked the bench hard, receiving for his troubles a painful reminder that his once-numb toe had regained its sensation. Cursing out loud, he started walking back to the guest-house. As he passed the stage, he noticed something lying on it. He went closer and bent down to pick it up. It was the bead bracelet he'd seen around Sati's right wrist. The string did not appear to be broken.

Did she purposely drop it here?

He brought the bracelet to his nose and inhaled: the fragrance of the Holy Lake on a sun-drenched evening. Bringing it reverently to his lips, he kissed it gently. Smiling, he dropped the bracelet into the pouch at his waist.

When I return from Mount Mandar I'll find her. I'll pursue her to the end of the world and fight the entire human race to have her, if that's what it takes.

For in his heart and soul, he knew that his journey in this life was incomplete without her.

— ⁂ —

'How much further is it, Madam Prime Minister?' asked Nandi, almost childlike in his excitement.

A visit to the almost mythical Mount Mandar was a rare honour for any Meluhan. Most Suryavanshis regarded Mount Mandar as the soul of their empire, for as long as it was safe, so was the *Somras.*

'We only left Devagiri an hour ago, Captain,' said Kanakhala, smiling indulgently. 'It's a day's journey to Mount Mandar.'

'Forgive me for asking, but with the blinds drawn I can't see the passage of the sun.'

'That's why there's a *prahar* lamp right behind you, Captain. The blinds are drawn for your own protection.'

Shiva smiled at Kanakhala, well aware that the blinds were drawn not for *their* protection, but to keep the location of Mount Mandar secret. If Chandravanshi terrorists attacked Mount Mandar, all would be lost for Meluha. With the exception of the scientists who manufactured the *Somras*, the elite team of soldiers known as the Arishtanemi who guarded the road to the mountain and the few people authorised by the emperor himself, nobody was allowed to know its location, let alone visit the mountain.

'Who will we be meeting there, Kanakhala?' asked Shiva.

'My Lord, tomorrow we will be meeting Chief Scientist Brahaspati, who leads the team of scientists who manufacture the *Somras*. Of course, they also conduct research in many other fields. A bird-courier has already been sent to inform him of your arrival.'

Shiva smiled and nodded his thanks, and as Nandi looked at the *prahar* lamp for the umpteenth time, he went back to his book. It was an interesting manuscript about the terrible war fought many thousands of years ago between the *Devas*, the gods, and the *Asuras*, the demons – an endless struggle between eternal opposites: good and evil. The *Devas*, with the help of Lord Rudra – the Mahadev, the God of Gods – had destroyed the *Asuras* and established righteousness in the world again.

— ⚡ ◎ ℧ ⚕ ⊕ —

'I hope you slept well, my Lord,' said Kanakhala as she welcomed Shiva and Nandi into the chamber outside Chief Scientist Brahaspati's office.

It was the beginning of the last hour of the first *prahar*. Days began early at Mount Mandar.

'I did,' said Shiva, 'though I could hear a strange rhythmic sound throughout the night.'

Kanakhala smiled but did not offer any explanation as she opened the door into the chief scientist's office and ushered him in. Various strange instruments were spread throughout the large room, neatly organised on tables of different heights. Palm-leaf notebooks sat alongside the instruments, presumably detailing experiments conducted and their results. The walls were painted a restrained blue and there was a breathtaking view of the dense forest at the foot of the mountain through the large picture window in the corner. In the centre of the room were some simple, low seats arranged in a square. The room looked characteristic of a culture which celebrated simplicity over style.

Brahaspati was standing in the centre of the room, his hands folded in a namaste. He was of medium height, much shorter than Shiva, and his wheat-coloured skin, deep-set eyes and well-trimmed beard gave Brahaspati a distinguished appearance. His head was clean-shaven except for a *choti* – a knotted tuft of hair at the crown of the head – and his serene expression made him look intellectual. He had broad shoulders and a barrel chest and he was a bit overweight. Brahaspati wore a typical white cotton *dhoti* and an *angvastram* draped loosely over his shoulders, with a *janau* tied from his left shoulder down to the right side of his hips.

'How are you, Kanakhala?' asked Brahaspati. 'It's been a long time.'

'Indeed it has,' said Kanakhala, greeting him with a namaste and a low bow.

Shiva noticed that the second amulet on Brahaspati's arm showed him to be a swan – a very select chosen-tribe amongst Brahmins, from what he had been told.

'This is Lord Shiva,' said Kanakhala.

'Just Shiva will do, thank you.' Shiva smiled and offered a polite namaste towards Brahaspati.

'As you wish: "just Shiva" it is. And who might you be?' asked Brahaspati, looking at Nandi.

'This is Captain Nandi,' answered Kanakhala for him, 'Lord Shiva's aide.'

'A pleasure to meet you, Captain,' said Brahaspati, before turning back to Shiva. 'I don't mean to sound rude, Shiva, but may I see your throat?'

Shiva removed his cravat as Brahaspati stepped forward to examine him. The scientist's smile disappeared as he saw the bright blue hue.

Brahaspati was speechless for a few moments, until, slowly gathering his wits, he said to Kanakhala, 'This is no trick – the colour comes from the inside. How is this possible? This means—'

'Yes,' said Kanakhala softly, her whole body radiating happiness, 'it means the Neelkanth has come. Our saviour has come.'

'Well, I don't know if I'm a saviour or anything like that,' said an embarrassed Shiva, retying the cravat around his throat, 'but I'll do what I can to help your wonderful country. I'm here because I have a feeling that knowing how the *Somras* works is vital if I'm to help you.'

Brahaspati still looked dazed. He continued to watch Shiva, but his attention was elsewhere: he appeared to be working out the implications of the arrival of the true Neelkanth.

'Brahaspati—?' said Kanakhala, gently calling the chief scientist back into the here and now.

He jumped when she lightly touched his arm, then, with obvious effort, refocused on the people before him.

'Can you tell me how the *Somras* works?' asked Shiva again.

'Of course,' he said, then paused when his eyes fell on Nandi. 'Is it all right to speak freely in front of the captain?'

'Captain Nandi has been a good friend to me since I arrived in Meluha,' said Shiva. 'I'd like him to stay.'

Touched by his Lord's open declaration of trust, Nandi vowed to himself once more, on pain of death, that he would never lie to Shiva again.

'As you wish, Shiva,' said Brahaspati.

Brahaspati's use of Shiva's given name made him realise the chief scientist had become neither submissive nor excessively deferential after discovering that he was the Neelkanth. There was a difference, though: while Parvateshwar's attitude was driven by a distrusting surliness, Brahaspati's was more a product of his natural assured affability.

'Thank you,' he said, smiling back. 'So, how does the *Somras* work?'

— ⚶ ⓂⓊ⇞⊛ —

The royal procession moved slowly along the road to Mount Mandar, surrounded by the legendary Arishtanemi, the most feared militia in all of India. The advance guard of one hundred and sixty cavalrymen in columns four abreast rode before the five royal carriages, and the same number followed in an identical formation as rearguard. Phalanxes forty strong marched to the left and right of each carriage, and three serving maids were seated on the side-supports of each vehicle.

The five carriages were made of solid wood, with no windows or apertures except for upward-pointing slits at the top for ventilation. Behind the driver was a grille to allow in light and air, which could be shut instantly in case of attack. All the carriages were of exactly the same dimensions and appearance, making it impossible to discern which one carried the royal family. Only someone with *divyadrishti* – divine vision – could see that the first, third and fourth carriages were empty. The second carried the royal family – Daksha, his wife Veerini and his daughter Sati. The last carriage carried Parvateshwar and some of his key staff.

'Father, I still don't understand why you insist on bringing me along to *pujas*. I'm not even allowed to attend the main ceremony,' said Sati.

'I've told you many times before,' replied Daksha as he patted Sati's hand fondly, 'none of my *pujas* are complete and pure until I've seen your face. I don't care about the damned law.'

'Father—' whispered Sati, reproachfully. She knew it was wrong of her father to insult the law.

Her mother looked at him, then gave Sati a kindly smile before returning to her book.

— ⚹ ◍U⇡❖ —

A short distance from the royal procession, hidden by the dense forest, a small band of fifty soldiers slunk along silently. They wore light leather armour and had their *dhotis* tied military-style to ensure ease of movement. Each of them carried two swords and a long knife, and had shields of metal and leather slung on their backs. Their specially made shoes had grooves to hold three small knives.

At the head were two men, one a handsome young captain, judging by his dark brown turban, whose face was embellished with a battle-scar. His leather armour had been tied on a little carelessly, and a pendant on a gold chain had slipped out. The pendant bore a beautiful white horizontal crescent moon, the Chandravanshi symbol.

Next to him walked a giant of a man, covered from head to toe by a long hooded robe, most of his face concealed behind a black mask. Very little of him was visible except for his strong fleshy hands and his expressionless almond-shaped eyes. A leather bracelet tied to his right wrist bore the serpent Aum symbol. Without turning to the captain, the hooded figure said, 'Vishwadyumna, your mark is visible. Put it in and tighten your armour.'

Embarrassed, Vishwadyumna immediately pushed the chain inside and pulled the two strings on the side of his shoulder to tighten the breastplate. 'My Lord,' he said, 'perhaps we should move ahead of the carriages to confirm our informant's claim that this is the route to Mount Mandar, and then return later to kidnap her? We're too dangerously outnumbered to attempt anything right now.'

The hooded figure replied calmly, 'I haven't ordered an attack, so why are you concerned about us being outnumbered? And we're definitely heading towards Mount Mandar. A few hours' delay at this point will not bring the heavens down. For now, we follow.'

Vishwadyumna swallowed hard. There was nothing he hated more than opposing his lord – after all, it was he who had found the rare Suryavanshi sympathetic to their cause, the one whose information would allow them to rip out and destroy the very heart of Meluha. Nevertheless, as captain he had a duty to voice his concerns. He spoke softly. 'But my Lord, you know the queen doesn't like delays. There is unrest brewing among the men; they are worrying that we are losing focus.'

The hooded figure turned sharply to face Vishwadyumna, his body conveying anger but his voice as composed as ever.

'I am *not* losing focus. If you want to leave, go – you'll still get your money. I'll do this alone if I have to.'

Vishwadyumna backed down immediately, shocked by his leader's rare – if tightly controlled – display of emotion. 'Forgive me, my Lord – of course I'll stay with you until you release me. And you're right – a few hours more will make no difference, not when we have waited centuries.'

The platoon continued silently tracking the royal caravan.

— Å ⍵U⌉❀ —

'The concept behind the *Somras* is ridiculously simple,' Brahaspati started, 'but making the concept a reality would have been impossible without Lord Brahma's genius. To understand how the medicine slows the ageing process, we need to understand what keeps us alive – that fundamental thing that none of us can live without.'

Shiva stared at him expectantly, waiting for him to expound further.

'Energy,' he said. 'When we walk, talk, think – that is, when we do *anything* that can be called being alive – we use energy.'

'We have a similar concept amongst our people,' said Shiva, 'we call it *shakti*.'

'*Shakti*?' Brahaspati sounded surprised. 'Interesting – that word came from the Pandyas, the ancestors of all the people of India, but it hasn't been used for centuries. Do you know the lineage of your tribe?'

'I don't, but one of our old women claims to know everything about our history – we could ask her when she comes to Devagiri.'

'Interesting,' he repeated, 'but let's get back to the subject at hand. Where does the energy our bodies need come from?'

'From the food we eat?' suggested Nandi timidly. He was finally gaining the confidence to speak in front of such important people.

'Absolutely right,' said Brahaspati. 'The food we eat stores energy, which we assimilate and expend – if we don't eat, we become weak. There's another important element in this process: food is converted into energy by the air we breathe. The air contains various gases, one of which we call oxygen, which reacts with our food and releases energy. Without this oxygen, our bodies would be starved of energy and we would die.'

'You're describing the process that keeps us alive,' said Shiva, 'but surely the *Somras* has to work on the process that causes us to grow old and die?'

He smiled. 'What I told you does have something to do with how we age – because it appears nature has a sense of humour. The very thing that keeps us alive is also what causes us to age and eventually die. When oxygen reacts with our food to release energy, it also releases something poisonous – we call them "oxidants". When you leave fruit out and it goes bad, it's because it has been "oxidised" – the "oxidants" have made it rot. It happens to metals too, especially with iron, the new metal we have discovered. We call that "rust". And the same thing happens to our bodies: we breathe in oxygen, which helps change the food we eat into energy – but it also releases these "oxidants" into our body which start reacting inside us. We rust from the inside out, if you like, and that's how we age and die.'

'By the holy god Agni,' exclaimed Nandi, 'so the very thing that gives us life also kills us?'

'Think about it for a moment,' said Brahaspati. 'The body tries to store enough food and water so that a few days without eating or drinking won't kill you. Logical, right?'

'Makes sense,' agreed Shiva.

'However, the body doesn't store more than a few minutes' worth of oxygen, the most crucial component for staying alive, and that makes no sense at all – unless the body realises that despite being an elixir, oxygen is also a poison, so it's dangerous to store. So what Lord Brahma did, after a lot of research, was to invent the *Somras*, which, when consumed, reacts with the oxidants, absorbs them and then expels them from the body as sweat or urine.'

'Is that why the sweat is poisonous the first time after a person drinks the *Somras*?'

'Yes, your sweat is particularly dangerous the first time after you drink the *Somras*, but even after a person has drunk the *Somras* for years, sweat and urine remain toxic, so you have to eject it from the body and make sure it doesn't affect anyone else.'

'So that's why Meluhans are obsessed with hygiene?'

'Indeed. All Meluhans are taught about water and hygiene from a very young age. Water absorbs the toxins released by the *Somras*, so we drink gallons of water every day. And everything that *can* be washed *should* be washed! Meluhans bathe at least twice a day — and all ablutions take place in specially designed rooms, so the waste can be carried safely out of the city via underground drains.'

'Strict hygiene standards,' Shiva said with a smile as he remembered his first day in Kashmir, and Ayurvati's strong words. 'So, what goes into manufacturing the *Somras*?'

'It's a difficult process requiring various ingredients that are not easily available. I'll give you an example. The branches of the Sanjeevani tree, which are grown on giant plantations, have to be churned with the waters of the Saraswati River before processing begins. Water from other sources doesn't work. The manufacturing process also generates a lot of heat, so more water is required during processing to keep the mixture stable.'

'I heard a strange noise throughout the night — was that the churners?'

'Yes — the giant churning machines are housed in a massive cavern at the base of this mountain. The Saraswati waters are channelled into the cavern via a complex system of canals and collected in an enormous pool which we affectionately call Sagar.'

'Sagar? An *ocean*? You have a pool as large as an ocean?'

Shiva had heard the legends of the massive, never-ending expanse of water called Sagar.

'It's a bit of an exaggeration,' admitted Brahaspati with a smile, 'but if you saw the pool, you would realise that we are not that far off the mark.'

'I would certainly like to see the whole facility. It was too late when we came in last night, so I haven't yet seen much of the mountain.'

'I'll take you around after lunch,' said Brahaspati, and Shiva grinned in reply. He was about to say something, but checked himself and glanced at Kanakhala and Nandi.

Brahaspati noticed the hesitation, and the glance. 'I think Shiva wants to ask me something in private. Nandi, Kanakhala – would you mind waiting outside for a moment?' he said courteously but firmly. He clearly commanded a great deal of respect amongst the Meluhans, for Kanakhala rose immediately and left the room after a formal namaste, closely followed by Nandi.

Once the door had closed behind them, Brahaspati turned to Shiva with a smile. 'Now why don't you ask me the real question you came to ask?'

CHAPTER 9

Love and Its Consequences

'I didn't want to question you in front of them – their faith is . . . overwhelming,' Shiva said with a wry grin. He was beginning to like Brahaspati. He was enjoying being around someone who treated him like an equal.

'I understand, my friend. What's your question?'

'Why did the *Somras* have this strange effect on me? I might have a blue throat, but I don't know how I'm going to become the saviour of the Suryavanshis. The emperor tells me I'm supposed to be the one who'll complete Lord Ram's unfinished work and destroy the Chandravanshis.'

'He actually said that?' asked Brahaspati, his eyes wide in surprise. 'The emperor can be tiresome – what he told you isn't completely correct. The prophecy doesn't exactly say that the Neelkanth will save the Suryavanshis. It says two things: first, that the Neelkanth will *not* be from the Sapt Sindhu, and second, the Neelkanth will be the "destroyer of evil". The

Meluhans believe this implies that the Neelkanth will destroy the Chandravanshis, since they are obviously evil. But destroying the Chandravanshis doesn't mean that the Suryavanshis will be saved – there are many other problems besides the Chandravanshis that we need to solve.'

'What kind of problems – like the Nagas?'

Brahaspati hesitated for a moment, then replied carefully, 'There are many problems, and we're working hard to solve them. But let's go back to your first question – why the *Somras* had this effect on you.'

'Yes – why did it turn my throat blue? And never mind that stuff about it stopping the degeneration of my body – the *Somras* has already repaired a dislocated shoulder and a frostbitten toe.'

'It repaired an injury?' asked Brahaspati, sounding incredulous. 'But that's impossible – it's only supposed to prevent diseases and ageing, not repair existing injuries.'

'Well, in my case it did just that.'

Brahaspati paused to gather his thoughts. 'We'll have to perform some experiments to come up with a definitive answer about that development. For now, though, I can think of only one explanation. You come from the high lands beyond the Himalayas, right?' And when Shiva nodded, he continued, 'The air gets thinner the higher you go, and there's less oxygen in thinner air, which means your body is used to surviving with less oxygen and consequently was less harmed by the "oxidants" – so therefore the "anti-oxidants" in the *Somras* might have had a stronger effect on you.'

'That sounds reasonable,' said Shiva, 'but why was *my* throat the only one to turn cold and blue?'

'A good point,' conceded Brahaspati. 'I have another question — did your tribe also experience improvements in any injuries?'

'Actually, they did.'

'Which suggests that the diluted air you all lived in had some role to play in the unusual effects of the *Somras*, but since you're the only one who developed a blue throat, the "thinner air" theory is clearly only a partial explanation. We can always research it more — I'm sure there's a scientific explanation for the blue throat.'

Shiva gazed at Brahaspati intently, reading between the lines of his last statement. 'You don't believe in the prophecy of the Neelkanth, do you?'

Brahaspati smiled awkwardly at Shiva. He was beginning to like the young man, and he didn't want to insult him — but he wasn't going to lie either. 'I believe in science. It provides a solution and a rationale for everything, and if something looks like a miracle, it's only because a scientific reason for it hasn't been discovered yet.'

'Then why do the Meluhans not look to science to solve their problems?'

'I'm not sure,' said Brahaspati thoughtfully. 'Perhaps it's because science is a capable but cold-hearted master. Unlike a Neelkanth, it won't solve your problems for you — it'll only provide you with the tools to fight your own battles. Perhaps it's easier for people to believe that someone else will come and solve their problems for them.'

'So what do you think the Neelkanth's role is in Meluha?'

Brahaspati looked at Shiva sympathetically. 'I'd like to think that true Suryavanshis would fight their own demons rather than pressuring someone else to do it. A true Suryavanshi's *duty* is to push himself to the limit of his abilities and strength. The coming of the Neelkanth should only redouble a Suryavanshi's efforts, since it's obvious that the time for the destruction of evil is near.' Brahaspati thought for a moment before asking, 'Are you concerned about the strain of taking up a responsibility you don't really want just because people say they have faith in you?'

'No, that's not it,' replied Shiva. 'This is a wonderful country and I want to do everything I can to help. But what if your people depend on me to protect them and I can't? Right now, I have no idea whether I can do everything they expect me to, so how can I give my word that I will?'

Brahaspati smiled. According to his rule-book, any man who took his own word seriously was worth respecting.

'You appear to be a good man, Shiva. You'll probably face a lot of pressure in the coming days. Be careful, my friend – the blue throat generates blind faith, and as a result your decisions will have ramifications for the entire land. Remember, whether a man is a legend or not is decided by history, not fortune-tellers.'

Shiva smiled, glad to have finally found a man who understood his predicament – and, more importantly, one who was willing to *offer* some advice at least.

— 🏹 ⵙⵓⵜ⊕ —

Late that evening, after a thoroughly enjoyable afternoon touring Mount Mandar with Brahaspati, Shiva lay on his bed, reading a book. A spent chillum rested on the side table.

He was reading *The Righteous War against the Asuras*, and some aspects of the story were troubling him. The *Asuras* were demons with a pathological hatred for the *Devas*, and they routinely attacked *Deva* cities in an attempt to force them to accept the *Asura* way of life. This was not a surprise to Shiva; he expected demons to behave – well, demonically. What he hadn't expected was that some of the *Devas* were prepared to go to unusually unethical limits in their blind pursuit of victory. And Lord Rudra, though personally a great man, appeared to have ignored the indiscretions of the *Devas* in the interest of the greater good.

Hearing a commotion outside the guest-house, Shiva looked down from his first-floor balcony to see the royal caravan arriving. Neat rows of Arishtanemi soldiers had formed an honour guard at the entrance and some people were disembarking from the far side of the second carriage – the royal family, Shiva assumed. The Arishtanemi accorded their royal family exactly the same courtesies they extended to every other arrival, regardless of rank – doubtless another manifestation of the customary Meluhan obsession with perceived equality.

Shiva's equality theory was challenged when Parvateshwar alighted from the fifth carriage and, as one, the Arishtanemi sprang to full attention while an officer rushed in front of Parvateshwar and executed what he guessed was the Meluhan military salute: with the body held rigidly at attention, the heels were clicked and the right hand, balled in a fist, was brought rapidly and violently to the left breast. After this dramatic salute the officer bent low in respect to the chief of the army, and the soldiers repeated their officer's greeting.

Parvateshwar formally saluted in return, accompanied with a slight bow of his head. He started towards his soldiers, inspecting the troops, while the officer fell in two steps behind him.

Shiva sensed there was admiration for the man himself rather than his rank. For all his surliness, Parvateshwar had a reputation as a brave warrior, and Shiva saw deep respect in each Arishtanemi's eyes as he bowed low to his general.

A little while later, Shiva heard a soft knock on his door. He didn't need to open it to know who was on the other side. Sighing softly, he let in his visitor.

Daksha's fixed smile disappeared and he started a little as the unfamiliar odour of marijuana assaulted his senses. Kanakhala, standing to the emperor's right, looked equally perplexed.

'What *is* that stench?' Daksha asked Brahaspati, who stood to the left. 'Perhaps you should change the Lord's room – how can you subject him to this discomfort?'

'I have a feeling Shiva is quite comfortable with this aroma, your Majesty,' said Brahaspati, and Shiva grinned.

'It's a smell that travels with me, your Majesty,' said Shiva. 'I like it.'

Daksha was baffled and his face did nothing to hide his revulsion, but he quickly recovered his composure. After all, if the Lord was happy with the malodour . . . 'I'm sorry to disturb you,' he started, his smile back in place, 'but I just wanted to tell you my family has arrived at the guest-house.'

'That's very thoughtful of you, your Majesty,' said Shiva with a formal namaste.

'We were hoping to have the honour of eating breakfast with you tomorrow morning.'

'The honour would be mine.'

'Excellent, excellent.' Daksha beamed as he moved on to the question that was dominating his mind. 'So what do you think of the *Somras*, my Lord? Is it not the drink of the gods?'

'Yes, your Majesty. It does indeed appear to be a miraculous drink.'

'It is the foundation of our civilisation,' continued Daksha. 'When you tour our land, you'll surely see the goodness of our way of life, and will find it in your heart to preserve it.'

'Your Majesty, I already think highly of your country – it truly is a great empire that treats its citizens well, and I've no doubt it's a way of life worth protecting. What I'm unsure of is exactly what I can do to help you. Yours is such an advanced civilisation and I am just a simple tribal man.'

'Faith is a very potent weapon, my Lord,' said Daksha, his hands joined in supplication. 'All that's needed is for you to have as much faith in yourself as we have in you. I'm sure that once you see the effect your presence has on our people, you'll realise what you can do.'

Shiva gave up arguing against Daksha's unshakeable belief.

Brahaspati winked at Shiva before coming to his rescue. 'Your Majesty, Shiva looks tired to me – it's been a long day. Maybe we should let him retire and meet again tomorrow?'

Daksha smiled. 'You're right, Brahaspati – my apologies for troubling you, my Lord. We'll see you at breakfast. Until tomorrow, then.'

'Until tomorrow, your Majesty,' replied Shiva.

Sati waited quietly at the table as Daksha glanced nervously at the *prahar* lamp. To his left were Kanakhala, Brahaspati and Parvateshwar; to his right, an empty chair. *For the Neelkanth*, thought Sati, who was seated next to the empty chair, with her mother on her right. Her father had agonised over the seating, trying to get it exactly right.

Sati looked over the arrangements. A formal table and chairs had been set, rather than the low table and floor cushions Meluhans normally used. Gold plates had replaced the beloved banana leaves, and instead of the taste-enhancing *kulhads*, or mud cups, there were refined silver goblets. Her father was stopping at nothing to make this breakfast meeting perfect. She had seen him pin his hopes on too many so-called Neelkanths already, 'miracle men' who all turned out to be frauds. She hoped he would not have to face this crushing disillusionment again.

As the crier announced Shiva and Nandi, Daksha rose with a reverential namaste to receive the Lord, and Parvateshwar rolled his eyes at his emperor's servile behaviour. At the same instant, Sati bent down to pick up a goblet she had knocked to the floor.

'My Lord,' said the emperor, pointing at people in turn, 'you already know Kanakhala, Brahaspati and Parvateshwar. Permit me to introduce my wife, Queen Veerini.'

Shiva smiled politely as he returned Veerini's namaste with a formal namaste and a low bow.

'And next to her,' said Daksha with a broad smile as Sati stood up, clutching the goblet she had retrieved, 'is my daughter, Princess Sati.'

Shiva's breath rushed out as he gazed at his life staring back at him. His heart beat a frantic rhythm, and he could have sworn he smelled his favourite fragrance in the whole world: the aroma of the Holy Lake at sunset. As before, he was mesmerised.

The uncomfortable silence that filled the room was broken by the clang of the unfortunate goblet as it fell once again to the floor from Sati's nerveless fingers. The rolling vessel brought Sati to her senses, and with a superhuman effort she managed to control the look of shock on her face. She was breathing heavily, as if she had just danced a duet with Shiva. She didn't realise her soul was doing exactly that.

Daksha gazed at the dumbstruck couple with the gleeful expression of a director watching his play being perfectly performed.

Nandi, standing right behind Shiva, could see Sati's expression, and suddenly everything became clear to him: the dance practices, the *vikarma* touch, the *shudhikaran* – and his Lord's anguish. While some part of him was afraid, he quickly reconciled himself to the situation. If his Lord wanted this, he would support it completely.

The chief scientist, Brahaspati, stared blankly at the couple, deep in thought about the implications of this unexpected situation.

And Parvateshwar could barely conceal his repugnance – this was wrong, immoral, and, worst of all, illegal.

'My Lord,' said Daksha, pointing to the empty chair, 'please, take your seat and we shall begin.'

Shiva didn't react – he hadn't heard Daksha's words. He was in a world where the only sound was the harmonious melody of Sati's heavy breathing, a tune he could blissfully dance to for his next seven lives.

'My Lord?' repeated Daksha, a little louder, and Shiva finally looked at him as if he had come from another world.

'Please, take your seat, my Lord,' Daksha said once again.

'Yes, of course, your Majesty,' said Shiva, averting his eyes in embarrassment. As he sat, the food, a delicacy known as *idli* that the Meluhans loved for breakfast, was brought in.

'*You're* the Neelkanth?' Sati, still shocked, whispered softly to Shiva as soon as she had willed some calmness into her breathing.

'Apparently so,' he replied with a playful grin. 'Impressed?'

Sati answered that question with a disdainful raised eyebrow. The mask was back in place. 'Why would I be impressed?'

What?

'My Lord,' said Daksha, and Shiva turned towards him.

'Yes, your Majesty?'

'Our *puja* to Lord Brahma should be over by this evening, but my reviews are going to take two more days. I don't see any point in Veerini and Sati staying any longer – they'll get thoroughly bored.'

'Thank you, your Majesty,' said Brahaspati with a sly grin. 'The royal family's interest in Mount Mandar is most reassuring.'

The entire table burst out laughing, and Daksha grinned too. 'You know what I meant, Brahaspati,' he said, smiling wryly. He turned back to Shiva and continued, 'Am I right in thinking that you're planning to leave for Devagiri tomorrow morning? I think it would be a good idea for Veerini and Sati to accompany you. The rest of us can catch up with you two days later.'

Sati looked up in alarm. She wasn't sure why, but something told her that she shouldn't agree to this plan – but another part of her said she had no reason to be scared: in her eighty-five years as a *vikarma* she had never broken the law. She had the self-control to know what was right, and what wasn't, and to do what was necessary.

Shiva had no such doubts. With very obvious delight he said, 'I think that is a very good idea, your Majesty.'

'It's settled, then,' said Daksha, looking visibly content. 'Parvateshwar, please ensure that the Arishtanemi escort are divided into two groups for the return journey.'

'My Lord, I don't think that's wise,' said Parvateshwar. 'Many of the Arishtanemi are still in Devagiri, preparing for the Sanjeevani material transfer. And we cannot reduce the standing contingent at Mount Mandar, not under any circumstances. We may not have enough soldiers for two caravans, so I would prefer us all to travel together when your reviews are concluded.'

'I'm sure there won't be a problem,' the emperor said firmly. 'Aren't you always telling me that each Arishtanemi is equal to fifty enemy soldiers? It's settled: the Lord Neelkanth, Veerini and Sati will leave tomorrow morning. Please make all the arrangements.'

Parvateshwar went unhappily back to his thoughts as Shiva and Sati started whispering to each other again.

'Please tell me you went for a *shudhikaran*,' she said seriously.

'I did,' said Shiva – and it was true, he had finally attended a purification ceremony on his last night at Devagiri. He still didn't believe he'd needed it, but he knew Sati would ask him the next time they met and he didn't want to have to lie to her. 'Although I think the concept of *shudhikaran* is completely absurd,' he whispered back. 'In fact, the entire concept of the *vikarma* is ridiculous. It's one of the few unfair things I've seen in Meluha and it should be changed.'

Sati's eyes locked with his. Her face was devoid of any expression and as Shiva returned her gaze, he tried to guess some of the thoughts running through her mind. But he hit a blank wall.

$$- \lambda \, \text{\textcopyright} \, \text{U} \, \text{\ding{58}} \, \text{\ding{192}} -$$

The following day, at the beginning of the second *prahar*, Shiva, Veerini, Sati and Nandi departed for Devagiri, accompanied by a hundred Arishtanemi. Daksha, Parvateshwar and Kanakhala stood outside the guest-house to see them off. Brahaspati had been detained by some scheduled experiments.

Since protocol required the emperor's caravan to include a minimum of four vehicles, Shiva and his companions would be travelling to Devagiri in the one remaining carriage. Parvateshwar was deeply unhappy about members of the royal family travelling without any dummy carriages, but Daksha had overruled his objections.

Sitting on one of the comfortably upholstered seats inside the carriage, Sati noticed that Shiva was wearing his cravat again. 'Why do you cover your throat all the time?'

'I'm uncomfortable with the attention the blue throat attracts,' replied Shiva.

'But you'll have to get used to it – it's not going to disappear.'

'True,' answered Shiva with a smile, 'but until then, the cravat is my shield.'

As the caravan departed, Parvateshwar and Kanakhala approached Daksha.

'Why do you have so much faith in that man, my Lord?' asked Parvateshwar. 'He's done nothing to deserve respect. How can he lead us to victory when he hasn't even been trained for it? The entire concept of the Neelkanth goes against our rules. In Meluha a person should only be given a task if he is found capable of it, and after he has been trained for it by the system.'

'We're at war, Parvateshwar,' Daksha said bluntly. 'An undeclared one, perhaps, but it's war all the same. We face terrorist attacks every other week because these cowardly Chandravanshis won't fight us in the open, and our army is too small to invade their territory successfully. Our "rules" aren't working. We need a miracle. And the first rule of serendipity is that miracles come when we forget rational laws and have faith. I have faith in the Neelkanth, and so do my people.'

'But Shiva has no faith in himself,' said Parvateshwar. 'How can you force him to be our saviour when he doesn't want to do it?'

'Sati will change that.'

'My Lord, surely you're not going to use your own daughter as bait?' He sounded as horrified as he felt. 'And do you really want a saviour who decides to help us just because of his lust?'

'It's not lust!'

Parvateshwar was shocked into silence by Daksha's vehement reaction.

'What kind of a father do you think I am?' asked Daksha. 'How dare you even *think* I would use my daughter so? My hope is that she'll find some comfort and happiness with the Lord. She's suffered enough – I want her to be happy. And if by encouraging her happiness I also help my country, where's the harm in that?'

Parvateshwar opened his mouth to reply, but thought better of it.

'We need to destroy the Chandravanshi ideology,' continued Daksha, 'and the only way we can do that is by giving the benefits of our lifestyle to the people of Swadweep. The common Swadweepans will be grateful for it, but their Chandravanshi rulers will do everything in their power to stop us. They might be able to resist us, but try as they might, they won't be able to stop a people led by the Neelkanth. And if Sati is with the Neelkanth, there's no way he'd refuse to lead us against the Chandravanshis.'

'Do you really think the Lord will aid us just because he's in love with your daughter?' asked Kanakhala.

'You've missed the point,' replied Daksha. 'The Lord doesn't need to be convinced to help us. He's already seen how great our civilisation is – maybe it's not perfect, but it's great all the same – and he's promised to help us any way he can. What the Neelkanth needs is the motivation and belief in himself. That belief in himself will assert itself the closer he becomes to Sati.'

'And how will that happen, your Majesty?' asked Parvateshwar, frowning slightly.

'What's the most powerful force in a man's life?' asked Daksha.

Kanakhala and Parvateshwar stared blankly at Daksha, utterly nonplussed.

'It's his intense desire to impress the person he loves most,' expounded Daksha. 'Look at me. I've always loved my father, and my desire to impress him hasn't lessened, even after his death. I still want to make him proud of me, and that desire drives me to my destiny as the king who will re-establish the pure Suryavanshi way of life across India. And when the Neelkanth develops a deep desire to make Sati proud of him, he will rise to fulfil his destiny.'

Parvateshwar frowned, but kept quiet, though he did not quite agree with his emperor's logic.

'But what if Sati seeks something different?' asked Kanakhala. 'Like a husband who spends all his time with her.'

'I know my daughter,' replied Daksha confidently. 'I know what it takes to impress her.'

'That's an interesting point of view, my Lord,' said Kanakhala, smiling to take any hint of an insult out of her words. 'Just out of curiosity, what do you think is the most powerful force in a woman's life?'

Daksha laughed out loud. 'Why do you ask? Don't you know?'

'The most powerful force in my life is the desire to get out of the house before my mother-in-law wakes up!'

Daksha laughed along with Kanakhala at her quip, but Parvateshwar didn't find it funny. 'I'm sorry, Kanakhala, but that's no way to speak about your mother-in-law.'

'Oh, relax, Parvateshwar,' said Kanakhala. 'You take everything too seriously.'

'I think,' said Daksha, with a grin, 'the most powerful force in a woman's life is the need to be appreciated, loved and cherished for who she is.'

Kanakhala smiled and nodded. Her emperor truly understood human emotions.

CHAPTER 10

The Hooded Figure Returns

As the caravan emerged from the depths of Mount Mandar, Veerini halted the carriage so that she and her companions could offer a prayer of gratitude to the mountain. Watching over them, on high alert, was the Arishtanemi Bhabravya, a strapping man of sixty years with an intimidating moustache and beard.

After a few moments, Bhabravya approached Veerini and said with barely concealed impatience, 'Your Majesty, perhaps it's time to get back into the carriage.'

Veerini looked up at the captain and rose, Sati, Shiva and Nandi following her, and the caravan resumed its journey.

'It's her,' said Vishwadyumna, putting down the scope and turning towards his Lord.

The platoon was positioned at a safe distance, concealed from the caravan by the dense, almost impenetrable foliage.

The hooded figure grunted his agreement, but his gaze lingered on Shiva's muscular body. Even without the scope he had no doubt this was the same man he'd fought at the Brahma temple a couple of weeks before. 'Who is that man?'

'I don't know, my Lord.'

'Keep your eye on him – he was the one who foiled the last attack.'

Vishwadyumna was of the firm opinion that the previous attempt had failed because it was unplanned, and that the presence of the caste-unmarked man had made little difference to the unsuccessful outcome. He had been puzzled by his Lord's recent irrational decisions – such carelessness was out of character for him – but perhaps the proximity of their ultimate objective was clouding his judgement. In spite of his misgivings, however, he was wise enough to keep his thoughts to himself. 'We should track them for an hour or so before we attack, my Lord – by that time they'll be a safe distance away from any Arishtanemi reinforcements. Then we can wrap this up quickly and report back to the queen.'

'No. We'll wait until they're at least half a day's distance from Mount Mandar – these new carriages have systems that can send an emergency signal the moment they're attacked. Our task must be finished before reinforcements arrive.'

'Yes, my Lord,' said Vishwadyumna, relieved to hear that his Lord hadn't lost his famed tactical brilliance after all.

'And remember – I want it done quickly,' added the hooded figure. 'The longer we take, the more people get hurt.'

'Yes, my Lord.'

— 𝕏 ⵔ ⵘ ⵔ ⊛ —

The caravan stopped for lunch at the beginning of the third *prahar*, in a clearing halfway between Mount Mandar and Devagiri, where the forest had been cut back to reduce any chance of a surprise attack. Veerini's maids quickly unpacked the food and started heating it in the centre of the clearing while the royal party made themselves comfortable. Bhabravya stood guard on the higher ground at the rear, keeping an eagle eye on their surroundings. Half the Arishtanemi soldiers had also sat down to eat, while the rest kept watch.

Shiva was about to take a second helping of rice when he heard the crack of a twig somewhere along the road. Stopping with his hand halfway to the dish, he listened intently for another sound. There was none. Probably some forest creature that had stumbled on them by mistake and was now keeping still. Shiva glanced at Sati to see if she'd heard the sound, and found her also staring intently down the road. The instant their eyes met, they both heard the soft crunch as the foot on the broken twig eased its pressure slightly.

Shiva immediately put his plate down and stood up, drew his sword and fixed his shield on his back. Bhabravya saw Shiva's actions and drew his sword, giving his men quick, silent signals to do likewise. The Arishtanemi were battle-ready in a matter of seconds. Sati and Nandi also drew their weapons and took up their traditional fighting positions.

Sati whispered to Veerini without turning, 'Mother, please get into the carriage and lock it. The maids will join you inside as soon as they've unhitched the horses. We have no intention of retreating, and we don't want the enemy kidnapping you either.'

'Come with me, Sati,' pleaded Veerini as her maids rushed to release the horses from the shafts.

'No, I'm staying here, Mother. Please hurry. We may not have much time.'

Veerini reluctantly complied, followed by the maids, who rushed into the carriage and quickly locked it from the inside.

Some distance from the royal carriage, Bhabravya whispered to his aide, 'I know their tactics – I've seen these cowards on the southern border. They'll send an advance suicide party, then pretend to retreat in an attempt to draw us into an ambush. I don't care how many men we lose – we'll chase those bastards down and destroy every single one of them. They'll pay for this mistake.'

Shiva turned to Sati and whispered carefully, 'I think they must be aiming for a high-profile target. Nothing would be more significant than the royal family. Do you think that you should wait in the carriage too?'

Sati looked at Shiva in surprise and a pained expression crossed her face, swiftly transforming into a defiant glare. 'No way! I'm going to fight—'

What's wrong with her? My suggestion is completely logical: make the main objective of the enemy difficult to get at and they will lose the will to fight.

He opened his mouth to argue, but the steel in her gaze told him he'd be wasting his breath, so he pushed these thoughts out of his mind and focused on the road, listening intently for any movement from the enemy. They were prepared for the ambush. It was the enemy's turn to make a move. Just as they thought that it might have been a false alarm, a loud sound reverberated from down the road – from the direction of Mount Mandar. Shiva turned around, but stayed where he was. Whatever was making the noise was moving rapidly towards them.

Shiva did not recognise the cacophony, but the Arishtanemi from the southern border knew exactly what it was: it was the sound of a *Nagadhvani* conch, blown to announce the launch of a Naga attack.

Though he was impatient to fight, Bhabravya did not forget the standard operating procedures. He whispered an order to an aide, who rushed to the carriage and pulled out the red box fixed to the bottom. Kicking it open, the aide pressed a button on the side, and a tubular chimney-like structure extended straight up from the box for nearly twenty-five feet. The chimney ensured that any smoke signal was not lost in the dense forest and could be seen by the scouts at both Devagiri and Mount Mandar.

The soldier picked a branch from the fire and pushed it into the last of the four slots on the right side of the box and red smoke fumed out of the chimney, signifying the highest level of danger. Help was six hours away – four, if the back-up rode hard.

But Bhabravya did not intend the battle to last that long. He intended to kill every one of the Nagas and the Chandravanshis long before that.

Then the attack began, coming from the side of the road leading to Mount Mandar. A small band of ten Chandravanshi soldiers charged at the Arishtanemi. One soldier was holding the Naga conch shell and blowing hard.

Shiva saw one amongst them had his entire face and head covered with a cloth, except for small slits left for his eyes: perhaps the Naga himself?

Shiva didn't move. The Arishtanemi could easily handle ten Chandravanshis. He signalled to Sati and Nandi to stay where they were, and there was no argument from Sati this time – she'd also concluded that this attack was a ruse.

The battle was short and fierce. The Chandravanshi soldiers fought viciously, but they were outnumbered, and just as Bhabravya had expected, they soon turned and beat a hasty retreat towards Mount Mandar.

'After them,' yelled Bhabravya, 'kill them all!'

The Arishtanemi dashed behind their captain in pursuit of the retreating Chandravanshis, deaf to Shiva's warning cry: 'No! Stay here – don't chase them.'

By the time the remaining Arishtanemi heard Shiva's order, the majority had already rushed off in pursuit of the Chandravanshis, and Shiva was left in the clearing with Sati,

Nandi and only twenty-five soldiers. He looked at the road leading to Devagiri – the direction from which the crack of the twig had come, then turned back to address the remaining men. Pointing behind him, his voice steady and calm, he said, 'This is where the actual attack will come from, so get into tight formations of four, facing that direction. Keep the princess in the middle. We'll have to hold them back for about five or ten minutes – the other Arishtanemi will return when they realise there are no Chandravanshis to fight in that direction.'

The Arishtanemi nodded respectfully at Shiva. They were battle-hardened men, and they appreciated a clear-headed, calm leader who obviously knew exactly what he was doing. They quickly got into formation and waited.

Then the real attack began. Forty Chandravanshi soldiers led by a hooded figure emerged from the trees and walked slowly towards the Suryavanshi caravan. The outnumbered Arishtanemi remained in position, waiting for their enemy to come to them.

'Surrender the princess and we'll leave,' said the hooded figure. 'We want no unnecessary bloodshed.'

So the earlier group had someone pretending to be a Naga. This must be the real one. It looks like the same joker from the Brahma temple. Strange costume, but he fought well.

'We don't want any bloodshed either,' said Shiva. 'Leave quietly, and we promise not to kill you.'

'*You're* the one looking death in the face, barbarian,' said the hooded figure, his posture conveying anger, though his voice remained eerily composed.

Shiva noticed a brown-turbaned officer watching the hooded figure impatiently. He clearly wanted to attack fast and get this over with.

Dissension amongst the ranks?

'The only face I'm looking at is your stupid festival mask, and soon I'll be shoving it down your throat. And you might want to tell your brainless brown-turbaned lieutenant not to give away your battle plans.'

The hooded figure didn't so much as flick his eyes at his lieutenant.

Damn! This man is good.

'This is your final warning, barbarian,' said the hooded figure. 'Hand her over immediately.'

Sati gasped suddenly, then shouted, 'Mother! The new emergency conch shell close to the front grille – blow it, now!'

Scant seconds later, the mournful sound of the conch emerged from the carriage, summoning Bhabravya and his men back to the clearing.

The hooded figure cursed as he realised he'd just lost his advantage. Very little time remained to complete his mission before the other Arishtanemi returned. Abandoning all hope of avoiding a fight, he gave the order: 'Charge!'

The Arishtanemi stayed in position.

'Steady,' said Shiva, 'wait for them. All you have to do is

buy time and keep the princess safe. Our friends will be back soon.'

But as the Chandravanshis came closer, Sati suddenly broke through the cordon and struck out at the hooded figure. Her surprise attack slowed the Chandravanshis, and left the Arishtanemi no choice – as one they charged like vicious tigers.

Shiva moved quickly to protect Sati's right flank as an advancing Vishwadyumna got dangerously close to her. Vishwadyumna swung his sword to force Shiva out of his way, but the speed of Shiva's advance left him unbalanced. Shiva parried the blow easily and as he pushed him back with his shield he saw Nandi moving rapidly to Sati's left to block the Chandravanshis trying to charge from that direction.

Sati was still attacking the hooded figure fiercely, but the hooded figure was only defending himself rather than striking back. He wanted her alive and unharmed.

Shiva cut Vishwadyumna savagely across his exposed shoulder. Grimacing, the Naga brought his shield up to fend off Shiva, and with the same movement, he brought his sword arm up to thrust at the barbarian's torso. Shiva quickly pulled his own shield in to protect himself – but not quickly enough. Vishwadyumna slashed Shiva's chest.

Stepping back and jumping to his right, Shiva brought his weapon down swiftly in a brutal jab. Though Vishwadyumna promptly brought his shield up to block the attack, Shiva's unorthodox move unsettled him and he staggered back, realising that Shiva was an excellent swordsman. It was going to be a hard and long duel.

Nandi had already brought down one Chandravanshi soldier who had broken a Suryavanshi law of combat by attacking below the waist and cutting Nandi's thigh. Though bleeding profusely, Nandi was ferociously battling another soldier who had attacked him from the left. The Chandravanshi brought his shield down hard on Nandi's injured leg, making him stagger and fall. The Chandravanshi thought he had his man. Raising his sword high with both hands, he was about to bring it down to finish the job when he suddenly arched forward as if a brutal force had pounded him from behind. As he fell, Nandi saw a knife buried deep in the Chandravanshi's back, and looking up, he saw Shiva's left arm descending in a smooth arc after releasing the dagger while, with his right hand, Shiva brought his sword up to block a vicious cut from the brown-turbaned captain. As Nandi stumbled to his feet, Shiva reached back to pull his shield in front of him again.

The hooded figure knew they were taking too long – the other Arishtanemi would be back soon. He tried to slip behind Sati, intending to club her on the back of the head and knock her unconscious, but she was too quick for him. Moving swiftly, she turned to face her enemy again, then, pulling a knife from the folds of her *angvastram* with her left hand, she slashed outwards across the hooded figure's immense stomach. The knife sliced through the robe, but the armour hidden beneath saved him from Sati's blade.

With a resounding roar, Bhabravya and the other Arishtanemi rushed back into the clearing to fight alongside their comrades. Suddenly vastly outnumbered, the hooded figure had no choice but to order a retreat.

Shiva stopped Bhabravya from chasing the Chandravanshis once again.

'Let them go, brave Bhabravya,' said Shiva. 'We'll have other chances to get them. Right now the primary objective is to protect the royal family.'

Bhabravya's look of admiration was for Shiva's skill in battle, not because of the blue throat, of which he was still unaware. He nodded politely. 'That makes sense, foreigner.'

He quickly formed the Arishtanemi soldiers into a tight defensive perimeter around the wounded, leaving the dead where they had fallen. At least three Arishtanemi bodies lay in the clearing, alongside nine Chandravanshi – the last, too wounded to escape, had taken his own life. Better to meet one's maker than fall alive into enemy hands and risk revealing secrets. Bhabravya ordered his soldiers to stay low with their shields in front to protect against arrows. And they waited so till the rescue party arrived.

$$- \lambda \, \text{\textcircled{0}} \, \text{U} \, \text{\textcircled{+}} \, \text{\textcircled{$\odot$}} \, -$$

'My God,' cried an anxious Daksha as he hugged Sati tight.

The rescue party of five hundred soldiers had arrived from Mount Mandar by the fourth hour of the second *prahar*. Despite Parvateshwar's warnings, Daksha, Brahaspati and Kanakhala had insisted on accompanying the soldiers. Releasing Sati from his grip, a tear escaped his eye as he whispered, 'You're not injured, are you?'

'I'm fine, Father,' said Sati self-consciously, 'just a few cuts. Nothing serious.'

'She fought very bravely,' said Veerini, beaming with pride.

'I think that's a mother's bias,' said Sati, her face gradually recovering its customary serious expression. 'It was Shiva who saved the day, Father – he figured out the Chandravanshis' real plan and rallied everyone at the crucial moment. We only beat them because of him.'

'I think she's being far too generous,' said Shiva modestly. *She's impressed – finally!*

'Not at all, my Lord,' said a visibly grateful Daksha. 'You've already begun to work your magic – we've actually beaten back a terrorist attack. You don't know how significant this is for us!'

'But it wasn't a terrorist attack, your Majesty,' said Shiva. 'It was an attempt to kidnap the princess.'

'A *kidnap* attempt?' asked Daksha, his grateful smile slipping a little.

'The hooded man leading the attack certainly wanted her alive and unharmed.'

'What hooded man?' he cried, now thoroughly alarmed.

'The Naga, your Majesty,' said Shiva, surprised at Daksha's hysterical response. 'I've seen that man fight before and he's an excellent warrior – a little slow, perhaps, but first-rate technique. But while he was fighting Sati he did his best not to hurt her.'

The colour drained completely from Daksha's face and Veerini glared at her husband with a strange mixture of fear and anger. The expressions on their faces made Shiva feel uncomfortable, as if he were intruding on a private family moment.

'Father?' asked Sati, worried, 'are you all right?'

When no response was forthcoming, Shiva turned to Sati and said, 'Perhaps it would be best if you speak to your family in private. I'll go and see how Nandi and the other soldiers are doing.'

Parvateshwar was inspecting his men, checking on the injured and ensuring they received medical help, with Bhabravya two steps behind. When he came to the Chandravanshi Shiva had killed while protecting Nandi, he roared in horror, 'This man has been stabbed in the back!'

'Yes, my Lord,' said Bhabravya, with his head bowed.

'Who did this? Who broke the sacred rules of combat?'

'I think it was the foreigner, my Lord, but I heard he was trying to protect Captain Nandi from this Chandravanshi. And the Chandravanshi himself was not following the combat rules – he'd already attacked Nandi below the waist.'

Parvateshwar turned and gave Bhabravya a withering look

that made him cower. 'Rules are rules,' he growled. 'They are meant to be followed, even if your enemy ignores them.'

'Yes, my Lord.'

'Go and make sure that the dead are properly cremated – including the Chandravanshis.'

'My Lord?' asked Bhabravya. 'But they're terrorists—'

'*They* may be terrorists,' snarled Parvateshwar, 'but *we* are Suryavanshis. We follow Lord Ram's rules, even with regard to our enemies. The Chandravanshis will receive proper cremations – is that clear?'

'Yes, my Lord,' replied Bhabravya, thoroughly abashed, and he hurried off to make the arrangements.

— ⚇ ꝏ Ս ⚵ ✹ —

'Why do you call the foreigner "my Lord"?' asked an injured Arishtanemi lying next to Nandi.

Shiva had just departed after spending half an hour with Nandi and the other injured soldiers. None of them were behaving as if they'd fought a battle just a few hours earlier; they were talking jovially with each other, some even teasing their comrades for falling for the red-herring diversion at the beginning of the battle. To the Kshatriya, laughing in the face of death was the ultimate mark of a real man.

'Because he *is* my Lord,' answered Nandi simply.

'But he's a foreigner – a caste-unmarked foreigner,' said the Arishtanemi. 'He's a brave warrior, no doubt, but there are so many brave warriors in Meluha. What makes him so special? And why's he spending so much time with the royal family?'

'I can't answer that, my friend. You'll find out when the time is right.'

The Arishtanemi looked at Nandi quizzically for a moment, then shook his head and smiled. He was a soldier. He concerned himself only with the here and now; bigger questions didn't linger too long in his mind. 'None of my business, I guess,' he said amicably. 'However, the time *is* right to tell you that you're a brave man, my friend. I saw you fight despite your injury – you don't know the meaning of the word "surrender". I'd be proud to have you as my *bhraata*.'

That was a huge compliment from the Arishtanemi. The *bhraata* system meant every soldier in the Meluhan army up to the rank of captain was assigned a partner of equal rank, and each pair of *bhraatas* would fight together and look out for each other like brothers.

The Arishtanemi were elite soldiers; customarily they became *bhraatas* only with other Arishtanemi. Nandi knew he could never really be the Arishtanemi's *bhraata* – he had to stay with the Lord – but the honour of being offered this brotherhood brought tears to his eyes.

'Don't get teary on me now,' said the Arishtanemi, chuckling and wrinkling his nose in amusement.

Nandi smiled and slapped his arm. 'What's your name, my friend?' he asked.

'Kaustav – and some day we shall battle the main

Chandravanshi army together, my *bhraata*, and by the grace of Lord Ram, we'll kill every last one of those bastards!'

'By Lord Agni, we will!'

— ⚓ ⓌU⚷⊕ —

'I'm curious to learn how you got into the Naga's mind,' said Brahaspati as he watched a medic clean and dress a gash on Shiva's torso. Shiva had insisted that every other soldier's wounds were tended before he received medical attention himself.

'I can't really explain it,' said Shiva. 'It was just obvious to me how the Naga would think.'

'I can explain it!'

'Go on, then.'

'The explanation is that you're the omnipotent "N", whose name cannot be spoken,' said Brahaspati, opening his eyes wide and waggling his fingers like a magician.

They both burst out laughing and Shiva rocked back slightly, earning himself a stern look from the military doctor tending his wound. Shiva settled down again while the medic finished his work.

Having applied the Ayurvedic paste, he covered it with a medicinal neem leaf and bandaged the wound with a cotton cloth. 'You'll need to change that every second day, foreigner,' he said, pointing at the bandage. 'The royal doctor in Devagiri will be able to do it for you. And don't get this area wet for a week. Also, avoid the *Somras* during this period since you won't be able to take a complete bath.'

'Oh, he doesn't need the *Somras*,' joked Brahaspati. 'It's already done him all the damage it can.'

Shiva and Brahaspati collapsed into helpless laughter again as the doctor walked away, shaking his head in exasperation.

'But seriously,' said Brahaspati, calming down, 'why would they attack you? You haven't harmed anybody.'

'They weren't attacking me; they were after Sati.'

'Sati – why Sati? That's even more bizarre.'

'In truth, I suspect they were targeting the royal family in general rather than Sati specifically,' said Shiva. 'The primary target was probably the emperor, but as he wasn't there, they went for Sati instead. I think they hoped to kidnap a royal to use as leverage.'

Brahaspati didn't respond, but he looked worried. Clasping his hands together and bringing them close to his face, he stared into the distance, deep in thought. Shiva reached into his pouch and pulled out his chillum, then carefully filled it with some dried marijuana. Brahaspati turned to look at his friend, clearly unhappy at what he was doing.

'I probably shouldn't say this,' said Brahaspati, 'but I consider you my friend, and as such it's my duty to tell you the truth. I've seen Egyptian merchants in Karachapa with this marijuana habit – it's not good for you.'

'You're wrong, my friend,' said Shiva, grinning broadly. 'This is actually the best habit in the world.'

'But it has many harmful side-effects – worst of all, it harms your memory, causing untold damage to your ability to draw on past knowledge.'

Shiva's face suddenly became uncharacteristically serious and he gazed back at Brahaspati with a melancholy smile. 'That's exactly why it's good, my friend. No idiot who smokes this is scared of forgetting.' He lit up his chillum, took a deep drag and continued, 'They're scared of *not* forgetting.'

Brahaspati stared sharply at Shiva, wondering what terrible event in his past could have prompted his friend to become addicted to the weed.

CHAPTER 11

Neelkanth Unveiled

The royal caravan resumed its journey to Devagiri the following morning. They had spent the night at a temporary camp in the clearing after the Arishtanemi and Parvateshwar agreed that it wasn't safe to travel at night. The wounded, including Nandi, occupied the first three carriages and the fifth, while the royal family travelled in the fourth with Shiva. All those soldiers who had fought in the previous day's battle were granted the privilege of riding horses, travelling in relative comfort, while Brahaspati and Kanakhala walked with the rest of the troops, in mourning for the three slain Arishtanemi. Parvateshwar, Bhabravya and two other soldiers bore a makeshift wooden palanquin that carried three urns containing the martyrs' ashes. The urns would be given to their families for ceremonial submersion in the Saraswati. Shiva, Sati and Nandi wanted to walk too, but the doctor insisted they were in no fit condition to do so.

Parvateshwar was filled with pride at the bravery of his soldiers. *His boys* had proved they were made of metal forged in Lord Indra's own furnace. He cursed himself for not being there to fight alongside them, to protect his goddaughter, *his* Sati, when she was in danger. He prayed for the day when he would finally get a chance to destroy the cowardly Chandravanshis himself – and he silently pledged that he would donate his salary anonymously for the next six months to the families of the slain soldiers.

'I never imagined he'd sink so low,' exclaimed Daksha in disgust, waking Shiva and Sati, who had been dozing comfortably in the carriage. Veerini looked up from the book she was reading, narrowing her eyes as she focused on her husband.

'Who, your Majesty?' asked Shiva groggily.

'Dilipa! That blight on humanity,' said Daksha, barely concealing his loathing.

Still staring hard at her husband, Veerini slowly reached out, grasped her daughter's hand in hers, brought it to her lips and kissed it gently. Then she put her other hand protectively on top of Sati's.

Sati gazed at her mother warmly, a hint of a smile on her face, and rested her tired head on her shoulder.

'Who's Dilipa, your Majesty?' asked Shiva.

'He's the Emperor of Swadweep,' replied Daksha. 'Everyone knows Sati is the apple of my eye – they were trying to kidnap her to force my hand!'

Shiva gazed sympathetically at Daksha. He understood the emperor's outrage at this latest Chandravanshi treachery.

'And using a Naga for this nefarious plan?' he continued, his voice furious. 'How low will they go?'

'I'm not so sure the Naga was being used, your Majesty,' said Shiva softly. 'He appeared to be the leader.'

But Daksha was too lost in his self-righteous anger to explore Shiva's suggestion. 'The Naga might have been the leader of this particular platoon, my Lord, but the Chandravanshis are in overall command. The cursed Nagas strike terror into the hearts of Meluhans and Swadweepans alike – but the Chandravanshis hate us so much that they don't care about the sins they're bringing on their own souls by consorting with those deformed demons. Do you see the kind of vermin we're up against, my Lord? They have no code, no honour, and they outnumber us ten to one. We need your help, my Lord: my people and my family are in mortal danger.'

'Your Majesty, I'll do everything in my power to help you,' Shiva replied, 'but I'm no general. I can't lead an army against the Chandravanshis. What difference can a simple tribal leader make?'

'At least let me announce your arrival to the court and the people, my Lord,' pleaded Daksha. 'Spend a few weeks travelling through the empire – your mere presence will raise morale. Look at the difference you made yesterday – we foiled a terrorist attack because of you, because of your presence of mind. Please, let me announce your arrival. That's all I ask.'

Shiva gazed at Daksha's earnest face with trepidation in his heart. He could feel Sati's and Veerini's eyes on him — especially Sati's.

What am I getting myself into?

'All right,' said Shiva at last, sounding resigned.

Daksha jumped up and embraced him in a fierce hug. 'Thank you, my Lord,' he exclaimed as Shiva struggled from his embrace for air. 'I'll announce your presence at court tomorrow, and in a few weeks you can leave for a tour of the empire. I'll personally make all the arrangements. You'll have a full brigade travelling with you for security — and Parvateshwar and Sati will also accompany you.'

'No,' protested Veerini in a harsh tone Sati had never heard her mother use before, 'Sati isn't going anywhere — I won't allow you to put our daughter's life in danger. She'll be staying with me in Devagiri.'

'Veerini, don't be silly,' said Daksha calmly. 'Do you really think anything bad will happen to Sati if she's with the Neelkanth?'

'She's not going, and that's final!' Veerini's steely glare matched her firm tone, and she was still clutching Sati's hand tightly.

The emperor waved his wife's concerns aside and turned back to Shiva. 'Don't worry, I'll make all the arrangements. Parvateshwar and Sati will be travelling with you. You may have to restrain Sati sometimes, though.'

Shiva frowned. So did Sati.

Daksha smiled genially. 'My darling daughter has a tendency to be a little too brave at times. Once, when she was just a child, she jumped in all by herself, with nothing but her short sword, to save an old woman being attacked by a pack of wild dogs. She nearly got herself killed for her pains. It was one of the worst days of my life. It is this impulsiveness which worries Veerini, I think.'

Shiva looked at Sati. There was no expression on her face.

'If you keep an eye on her,' continued Daksha, 'you shouldn't have a problem.'

Shiva glanced at Sati again, and a surge of admiration joined the boundless love he already felt for her. *She did what I couldn't do.*

— ☩ ⓪ U ⌖ ✦ —

The following morning, Shiva found himself seated next to Daksha in the Meluhan royal court. The magnificence of the building left him wonderstruck. This was a public building, and the usual Meluhan reticence and understated designs had been bypassed. It was built next to the Great Public Bath. The platform had been constructed of the standard kiln-bricks, but the structure itself, including the floor, was made of teak, which was easily carved and shaped, yet strong. Huge wooden pillars extravagantly sculpted with images of celestial nymphs, gods, saints and other divine beings had been set into grooves on the platform. An ornately carved wooden roof inlaid with gold and silver designs crowned the pillars, and pennants of holy blue and royal red hung from the ceiling. Every wall-niche contained a painting depicting a scene from the life of Lord Ram.

But Shiva had little time to admire the court's glorious architecture. Daksha was about to reveal that he was the long-awaited Neelkanth, and the expectations that would doubtless generate in the gathered Meluhans were causing him considerable discomfort.

'As you may have heard,' the emperor began, addressing the assembled crowd, 'there was another terrorist attack yesterday. The Chandravanshis tried to harm the royal family near Mount Mandar.'

Murmurs of dismay filled the court. The question troubling everyone was how the Chandravanshis had discovered Mount Mandar.

'The Chandravanshis' attack was devious,' the emperor went on, his booming voice drowning out the murmurs. The hall was designed to make any words spoken from the platform resonate around the entire hall. 'But we beat them back. For the first time in decades, we beat back one of their cowardly terrorist attacks.'

An exultant roar filled the court at this announcement. They had beaten back open military assaults from the Chandravanshis before, but until this day, the Meluhans had found no answer to the dreaded terrorist strikes.

Raising his hand to quiet the crowd, he continued, 'We beat them back because the time for truth to triumph is upon us at last. We beat them back because we were led by Father Manu's messenger. We beat them back because the time for justice has come!'

The murmurs grew louder. Had the Neelkanth finally arrived? Everyone had heard the rumours, but nobody believed them. There had been too many false declarations in the past.

Daksha waited for the anticipation to build, then jubilantly bellowed, 'Yes, the rumours are true: our saviour has come! *The Neelkanth has come!*'

Shiva was deeply uncomfortable to be put on display on the royal platform without his cravat. The Meluhan elite thronged around him, their excited chatter buzzing in his ears:

'—we'd heard the rumours, my Lord, but we didn't believe them—'

'—we have nothing more to fear, my Lord – the days of evil are numbered—'

'—where are you from, my Lord—?'

'—Mount Kailash? Where's that, my Lord? I'd like to take a pilgrimage there—'

Shiva found the Meluhans' endless questions and blind faith in him deeply disturbing. At the earliest opportunity, he asked the emperor for permission to leave the court.

— ⁂ ⯑ Ⓤ ⯑ ⊛ —

A few hours later, sitting in the quiet comfort of his chamber, Shiva contemplated what had happened at the court. The cravat was back around his neck.

'By the Holy Lake, can I really deliver these people from their troubles?' he murmured to himself.

'What did you say, my Lord?' asked Nandi, who was sitting patiently at a distance.

'The faith your people are putting in me makes me anxious,' said Shiva, loud enough for Nandi to hear. 'In a one-on-one battle, I could take on any enemy to protect your people – but I'm no great leader, and I'm certainly no "destroyer of evil".'

'I'm sure you can lead us to victory against any foe, my Lord. You beat the Chandravanshis back on the road to Devagiri.'

'That wasn't a genuine victory,' said Shiva dismissively. 'We routed a small platoon sent to kidnap rather than kill. If we'd faced a well-organised army hell-bent on killing, the outcome would likely have been very different. Meluha is facing a formidable and ruthless enemy and blind faith in one man isn't the answer. Maybe you're too innocent to take on such a cold-blooded foe. You need to adapt to the changing times and develop a new way of living. I'm not some god who will magically solve all your problems.'

'You're right, my Lord,' said Nandi, with all the conviction of a simple man fortunate not to be troubled by too many complicated thoughts, 'we do need a new way of living – although I've no idea what that would look like. But I do know one thing: more than a thousand years ago, we faced a similar situation, and Lord Ram came and taught us a better way. I'm sure you, in turn, will lead us to a superior path.'

'I'm no Lord Ram, Nandi!'

How can this fool even compare me to Lord Ram, the Maryada Purushottam, the Ideal Man?

'You're better than Lord Ram, my Lord,' said Nandi.

'Stop this nonsense, Nandi! What have I done that warrants comparison with the great Lord Ram's achievements, let alone be considered better than him?'

'But you *will* perform deeds that will place you above him, my Lord.'

'Just shut up!'

The preparations for Shiva's tour of the empire were in full swing, but he still made time every afternoon for Sati's dance lessons. They were developing a quiet friendship, but while Sati was respectful and courteous towards him, he still longed for a more intimate relationship. But there was no softening of emotions from Sati.

Shiva's tribe had arrived in Devagiri, where they were given comfortable accommodation and jobs suited to their talents. Bhadra was the exception; Shiva's old friend was to accompany the Neelkanth on his grand tour.

'*Veer*bhadra! When the hell did you get *that* name?' Shiva asked Bhadra, happily embracing him. The first thing Shiva noticed was that his friend's hump had completely disappeared, thanks to the magical *Somras*.

'Stupid reason, actually.' Bhadra said, stepping back from

the embrace, smiling shyly. 'On the journey here, I saved the caravan leader from a tiger attack. He gave me the title *Veer*. It means "a brave man".'

'You fought a tiger single-handed?' Shiva was clearly impressed.

Bhadra nodded, feeling awkward.

'Then you are indeed a brave man, Veerbhadra!'

'Yeah, right.' Bhadra stared at Shiva, his smile fading and his expression becoming more serious. 'You've got your own crazy label, apparently – "destroyer of evil" . . . Are you okay with all this? Tell me you're not just going along with it because of your past—'

'I'm simply going with the flow right now, my friend. These Meluhans are completely mad, no doubt, and I certainly can't do everything they expect me to. But something tells me that despite my misgivings, I can actually help these people somehow. And if I can make a difference, however small, I have a chance of reconciling with my past.'

'If you're sure, then so am I. I'll follow you anywhere.'

'Don't follow – walk beside me!'

Veerbhadra laughed and embraced his friend again. 'I missed you, Shiva.'

'Me too, Bhadra.'

'Let's meet in the garden this afternoon – I've got a great batch of marijuana.'

'It's a deal!'

Three weeks after Daksha had revealed the Neelkanth to the court and proposed his grand tour of the empire, the day finally dawned for Shiva's departure. On the morning of the day itself, the emperor visited Shiva in his chambers.

'You could have summoned me, your Majesty,' said Shiva with a namaste.

'It's my pleasure to come to you, my Lord,' replied Daksha, smiling as he returned Shiva's greeting with a low bow. 'I'd like to introduce the physician who'll be travelling with your entourage – she arrived from Kashmir last night.' Daksha moved aside as his escort showed the doctor into the room.

'Ayurvati,' exclaimed Shiva, his face lighting up with a brilliant smile. 'It's so good to see you again'

'The pleasure is all mine, my Lord,' Ayurvati replied as she bent down to touch his feet.

Shiva immediately moved back. 'I've told you before, Ayurvati, you're a giver of life. Please don't embarrass me by touching my feet.'

'And you're the Neelkanth, my Lord, the destroyer of evil – how can you deny me the privilege of your blessing?'

Shiva shook his head in despair, but he let Ayurvati touch his feet and gently laid his hand on her head and blessed her.

A few hours later, Shiva set off, accompanied by an entourage that included Sati and her maid Krittika, Parvateshwar, Brahaspati, Ayurvati, Nandi and Veerbhadra. A brigade of fifteen hundred soldiers, twenty-five handmaidens and fifty support staff would take care of their security and comfort. They planned to travel by road to the city of Kotdwaar on the Beas River, and then by boat to the port city of Karachapa, where Brahaspati hoped to meet a vessel from Mesopotamia delivering rare chemicals. From Karachapa they would travel due east to the city of Lothal, and finally north by road to the inland delta of the Saraswati before returning to Devagiri by boat.

CHAPTER 12

Journey through Meluha

'I have a question about Manu,' asked Shiva. 'Why is he often referred to as "the Father"?'

For the last few days the caravan had been travelling along the broad road from Devagiri to Kotdwaar. In the middle were seven carriages, identical to those used on the trip to Mount Mandar. Five of them were empty; Shiva, Sati, Brahaspati and Krittika were in the second carriage, and Parvateshwar rode in the fifth along with Ayurvati and his chief officers. The general insisted on strict adherence to every rule and protocol; consequently Nandi, whose rank did not allow him to travel in a carriage, was riding alongside the rest of the cavalry. Veerbhadra had been inducted as a soldier in Nandi's platoon. All the foot soldiers, led by their respective captains, marched in standard forward-, rear- and side-defence formations around the caravan.

'Lord Manu was the—' began Brahaspati and Sati, simultaneously. They both stopped talking.

'After you, please, Brahaspatiji,' said Sati.

'No, no,' he replied with a warm smile, 'why don't you tell him the story?' He knew whose voice the Neelkanth would prefer to hear.

'I can't do that, Brahaspatiji. It would be completely improper for me to—'

Shiva, exasperated, interrupted, 'Will one of you answer me, for the Holy Lake's sake – or are you planning to keep up this elaborate protocol nonsense for ever?'

'All right, all right,' said Brahaspati, smiling. 'Don't go turning blue all over now.'

'That's hilarious, Brahaspati,' said Shiva, laughing softly. 'Keep it up and you might actually get someone to laugh in a hundred years.'

Sati was astounded by the utterly inappropriate tone of Shiva and Brahaspati's banter, but if the revered chief scientist was comfortable with it, she would keep her opinions to herself. Regardless, how could she reprimand Shiva? Honour forbade it. He had saved her life – twice.

Seeing that Sati was intent on following protocol, Brahaspati said, 'Lord Manu is called "the Father" because the people of India consider him the progenitor of our civilisation.'

'Including the Swadweepans?' asked Shiva incredulously.

'We believe so. Lord Manu lived more than eight and a half thousand years ago. He was a prince from south India, from a land known as the Sangamtamil, way beyond the Narmada River where the land ends and the great ocean begins.

Sangamtamil was at that time the richest and most powerful country in the world, and Lord Manu's family, the Pandyas, had ruled there for many generations. But from the records left by Lord Manu, we know that by his time the kings had abandoned their ancient code of honour and had fallen into corrupt ways, spending their days lost in the pleasures of their fabulous wealth rather than attending to their duties and spiritual lives. Then a terrible calamity occurred: the seas rose and destroyed their entire civilisation.'

'My God!' Shiva exclaimed.

'Lord Manu knew this day would come, and he had prepared for it. He believed that his people's decadence had incurred the wrath of the gods. To escape the calamity, he led a band of his followers to higher lands in the north, aboard a fleet of ships. He established his first camp at a place called Mehragarh, deep in the western mountains of present-day Meluha. He was determined to establish a moral and just society, so he gave up his princely robes and became a priest. The term for priests in India – pandit – is a derivation of Lord Manu's family name, Pandya.'

'Interesting. So how did Lord Manu's little band grow into the formidable India we see today?'

'The years immediately following their arrival at Mehragarh were harsh. Every year's monsoon brought stronger flooding and higher sea tides. But after many years, Lord Manu's fervent prayers abated the gods' anger and the waters stopped advancing – though the sea never receded to its original levels.'

'So somewhere in the deep south, the sea still covers the ancient Sangamtamil cities?'

'We believe so,' replied Brahaspati. 'Once the sea stopped rising, Lord Manu and his men came down from the mountains. They were shocked to see that the minor stream of the Indus had become a massive river. Many other rivulets across northern India had also swollen and six great rivers had emerged: Indus, Saraswati, Yamuna, Ganga, Sarayu and Brahmaputra. Villages established on the banks of these rivers gradually became cities: thus, our land of the seven rivers, Sapt Sindhu, was born out of the destruction of the Sangamtamil.'

'You mentioned the creation of only six rivers in North India.'

'Indeed, for the seventh river already existed – the Narmada, which became our southern border. Lord Manu strictly forbade his descendants to go south of the Narmada, and if they did so, they could never return. We believe even the Chandravanshis adhere to this law.'

'Did Lord Manu lay down other laws?'

'Many, all of them listed in an extensive treatise called the *Manusmriti*. Would you be interested in listening to the entire text?'

'Tempting,' said Shiva, 'but I think I'll pass for now.'

'With your permission, my Lords,' suggested Krittika, 'perhaps we can continue this discussion of Lord Manu's laws over lunch?'

— ⚬ ⊛ —

A short distance from the road along which the Neelkanth's caravan was travelling, a small band of about forty men trudged silently along the Beas. Every other man carried a small bamboo coracle on his head, each of which could transport two people with relative safety and speed. Leading the platoon was a young man with a battle-scarred face, his head crowned with a brown turban. A little ahead of him walked a hooded figure, head bowed, eyes scrunched, taking slow, methodical steps, his mind lost in unfathomable thoughts. As he languidly raised a hand to rub his masked forehead, his cuff slipped back to reveal a leather bracelet embroidered with the serpent Aum symbol.

'We'll enter the river here, Vishwadyumna,' said the hooded figure. 'Whenever we approach populated areas, we'll move away from the river to avoid detection. We have to reach Karachapa within two months.'

'Karachapa, my Lord?' asked Vishwadyumna, surprised. 'But I thought we were to meet the queen outside Lothal.'

'We'll meet her outside Karachapa,' said the hooded figure, his tone brooking no further debate.

'Yes, my Lord,' replied Vishwadyumna, looking wistfully back in the direction of the Kotdwaar Road. He knew his Lord would have preferred to make one more attempt to kidnap the princess, but it would be a foolhardy endeavour considering the strength of the force now accompanying the caravan. Regardless, they were behind schedule for their main mission. Their most urgent priority now was to meet with the queen.

Turning towards one of his soldiers, Vishwadyumna ordered, 'Sriktaa, place your coracle in the river and give me your oar – I'll row the Lord for this part of the journey.'

Sriktaa obeyed immediately, and Vishwadyumna and the hooded figure were the first of the platoon to enter the river. A short distance ahead, the hooded figure observed two women lounging carelessly on a boat. One of them was sloppily splashing water at her friend, who was making a hopeless attempt to avoid getting wet, and their childish game was rocking their boat dangerously from side to side. They hadn't noticed a crocodile that had slipped into the river from the opposite bank and which was now swimming swiftly towards the women's boat in pursuit of an appetising meal.

'Look behind you!' shouted the hooded figure to the women, simultaneously gesturing at Vishwadyumna to row rapidly in their direction.

The women were too far away to hear his warning, but the sight of two men rowing towards them at speed certainly got their attention – particularly the one making frantic gestures: a giant covered from head to toe in a strange robe, his face hidden beneath a mask. Behind the duo, a large number of soldiers were swiftly pushing their own coracles onto the river. Thinking the men were approaching them with evil intent, the women put all their efforts behind the oar and started hastily rowing away from the hooded figure's boat – straight into the path of the crocodile.

'No,' shouted the hooded figure, grabbing the oar from

Vishwadyumna. His powerful strokes rapidly shortened the distance between the two boats – but not fast enough. Closing in on the women's craft, the crocodile dived under water and charged. Its massive body tilted and capsized the tiny vessel, throwing the women into the Beas.

The women's screams of terror rent the air as they fought to stay afloat. The crocodile's charge had taken the beast beyond them, but it quickly turned and swam back towards them. In those crucial seconds, the rescue boat arrived between the crocodile and its intended victims. Turning towards Vishwadyumna, the hooded figure shouted, 'Save the women!'

But before Vishwadyumna could react, the giant had already flung his robe aside and dived into the river. Holding his knife tightly between his teeth, he swam towards the advancing crocodile.

One of the women had lost consciousness. Vishwadyumna quickly pulled her into the boat and told the other, 'I'll be back soon.' Then he turned the coracle and paddled vigorously towards the bank. On his way there he crossed paths with some of his men and shouted, 'Row quickly – the Lord's life is in danger!'

The other soldiers hastened towards the area where the strange man had dived into the river. The water had turned red with blood from the battle raging under water. The soldiers said a silent prayer to Lord Varun, the god of the water and the seas, fervently hoping that the blood did not belong to their Lord.

One of the soldiers had drawn his sword and was about to jump into the water himself when the masked figure surfaced, soaked in blood – the crocodile's. He swam quickly towards the other remaining woman, who looked to be on the verge of losing consciousness. Reaching her in the nick of time, he lifted her head from the water.

Two of the Chandravanshi soldiers dived off their coracle. 'My Lord, please get into the boat,' said one. 'We'll swim ashore.'

'Help the woman first,' replied the masked figure, and helped the soldiers to manoeuvre the semi-conscious woman into the coracle before carefully climbing aboard himself and rowing towards the shore. By the time they reached the riverbank, Vishwadyumna had revived the other woman, who was clearly in shock, disorientated by the rapid chain of events.

'Are you all right?' Vishwadyumna asked, but she screamed as she looked beyond him and he turned around to see the masked figure carrying the other woman's limp body ashore. His wet, bloody clothes were glued to his massive body, and it was clear the woman thought the blood was her friend's.

'What have you done, you beast?' she shrieked, and the Naga looked up abruptly, his eyes showing mild surprise, but he remained silent.

As he gently laid the woman on the ground, the mask covering his face came undone and the woman next to Vishwadyumna stared at him in horror.

'Naga,' she screeched, and before Vishwadyumna could react, she had leapt to her feet and run off screaming, 'Help! Help! A Naga is eating my friend!'

The Naga watched the fleeing woman with melancholy eyes. Sighing, he blinked and shook his head slightly.

Vishwadyumna had just seen his Lord's face, for the first time in years. He immediately lowered his gaze, but not before he had glimpsed the rare flash of intense pain and sorrow in his Lord's normally expressionless eyes. Seething with anger, Vishwadyumna drew his sword to slay the ungrateful woman they had just saved.

'No,' the Naga said firmly. Pulling his mask back on, he turned to the other soldiers. 'Revive her.'

'My Lord, her friend will bring others here,' argued Vishwadyumna. 'Let's leave this woman to her fate and go.'

'No.'

'But my Lord — we must escape before someone comes.'

'Not until we're sure she's safe,' said the Naga, his voice as calm as ever.

— ⚶ ◍ Ⴎ ⚶ ◉ —

The royal party had broken their journey at a rest-house and were enjoying their lunch in the courtyard. Half of the soldiers were also eating their meal, while the rest stood guard. Parvateshwar had made sure everyone in the royal encampment was comfortable, but he refused to join them, preferring to eat later with his soldiers.

Shiva's peaceful repast was disturbed by a loud commotion from the location of one of the perimeter guards. He rose to investigate, motioning for Brahaspati, Nandi and Veerbhadra to remain seated. Parvateshwar had also heard the racket and was already moving towards the uproar.

'Please save her,' cried the woman. 'A Naga is eating her alive!'

'My apologies,' answered the captain, 'but we have strict orders not to leave the vicinity of this rest-house under any circumstances.'

'What's going on here?' demanded Parvateshwar.

Turning in surprise, the captain saluted and bowed low. 'My Lord, this woman alleges that a Naga has attacked her friend. She's asking for our help.'

Parvateshwar stared hard at the woman. He would have liked nothing better than to chase a Naga party and destroy them, but his orders were crystal-clear: he was not to leave the Neelkanth and Sati. Their protection was his only objective. But he was still a Kshatriya – and what kind of Kshatriya would he be if he didn't fight to protect the weak? Seething at the restrictions forced upon him, Parvateshwar was about to say something when Shiva appeared.

'What's the matter?' asked Shiva.

The captain couldn't believe he was actually getting to talk with the Neelkanth. 'My Lord, this woman claims that her friend has been attacked by Nagas, but we're concerned it might be a trap – we've heard about the Chandravanshi duplicity on the way from Mount Mandar'

Shiva's inner voice cried from an ancient memory, 'Go back – help her!' And drawing his sword in one smooth motion, he said, 'Take me to your friend.'

Parvateshwar looked at Shiva, grudging respect in his eyes, and he unsheathed his own weapon and turned to the captain. 'Follow us with your platoon.' To Brigadier Vraka, he said, 'Put the entire brigade on alert for any surprise attack. The princess must be kept safe at all costs!'

Shiva and Parvateshwar ran behind the woman, the captain trailing after with his platoon of thirty soldiers. A half-hour sprint finally brought them to the riverside, where they found a dazed woman sitting on the ground, breathing heavily and staring in shock at some imaginary vision in the distance. Her clothes were soaked with blood, but strangely they could find no injury. A great many footprints trailed in and out of the river.

The captain looked suspiciously at the woman who had led them there. Turning to his soldiers, he ordered, 'Form a perimeter around the general and the Neelkanth. It could be a trap.'

'She was being eaten alive, I tell you!' screeched the woman, absolutely stunned to see her friend conscious and unharmed.

'No, she wasn't,' said Shiva calmly. He pointed at the corpse of a crocodile floating in the river. A large flock of crows had settled on the carcase and were fighting viciously over its entrails. 'Somebody just saved her from that crocodile.'

'Whoever it was has rowed across the river, my Lord,' said the captain, pointing towards the collection of footprints close to the riverbank.

'Why would a Naga risk his own life to save this woman?' asked Shiva.

Parvateshwar was equally surprised. This was completely unlike the usual bloodthirsty Nagas they had dealt with until now.

'My Lords,' said the captain, 'the women appear to be safe. I don't think it's wise to linger here. With your permission, I'll escort them back to their village and rejoin the caravan at Kotdwaar while you return to the rest-house.'

'Take four soldiers with you, just in case,' said Parvateshwar.

With that, Shiva and Parvateshwar walked back to the rest-house, baffled by the bizarre event.

— ◈ ⚷ ◍ ∪ ⚶ ✦ —

Later that evening, Shiva, Brahaspati, Nandi and Veerbhadra were relaxing quietly around the campfire while Parvateshwar was moving amongst his soldiers, personally supervising the camp's security arrangements and the comfort of his boys. Shiva was watching Sati, who was sitting at a distance on the rest-house verandah, deep in serious conversation with Ayurvati and Krittika.

'It's ready, Shiva,' said Veerbhadra, handing the chillum to the Neelkanth.

Shiva brought the pipe up to his lips and pulled hard, visibly relaxing with his first long inhalation. Feeling like he needed more relief than usual after the day's exertions he took a couple more puffs before passing it back to his friend. Veerbhadra offered the pipe to Brahaspati and Nandi, who both declined. Brahaspati was watching Shiva stealing glances at Sati. He smiled and shook his head.

'What?' asked Shiva, noticing Brahaspati's gesture.

'I understand your longing, my friend,' whispered Brahaspati, 'but what you're hoping for is difficult – impossible, perhaps.'

'Things of true value are always difficult to win.'

Brahaspati smiled and patted Shiva's hand.

Veerbhadra knew what his friend needed: dancing and music – they always improved his mood. 'Don't people sing and dance in this wretched country?' he asked.

'Private Veerbhadra,' said Nandi, his tone firm as he addressed his subordinate, 'firstly, this country is not wretched – it's the greatest land in the world.'

Veerbhadra playfully put his hands together in mock apology.

'Secondly,' continued Nandi, 'we dance only when occasion demands it, like the *Holi* festival or a public performance.'

'But, Captain – the greatest joy of dancing is when you do it for no reason at all,' said Veerbhadra.

'I agree,' said Shiva, and Nandi immediately fell silent.

Without any warning, Veerbhadra suddenly burst into one of the folk songs of his region, making Shiva smile, for it was one of his favourites. As he sang, Veerbhadra rose slowly and began dancing to the lilting tune, and Shiva accompanied him, the combination of marijuana and music immediately changing his mood.

Brahaspati stared at Shiva, first in shock and then with pleasure. After a while he noticed a pattern to the dance, a smooth six-step combination, repeated again and again.

Shiva reached out and pulled Brahaspati and Nandi to their feet and they joined in, tentatively at first, but soon dancing with abandon, even the initially reluctant Brahaspati. The group began to circle around the fire, their singing growing ever louder and livelier, until Shiva suddenly darted out of the ring towards Sati.

'Dance with me.'

A flabbergasted Sati shook her head.

'Oh come on! If you can dance while your Guruji and I watch, why not here?'

'That was for *knowledge*,' she said.

'So is it wrong to dance for something other than knowledge?'

'I didn't say that.'

'Fine, have it your way,' said Shiva with a frustrated gesture. 'Ayurvati, come!'

And before the startled doctor could react, Shiva had grabbed her hand and pulled her into the circle. Veerbhadra lured Krittika in as well, and together they danced boisterously and sang loudly, making a racket in an otherwise quiet night.

Sati got up, clearly agitated, glared at Shiva's back and ran into the rest-house, and Shiva's anger rose even higher as he noticed her absence when he turned towards the verandah.

Damn!

He returned his attention to the dance, his heart filled with a strange mixture of pain and joy. He glanced at the verandah again. Still nobody there.

But who's behind that curtain . . . ?

Veerbhadra dragged Shiva into the next move and a few moments passed before Shiva could look at the verandah again. He saw Sati, outlined behind the curtain, staring at him. Only at him.

Surprised and delighted, Shiva swung fluidly back into the dance, determined to impress her.

CHAPTER 13

Blessings of the Impure

Kotdwaar was decked in all its glory to receive the Neelkanth. Torches had been lit around the fort's perimeter and the walls hung with red and blue pennants embellished with the Suryavanshi sun as if it was Diwali. In a rare breach of protocol, the governor had come outside the city to personally receive the Neelkanth. After the formal exhibition of the Neelkanth for the Kotdwaar elite at the local court, a public function had been arranged for the following day. Sixty-five thousand people – practically the entire population of Kotdwaar – had converged for the event, which had been organised outside the city platform to ensure that every person could be accommodated.

The remarkable effect Shiva had on the people was a revelation to him. Though he was careful with his words, telling them only that he would do all he could to support the people of Meluha, the public made their own interpretations, allowing

Shiva's speech to convince them that Meluha's troubles would soon be at an end.

'The cursed Chandravanshis will finally be destroyed,' said one man triumphantly.

'We don't have to worry about anything ever again,' said a woman. 'The Neelkanth will take care of everything!'

Parvateshwar, seated with Brahaspati and Sati on the speakers' platform, was deeply unhappy with the public's reaction. Turning to the chief scientist, he said, 'Our society is based on tried and tested laws that expect us to solve our own problems, not hope for miracles from some stranger. What has this man done to deserve such blind faith?'

'Parvateshwar,' said Brahaspati politely, for he greatly respected the general, 'I think Shiva is a good man, and I think he cares enough to want to help us. Aren't good intentions the first step towards any good deed?'

Parvateshwar wasn't so sure. He had never been a believer in the prophecy of the Neelkanth, and he thought that every man and woman must earn their station in life through training and application, not just be handed it on a silver platter because of a blue throat. 'That may be true to a point, but intentions aren't enough – they have to be backed by ability. Here we are, putting an untrained, untested stranger on a pedestal and acting as though he's our saviour. For all we know, he might lead us to complete disaster. We're acting on faith alone, not logic or laws or even experience.'

'Sometimes one needs a little faith when faced with a diffi-cult situation. Rational answers don't always work. Sometimes we need a miracle.'

'*You're* talking about miracles? A scientist?'

'You can have scientific miracles, too, Parvateshwar,' Brahaspati said with a smile.

Parvateshwar was distracted by the sight of Shiva stepping off the platform into a surging crowd of people wanting to touch him. The soldiers, led by Nandi and Veerbhadra, were holding them back. There was a blind man amongst them who looked like he might get injured in the mêlée.

'Nandi, let that man through,' said Shiva, and Nandi and Veerbhadra immediately lowered the rope to let him pass.

Another man shouted, 'I'm his son – he needs me to guide him.'

'Let him in as well,' said Shiva, and the son rushed in and grasped his father's hand. The blind man, who had looked lost without his son's guidance, smiled warmly as he recognised the familiar touch.

Leading him close to Shiva, the son said, 'Father, the Neelkanth is right in front of you. Can you sense his presence?'

Tears flowed from the blind man's eyes, and without thinking, he bent down to try to touch Shiva's feet. His son cried out in shock and pulled the man back, scolding him sharply.

Shiva was stunned by the harshness in the son's tone

compared to the loving way he had been speaking earlier. 'What just happened?' he asked.

'I'm sorry, my Lord,' apologised the son, 'my father didn't mean to – he just forgot himself in your presence.'

'Forgive me, my Lord,' begged the blind man, his tears flowing faster.

'For what?' Shiva was baffled.

'He's a *vikarma*, my Lord,' said the son, 'ever since disease blinded him twenty years ago. Obviously he shouldn't have tried to touch you.'

Sati, who was standing near Shiva, had heard the entire conversation, and she felt deep sympathy for the blind man – she understood his torment only too well – but what he'd tried to do was illegal.

'I'm sorry, my Lord,' continued the blind man, 'but please, don't let your anger with me stop you from protecting our country. It's the greatest land Parmatma created – save it from the evil Chandravanshis. Save *us*, my Lord.' And the blind man folded his hands in a penitent namaste, still crying.

Shiva was moved by his dignity, but he couldn't help but wonder, *Why does he still love a country that treats him so unfairly? Even worse, he doesn't even appear to think he's being treated unfairly.*

Shiva realised he was looking at a man to whom fate had been very unkind. *I will stop this nonsense*, he promised himself.

He stepped forward and bent down, and the flabbergasted son trembled in disbelief as he saw the Neelkanth touch his *vikarma* father's feet. The blind man was confused for a moment, but when he understood what the Neelkanth had done, his hand shot up to cover his mouth in shock.

Shiva rose and stood in front of the blind man. 'Bless me, sir, so that I may find the strength to fight for a man as patriotic as you.'

The blind man stood dumbstruck, his tears drying on his bewildered face. He was about to collapse when Shiva took a quick step forward to catch him, lest he fall to the ground. The blind man found the strength to say, '*Vijayibhav.*' *May you be victorious.*

Shiva released the man into his son's arms.

The entire crowd was stunned into silence by what the Neelkanth had done. Forget the gravity of touching a *vikarma* – the Neelkanth had just asked one for his blessing!

Shiva turned to see Parvateshwar's enraged face. Shiva had broken the law – broken it brazenly, and in public. Next to him, Sati's face, her eyes, her entire demeanour, was expressionless.

What the hell is she thinking now?

Brahaspati and Sati entered Shiva's chambers as soon as he was alone. Shiva smiled at seeing his two favourite people in the world, but his face fell when Sati said, 'You must get a *shudhikaran* done.'

He looked at her and answered simply, 'No.'

'No? What do you mean, no?'

'I mean no. *Nahin. Nako,*' said Shiva, adding the words for 'no' in the Kashmiri and Kotdwaar dialects for good measure.

'Shiva,' said Brahaspati, struggling to keep his composure, 'this is no laughing matter. I agree with Sati. The governor is also worried about your safety – he has summoned a pandit. He's waiting outside as we speak. Get the ceremony done now. '

'Did you not hear me say no?'

'Shiva,' said Sati, her tone a little softer, 'I respect you immensely – your valour, your intelligence, your talent – but you're not above the law. You've touched a *vikarma*, so you have to get a *shudhikaran* – that's the law.'

'If the law says that touching that poor blind man is illegal, then the law is wrong!'

Shiva's vehemence stunned Sati into silence.

'Shiva, listen to me,' said Brahaspati, 'not doing a *shudhikaran* might be harmful to you. You're important to India's future – you're destined for great things – don't put yourself at risk out of obstinacy.'

'It's not obstinacy. Tell me, honestly, how I can be harmed simply by touching a wronged man – who, I might add, still loves his country despite the way he has been ostracised and ill-treated?'

'He may be a good man, Shiva,' said Brahaspati, 'but the sins of his previous birth will contaminate your fate.'

'Let them! If that lessens the weight on that man's shoulders, I will feel blessed indeed.'

'I don't understand, Shiva,' said Sati. 'Why should you bear the punishment for someone else's sins?'

'Firstly, I don't believe in this nonsense about his blindness being a punishment for the sins of his previous birth. He was infected by a disease, plain and simple – it could have happened to anyone. Secondly, if I choose to carry the weight of some-one else's so-called sins, why should that matter to anyone but me?'

'It matters because we care about you,' cried Brahaspati.

'Come on, Sati,' said Shiva, 'don't tell me you believe in this rubbish.'

'It's not rubbish.'

'But don't you want me to fight for you? To stop this unfair-ness your society has subjected you to?'

'Is that what this is about? *Me?*' asked Sati, outraged.

'No,' retorted Shiva, then changed his mind. 'Actually, yes – this is also about you. It's about all the *vikarma* and the unfairness they have to endure. I want to save them from leading outcast lives.'

'I don't need your protection,' shouted Sati, 'I cannot be saved!' And with that, she stormed out of the room.

Shiva glared at her retreating form in irritation. 'What the hell is wrong with that woman?'

'She's right, Shiva,' advised Brahaspati. 'Don't go there.'

'You agree with her about this *vikarma* business? Answer with your heart, Brahaspati: don't you think it's unfair?'

'I wasn't talking about that. I was talking about Sati.'

Shiva continued to glare defiantly at Brahaspati. Everything in his mind, body and soul told him that he should pursue Sati. That his life would be meaningless and his soul's existence incomplete without her.

'Don't go there, my friend,' Brahaspati repeated.

The caravan left the river city of Kotdwaar on a royal barge: identical boats preceding and following, in keeping with the Meluhan military protocols, to confuse any would-be attacker. Each of the three large boats was manned by a full brigade of soldiers, and five small, quick cutters kept pace on each side of the royal convoy.

'When the monsoon is not active, my Lord,' Ayurvati explained, 'the rivers are the best way to travel. Though good roads connect all the major cities, they can't match the rivers for speed and safety.'

Shiva smiled politely at Ayurvati, but he was not in the mood for much conversation. Sati had not spoken to him since he'd refused to undergo a *shudhikaran*.

The royal barge stopped at many cities along the river and at every one the Neelkanth's arrival was met with excessive celebration. Such exuberant reaction was unnatural in Meluha – but then, it wasn't every day that a Neelkanth graced the land.

Shiva kept the troubles of his heart to himself for many days, but finally he asked Brahaspati, 'Why?'

'Why what?'

'You know what I'm talking about, Brahaspati,' said Shiva, narrowing his eyes in irritation.

Brahaspati smiled sadly and replied, 'She genuinely believes she deserves to be a *vikarma*.'

'Why?'

'Perhaps because of the manner in which she became one.'

'So how did it happen?'

'It was during her earlier marriage—'

'What! Sati was married?'

'Indeed, around ninety years ago – a political marriage with one of the other noble families of the empire. Her husband's name was Chandandhwaj. She became pregnant and went to Maika during the monsoon season to deliver the child. Unfortunately, the child was stillborn.'

'Oh my God,' said Shiva, imagining the pain Sati must have felt.

'That wasn't the only bad news. Her husband had gone to the Narmada to pray for the safe birth of their child, and on the same day as the babe was stillborn, he drowned. On that cursed day, her life was destroyed.'

Shiva stared at Brahaspati, too stunned to react.

'She became a widow and was declared a *vikarma* that same day.'

'But how can her husband's death be considered her fault?' Shiva asked. He was outraged. 'That's completely ridiculous.'

'She wasn't declared a *vikarma* because of her husband's death, but because she gave birth to a stillborn child.'

'But that could have happened for any number of reasons – maybe the local doctors made a mistake—'

'That doesn't happen in Meluha, Shiva,' said Brahaspati calmly. 'Only giving birth to a Naga child would be considered worse than a stillborn babe. Thank God that didn't happen, for then she would have been completely ostracised from society and banished to the land of the Nagas.'

'This concept of *vikarma* is utterly unfair – it has to be changed,' Shiva announced firmly.

Brahaspati stared intently into his friend's eyes. 'You might save the *vikarma*, Shiva, but how do you save a woman who doesn't want to be saved? She genuinely believes she deserves this punishment.'

'But why? She can't be the first – or the last – Meluhan woman to have given birth to a stillborn child.'

'She was the first *royal* woman to have a stillbirth, and her fate has been a source of embarrassment to the emperor ever since – it raises serious questions about his ancestry.'

'How would it raise questions about his lineage? Sati is not his birth-daughter – she would also have come from Maika, right?'

'No, my friend: that law was relaxed for noble families around two hundred and fifty years ago. Meluhan laws *can* be amended, provided ninety per cent of the Brahmins, Kshatriyas and Vaishyas above a particular chosen-tribe level and job status vote for the change. There have been rare instances of such unanimity, and this was one of them – in the "national interest", noble families were granted permission to keep their birth-children. Only one man opposed this change.'

'Who?'

'Lord Satyadhwaj, Parvateshwar's grandfather. Their family vowed not to have any birth-children after this law was passed, and Parvateshwar honours that promise to this day.'

'But if the birth-law could be changed,' said Shiva, his mind racing through the possibilities, 'why not the law of *vikarma*?'

'Because not enough noble families are affected by that law to make it an issue for them. That's the harsh truth.'

'But all this goes completely against Lord Ram's teachings!'

'Actually, Lord Ram's teachings support the concept of the *vikarma* – are you questioning his wisdom?'

Shiva glanced silently at Brahaspati before looking out over the river.

'There's nothing wrong with questioning Lord Ram's laws, my friend,' Brahaspati said. 'There were many times when he himself changed his mind because of someone else's views. The question is: what are your motives for wanting to change the law? Is it because you genuinely think the law itself is unfair – or is it because you're attracted to Sati and you want to remove an inconvenient law which stands in your path?'

'I genuinely think the *vikarma* law is unfair,' Shiva said firmly. 'I felt that from the moment I found out about it – which was before I knew Sati was a *vikarma* herself.'

'Sati doesn't think the law's unfair.'

'But she's a good woman – she doesn't deserve to be treated this way.'

'She's not just a good woman: she's one of the finest I have ever met. She's beautiful, honest, straightforward, brave and intelligent – everything a man could want in a woman. But you're not just any man; you're the Neelkanth.'

Shiva turned around and rested his hands on the boat's railing, not even seeing the dense forest that lined the riverbanks as their vessel glided through the water. The soothing evening breeze fanned his long hair.

'I've told you before, my friend,' said Brahaspati, 'that unfortunate blue throat affects every decision you make. You have to think many times before you act.'

— ⚡ 𝍐 𝌄 ♰ ⊛ —

It was late in the night when the royal convoy set sail along the Indus from the city of Sutgengarh. The city's inhabitants had greeted the Neelkanth with the now predictable exuberance that erupted everywhere he went. Their civilisation's saviour had finally arrived.

That saviour, however, was in his own private hell. Sati had maintained her distance for weeks now, and he was riven by pain and dismay.

Their next stop along the mighty Indus was the famous city of Mohan Jo Daro, or the Platform of Mohan: a city dedicated to a great philosopher-priest called Lord Mohan who had lived in that region many thousands of years ago. Once Shiva had met with the local people, he expressed a desire to visit the temple of Lord Mohan which stood outside the main city platform, further along the Indus. The governor offered to take the Lord Neelkanth there in a grand procession, but Shiva insisted on making his own way there. For some reason he felt drawn to the temple, sensing that it might offer some solutions for his troubled heart.

The temple itself was simple, much like Lord Mohan himself was reputed to have been: a small, nondescript structure that announced itself as the birthplace of the sage. The only sign of the temple's significance was the massive gates at the compound's four cardinal points. Shiva entered the temple alone, leaving Nandi, Veerbhadra and a platoon of soldiers outside.

Shiva had put his comforting cravat back around his neck, and now he walked up the steps feeling the first tranquillity he had experienced for longer than he could remember. He rang the bell at the entrance, and then sat down, his back against a pillar, to wait. He shut his eyes in quiet contemplation.

Suddenly, an oddly familiar voice asked, 'How are you, my friend?'

CHAPTER 14

The Pandit of Mohan Jo Daro

Shiva opened his eyes to behold a man who was the double of the pandit he had met at the Brahma temple in what felt like another life. He sported the same long, flowing white beard and a big white mane of hair, and wore a saffron *dhoti* and *angvastram*. His wizened face bore a calm and welcoming smile. If it wasn't for this pandit's much taller frame, Shiva could have easily mistaken him for the other one.

'How are you, my friend?' repeated the pandit, sitting down next to him.

'I am all right, Panditji,' he said, using the Indian term *ji* as a form of respect. The intrusion was welcome to him, though he didn't quite know why – it felt almost as though he had been drawn to this temple because he was destined to meet the pandit. 'Do all pandits in Meluha look alike?'

The man smiled warmly. 'Not all the pandits. Just us.'

'And who might "*us*" be, Panditji?'

'The next time you meet one of us, we will tell you,' said the pandit cryptically. 'That's a promise.'

'Why not now?'

'At this point in time, our identity isn't important. What is important is that you are disturbed about something. Do you want to talk about it?'

Shiva took a deep breath. Gut instinct told him he could trust this man. 'There's a task I supposedly have to perform for Meluha,' he started.

'That much I know — although I wouldn't limit the Neelkanth's role to the discharge of a mere "task". He does much more than that.' Pointing at Shiva's throat, the pandit continued, 'Pieces of cotton can't cover divine brilliance.'

Shiva looked up with a wry smile. 'From what I've seen, Meluha does appear to be a wonderful society, and I want to do all I can to protect it from evil.'

'Then what's the problem?'

'The problem is that I've discovered some grossly unfair practices in this nearly perfect society — practices inconsistent with the ideals to which Meluha aspires.'

'And what would these practices be?' asked the pandit.

'The way the *vikarma* are treated, for a start.'

'And why is that unfair?'

'How can anyone be sure that these people committed sins in their previous births, and that their present sufferings are a result of that? It might be sheer bad luck — or a random act of nature.'

'You're right, it could be – but do you think that the fate of the *vikarma* is about them personally?'

'Isn't it?'

'No, it isn't,' explained the pandit. 'It's about the society as a whole. The *vikarma* acceptance of their fate is integral to Meluha's stability.'

Shiva frowned. That didn't make much sense to him.

'Every successful society, O Neelkanth, needs both flexibility and stability. Flexibility is vital because every single person has different dreams and capabilities. The birth-son of a warrior could have the talent to be a great businessman, in which case society needs to be flexible enough to allow this son to pursue a different vocation from his father's. Flexibility in a society allows change, giving all its members the opportunity to discover their true selves and grow to their full potential. And if every person in a society achieves his true potential, society as a whole also achieves its true potential.'

'I agree,' replied Shiva. *But what does this have to do with the* vikarma?

'Bear with me,' the pandit said, responding to Shiva's unspoken question. 'I'll come to the obvious question in a bit. If we believe that flexibility is key to a successful society, the Maika system is designed to achieve it in practice. No child knows its birth-parents' professions, and as a result they are free to pursue whatever their natural talent inspires them to do.'

'That makes total sense to me. The Maika system is almost breathtakingly fair – the only person an individual can credit or blame for what he does with his life is himself. So much for flexibility. What about stability?'

'Stability allows a person the freedom of choice, my friend. People can pursue their dreams only when they are living in a society where survival is not threatened on a daily basis. In a society without security and stability, there are no intellectuals or businessmen or artists. When man is constantly in fight-or-flight mode he is no better than an animal, with no chance for ideas to be nurtured or dreams to be pursued. That is the way all humans were before we formed societies, but civilisation is very fragile and our base natures can seize control very fast. It would take only a few decades of chaos to make us forget our humanity and turn back into animals. Our base natures can take over very quickly, make us forget that we are sentient beings, with laws and codes and ethics.'

'I understand. The tribes in my homeland are no better than animals right now – they don't even *want* to live a better life!'

'They don't know a better life is possible, Neelkanth,' the pandit said gently. 'Such is the curse of constant strife – it makes us forget the most beautiful part of being human. That's why a society must remain stable – so that we don't put each other in a situation where we *have* to fight for survival.'

'I'll agree with you there – but why would letting people achieve their potential cause instability? Wouldn't that make people happier with their lives, and consequently have an ever-increasing stabilising effect on society?'

'It would – but only to a point. People are happy when they change their lives for the better – but there are two situations in which change can lead to chaos. The first is when people face a change imposed on them by others, or find themselves in situations they can't understand. This scares them almost as much as death. When change happens too fast, they resist it.'

'Yes, change forced by others is difficult to accept,' Shiva agreed.

'And too rapid a change causes instability. The bedrock of Lord Ram's way of life is designed to prevent this situation from occurring. There are laws which help a society change slowly, allowing it to remain stable – and at the same time, grant its citizens the freedom to follow their dreams. He created an ideal balance of stability and flexibility.'

'You mentioned a second situation—?'

'The second occurs when people *can't* make the transition they want to improve their lives, for reasons beyond their control. Let's say there's an exceptional warrior who loses his hand–eye coordination due to a disease. He's still a fighter, but he's no longer an extraordinary one. The odds are that he'll be frustrated by what he might perceive as an injustice meted out to him. He's likely to blame his doctor, or even society at large. Such discontented people can become a threat to society as a whole.'

Shiva frowned. He didn't like the logic, but he knew that one of the main reasons the Pakratis had rejected his uncle's peace offer all those years ago was because their diseased old chief was desperate to live up to his youthful reputation as an exceptional warrior who could defeat the Gunas.

'Their combined rage can lead to unrest, even violence,' the pandit continued. 'Lord Ram sensed that, and that's why the concept of *vikarma* came into being: if you make a person believe that his misfortune in this birth is due to his sins in his previous birth, he'll resign himself to his fate and not vent his fury on society at large.'

'But how does ostracising the *vikarma* not lead to more suppressed anger?'

'They're not ostracised, my friend: their living costs are subsidised by the government. They can still interact with family members. Whenever possible, they're allowed to achieve personal excellence in their chosen fields. They're also permitted to fight to protect themselves. What they *can't* do is to be in a position to influence others.'

He paused, and then looked at Shiva. 'This system has worked for a thousand years. Do you know how common rebellion was in India before Lord Ram created this empire? And most of the time, these rebellions weren't led by far-sighted men who thought they could create a better way of life for the common man; they were led by men discontented with their lot in life – people very much like the *vikarma*. And these rebellions usually caused chaos that lasted decades before order could be restored.'

'So you're saying that anyone who's frustrated with his lot

in life should simply resign himself to being a *vikarma* for the larger good of society?'

'Yes.'

Shiva was aghast – he couldn't believe what he was hearing, and he deeply disliked the arguments being presented to him. 'I'm sorry, but this system sounds completely unfair to me. I've heard that almost one-twentieth of the people in Meluha are *vikarma*. Surely you can't treat so many people as outcasts for ever? This system needs to change.'

'And you can change it – you're the Neelkanth. But remember, no system is perfect. In Lord Ram's time, there was a lady called Manthara who suffered terribly, because of her physical deformities. And then fate put her in a position of influence over a powerful queen, and thus over the entire kingdom. The karma of one maladjusted victim of fate triggered a series of events that led to mass destruction, and the loss of millions of lives. Wouldn't it have been better for everybody if this person had been declared a *vikarma* and banned from having influence over others? But you do have a point: maybe there are so many *vikarma* now that it might lead to a tipping point of a different kind, and one that might tumble our society into chaos. There are no easy answers, O Neelkanth. I do not have the solution to this problem. Maybe you can find it.'

Shiva turned his face away. He still believed in his heart that the *vikarma* system was unfair.

'Are you concerned about *all* the *vikarma*, O Neelkanth?' asked the pandit, finally, 'or just one in particular?'

'What is the Lord doing in there?' asked Nandi. 'He's taking far too long.'

'I don't know,' said Veerbhadra. 'All I know is that if Shiva says he needs to do something, I accept it.'

'Why do you call the Lord by his name?'

'Because that's his name!'

Nandi smiled at the simple answer and turned to look at the temple.

'Tell me, Captain,' said Veerbhadra, leaning in close to Nandi and lowering his voice, 'is Krittika spoken for?'

'"Spoken for"?'

'I mean,' continued Veerbhadra, 'is she off limits?'

'"Off limits"?'

'You know what I mean,' said Veerbhadra, turning beet-red.

'She's a widow,' said Nandi. 'Her husband died fifteen years ago.'

'Oh – that's terrible!'

'Yes, it is,' said Nandi, smiling at Veerbhadra, 'but to answer your question, no, she is not "spoken for" right now.'

'My lady, may I say something?' asked Krittika.

Sati turned from the guest-room window to look at Krittika with a surprised frown. 'Have I ever stopped you from speaking your mind? A true Suryavanshi always speaks her mind.'

'In that case,' said Krittika, 'I think that sometimes it may not be harmful for you to lose control of yourself.'

Sati's frown deepened even more.

Krittika spoke quickly, before her courage deserted her. 'Forget about him being the Neelkanth, my lady. As a man, I think he's the finest I've met: he's intelligent and brave and funny and kind, and he worships the ground you walk on. Is that really so bad?'

Sati glared at Krittika; she didn't know if she was more upset about what she was saying, or with herself for having such transparent feelings.

Krittika, oblivious to Sati's growing anger, continued, 'Maybe – just maybe – breaking the rules this once might lead to happiness.'

'I'm a Suryavanshi,' said Sati, her voice low and cross. 'Rules are *all* I live by. What's happiness got to do with it? Don't ever dare mention this to me again!'

— ⚕ ⑳Ⓤ⚜⊕ —

'Well, there is one particular *vikarma*,' admitted Shiva, 'but that's not why I think the *vikarma* law is unfair.'

'I know that,' said the pandit, 'but I also know that what's troubling you right now is your relationship with this particular individual: you don't want her to think that you would change the law, however justified that change might be, just to get her – because if Sati believes that, you will never win her.'

'How do you know her name?' asked Shiva, flabbergasted.

'We know many things, my friend.'

'My entire life is meaningless without her.'

'I know.' The pandit smiled. 'Perhaps I can help you.'

Shiva frowned at this unexpected development.

'You want her to reciprocate your love – but how can she when you don't even understand her?' the pandit started.

'I think I understand her – I know I love her.'

'Yes, you may well love her – but you don't understand her. You don't know what she wants.'

Shiva kept quiet. He knew the pandit was right; Sati thoroughly confused him.

'You might be able to guess what she wants,' continued the pandit, 'with the help of the theory of transactions.'

'With the what?' Now he really was lost.

'The theory of transactions, my friend, is responsible for the very fabric of society.'

'Forgive me, but I have no idea what you're talking about. What does this theory have to do with Sati?'

'Indulge me for a little while, Neelkanth,' said the pandit. He touched Shiva's robe. 'This cloth you're wearing – it is created by cotton threads being woven together, right?'

'Of course.'

'In the same way, transactions are threads that, when woven together, make up a society, its culture, and, on an individual level, a person's character.'

Shiva thought he was beginning to understand, and he gestured for the pandit to continue.

'If you want to know the strength of a cloth, you inspect the quality of its weave. If you want to understand an individual's character, look closely at their interpersonal behaviour – their "transactions".'

'All right,' said Shiva slowly, absorbing the pandit's words, 'so "transactions" are—'

'I'll explain,' interrupted the pandit. 'Transactions are interactions between individuals – it could be trading goods, like a Shudra farmer offering grain in return for a Vaishya's money. But it could also be something beyond the material, like a Kshatriya offering protection to a society in return for power.'

'So transactions are about give and take?'

'Exactly – so using this logic, if you want something from someone, you have to give that person something they want in return.'

'So what do you think she wants?' asked Shiva.

'Try to understand Sati's transactions. What do *you* think she wants?'

'I've no idea. She's very confusing,' he admitted.

'No, she isn't; there's always a pattern. Think: she's probably the most eminent *vikarma* in history. She has the power to rebel if she wants to – and she certainly has the spirit, since she never backs off from a fight – but she chooses *not* to rebel against the *vikarma* law. But nor does she fade into the background like most *vikarmas* – she does not live her life in anonymity. She follows the commandments, but she doesn't whine and complain to others about her lot; however unfairly life treats her, she conducts herself with dignity. Why?'

'Because she's a righteous person?'

'That she is, no doubt. But that's not the reason. Remember, in a "transaction" you *give something* because you *want something* in return. She's accepting an unfair law without trying to make anyone feel guilty about it, and most importantly, she continues to use her talents to contribute to the good of society whenever she can. What do you think a person who is giving all this in her transactions with society wants in return?'

'Respect,' answered Shiva immediately.

'Exactly!' The pandit beamed. 'And what do you think you do when you try to *protect* such a person?'

'Disrespect her.' He grimaced.

'Absolutely! I know it comes naturally to you to want to protect any good person who appears to be in need, but I suggest you control that noble urge where Sati is concerned. Respect her, and she'll be drawn to you. She gets many things from the people who love her, but not this thing she craves the most.'

Shiva looked at the pandit with a grateful smile. He had found his answer.

— ✶ ⍵∪♀❋ —

Another two weeks of travel brought the Neelkanth's convoy to the glittering city of Karachapa, which stood at the point where the Indus flowed into the Western Sea. It had long since grown beyond the original platform on which it had been founded and now the *Dwitiya*, or second platform, built fifty years ago on an even grander scale than the first, was home to the Karachapa elite.

Following the precedent established along the route, the governor, a diminutive Vaishya called Jhooleshwar, accompanied by a fair number of its hundred thousand citizens, received the Neelkanth outside the city,

Karachapa was at heart a frontier trading city, and in an act of foresight, Emperor Daksha's father, Emperor Brahmanayak, had appointed a Vaishya as its governor more than a hundred years before. Jhooleshwar had ruled extraordinarily well – he was considered the wisest and most efficient governor in the city's history – and Karachapa had long overtaken Lothal in the east to become Meluha's premier city of commerce, even welcoming foreigners like Mesopotamians and Egyptians – although they were allowed into this liberal city, they were not permitted to travel further into Meluha without express royal permission.

On his very first day, Jhooleshwar escorted the Neelkanth and Brahaspati – who wanted to check on the imports he was expecting from the Mesopotamian merchants – on an excursion to the Western Sea. Shiva had never seen the sea, and he was fascinated by what looked like an infinite expanse of water.

They spent many hours at the port, where Jhooleshwar

proudly expounded on the various types of ships and vessels manufactured at Karachapa's shipyards.

At that evening's state dinner, Jhooleshwar proudly announced that a *yagna*, a ceremonial fire-sacrifice, was being organised the next day in honour of the Neelkanth, under the auspices of Lord Varun, god of the water and the seas, and the legendary Ashwini Kumar twins, the celebrated ancient seafarers who had navigated the ocean routes from Meluha to Mesopotamia and beyond. Their maps, guidance and stories were still a source of inspiration and learning for this city of seamen.

After dinner, Shiva visited Sati's chambers. 'I was wondering if you'll be coming to the *yagna* tomorrow,' he said, choosing his words with care, as he had ever since Sati had gone back to being formal with him.

'I'm very sorry, Lord Neelkanth,' she replied courteously, 'but I'm not allowed to attend such ceremonies.'

He was about to say that nobody would question her if she was attending with the Neelkanth – then he remembered the pandit's advice. 'Perhaps we could have a dance practice tomorrow?' he suggested. 'I can't remember the last time we danced together.'

'That would be agreeable – I've not had the benefit of your instruction in a long time,' said Sati.

Shiva smiled unhappily at Sati, tormented by the icy formality of their relationship, and bade her goodbye.

As he turned to leave, Krittika glanced at Sati, shaking her head imperceptibly.

CHAPTER 15

Trial by Fire

The little boy hurried along the dusty goat trail, trying to avoid the sharp stones, bundling his fur coat around his small frame. The dense, wet forest encroached menacingly on the narrow path. The boy was sure there were terrible monsters lurking in the trees, waiting to pounce on him if he slowed down. His village was only a few hours away but the sun was setting fast behind the mountains and monsters loved the darkness – he'd heard his mother and grandmother say that often enough, especially when he was being difficult. He'd have liked the company of an elder. Everyone knew monsters didn't trouble the elders.

His heart skipped a beat as he heard a strange heaving sound and immediately drew his short sword, anticipating an attack from behind. His friends had heard many stories about the monsters of the forests – the cowardly creatures never attacked from the front.

He stood still, straining to determine where the sound was coming from. It was vaguely familiar, a peculiar repetitive rhythm he thought he'd heard before, and now it was accompanied by a heavy grunting male voice – this was no monster! Excitement thrilled through his body: his friends had whispered and giggled about this, but he'd never seen the act himself. This was his chance!

He crept slowly into the bushes, his sword dangling by his side. He hadn't gone far from the path when he came upon a small clearing where the sound was coming from.

He peeped around a tree-trunk and saw a couple – they looked like they were in a hurry; they hadn't even disrobed completely. The man was extraordinarily hairy, almost like a bear – he could only see his back from here – but the woman was astonishingly beautiful, with long, lustrous wavy hair. Her torn blouse revealed a firm breast – with deep red welts gouged into her smooth skin – and her skirt had been ripped too, exposing long, slim legs. He was so excited – wait till Bhadra heard about this!

But even as he was enjoying the show, he started to think something was amiss. The man was in the throes of passion, but the woman was just lying there, almost like a dead body. She wasn't clutching the man to her; instead, her hands just flopped at her sides; instead of whispering encouragements to her lover, her mouth was pressed tightly shut.

Were those tears of ecstasy rolling down her cheeks – or was she being forced? But how could that be, when the man's knife was within the woman's reach – she could have picked it up and stabbed him, if she'd wanted.

The boy tried to silence his conscience; Just shut up and let me look, *he told himself.*

Then the woman's eyes suddenly fell upon him, the moment that

*would haunt him for the rest of his life. 'Help,' she cried out, 'please,
help me!'*

*Startled, he fell back, dropping his sword, as the hairy monster
turned to see who the woman was calling to.*

*The boy quickly picked up his sword and fled, ignoring the searing
pain in his frostbitten foot as he ran. He was terrified, thinking that
the man was chasing him – he could hear the heavy breathing—*

*The boy sprinted along the goat trail towards his village, the heavy
breathing drawing closer with every second, until he suddenly swerved
to his left, pivoted, and slashed back with his sword—*

*—but there was nobody there – no hairy man; no heavy breathing.
The only sound was the haunting plea of the distraught woman, echoing
in his head: 'Help! Please help me!'*

The little boy looked back. That poor woman.

Go back – help her! *cried his inner voice.*

*He hesitated for a moment, then he turned and fled towards to his
village.*

—☆ⓜ∪↑⊛—

No – go back! Help her!

Shiva woke up sweating, his heart pounding madly, and
instinctively he turned around, as he always did, wanting
desperately to revisit that dreadful day – to redeem himself.
But there would be no redemption for him.

The woman's terrified face came flooding back and he shut
his eyes – but how do you shut your eyes against an image
branded on your very soul?

He pulled his knees up to his chest and rested his head on them. Then he did the only thing that helped: he cried.

The *yagna* platform had been set up in the central square of the *Dwitiya* platform. For Karachapa, this was not the usual austere affair typical of Meluha; instead, the city had decorated the area with bright colours and the platform itself had been painted in a bright golden hue. Colourfully embellished poles festooned with flowers held aloft a *shamiana*, a cloth canopy, and red and blue pennants bearing the Suryavanshi symbol hung proudly. There was a happy atmosphere of pomp and ceremony everywhere.

Jhooleshwar received Shiva and guided him to his ritual seat at the *yagna*. Finally giving in to the governor's repeated requests, Shiva had removed his cravat for the duration of the ceremony.

Parvateshwar and Brahaspati sat on the Neelkanth's right, with Jhooleshwar and Ayurvati to his left. Nandi and Veerbhadra had also been invited, and now they sat behind Shiva – though he'd got the impression his request had been considered somewhat unorthodox. But Jhooleshwar governed a cosmopolitan border city, and he believed that many of the strict Meluhan laws could be bent a little for the sake of expediency. His liberal attitude had made Karachapa a magnet for people from a wide variety of races, and turned the city into a thriving hub for the exchange of goods, services and ideas.

Shiva glanced towards Sati's balcony, which overlooked the central square. She was not allowed to step onto the platform while the *yagna* was being conducted, but she could watch from the safe distance of her chambers, and he could see her standing behind the balcony curtain, with Krittika by her side, observing the proceedings.

Now, as was the custom before such a *yagna*, the presiding pandit stood up and asked formally, 'If anybody present has an objection to this *yagna*, please speak now, or for ever hold your peace.'

This traditional question was entirely rhetorical, not requiring any response – so there was a loud collective groan when a voice cried out loudly, 'I object!'

Jhooleshwar quickly leaned over and said quietly to Shiva, 'Tarak – he's an immigrant from the ultraconservative north-west region of the empire. Since he's been here, he's taken it upon himself to become the "moral police" – he calls us "this decadent city of sin".'

Shiva craned his neck to see the dissenter. Tarak was standing at the back, at the edge of the *puja* platform, very close to Sati's balcony. He was a giant of a man with an immense stomach and a miner's bulging, muscular arms. His fair face was brutally wrinkled by a lifetime of strife, and it was obvious without even looking at his amulets that Tarak was a Kshatriya who had spent his life in the lower echelons of the army.

Jhooleshwar glared at the man in exasperation. 'What is it

now? We didn't use white – the Chandravanshi colour – in our decorations this time, did we? Or do you think the water being used for the ceremony is not at the correct temperature stipulated by the Vedas?'

The gathering sniggered and Parvateshwar looked sharply at Jhooleshwar; before he could reprimand the governor for his cavalier reference to the Vedas, Tarak spoke up. 'The law says that no *vikarma* should be allowed on the *yagna* platform.'

'Indeed,' said Jhooleshwar, 'but unless you've been declared a *vikarma*, I don't think that law is being broken.'

'Yes, it is,' he declared dramatically, and shocked murmurs rose from the congregation.

Jhooleshwar raised his hand. 'Nobody here is a *vikarma*, Tarak,' he said firmly. 'Now please sit down.'

'Princess Sati defiles the *yagna* with her presence.'

Shiva and Parvateshwar looked sharply at Tarak. Jhooleshwar was as stunned as the rest of the assembly by Tarak's statement.

'You go too far,' said the governor. 'Princess Sati *is* abiding by the laws of the *yagna* – she's confined to the guest-house, not present on the *yagna* platform. Now sit down before I have you whipped.'

'On what charge will you have me whipped, Governor?' yelled Tarak. 'Standing up for the law is no crime in Meluha.'

'But the law has not been broken!'

'Yes, it has: the *exact* words of the law state that no *vikarma* can be on the platform while a *yagna* is being conducted. The *yagna* is being conducted on the *Dwitiya* platform of the city, therefore by being on the same platform, the princess defiles the *yagna*.'

Shiva realised that Tarak was technically correct; like most people would, the governor had interpreted that law to mean that a *vikarma* couldn't be on the prayer ceremony platform, but a stricter interpretation of the law would mean that Sati should not be *anywhere* on the entire *Dwitiya* platform. To fulfil the absolute letter of the *yagna* law, she would have to move either to the city's other platform, or outside the city walls.

Jhooleshwar was momentarily taken aback, but he tried a weak rally. 'Come, come, Tarak – you are being too conscientious. Surely that is much too strict an interpretation. I think—'

'No, Shri Jhooleshwarji.' A new voice cut through the murmuring gathering and everybody turned to see where the sound was coming from.

Sati had stepped out onto her balcony; now she offered a formal namaste and continued, 'Please accept my apologies for interrupting you, Governor, but Tarak's interpretation of the law is fair. I am terribly sorry to have disturbed the *yagna*. My entourage and I will leave the city immediately; we will return at the beginning of the third *prahar*, by which time I believe the ceremony should be over.'

Shiva clenched his fists. He desperately wanted to wring Tarak's neck, but with a superhuman effort he managed to control himself. Within minutes, Sati had left the guest-house, accompanied by Krittika and five of their personal bodyguards. Shiva glanced behind him and Nandi and Veerbhadra both rose to join Sati, understanding that Shiva would want them to ensure she was safe while she was outside the city.

'It's disgusting that you didn't realise this yourself,' Tarak said scornfully to Sati. 'What kind of a princess are you? Don't you respect the law?'

Sati stared at Tarak, her face calm, saying nothing, refusing to be drawn into a debate as she waited patiently for her guards to prepare the horses.

'I don't understand what a *vikarma* woman is doing travelling with the Neelkanth's entourage in the first place,' Tarak raged. 'She's polluting the entire journey—'

'Enough,' Shiva shouted loudly. 'Princess Sati is leaving with dignity, so you can stop your diatribe right now.'

'I will not,' Tarak screeched. 'What kind of a leader are you, challenging Lord Ram's laws?'

'The Lord Neelkanth is the one person who has the right to challenge the law,' the governor interrupted. 'If you value your life, you will not defy his authority.'

'I'm a Meluhan,' shrieked Tarak, 'and it's my *right* to challenge anyone breaking the law. A *dhobi*, a mere washerman, challenged Lord Ram, and in his greatness, he listened to the man's objection and renounced his wife. I would urge the Neelkanth to learn from Lord Ram's example and use his brains for making decisions—'

'Enough, Tarak!' Sati erupted.

Tarak's vehement rant had stunned the entire congregation into silence – but now something inside Sati had snapped. She had tolerated too many insults for too long, enduring them all with quiet dignity – but this man had gone too far. He had insulted Shiva – *her* Shiva, she finally acknowledged to herself.

'I invoke the right of *Agnipariksha*,' she said, back in control of her emotions.

The stunned onlookers couldn't believe their ears: *a trial by fire!*

This was getting worse and worse: *Agnipariksha* gave an unfairly injured soul the right to challenge their tormentor to a duel. Combat would take place within a ring of fire from which there was no escape – the duellists had to keep fighting until one person surrendered or died. *Agniparikshas* were extremely rare – and it was almost unheard of for a woman to invoke that right.

'There's no reason for this, my lady,' pleaded Jhooleshwar, terrified that Princess Sati would be killed in his city. The gargantuan Tarak would surely slay her, and the emperor's wrath would be terrible.

Turning to Tarak, Jhooleshwar ordered, 'You will not accept this challenge.'

'And be called a coward?'

'You want to prove your bravery?' said Parvateshwar, speaking for the first time. 'Then fight me. I will act as Princess Sati's second for the challenge.'

'Only I have the right to appoint a second, *Pitratulya*,' said Sati. The honorific meant 'like a father', and she smiled at the general as she said it. Turning back to Tarak, she said, 'I am appointing no second. You will fight with me.'

This time the chief scientist objected. Brahaspati said firmly, 'Tarak, you will do no such thing.'

At last Shiva spoke. 'Tarak, the only reason you wouldn't want to fight is if you are afraid of being killed.'

Every person turned towards the Neelkanth, shocked by his words. Turning to Sati, Shiva continued, 'Citizens of Karachapa, I've seen the princess fight. She can defeat anyone – even the gods.'

Sati stared at Shiva, shocked.

'I accept the challenge,' growled Tarak.

Sati nodded at Tarak, climbed on her white steed and started to leave. At the edge of the square, she pulled up her horse and looked at Shiva one more time. She smiled at him, then turned and rode away.

— ⚕ Ⓤↂ⊛ —

At the beginning of the third *prahar*, Shiva and Brahaspati stole quietly into the local *varjish graha*, the exercise hall, to observe Tarak practising with two partners. The *yagna* had been a disaster – with everyone petrified that the princess would die the next day, no one was inclined to participate in the ceremony, but the *yagna* had been called, so it had to be conducted or the gods would be offended. The congregation reluctantly went through the motions until finally the *yagna* was called to a close.

Watching Tarak's fearsome blows rain down on his hapless partners, Brahaspati's soul filled with dread and he came to an immediate decision. 'I'll assassinate him tonight. She won't die tomorrow.'

Shiva turned to the chief scientist in stunned disbelief. 'Brahaspati – what are you saying?'

'Sati's too good, too noble to suffer this fate and I am willing to sacrifice my life and reputation for her.'

'But you're a Brahmin – you're not supposed to kill—'

'I'll do it for you,' whispered Brahaspati. Strong emotions were obviously clouding his judgement. 'You won't lose her, my friend.'

Shiva came close to Brahaspati and hugged him. As the chief scientist clung to him, he whispered, 'Don't corrupt your soul, my friend. I'm not worth such a big sacrifice.' He stepped back and added, 'In any case, your generous sacrifice will not be required, for as sure as the sun rises in the east, Sati will defeat Tarak tomorrow.'

— ⅄ ◍ Ʊ ⅄ ⊛ —

A few hours into the third *prahar*, Sati returned to the guest-house and summoned Nandi and Veerbhadra to the central courtyard. She drew her sword and began to practise with them.

When Parvateshwar walked in a little later, he looked like

a broken man. His expression made it clear that he feared this might be the last time he would talk to Sati.

When she saw him she sheathed her sword and folded her hands into a respectful namaste. '*Pitratulya*,' she whispered.

He approached, his face distraught; she couldn't be sure but it looked as if he'd been crying – she'd never before seen even a hint of a tear in his confident eyes.

'My child,' he mumbled.

'I'm doing what I think is right,' said Sati quietly. 'I'm happy with my choice.'

Parvateshwar couldn't find the words. For a brief moment, he considered assassinating Tarak himself, that very night – but such an act would be illegal . . .

At that moment, Shiva and Brahaspati walked in, and Shiva immediately noticed the expression on the general's face. Like Sati, he thought this was the first time he'd seen any sign of weakness in the man. While he could understand how Parvateshwar felt, he didn't like the effect it was clearly having on Sati.

'I'm sorry I'm late,' he said cheerily.

Everyone turned to look at him.

'Brahaspati and I have been to Lord Varun's temple to pray for Tarak,' he went on. 'We prayed for his soul, that it will have a comfortable journey to the other world.'

Sati burst out laughing, and after a moment the rest of the party gathered in the courtyard joined her.

'Bhadra,' said Shiva, 'you're not the right opponent for this practice. You move too quickly. Nandi, you duel with the princess – and control your agility, will you?'

Turning to Sati, he continued, 'I was watching Tarak practise: his blows have tremendous power, but the force he exerts slows him down and turns his strength into his weakness. Use your agility against his strength.'

Sati listened, absorbing every word, then resumed her practice with Nandi, following Shiva's advice. He was right: her quickness against Nandi's slower movements meant she was able to land several killing strikes.

Suddenly, an idea struck Shiva. He told Nandi to stop, then asked Sati, 'Are you allowed to choose the combat weapon?'

'Yes – that's my prerogative as I issued the challenge.'

'Then choose the knife – it'll reduce the reach of his strikes, and you can move in and out much more quickly than he can shift himself.'

'That's brilliant,' concurred Parvateshwar, and Brahaspati nodded too.

Even as Sati signalled her agreement, Veerbhadra emerged with two knives. Giving one to Nandi and the other to Sati, he said, 'Practise, my lady.'

— ⟶ ⚨ ◍ Ʊ ⚷ ✸ ⟵ —

Sati and Tarak stood at the centre of the *Rangbhoomi*. The circular stadium was the exact dimensions required for an *Agnipariksha*: not so big that a person could simply steer clear of the other contestant, nor so small that the combat would end too quickly. A capacity crowd of more than twenty thousand people filled the stands; they'd come to watch the most important duel to take place in Karachapa for the last five hundred years.

There was a prayer on every lip: let Father Manu cause a miracle so that Princess Sati would win – or at the very least, live. A bird-courier had been sent to Emperor Daksha the previous day, informing him of the duel, but it was too soon to expect a reply.

Tarak and Sati greeted each other with a namaste and repeated the ancient pledge: that each would fight with honour. Then they turned to the statue of Lord Varun at the top of the main stand and bowed, asking for blessings from the god of the water and the seas.

Jhooleshwar had ushered Shiva into his own ceremonial seat right below the statue of Lord Varun. He sat on Shiva's left, with Ayurvati and Krittika on his left. Brahaspati and Parvateshwar sat on Shiva's right, and Nandi and Veerbhadra took up their now familiar position behind the Neelkanth.

At long last, Governor Jhooleshwar stood up. Despite his apprehension, he appeared composed. As custom demanded, he raised a balled fist to his heart and boomed: '*Satya! Dharma! Maan!*' – an invocation to *Truth, Duty, Honour.*

The rest of the stadium rang out, repeating the mantra: '*Satya! Dharma! Maan!*'

Tarak and Sati echoed the words, '*Satya! Dharma! Maan!*'

Jhooleshwar gestured to the stadium keeper, who lit the ceremonial oil-lamp with the holy flame; the lamp spilled its fire onto the oil-channel and within seconds the periphery of the central ground was aflame.

The ring for the *pariksha* had been set.

Jhooleshwar turned to Shiva. 'My Lord, will you start the duel?'

Shiva stood up and looked at Sati with a confident smile, then he declared loudly, 'In the purifying fire of Lord Agni, truth will always triumph!'

Tarak and Sati immediately drew their knives. Tarak held his knife in front of him, like most traditional fighters. He'd chosen a strategy that played to his strengths: keeping his knife in front of him would allow him to strike the moment Sati came close. He stood still, making Sati move towards him.

Sati, breaking all the Meluhans' usual rules of combat, held her knife behind her, shifting it continually from one hand to the other, all the while keeping a safe distance from her opponent, trying to confuse Tarak about the direction of her attack.

Tarak, watching her movements like a hawk, saw her right arm flex; the knife was now in her right hand.

Suddenly Sati leapt to the left – but Tarak, seeing through her opening gambit, remained stationary; with the knife in her right hand, the leftwards movement was a feint, because she would have to move to the right to bring her knife into play.

Sure enough, Sati darted to the right and brought her arm up in a stabbing motion – but Tarak was prepared, and shifting his knife quickly to his left hand, he slashed viciously, cutting Sati across her torso. It wasn't a deep cut, but it appeared to hurt.

A collective gasp went up from the audience.

Sati retreated and rallied, moving the knife behind her back again and once more transferring it from one hand to the other.

Tarak kept a close eye on her arms, watching the way her muscles flexed. The knife was in her left hand. He expected her to move to the right, which she did, and as before he remained immobile, waiting for her to swerve suddenly to her left – and so she did, swinging her left arm as she moved, but he acted before her arm could come close enough to do any damage. Swinging out ferociously with his right arm, he cut her, this time catching her deep in the left shoulder.

Sati retreated rapidly as the audience moaned in horror. Some shut their eyes; they couldn't bear to look any more. Most were praying fervently. If it had to be done, let it be done swiftly.

'What's she doing?' whispered a panic-stricken Brahaspati to Shiva. 'Why is she charging in so recklessly?'

As Shiva turned to answer Brahaspati, he noticed the surprised yet admiring grin on Parvateshwar's face. Unlike Brahaspati, he knew exactly what was going on. Turning back to look at the duel, Shiva whispered, 'She's laying a trap.'

At the centre of the combat circle Sati was still transferring the knife between her hands behind her back, but this time though she flexed her left arm, keeping her right arm loose and relaxed, she did not transfer the knife.

Tarak was watching Sati closely. He was confident that he had her measure – and that he was going to slowly and painfully bleed her to death.

Now he waited for her to move right, then left, and she did just that, in a swift veer. Expecting her left arm to come in as before, he sliced with his right hand – and this time Sati pirouetted neatly and before a surprised Tarak could react, she had leapt to her right and thrust the knife in her right hand deep into his chest. The shock of the blow immobilised him. The knife pierced his lung, and blood spurted from his mouth. He dropped his own blade and staggered back.

Sati moved towards him and ruthlessly pushed her own knife in deeper, until it was buried right up to its hilt in his chest.

Tarak stumbled back and collapsed to the ground and lay there, motionless.

The entire stadium was stunned into silence.

Sati's face bore the expression of the Mother Goddess in fury as eighty-five years of repressed anger surfaced in that very instant. Slowly she pulled out the knife, twisting it as she did so to inflict maximum damage. Blood spewed from Tarak's mouth at an alarming rate. She raised the knife with both her hands. All she had to do was bring it down, piercing his heart, and Tarak would meet his maker.

Then, suddenly, her expression became calm again, almost as if someone had sucked out all the negative energy inside her. She turned around and looked up: Shiva, the destroyer of evil, was sitting on his throne, watching her. A slight smile tugged at his lips.

Sati looked at Tarak and whispered, 'I forgive you,' and though she had spoken so quietly, her words echoed around the stadium and the onlookers erupted in joy. Even if Lord Varun himself had scripted the fight, it could not have been more perfect. This had everything the Suryavanshis held dear: defiance under pressure, magnanimity in victory.

Sati raised her knife and shouted, '*Jai Shri Ram!*' and the entire stadium echoed her triumphant cry. She turned towards Shiva and roared once again, '*Jai Shri Ram!*'

'*Jai—*' Shiva began, but the words were clogged by the knot of emotion in his throat. He glanced away from Sati, lest the woman he loved see his tears.

Regaining control of himself, he looked back at her with a radiant smile, and she stared deeply into his eyes as emotions dormant for far too long rippled through her. At last she couldn't bear it any longer, and she shut her eyes.

CHAPTER 16

The Sun and Earth

An impromptu celebration was held that night in the jubilant city: their princess was safe and the insufferable Tarak had been defeated. He had few supporters in Karachapa; many believed that even his own mother must have loathed the surly preacher. But as with all Meluhan life, strict rules governed duels, and the moment Sati publicly forgave Tarak, doctors had rushed in. They had laboured for hours to save his life, and to the dismay of many of the townsfolk, they had succeeded.

'Have you heard the poem of the sun and the earth?' Sati asked Shiva. They were sitting quietly on the balcony of the governor's palace while a boisterous party raged inside.

'No,' he said with a seductive grin, moving a little nearer to her, 'but I'd love to hear it.'

Sati absentmindedly stroked the thick dressing that covered the gash in her abdomen, 'Sometimes the earth thinks about coming closer to the sun,' she started, 'but she can't do that; she is so base and his brilliance so searing that she will cause destruction if she draws him closer.'

Where is this leading? Shiva wondered. He didn't have a great feeling about this.

'I disagree,' he said. 'I think the sun burns only as long as the earth is close to him. Without the earth, there would be no reason for the sun to exist.'

'The sun doesn't exist just for the earth. It exists for every single planet in the solar system.'

'Isn't it really the sun's prerogative to decide for whom he exists?'

'No,' said Sati, a melancholy expression in her eyes as she looked at Shiva. 'The moment he became the sun, he accepted a higher calling. He no longer exists for himself, but for the greater good of everyone. His radiance is the lifeblood of the solar system. And if the earth has any sense of responsibility, she won't do anything to destroy this balance.'

'So what should the sun do?' asked Shiva, hurt and anger colouring his face. 'Waste his entire life burning away, looking at the earth from a distance?'

'The earth isn't going anywhere – the sun and the earth can still share a warm friendship. But anything more would be against the law, and against the interests of others.'

Shiva turned away from Sati and looked north to seek solace from his Holy Lake. Feeling nothing, he looked up at the skies, towards the gods he didn't believe in.

Dammit!

He got up, thumped the balcony railing with his powerful fist, dislodging some bricks, and stormed off.

In a forested area outside the city walls, a few soldiers lay in wait. Two hooded figures sat on large rocks a little way away, and the captain of the platoon stood rigidly to attention next to them. He could not believe that he was standing next to the queen herself. The privilege almost overwhelmed him.

One of the hooded figures raised his hand to motion for the captain to step closer, revealing a leather bracelet decorated with the serpent Aum. 'Are you sure this is where we're supposed to meet him, Vishwadyumna? He's nearly an hour late.'

'Yes, my lord,' the captain replied nervously, 'this is the exact location he specified.'

The other hooded figure turned and in a commanding voice – a voice used to being obeyed without question – said, 'I trust you have worked this out in detail. I hope I haven't entered this vile territory in vain.' Then she growled, 'I cannot believe that man makes the Queen of the Nagas wait!'

The other hooded figure moved his fleshy hands in a gesture that asked the queen for patience. 'Have faith, your Majesty. This man is our key to giving the Suryavanshis a blow from which they will never recover.'

'Apparently, there was an *Agnipariksha* fight between the princess and a man in the city yesterday,' said Vishwadyumna suddenly, trying to impress the queen with his local know-ledge. 'I don't have all the details – I hope our man wasn't involved in it.'

The queen glanced swiftly at the other hooded figure, then returned her attention to Vishwadyumna. 'Leave us.'

Vishwadyumna, realising he'd said something he shouldn't have – although he had no idea what it was – quickly retreated. *This* was why the training officers always said a good soldier never speaks unless spoken to.

'*She's* here?' asked the queen, her voice thick with barely suppressed anger, and when her companion nodded, added sternly, 'I told you to forget about this. This pointless quest will gain us nothing. Your stupid attack at Mount Mandar might already have left them suspecting that we have a mole in their midst.'

As he started to speak she interjected, 'Did you come here for her?'

'No, your Majesty,' said the hooded figure, his tone both respectful and apologetic. 'This truly is the place where he asked us to meet him.'

The queen reached out and gently patted the man's shoulder. 'Stay focused, my child,' she said softly. 'You are correct: if we pull this off, it will be our biggest victory ever.'

As the man nodded his agreement, she said contemplatively, 'Your preoccupation with her makes you take uncharacter-istic decisions. He has sent a clear message that she cannot be touched – otherwise, the deal is off.'

The hooded figure stared at the queen in surprise. 'How did you get to hear from him directly?'

'I am the Queen of the Nagas, my child, not just your mother's sister,' she interrupted, 'and like any competent ruler, I have more than one piece on the chessboard.'

In the shadow of his hood he flushed, filled with shame for his poor judgement at Mount Mandar. The queen's next words only added to his embarrassment.

'You are making surprising mistakes, my child,' she said softly. 'You have the potential to be the greatest Naga ever. Don't waste that potential.'

He swallowed hard. 'Yes, your Majesty,' he said, and a smile finally reached his eyes as he stared at his *mausi*, his mother's sister. 'Whatever you say, *Mausi*.'

— ⋏ ⑩ Ⴄ � ⊛ —

It had been two weeks since the *Agnipariksha*, and Sati had recovered sufficiently for the convoy to consider leaving for the next destination. 'It's agreed, then,' said Parvateshwar to Shiva and Brahaspati. 'I'll make the arrangements for us to start a week from today. By that time, Sati should have recovered completely.'

'That sounds like a plan,' agreed Shiva.

'I'm afraid I won't be travelling any further with you,' said Brahaspati.

'Why not?' asked Parvateshwar, looking surprised.

'The new chemicals I ordered have finally arrived, and

I really want to get them back to Mount Mandar so the experiments can begin as soon as possible. If we can get this right, we'll need much less water for making the *Somras*.'

Shiva smiled sadly. 'I'm going to miss you, my friend.'

'And I you,' said Brahaspati. 'But I'm not leaving the country – when you finish your tour, come back to Mount Mandar. I'll show you around the forests near our facility.'

'I'd like that,' said Shiva with a grin. 'Perhaps your scientific skills will even discover a plausible reason for my blue throat!'

Shiva and Brahaspati shared a laugh, but Parvateshwar, not understanding the private joke, just looked on politely. Then, as if he'd just thought of it, he said, 'I should mention one thing, Brahaspati: I won't be able to divert any soldiers from the royal entourage to accompany you – but I'll ask Governor Jhooleshwar to send some soldiers along for your return journey.'

Brahaspati clapped him on the shoulder. 'Thank you, Parvateshwar, but I'm sure I'll be fine – why would any terrorist be interested in me?'

'There was another attack yesterday – a village some twenty miles from Mohan Jo Daro,' he said quietly. 'The entire temple was destroyed, and all the Brahmins were murdered.'

'Another one?' exclaimed Shiva angrily. 'That's the third this month!'

'They're getting bolder,' the general said, 'and as usual, they managed to escape before any back-up could arrive to give them a real fight.'

Shiva clenched his fists. He had no idea how to counter these terrorist attacks – since nobody knew where they would strike next, there was no way to prepare for them. He was beginning to wonder if attacking Swadweep was the only way to stop this.

Brahaspati, sensing Shiva's inner turmoil, kept quiet. He knew there were no easy answers.

Looking at Shiva, Parvateshwar continued, 'I will also get my people to make preparations for our journey. I'll meet you tonight for dinner – I think Sati is finally well enough to join us, and I thought I might invite Nandi and Veerbhadra too – I know you enjoy their company.'

Startled by the general's uncharacteristic thoughtfulness, Shiva said, 'Thanks, Parvateshwar, that's very kind of you – but I believe Krittika, Nandi and Veerbhadra are going to a flute recital tonight. Veerbhadra's even bought some jewels so he won't look like a country bumpkin next to Nandi!'

Parvateshwar smiled politely, not getting the joke.

'But it will be my pleasure to dine with you,' Shiva finished.

'Until this evening, then,' said Parvateshwar, standing to take his leave. After a few steps, he stopped and turned around. He started, 'Shiva—', then hesitated.

'Yes?' said Shiva as he too rose to his feet.

'I've never said this' – the general was clearly uncomfortable – 'but I would like to thank you for helping Sati in her *Agnipariksha* – your clear thinking led to victory.'

'No, no,' said Shiva, 'it was her own brilliance.'

'Of course it was,' Parvateshwar agreed, 'but you gave her the confidence and the strategy that allowed her brilliance to shine. I love Sati like a daughter, and I thank you for helping her.'

'You're welcome.' Shiva smiled and said no more; lengthening this conversation would only embarrass Parvateshwar further.

Parvateshwar smiled and folded his hands into a namaste. While he had still not fallen prey to the countrywide 'Neelkanth fever', he was beginning to respect Shiva.

Earning Parvateshwar's esteem was going to be a long journey, Shiva thought as the general turned around and walked out of the room, *but at least he'd begun it.*

'He's not a bad sort,' said Brahaspati, looking at Parvateshwar's retreating back. 'A little surly, perhaps, but he's one of the most honest Suryavanshis I've ever met, and he's a true follower of Lord Ram. I hope his ill-tempered comments don't upset you too much.'

'Not at all,' said Shiva. 'In fact, I think very highly of Parvateshwar. He's one man whose respect I'd certainly like to earn.'

Brahaspati smiled and said, 'You're a good man.' Shiva returned his smile. 'To be honest,' he continued. 'I've never believed in the prophecy of the Neelkanth. I still don't.' Shiva's smile widened. 'But I do believe in you. If there's one person capable of sucking the negative energy out of this land, it's you, and I'll do everything I can to help you.'

'You're the brother I never had, Brahaspati. Your presence alone is all the help I need.' He embraced the chief scientist, and Brahaspati hugged him back warmly, feeling a sense of renewed energy course through him. He swore to himself once again that he'd never back off from his mission, no matter what. It wasn't just for Meluha, it was also for Shiva. His friend.

— ♈ ◍Ʊ♌⊛ —

More than three weeks after the *Agnipariksha*, the convoy finally set off from Karachapa. This time six of the seven carriages were decoys, and Shiva and Sati sat in the third with Parvateshwar and Ayurvati; this was the first time Parvateshwar had travelled in the same carriage as Shiva. Krittika had volunteered to ride, claiming that she was missing the scenic beauty of the countryside, and Veerbhadra was delighted to ride with her, alongside Nandi's platoon.

A few days out from Karachapa, the convoy was brought to a halt by a large caravan travelling hurriedly in the opposite direction.

Brigadier Vraka came up to Parvateshwar and executed a crisp military salute before reporting, 'My Lord, they're refugees from the village of Koonj. They claim they are escaping a terrorist attack.'

'*Escaping?*' Parvateshwar asked, 'you mean the attack's still in progress?'

'I think so, my Lord,' said Vraka, his face filled with rage.

'Goddammit,' Parvateshwar swore. This was an opportunity no Meluhan warrior had ever had before: to be in the right place at the right time – while a terrorist attack was actually in progress – with fifteen hundred soldiers. But his hands were tied. His sole mission was to protect the Neelkanth and the princess.

What nonsense, he thought to himself. *My orders forbid me from following my Kshatriya dharma!*

'What's the matter, Parvateshwar?'

He turned to find Shiva standing right behind him, and Sati and Ayurvati climbing out of the carriage to join them – but before he could reply, a horrible noise echoed along the quiet forest road, a sound Shiva had come to recognise.

A conch-shell bearer was heralding a Naga attack.

CHAPTER 17

The Battle of Koonj

'Where are they?' asked Parvateshwar.

'My village is a short distance from here, my Lord,' said the scared headman. 'There are around five hundred Chandravanshi soldiers led by Nagas – five or six, I think. They gave us thirty minutes to leave, but the Brahmins at the temple were detained.'

Parvateshwar clenched his fists to rein in his fury.

'Our panditji is a good man, my Lord,' said the headman, trying not to let the tears spill from his eyes as the brigadier put a comforting hand on his shoulder.

'We wanted to stay and fight alongside our pandit and the other Brahmins,' he said hoarsely. 'They're men of God – they don't even know how to raise a weapon – how can they fight this horde? But Panditji ordered us to take the women and children and run – he said he'd face whatever fate Lord Brahma decrees – but if anyone can be saved, they should be.'

Parvateshwar dug his nails into his palms. He was livid at the cowardly Chandravanshis for yet again attacking defence-less Brahmins and not Kshatriyas who could retaliate. He was incensed for being put in this position, where he could not take action. Though part of him wanted to ignore his orders, he was bound by oath not to break the law.

'This nonsense has to stop!'

Parvateshwar looked up to see whose voice was echoing his thoughts. When he saw the expression on Shiva's face, he involuntarily stepped back for a moment. The intense fury visible on the Neelkanth's face would have brought even a *Deva* to a standstill.

'We are good people,' raged Shiva. 'We are not scared chicken who should turn and flee – those terrorists should be the ones on the run. They should be the ones feeling the wrath of the Suryavanshis!'

A villager standing behind the headman said, 'But they're terrorists – we can't defeat them; the panditji knew it – that's why he ordered us to run.'

'But we have fifteen hundred soldiers,' said Shiva, irritated by the man's cowardice, 'and there are another five hundred of you: we outnumber them, four to one. We can crush them, teach them a lesson they'll never forget.'

'But there are *Nagas* there,' the headman said, aghast. 'They're supernatural, bloodthirsty killers – what chance do we have against such evil?'

It's time. Superstition could only be countered by another, stronger belief. Shiva climbed onto the roof of the carriage so that everyone could see him, then ripped off his cravat and threw it away. He didn't need it any more.

'I am the Neelkanth!' he cried.

Every soldier looked up at the destroyer of evil, overjoyed to see him truly accept his destiny. The villagers, who had not heard of the Neelkanth's arrival, were stunned to see the prophecy come alive, right before their very eyes.

'I am going to fight these terrorists,' Shiva roared. 'I am going to show them that we are not scared of them. I am going to make them feel the pain we feel, and let them know that Meluha is not going to capitulate to them.'

Pure energy coursed through the huddled mass of villagers standing in front of him; straightening their spines and inspiring their souls.

'Who's coming with me?' Shiva shouted.

'I am,' bellowed Parvateshwar, feeling the suffocating restraints imposed on him fall away.

'I am,' echoed Sati, Nandi, Veerbhadra and Vraka.

'I am,' echoed every single soul standing there.

Suddenly the scared villagers and soldiers had turned into a righteous army. The soldiers drew their swords and the villagers grabbed whatever weapons they could from the travelling armoury.

'To Koonj,' yelled Shiva, mounting a horse and galloping ahead.

Parvateshwar and Sati quickly unharnessed the horses from

their carriage and raced after Shiva, with the Suryavanshis charging behind them, raising a battle-cry louder than any Naga conch shell.

As they stormed into Koonj, the true horror of what had happened there hit them. The Chandravanshis had focused their attack on the place that would cause the Meluhans the most distress: their venerated temple. The decapitated bodies of the Brahmins lay around the shrine, and the temple itself was aflame. The Suryavanshis, further enraged by the grue-some sight, charged like crazed bulls.

The Chandravanshis had no chance. They were taken by surprise, completely outnumbered and overwhelmed, and they lost ground immediately. Some tried to retreat, but the five Nagas rallied them back into the fray and they fought on against the crushing odds with unexpected courage, clashing against the righteous Suryavanshis.

Parvateshwar fought like a man possessed, and Shiva, who had never seen the general in battle, was awed by his skill and valour. Like Shiva, he knew the Nagas were the key to Chandravanshi victory; as long as they were alive, they would strike terror into the Suryavanshis, all the while inspiring the Chandravanshis to fight even harder.

He singled one out and attacked with frenzied aggression. The Naga skilfully parried Parvateshwar's attack with his shield and brought his sword down on the general's exposed shoulder – but Parvateshwar had deliberately left his flank exposed. Swinging nimbly to the side to avoid the blow, he swiftly drew a knife from a sheath hidden below the shield on his back and hurled it at the Naga's exposed right shoulder.

The Naga roared in fury and pain, letting Parvateshwar know that the knife had penetrated deep, but to his surprise – and admiration – the wounded man ignored the knife still buried in his shoulder and swung his sword-arm, rejoining the battle.

Parvateshwar brought his shield back in front of him and blocked the Naga's slightly weaker strike. He thrust his sword up and stabbed, but the Naga was too quick, and deflected it. Parvateshwar swerved left and rammed his shield down hard on the knife stuck in the Naga's shoulder, feeling the blade chipping through bone. The Naga snarled in pain and stumbled, and that gave him the opening he needed. He brought up his sword and thrust it forward, pushing it ruthlessly through the Naga's heart.

The Naga froze as Parvateshwar's sword ripped the life out of him, then fell back, dead.

Even Parvateshwar shared the Meluhan fascination with the Nagas' deformities, and he knelt to tear off the Naga's mask – revealing a truly horrifying countenance. The Naga's nose was pure bone, resembling a bird's beak. His ears were ridiculously large, his mouth grotesquely constricted. He looked like a vulture in human form.

Parvateshwar quickly whispered the words every Suryavanshi said when he brought down a worthy opponent: 'Have a safe journey to the other side, brave warrior.'

One down, four to go, he thought, rising swiftly, and as he scanned the battlefield, he saw Shiva bringing down a gigantic Naga in the distance. *Correction – two down, three to go*.

Their gazes locked, and they both nodded. Shiva pointed behind him and Parvateshwar turned to see a ferocious Naga singlehandedly fighting five Suryavanshis.

He turned back and signalled his understanding, and as Shiva charged another of the deformed warriors, Parvateshwar set off towards the Naga earmarked for him.

— ⚱ ⦿⋃⥮⊕ —

Shiva dashed through the pitched battle towards a Naga who had just killed a Suryavanshi soldier. He leaped high as he approached, holding his shield in front of him to counter the Naga's standard swinging strike. The Naga had brought his own shield up to block what he expected from Shiva: the orthodox up-and-down swinging strike from a good height – but Shiva surprised him by thrusting his sword sideways, neatly bypassing the Naga's shield and badly gashing his arm.

The Naga bellowed in pain and fell back, before straightening and holding his shield high again. He'd just realised that this big Meluhan with the strange blue-stained throat was going to be a far more formidable enemy than any Suryavanshi he'd fought before.

As Shiva grimly battled the fearless Naga, he failed to notice another, observing from a distance. This Naga could see that their assault was being progressively pushed back, and that it was only a matter of time before they would have to retreat – and then he would have to face the ignominy of having led the first failed destruction attack. It was clear that this big man was leading the counter-offensive, and it was equally clear that the man had to be destroyed, for the future of the mission. The Naga drew his bow and nocked an arrow.

Shiva, unaware of the danger, had pierced the Naga's stomach with his sword, but the injured man grimly fought on, stepping back slowly and all the while ramming Shiva with his shield. He tried in vain to get his sword around to slice Shiva, who fended off the Naga's blows while pushing the sword in deeper and deeper. It took just a few more seconds; the Naga's soul finally surrendered, slipping away as his body collapsed and bled to death. Shiva looked down at the fallen warrior in awe.

These people may be evil, but they're fearless soldiers, he thought.

Shiva looked for Parvateshwar, and seeing that he had killed the Naga he had engaged, he continued to turn slowly, trying to find the last Naga. Then he heard a loud shout from the person he had come to love beyond reason.

'S-H-I-V-A!'

As he turned to his right, he saw Sati racing towards him, and he looked behind her to see if anyone was chasing her, but there was no one in obvious pursuit. He frowned, but before he could do or say anything, Sati had leapt forward.

Her jump was timed to perfection.

The remaining Naga had released an *agnibaan* – a fire-arrow, one of his people's legendary poisoned arrows. The venom on the tip burned the victim's body from the inside, causing a slow, painful death that would scar the soul for many births. The arrow had been aimed precisely at Shiva's neck, and it sped unerringly on its deadly mission – but the Naga had not considered the possibility of someone obstructing its path.

Sati twisted her body in mid-air as she leapt in front of Shiva and the arrow slammed into her chest with brutal force, propelling her airborne body backwards. She fell to the left, her body already limp.

Shiva, stunned, stared at Sati's prone body, his heart shattering into a million pieces. Then the destroyer of evil roared in a furious rage, raised his sword and charged at the Naga like a wild elephant on the brink of insanity. The Naga was momentarily staggered by the fearsome sight of the charging Neelkanth, but he rallied and swiftly drew another arrow from his quiver, nocked it and let it fly. Shiva swung his sword, barely missing a step as he deflected the arrow, never decreasing his manic speed.

The increasingly panic-stricken Naga nocked a third arrow and Shiva swung his sword once more, and this time he picked up his speed as he knocked the shaft aside.

The Naga reached back to draw again, but it was too late. With a fierce yell, Shiva leapt high as he neared the Naga and decapitated him with one vicious swing of his sword. The Naga's lifeless body slumped to the ground and as his severed head flew through the air, his still-pumping heart spewed blood through his gaping neck.

But the Neelkanth's vengeance was not yet quenched. Screaming at the top of his lungs, Shiva repeatedly hacked at the Naga's inert body, carving it into bloody chunks. No assertion of reason, no articulation of sanity could have penetrated Shiva's enraged mind – except for a soft, pained voice that was barely audible over the din of battle . . . except to him.

'Shiva . . .'

He stopped and turned back to see Sati, in the distance, her head raised slightly.

'Sati,' he cried, and instantly forgetting the Naga's mutilated corpse, he sped towards her, bellowing, 'Parvateshwar – get Ayurvati! Sati has fallen!'

Ayurvati had already seen Sati fall and was running towards her, and Parvateshwar, hearing Shiva's call, did the same, even as the Chandravanshis retreated in haste.

Shiva reached her first. She was alive, but breathing heavily, for the arrow had pierced her left lung. Blood gushed from her mouth as she bled internally, but her face had a strange smile, almost serene, as she stared at Shiva.

Shiva desperately wanted to hold her, but he kept his hands locked together for fear of hurting her more and tried frantically to control his tears.

'O Lord Brahma,' cried Ayurvati as she reached Sati and recognised the arrow. 'Mastrak, Dhruvini – get a stretcher! Now!'

Shiva followed close behind as Parvateshwar, Ayurvati, Mastrak and Dhruvini carried Sati to one of the village houses, where Ayurvati's other assistants had already begun cleaning the hut and setting out the instruments for surgery.

'Wait outside, my Lord,' said Ayurvati to Shiva, raising her hand to stop him as he tried to enter the room.

Parvateshwar held him back with a firm but gentle hand on his shoulder. 'Ayurvati's one of the best doctors in the world, Shiva. Let her use her skills,' he said quietly.

Shiva turned to look at Parvateshwar. The general was doing an admirable job of controlling his emotions, but one look told Shiva that Parvateshwar was as afraid for Sati as he was – maybe even more than he'd been before her *Agnipariksha*.

A sudden thought hit Shiva. He turned and hurried to the closest Naga body and checked the right wrist. Finding nothing there, he made for the other dead Nagas.

Parvateshwar rallied himself enough to recognise there were important tasks that needed to be done. He called Vraka and ordered, 'Place guards over the prisoners of war. Get doctors to attend to all the injured, including the Chandravanshis.'

'The injured Chandravanshis have already taken their poison, sir,' said Vraka. 'You know they never want to be taken alive.'

Parvateshwar gave Vraka a withering look, clearly indicating that he had no interest in petty details and the brigadier should just get to the task at hand.

'Yes, my Lord,' said the officer, acknowledging Parvateshwar's unspoken order.

'Arrange a perimeter in case of further attack,' the general continued, wanting to return his attention to Sati, in the house behind him. 'And . . .'

Vraka looked up at Parvateshwar, surprised; he had never seen his general hesitate before. He waited silently for Parvateshwar to complete his order.

After a moment, Parvateshwar said softly, 'If there are any courier-pigeons still alive, send a letter to Devagiri – to the emperor. On red paper. Tell him . . . tell him Princess Sati is seriously injured.'

Vraka looked up in disbelief – this was the first he'd heard about Sati's injury. But once again he said nothing.

'Tell the emperor,' continued Parvateshwar, 'that the princess has been shot by an *agnibaan*.'

'O Lord Indra,' blurted Vraka, unable to control his shocked dismay.

'Do it now, Brigadier,' snarled Parvateshwar.

'Yes, my Lord,' Vraka said, pulling himself together. He saluted weakly before heading off to carry out his duties.

Shiva had checked four of the Nagas, but none of them wore the leather bracelet with the serpent Aum that he had seen before. He came to the last one, the one who had shot Sati – the one he had hacked to pieces – and kicked the Naga's torso with intense hatred. Then he hunted around for the severed limb and lifted it to check the wrist. No leather bracelet. It wasn't him.

When he returned to the hut he found Parvateshwar seated on a stool outside. Krittika was standing beside him, sobbing uncontrollably, and Veerbhadra was holding her gently, comforting her. Nandi, looking distraught, stood at Veerbhadra's side. Parvateshwar looked up at Shiva and pointed to the empty stool next to him with a weak smile. He was making a brave attempt to appear in control of his emotions. Shiva sat down slowly and looked into the distance while they all waited for Ayurvati to come out.

— ⁂ —

'We've removed the arrow, my Lord,' said Ayurvati as Shiva and Parvateshwar stood looking at the unconscious princess. Nobody else had been allowed in; Ayurvati had made it clear that Sati didn't need the increased risk of infection, and nobody dared argue with the formidable Ayurvati on medical matters. Mastrak and Dhruvini had already left, ordered to support the other medics treating the injured Suryavanshi soldiers.

Beside the bed, Shiva could see the bloodied instrument that had been used to pull out the arrow. Those tongs would never be used again; they were contaminated with the *agni-baan* poison. Ayurvati had said there were no chemicals, and no amount of heat that could make the instruments sterile and safe again.

Next to the tongs lay the offending arrow, wrapped in neem leaves. It would stay there for one full day before being buried deep in a dry grave, to ensure it wouldn't cause any more harm.

Shiva looked pleadingly at Ayurvati, unable to find the strength to ask the question that raged in his heart.

'I won't lie to you, my Lord,' the doctor said, in the detached manner medics used to give themselves the strength to deal with traumatic circumstances like these. 'It doesn't look good. Nobody has ever survived an *agnibaan* that's penetrated one of the vital organs. In a while the poison will cause an intense fever, and that will result in the failing of one organ after another.'

Shiva looked down at Sati and then pleadingly at the doctor, who was fighting hard to rein in her tears and keep her composure. She couldn't afford to lose control. She had many lives to save in the next few hours.

'I'm sorry, my Lord,' she said once she was sure she wasn't going to break down and sob, 'but there's no known cure. We can only give her something to make her end easier.'

Shiva glared at her angrily. 'We are not giving up. Is that clear?'

Ayurvati looked at the ground, unable to meet Shiva's gaze.

'If the fever is kept under control, then her organs won't be damaged, is that right?' Shiva asked suddenly as an idea occurred to him. A glimmer of hope lit his eyes.

Ayurvati looked at him. 'Yes – but the fever caused by an *agnibaan* can only be delayed, not broken. If we try to control the fever, it'll come back even stronger once the medicines are stopped.'

'Then we'll control the fever for ever,' Shiva said fiercely. 'I'll sit by her side for the rest of my life, if necessary. The fever will not rise.'

Ayurvati opened her mouth, then thought better of it and kept silent. She'd give him a few hours. She knew Sati could not be saved; it was impossible. Precious time was being wasted in this futile discussion — time that could be used to save other lives.

'All right, my Lord,' she said, quickly administering drugs that would keep Sati's fever down. 'This should make her comfortable for a few hours.'

She glanced quickly at Parvateshwar, who was standing at the back of the hut. He knew reducing the fever would only lengthen Sati's agony, but she could see that he had also felt that same glimmer of hope.

Turning back to Shiva, Ayurvati said, 'My Lord, you're also injured — let me dress your wounds, and then I'll leave you in peace with Sati.'

'I'm fine,' he said, not taking his eyes off Sati for an instant.

'No, you're not,' she said firmly. 'Your wounds are deep, and if they become infected, they could be life-threatening.'

Shiva waved his hand dismissively, his eyes never leaving Sati.

'Shiva!'

Ayurvati's unexpected shout finally got his attention.

'You cannot help Sati if you yourself become sick!'

Her harsh tone had the desired effect, and Shiva let the doctor dress his wounds, then tend to Parvateshwar before she left the hut.

Shiva glanced at the hut's *prahar* lamp. It had been three hours since Ayurvati had removed the arrow.

Parvateshwar had left the hut a while earlier to check on his injured men and get the camp set up. Given the number of injured men, the convoy would be remaining in Koonj for some time. That was Parvateshwar's way, Shiva realised: when confronted with an ugly situation he could do nothing about, he refused to wallow in his misery but instead drowned himself in his work as a way to avoid dwelling on the crisis.

Shiva was the exact opposite. He had sworn, many years ago, that he would never run from a difficult situation, even if there was absolutely nothing he could do, and so he had not left Sati's side, even for a moment. He sat patiently by her bed, waiting – praying – for her to recover.

'Shiva . . .' A barely audible whisper broke the silence.

Sati's eyes were slightly open, and one hand had moved slightly, almost indiscernibly.

He pulled his chair closer, careful not to touch her. 'I'm so sorry,' he whispered. 'I should never have got us into this fight.'

'No, no,' murmured Sati, 'you did the right thing – someone had to make a stand. You've come to Meluha to lead us, to destroy evil – you did your duty.'

Shiva stared at Sati, overcome by grief, as she opened her eyes a little wider, trying to take in as much of Shiva as she could in what she knew were to be her last moments. The irony of death was not lost on her: that the ultimate destroyer of a soul's aspirations also gave that soul the courage to challenge every constraint, to express even the most long-denied dream.

'It's my time to go, Shiva,' whispered Sati, 'but before I leave you, I wanted you to know that the last few months have been the happiest of my life.'

Shiva's tear-filled eyes never left Sati's. His hands developed a life of their own and moved towards her, but he checked himself in time and didn't touch her; he knew that Sati wouldn't like the *vikarma* law to be broken, no matter what the circumstances.

'I wish you'd come into my life sooner,' said Sati, revealing a secret she hadn't even acknowledged to herself. 'My life would have been so different.'

Shiva fought against the despair that welled up inside him at her words.

'I wish I had told you my true feelings earlier,' she murmured. 'Because the first time I tell you this will also probably be the last.'

Shiva gazed at her, grief choking his voice in his throat, as she looked deeply into his eyes and whispered softly, 'I love you.'

The dam finally broke and tears of utter grief poured down Shiva's face. 'You're going to repeat those words for at least another hundred years,' he sobbed. 'You're not going anywhere – I'll fight the god of death himself if I have to. You're not going *anywhere*.'

Sati smiled sadly and put her hand in Shiva's. Her flesh was on fire. The fever had begun its final assault on her body.

CHAPTER 18

Sati and the Fire Arrow

'Nothing can be done, my Lord,' said Ayurvati, who looked visibly uncomfortable. She, Shiva and Parvateshwar were standing in a corner of the hut, trying to be out of range of Sati's hearing.

'Come on, Ayurvati,' urged Shiva. 'You're the best doctor in the land. All we have to do is break the fever—'

'This fever cannot be broken,' she repeated for what felt the hundredth time. 'There is no cure for the *agnibaan* poison; all we are doing is lengthening Sati's agony by keeping the fever low. The moment the medicines are stopped, the fever will come back with a vengeance.'

'Let me go, Shiva,' mumbled a frail voice and everyone turned to stare at Sati. Her face bore the smile that came only with the acceptance of the inevitable. 'I have no regrets. I've told you what I needed to and I'm content. My time has come.'

'Don't give up on me, Sati,' Shiva cried. 'You're not gone yet – we'll find a way – *I'll* find a way. Just hold on for me, please.'

Sati gave up; she didn't have the strength to argue. And she also knew Shiva would have to make his own peace with her death – and he never would unless he felt he'd tried everything possible to save her.

'I can feel the fever rising,' she said. 'Please, give me the medicines.'

Ayurvati glanced at her, clearly uncomfortable with the request. All her medical training told her that she shouldn't do this; the medicines would only prolong Sati's suffering.

But Sati stared hard at Ayurvati. She couldn't give up now, not when Shiva had asked her to hang on.

'Give me the medicines, Ayurvatiji,' she repeated. 'I know what I'm doing.'

Sighing, Ayurvati did as Sati asked. She gazed into her patient's eyes, expecting to find some trace of fear or anguish, but there was none, and she smiled gently and returned to Shiva and Parvateshwar.

'I know,' exclaimed Shiva 'why don't we give her the *Somras*?'

'What effect do you think that will have, my Lord?' Ayurvati sounded surprised. 'The *Somras* only increases a person's lifespan – it has no effect on injuries.'

'I don't think anyone truly understands everything about the *Somras*, Ayurvati – not even you. I didn't get the chance to tell you that the *Somras* repaired the frostbitten toe I had lived with all my life – and it also repaired my dislocated shoulder.'

Parvateshwar's eyes widened in surprise and he exclaimed, 'That's impossible! The *Somras* doesn't cure physical disabilities—'

'It cured mine.'

'But that could also be because you're special,' said Ayurvati gently. 'You're the Neelkanth, after all.'

'I didn't drop from the sky, Ayurvati – my body is as human as Sati's, as human as yours. Let's just try it!'

Parvateshwar didn't need any more convincing. He dashed out to find Vraka, who was sitting on a stool by the door. The brigadier immediately rose and saluted hiscommander.

'Vraka,' said Parvateshwar, 'there might still be some *Somras* powder hidden in the temple – well, what's left of the temple. It was the main production centre of this area. I need that powder – *now!*'

'You'll have it, my Lord,' boomed Vraka as he rushed off with his guards.

— ⁂ ◍ � ⌖ ⊕ —

'There's nothing else we can do but wait,' said Ayurvati as Sati fell asleep. The *Somras* had been administered, a stronger dose than usual. 'Parvateshwar, you're wounded and exhausted – please, get some sleep.'

'I don't need sleep,' the general said stubbornly. 'I'm staying on guard with my soldiers at the perimeter. You can't trust those Chandravanshis – they may launch a counter-attack at night.'

Frustrated, Ayurvati glared at him. The Kshatriyas' machismo made them impossible patients. Then she turned to Shiva. 'Are you going to bed, my Lord?' asked Ayurvati, hoping that he at least would listen. 'There's nothing more you can do now. We just have to wait – and you need the rest.'

Shiva just shook his head. Wild horses couldn't drag him away from Sati.

'At least let us bring you a bed,' she suggested, 'and you can sleep here, and keep an eye on Sati.'

'Thank you, but I'm not going to sleep,' said Shiva, glancing briefly at Ayurvati before returning his gaze to Sati. 'I'm staying here. You get some rest – I'll call you if there's any change.'

Ayurvati glared at him, and then whispered, 'As you wish, my Lord.'

As the doctor walked towards her own hut, a wave of exhaustion washed over her. She needed to rest, for the next day she would be busy checking all the injured. The first twenty-four hours were crucial to any recovery and her medical corps had been split into groups to keep a staggered all-night vigil in case of emergencies.

'I'll be with my men, Shiva,' Parvateshwar announced after a few minutes. 'Nandi and Veerbhadra are on duty outside, along with some of my personal guards.'

Shiva knew what Parvateshwar really wanted to say. 'I'll

call you the moment there's any change,' he said, looking up sympathetically at the general, who smiled weakly, then rushed out before his feelings overwhelmed and embarrassed him.

— ☀ ◉ ∪ ✝ ⊕ —

Parvateshwar sat silently in the darkness, his soldiers at a respectful distance. They could tell when their commander wanted to be left alone. The general was lost in thoughts of Sati. Why would the Almighty put someone like her through so much suffering? He remembered her childhood, and the day he decided that here was a girl he'd be proud to have as his goddaughter.

That fateful day was the first and only time he had ever regretted his vow not to have any progeny of his own. What foolish man wouldn't want a child like Sati?

It had been a lazy afternoon more than a hundred years ago, and Sati had just returned from the Maika national school at the tender age of sixteen, full of energy and a passionate belief in Lord Ram's teachings. Her grandfather, Emperor Brahmanayak, still reigned over the land of Meluha, and her father, then Prince Daksha, was content being a family man, spending his days with his wife and daughter. He was showing neither the inclination to master the warrior ways of the Kshatriya nor the slightest ambition to succeed his father.

On that day, Daksha had settled down for a family picnic on the bank of the River Saraswati, a short distance from Devagiri. Parvateshwar had been the prince's bodyguard back then, and he was sitting close enough to protect him but far enough away to give the family some privacy. Sati had wandered off to explore the edge of the forest, but she stayed close to the riverbank, so she was always visible.

Suddenly the girl's cry ripped through the silence, and Daksha, Veerini and Parvateshwar rushed to the water's edge, where they saw Sati at a distance, battling a ferocious pack of wild dogs which was large enough to bring down even a charging lion. The princess was fighting to protect a severely injured woman, marked out by her fair skin as a recent immigrant.

Drawing his sword, Daksha charged along the bank to save his daughter, closely followed by Parvateshwar, and within moments, they had leapt into the fray. Parvateshwar charged forward aggressively, striking out all about him, and Sati, rejuvenated by the sudden support, turned the attack back against the four dogs menacing her.

But Daksha, despite fighting with all the passion of a parent's protective spirit, was the weakest of them, and the animals recognised that.

Before Daksha realised quite what was happening, six of the feral dogs charged at him at the same time. He thrust his sword at the dog right in front of him, felling the animal, but that proved to be a costly mistake for his sword got stuck between the dead animal's ribs.

That gave the rest of the pack the opening they needed. One charged viciously from the side and seized Daksha's right forearm in its jaws. Daksha roared in pain, but he held fast to his sword, even as he tried to wrestle his arm free. Another dog bit Daksha's left leg, tearing a chunk of flesh free.

Seeing his prince in trouble, Parvateshwar yelled in fury and swung hard at the dog clinging to Daksha's arm, cutting deep into the beast's back, then he pirouetted and slashed at the animal charging Daksha from the front.

Sati moved in to protect her father's left flank as Daksha finally managed to extract his sword and angrily stabbed the dog clinging to his leg. Seeing their numbers rapidly depleting, the remaining dogs retreated, growling and yelping.

'Daksha,' sobbed Veerini as she rushed to her husband, who was losing blood at an alarming rate from his numerous wounds, especially the ragged gash in his leg – the dog must have bitten through a major artery. Parvateshwar quickly blew his conch-shell to alert the scouts at the closest crossing-house; with any luck soldiers and medical staff would get there within a few minutes.

Parvateshwar whipped off his *angvastram* and bound it tightly around Daksha's thigh, to stem the bleeding. Then he quickly checked out the injured foreign woman.

'Father, are you all right?' whispered Sati as she held his hand.

'Dammit, Sati,' her father shouted. 'What do you think you were doing?'

This furious response from her doting father shocked and silenced Sati, and she dropped her gaze in shame.

'Who asked you to be a hero?' he went on, fuming at his

daughter. 'What if something had happened to you – what would I do? Where would I go? And for whom were you risking your life? What difference does that immigrant woman's life make in comparison to yours?'

Sati continued to look down, distraught at the scolding when she'd been expecting praise.

The crossing-house soldiers and doctors arrived at that moment and efficiently dressed Daksha's wounds. After seeing to Parvateshwar and Sati's far more minor injuries, they placed Daksha on a stretcher and bore him off to see the royal physician. Another group of soldiers placed the immigrant woman on another stretcher to carry her to a public doctor in Devagiri.

Sati stayed rooted to the spot as she watched her father being carried away, followed by her mother. She felt dreadfully guilty about the harm her actions had caused – she'd only been trying to save a woman in distress. Wasn't that one of Lord Ram's primary teachings, that it was the duty of the strong to protect the weak?

She felt a soft touch on her shoulder, and steeling herself for another scolding, she turned to face Captain Parvateshwar, her father's stern bodyguard. To her surprise, though, his face sported a rare smile.

'I am proud of you, my child,' whispered Parvateshwar. 'You are a true follower of Lord Ram.'

Tears suddenly welled and Sati quickly looked away until she could control herself, then she looked up with a wan smile at the man she would grow to call *Pitratulya*, like a father to her.

Jolted back into the present by a bird call, Parvateshwar scanned the perimeter, his eyes moist at the ancient memory. He clasped his hands in a prayer and whispered, 'She's your true follower, Lord Ram. Fight for her, I beg you.'

Shiva had lost track of time – resetting the *prahar* lamps was a low priority when so many lives were still in danger – but looking out of the window, he could see the early signs of dawn. His wounds burned, but he refused to give in to them. Instead, he sat quietly on his chair next to Sati's bed, restraining himself from making any noise that would disturb her. She held his hand tightly in hers, and despite the searing heat radiating from her feverish body, Shiva didn't move his sweating hand away.

He looked longingly at Sati and softly whispered, 'Either you stay here, or I leave this world with you. The choice is yours.'

Feeling a slight twitch, he looked down to see Sati's hand move slightly, allowing the sweat to drip from between their clasped palms.

Her sweat or mine? Shiva wondered idly. It was impossible to say. He touched her forehead gently with his other hand. Her flesh was burning even more strongly. But there were soft beads of perspiration on her temples, and a burst of elation shot through Shiva's being.

'By the great Lord Brahma,' whispered Ayurvati in awe, looking down at Sati. 'I've never seen anything like this.'

The princess was still sleeping, but she was now sweating profusely. Her garments and sheets were soaked through. Parvateshwar was standing by Ayurvati's side, his face aglow with hope.

'The *agnibaan* fever *never* breaks.' Ayurvati sounded stunned. 'This is a miracle.'

Shiva looked up, his face flushed with the ecstasy of a soul that had salvaged its reason for existence. 'May the Holy Lake bless the *Somras*.'

Parvateshwar noticed Sati's hand clutched tightly in Shiva's, but he made no comment. The bliss of this moment had finally crowded out his instinctive desire to stop something deemed unacceptable by the laws of the land.

'My Lord,' said Ayurvati softly, 'the sweat must be removed since it is toxic, but her wounds must be kept dry. So she cannot bathe. My nurses will have to rub her down.'

Shiva looked up at Ayurvati and nodded, not understanding the implication.

'Um, my Lord?' And when he still didn't move, she said patiently, 'That means you'll have to leave the room.'

'Oh,' said an abashed Shiva, 'of course.'

As he got up to leave, the doctor said gently, 'My Lord, your hands need to be washed as well.'

Shiva looked down at the commingled sweat dripping from his palm. 'I'll do so immediately.'

'This is a miracle, Sati,' said Ayurvati, beaming from ear to ear. 'Nobody has ever recovered from an *agnibaan* fever! I'll be honest – I'd given up hope. But the Lord's faith has kept you alive.'

Sati had been cleaned – she still couldn't be bathed because of her deep wounds – and dressed in freshly washed clothes, and now she was lying on a new bed made up with sterilised linen. All traces of the toxic sweat triggered by the *Somras* had been removed. Like everyone else in the room, she too was smiling.

'Oh no,' said Shiva self-consciously, 'I did nothing – it was Sati's fighting spirit that saved her.'

'No, Shiva – it was you, not me,' said Sati, holding his hand without the least hint of tentativeness. 'You've saved me on so many levels. I don't know how I can even begin to repay you.'

'By never saying again that you have to repay me.'

Sati smiled even more broadly and gripped Shiva's hand even tighter. Parvateshwar looked on gloomily, unhappy in spite of himself at their open display of affection.

'All right,' said Ayurvati, clapping her hands decisively, 'much as I would like to sit here and chit-chat with you, I have work to do.'

'What work?' asked Shiva playfully. 'You're a brilliant doctor with an exceptional team. I know that every single injured person has been saved. Surely there's nothing more for you to do?'

'Oh, but there is, my Lord,' said Ayurvati with a smile. 'I have to write up my report on how the *Somras* cured an *agnibaan* wound; I need to present it to the medical council as soon as I return to Devagiri. This is big news – we must start researching the curative properties of the *Somras* – there's a lot of work to do!'

Shiva smiled fondly at Ayurvati.

Sati whispered, 'Thank you, Ayurvatiji. Like thousands of others, I too owe my life to you.'

'You owe me nothing, Sati. I only did my duty.' Ayurvati bowed with a formal namaste and left the room.

'Well, even I should leave . . .' mumbled Parvateshwar awkwardly, as he walked out.

He was surprised to find Ayurvati waiting for him outside. She was standing some distance from the guards, and clearly did not want them to overhear whatever she had to say.

'What is it, Ayurvati?' he asked quietly when he reached her.

'I know what's bothering you, Parvateshwar,' she said.

'Then how can you just stand by and watch while the *vikarma* law is broken? I don't think it's right. I know this isn't the time to say anything, but I'll raise the issue at the first appropriate opportunity.'

'No, you shouldn't.'

'How can you say that?' he asked, shocked. 'You come from a rare family that didn't have a single renegade Brahmin during the rebellion. Lord Ram insisted that the laws must be followed strictly, and demonstrated repeatedly that even he wasn't above the law. Shiva's a good man, I won't deny that, but even he can't be above the law. Our laws must apply to every citizen or our society will collapse. You above all should know this.'

'I know only one thing,' she said looking determined, 'and it's this: if the Neelkanth feels it's right, then it *is* right.'

Parvateshwar stared at Ayurvati as if he didn't recognise her. What had happened to the woman he knew and admired, the woman who followed the laws of the land to a T? Parvateshwar had begun to respect Shiva, but that respect had not turned into unquestioning faith; he still did not believe Shiva was the one who would complete Lord Ram's work. In Parvateshwar's eyes, no one but Lord Ram deserved absolute obedience.

'In any case,' said Ayurvati, 'I have to take my leave of you. I have a theory to think about.'

— ⋏ ◍Ʊ⋔◈ —

'Really?' asked Shiva. 'So in Meluha, the emperor's first-born son doesn't automatically succeed him.'

'Correct,' replied Sati, smiling. She shifted slightly to relieve the soreness in her back, all the while keeping Shiva's hand firmly clasped in her own. He leaned forward and pushed back a strand of hair that had slipped onto her face as she continued, 'Until around two hundred and fifty years ago, the king's children weren't his birth-children, remember, but drawn from the Maika system, so there was no way to determine the king's first-born – we could only ever know his first-adopted.'

The pair had spent many hours over the previous week talking about matters important and mundane. Although Sati was recovering quickly, she was still bedridden. Shiva and Parvateshwar had decided to cancel the planned trip to Lothal and return to Devagiri instead; the convoy would remain at Koonj until all the injured were ready to travel.

In the meantime, this was the perfect time for him to find out all he could about Meluha, and Sati was delighted to be able to teach him.

'But not even the first-*adopted* child would necessarily succeed,' she explained. 'This was another of the laws Lord Ram instituted for stability and peace. There used to be many royal families, each with their own small kingdoms—'

'—and their kings,' Shiva interjected, paying as much attention to the hypnotising dimples in Sati's cheeks when she spoke as to her words, 'These kings would probably be at war all the time, just so that one of them could be overlord for however short a period.'

'Exactly.' She shook her head sadly at such a foolish concept.

'It's the same everywhere,' said Shiva, remembering the never-ending power struggles in his part of the world.

'Battles for supremacy led to many unnecessary and futile wars,' Sati continued, 'and the only ones who suffered were the common people. Lord Ram felt it was ridiculous for the kings' egos to be fed by their people's suffering, so he created the *Rajya Sabha* – a ruling council – consisting of Brahmins and Kshatriyas of a specific rank. Whenever an emperor died or took *sanyas* to meditate in the wilderness, renouncing all worldly ambition, the council would meet and elect a new emperor from amongst the Kshatriyas of the rank of brigadier or above. The council's decision was final; it could not be contested.'

'I'll say it again,' said Shiva with a broad smile, 'Lord Ram was a genius.'

'Indeed he was,' agreed Sati enthusiastically. '*Jai Shri Ram.*'

'*Jai Shri Ram,*' echoed Shiva. 'So, how did your father become emperor after Emperor Brahmanayak? Your father was his first-born son, wasn't he?'

'Yes, but he was still elected, just like every other Meluhan emperor – it was actually the first time in Meluhan history that a ruling emperor's son was elected,' she said proudly.

'Perhaps your grandfather helped him get elected?'

'I couldn't say – I know my grandfather would have liked my father to become emperor after him, but I also know that he was a great man who followed the laws of Meluha; he would not have helped openly. But I know who did: Lord Bhrigu, a great sage respected across the land, gave him a great deal of aid during the election.'

Shiva smiled at her tenderly as he caressed her soft cheek, and Sati closed her eyes, luxuriating in the sensation. He ran his fingertips down to rest on her hand again and squeezed it softly.

He was about to ask more about Lord Bhrigu when the door suddenly swung open and Daksha himself stormed in, looking utterly exhausted, followed closely by Veerini and Prime Minister Kanakhala.

Shiva swiftly withdrew his hand, hoping Daksha hadn't seen where it was resting, but Daksha noticed the movement.

'Father,' cried Sati as Daksha knelt beside her bed and Veerini, tears in her eyes, dropped to her knees beside him and lovingly caressed her daughter's face.

Kanakhala remained at the door, giving the royal family space for their private moment. She greeted Shiva with a formal namaste, which he returned with a beaming smile. Now he could see Parvateshwar and Ayurvati were standing behind Kanakhala, with Nandi, Veerbhadra and Krittika crowded in behind them. A discreet aide silently brought in two chairs for the emperor and his wife, placed them next to the bed and left just as quietly.

Speaking softly, Kanakhala told Shiva that they had left Devagiri the moment they heard the news of Sati's injury. Together with two thousand soldiers, they had sailed down the Saraswati to the inland delta, then ridden night and day to reach Koonj.

'I'm all right, Father,' said Sati, holding her mother's hand. 'Seriously, Mother – I'm feeling better than ever. One more week and I'll dance for you!'

Shiva smiled tenderly at her as everyone laughed weakly.

Looking at her father, Sati said, 'I'm sorry to have caused

so much trouble – I know you must have abandoned important business to rush here—'

'Trouble?' Daksha interrupted her, 'my child, you're my life – you are nothing but a source of joy for me. You can't begin to imagine how proud I am of you.'

Veerini leaned over and laid a soft kiss on Sati's forehead.

'I'm proud of all of you,' the emperor continued, looking back at Parvateshwar and Ayurvati. 'Proud that you supported the Lord in what had to be done. We actually fought off a terrorist attack – you can't imagine how much this has electrified the nation!' He continued to pat Sati's hand soothingly as he turned to Shiva and said, 'Thank you, my Lord – thank you for fighting for us. Now we know for sure that we've put our faith in the right man.'

Shiva smiled awkwardly and acknowledged Daksha's faith with a courteous namaste.

Turning to Ayurvati, Daksha asked, 'How is Sati now? I'm told she's on her way to a total recovery.'

'Yes, your Majesty,' said Ayurvati, 'she should be well enough to travel in another week, and in three weeks the only memory of the wound will be a scar.'

'You're not just the best doctor of this generation, Ayurvati,' said Daksha proudly, 'you're the best doctor of all time.'

'Oh no, your Majesty,' she cried, holding the tips of her ears to ward off any evil spirits that might be angered by this undeserved compliment. 'There are many far greater than me – and in this case, it was the Lord Neelkanth who worked the miracle, not me.' Glancing briefly at the increasingly embarrassed Shiva, Ayurvati continued, 'I thought we'd lost her – but the Lord refused to lose hope. It was his idea to give her the *Somras*.'

Daksha turned to Shiva with a grateful smile. 'I have yet another thing to thank you for, my Lord. My daughter is part of my soul. I would not be able to survive without her.'

'Oh, I didn't do anything,' said Shiva, feeling horribly self-conscious. 'It was Ayurvati who treated her—'

'That's just your humility speaking, my Lord,' said Daksha. 'You truly are a worthy Neelkanth – in fact, you're a worthy Mahadev!'

Astounded, Shiva stared at the emperor. He knew he did not deserve to be compared to Lord Rudra, the previous Mahadev, the God of Gods; his deeds did not qualify him for that. 'Thank you, your Majesty, but you speak too highly of me,' he said firmly. 'I'm no Mahadev.'

'Oh, but you *are*, my Lord,' said Kanakhala and Ayurvati almost simultaneously.

But Parvateshwar remained silent, his brows furrowed by dark thoughts.

Finally realising that Shiva was uncomfortable being called Mahadev, Daksha turned to Sati. 'What I don't understand is why you jumped in front of the Lord to take the arrow. You've never believed in the prophecy – you've never had my faith in the Neelkanth – so why did you risk your own life for him?'

Sati remained silent, her eyes downcast, feeling embarrassed and ill-at-ease. Daksha looked at Shiva, who was wearing the very same sheepish expression. Veerini was staring intently at her husband. At last, finally noticing his wife, Daksha stood up suddenly and walked around the bed towards Shiva, holding his hands in a formal namaste.

Shiva got up and returned his namaste.

'My Lord,' said Daksha, 'for perhaps the first time in her life, my daughter is tongue-tied in front of me. And over time I have come to understand you: you give to others, but never ask anything for yourself. Understanding that, I am going to make the first move here.'

Shiva continued to stare at Daksha, frowning slightly as he continued, 'I won't lie to you, my Lord: our law classifies my daughter as a *vikarma* because decades ago she gave birth to a stillborn child. It is not that serious a crime – it could even have been the result of the past-life karma of the child's father – but the law of our land blames both father and mother.'

His expression clearly showed that he thought the *vikarma* law unfair.

'It is believed that a *vikarma* is a carrier of bad fate, so if Sati marries again, she will pass on her bad fate to her husband, and possibly her future children.'

Veerini looked at her husband, her eyes inscrutable.

'I know my daughter, my Lord.' Daksha looked at Sati proudly. 'I have never seen her do anything even remotely wrong. She's a good woman and in my opinion, the law that condemns her is unfair. But I am only the emperor. I cannot change the law.'

Parvateshwar glared at Daksha, upset that he would even consider changing the law just because he did not agree with it.

'It breaks my heart that I cannot give my daughter the happy life she deserves,' he said with a sigh, 'that I can't save her from the daily humiliation she suffers. What I can do, though, is ask you for help.'

Sati looked at her father with loving eyes.

'You are the Neelkanth. More than that, I genuinely believe you're a Mahadev, even though I can see that the title makes you uncomfortable. But as such, you are above the law – *you* can change the law, if you wish.'

Aghast, Parvateshwar glowered at Daksha. How could the emperor be so dismissive of the law? Then his eyes fell on Shiva and his heart sank further.

Shiva was staring at Daksha with undisguised delight. He'd thought he would have to work hard to persuade the emperor to let him marry Sati, but now he was quite sure that the emperor was about to offer him his daughter's hand.

'If you decide to make my daughter your wife, no power on earth can stop you,' said Daksha. 'The question is: do you want to?'

All the emotions in the universe surged through Shiva's being and shone out in his ecstatic smile. He tried to speak, but the overwhelming rush of feelings choked his voice in his throat. Instead, he bent down, gently clasped Sati's hand in his own, drew it to his lips and kissed it lovingly. Then he looked up at Daksha and whispered, 'I will never let go of her. *Never.*'

Sati stared at Shiva, stunned. She had dared to love him over the last week, but she had not dared to hope – and yet now her wildest dream was coming true. She was going to be Shiva's wife . . .

Daksha hugged Shiva tightly and whispered, 'My Lord!' as Veerini started sobbing uncontrollably. The unfairness Sati had endured for most of her life was finally being set right. She looked up at Daksha, almost willing to forgive him.

Ayurvati and Kanakhala approached and offered congratulations to the emperor, the queen, Shiva and Sati; and Nandi, Krittika and Veerbhadra, still standing in the doorway, also expressed their joy.

Only Parvateshwar was silent as he stood rooted near the door, furious at such arrant disregard for Lord Ram's laws.

At long last, Shiva regained control of himself. Firmly gripping Sati's hand, he looked at Daksha. 'Your Majesty, I do have one condition.'

'Anything, my Lord.'

'The *vikarma* law—'

'It doesn't need to be changed, my Lord,' said Daksha. 'If you decide to marry my daughter, then the law cannot stop you.'

'All the same,' said Shiva, 'that law must be changed.'

'Of course, if that's your wish—' Beaming, Daksha turned to Kanakhala. 'Draw up a proclamation, to be signed by the Neelkanth: from now on any noble woman who gives birth to a stillborn child will not be classified as *vikarma*.'

'No, your Majesty,' Shiva interrupted, 'that's not what I meant. I want the entire *vikarma* law scrapped: nobody will be a *vikarma* from now on. Bad luck can strike anyone – it's ridiculous to blame their past lives for it.'

Parvateshwar looked at Shiva in surprise. Though he was against even a comma being changed in any of Lord Ram's laws, Shiva was at least remaining true to Lord Ram's fundamental principle: the same law must apply to everybody, equally and fairly, without exception.

But the emperor was shocked: he, like all Meluhans, was superstitious about the *vikarma*; his displeasure was not with the *vikarma* law itself, but with his daughter being so classified. He quickly recovered his composure, however. 'Of course, my Lord. The proclamation will state that the entire *vikarma* law has been scrapped. Once you sign it, it will become law.'

'Thank you, your Majesty.' Shiva smiled gratefully.

'My daughter's happy days are starting again.' Daksha sounded exultant. 'Kanakhala – I want a grand ceremony at Devagiri when we return, a wedding the like of which the world has never seen, the most magnificent wedding ever! Summon the best organisers in the land. I want no expense spared.' He glanced at Shiva for affirmation, but Shiva was once again entranced by Sati's joyous smile and glorious dimples.

Reluctantly tearing his eyes from his beloved, he smiled and said, 'All I want is to marry Sati. I don't care whether it's the simplest ceremony in the world or the most magnificent – as long as all of you, Brahaspati and the Gunas are present, I will be happy.'

'Excellent,' rejoiced Daksha.

CHAPTER 19

Love Realised

An air of celebration greeted the royal caravan when it arrived in Devagiri three weeks later. The Prime Minister had travelled ahead, arriving a few days before the main convoy to ensure that all the preparations were in hand for the most eagerly awaited wedding in a millennium. Her arrangements, as always, had been impeccable.

The ceremonies and celebrations had been spread over seven days, each day filled with an exuberant variety of events. All the restaurants and shops were subsidised by the state to serve their customers free of charge for the seven days of revelry, and the city had been decorated extravagantly, with colourful banners hanging from the city walls, enlivening the sober grey exteriors. The roads had been freshly tiled in sacred blue, and every building had been freshly painted at government expense, making Devagiri look like it had been finished only the previous day.

Some of the giant protective spikes had been cleared from around the platforms' entry drawbridges and in their stead, giant *rangolis*, sacred decorative floor designs, visible from miles away had been drawn to welcome everyone into the capital. Kanakhala had wanted to clear all the spikes surrounding Devagiri, but Parvateshwar had vetoed it, for security reasons.

Elite families from across the empire had been invited to attend the festivities, and governors, scientists, generals, artists, even ascetics, all trooped into Devagiri to celebrate this momentous occasion. Mesopotamia and Egypt were amongst those countries whose ambassadors had been granted permits for a rare visit to the Meluhan capital, and Jhooleshwar cannily used the opportunity to wrangle some additional foreign trade quotas. Brahaspati had come down from Mount Mandar with his retinue, leaving only a skeleton security staff of Arishtanemi soldiers behind at the *Somras*-manufacturing facility; it would be the first time that seven whole days would elapse at Mount Mandar without any experiments being conducted.

The first day, two *pujas* were offered to Lord Indra and Lord Agni, the main gods of the people of India, whose blessings were sought before any event. The wedding of the millennium could only begin with their sanction. These particular *pujas* also celebrated the gods' warrior forms – the Meluhans were celebrating not only the marriage of the Neelkanth and their princess, but also the momentous defeat of the despised terrorists at Koonj; the echoes of Koonj would reverberate deep in the heart of Swadweep. The Suryavanshi vengeance had begun!

These *pujas* were followed by the formal marriage ceremony. While the celebrations were still in full swing, Shiva excused himself and tugged Sati along with him.

'By the Holy Lake,' he exclaimed, shutting the door to their private chamber behind him, 'this is only the first day! Is every day going to be as long?'

'Like you care! You just walked out when you pleased,' Sati teased him.

'Those damn ceremonies don't mean a thing to me,' he growled, ripping off his ceremonial turban and flinging it aside. He gazed longingly at Sati as he moved slowly towards her, his eyes ardent, his breathing heavy.

'Oh, but of course,' she mocked. 'The Neelkanth gets to decide what's important and what isn't – the Neelkanth can do anything he wants.'

'Oh yes he can!' he cried as Sati laughed mischievously and ran to the other side of the bed. He dashed towards her from the opposite side, pulling his *angvastram* off in one smooth motion.

'Oh yes he can . . .'

— ⟁⟁⟁⟁⟁ —

'Remember what I told you to say,' whispered Nandi to Veerbhadra. 'Don't worry – the Lord will give his permission.'

'What—?' whispered Shiva groggily as Sati gently roused him.

'Wake up,' she whispered tenderly as her hair fell over his face, teasing his cheeks. 'Careful now,' she murmured as Shiva looked at her longingly. 'Nandi, Krittika and Veerbhadra are waiting at the door. They have something important to tell you.'

Shiva pulled on a robe, walked to the door and glared at the trio. 'What is it, Nandi?' he growled. 'Isn't there someone beautiful in your life you'd rather be bothering at this hour instead of troubling me?'

'There's nobody like you, my Lord,' said Nandi, with a low bow and a chaste namaste.

'Nandi, if you keep this nonsense up you'll remain a bachelor all your life.'

Only Krittika, anxious about the task in hand, did not join in the laughter.

'All right, get on with it,' said Shiva. 'What's so important that you have to talk to me about it right now?'

Nandi nudged Veerbhadra roughly and Shiva turned a quizzical expression on his best friend.

'Bhadra, since when do you need the support of so many people to speak to me?' asked Shiva.

'Shiva—' he started nervously.

'Yes?'

'It's like this—'

'Like what?'

'Well, you see—'

'I can see you just fine, Bhadra.'

'Shiva, please don't make him more nervous than he already is,' chided Sati. 'Veerbhadra, speak fearlessly. You haven't done anything wrong.'

'Shiva,' whispered Veerbhadra timidly, his cheeks the colour of beetroot, 'I need your permission—'

'Permission granted,' said Shiva, thoroughly amused now and barely suppressing a grin. 'Whatever it is you want it for.'

'Actually, I'm considering getting married—'

'A capital idea,' said Shiva, 'so now all you have to do is convince some blind woman to have you!'

'Shiva,' Sati said, a warning tone in her voice.

'Actually, I've already found a woman,' said Veerbhadra before his courage could desert him, 'and she's not blind—'

'Not blind?' exclaimed Shiva, arching his eyebrows in mock disbelief. 'Then she's stupid enough to tie herself for the next seven births to a man who wants someone else to choose his bride for him?'

Veerbhadra gazed at Shiva with an odd mixture of embarrassment, contrition and incomprehension.

'I've told you before, Bhadra,' said Shiva, 'our tribe has many customs I don't like, chief amongst them the one that says the leader has to approve the bride of any tribesman. Don't you remember how we made fun of that ridiculous tradition as children?'

Veerbhadra looked at his feet, still unsure.

'For God's sake, man' – now he was sounding exasperated

– 'if you're happy with her, then I'm happy for you. You have my permission.'

Veerbhadra looked up, his expression a bizarre mix of surprise and ecstasy.

Krittika released a long-held breath with relief, then turned to Sati and silently mouthed, *Thank you*.

Shiva walked to Krittika and hugged her warmly. She stiffened for an instant, startled, before the Neelkanth's warmth conquered her cool Suryavanshi reserve and she returned the embrace.

'Welcome to the tribe,' whispered Shiva. 'We're quite mad, but good people at heart!'

'But how did you know?' said Veerbhadra. 'I never told you I loved her—'

'I'm not blind, Bhadra,' said Shiva, smiling at his old friend.

'Thank you, Lord Neelkanth,' said Krittika. 'Thank you for accepting me.'

Shiva stepped back and replied, 'No – thank *you*. Truthfully, I've always been concerned about Bhadra. He's a good, dependable man, but far too simple-minded when it comes to women. I was worried about how married life would treat him, but there's no reason for me to worry any more.'

'I must tell you something in return,' said Krittika. 'I never believed in the prophecy of the Neelkanth, but if you can save Meluha the way you've saved my lady, then you're worthy even of the title Mahadev!'

'I don't want to be called the Mahadev, Krittika. You know

I love Meluha as much as I love Sati, and I'll do everything I possibly can for this country.'

Turning towards Veerbhadra, Shiva ordered, 'Come here, you stupid oaf!'

Veerbhadra shuffled forward, embraced Shiva affectionately and whispered fervently, 'Thank you.'

'Don't be stupid,' said Shiva with a grin. 'There's no need to thank me.'

Veerbhadra smiled broadly.

'Just remember this,' snarled Shiva, his voice suddenly rough with mock-anger, 'you're going to have to explain to your best friend over the next chillum we share *exactly* how you dared to love a woman for so long without ever mentioning her to me!'

'Will a good batch of marijuana make up for my transgression?' asked Veerbhadra, his lips quirking in a smile.

Shiva grinned. 'I'll think about it!'

— ♈ ◑◐Ʊ⚥ ◉ —

'Doesn't she look tired?' Ayurvati studied Sati with her physician's eye.

Sati and her mother had been excused from this particular *puja*, which was for the bridegroom and father-in-law only.

'I'm not surprised – this is the sixth day of almost continuous celebrations and *pujas*,' Kanakhala observed. 'I know it's the custom for a royal wedding, but it must be exhausting.'

'Oh, I wouldn't say her condition has anything to do with the six *days* of *pujas*,' said Brahaspati with a mischievous grin.

'No?'

'No.' Brahaspati's smile grew even wider. 'I think it has to do with the five *nights*.'

'What do you—?' Then she blushed a deep red as the meaning of his words dawned on her.

Parvateshwar, sitting next to Kanakhala, glared at Brahaspati for the highly improper remark, but the chief scientist ignored him, his guffaw a loud counterpoint to the ladies' quiet giggles. An assistant pandit turned around in irritation, but seeing the seniority of the Brahmins sitting behind him, he immediately swallowed his annoyance and returned to his preparations.

Parvateshwar had no such compunctions. 'I can't believe the kind of conversation I'm being forced to endure!' he grumbled. He rose and walked huffily to the back of the congregation, which further amused Kanakhala and Ayurvati.

Then one of the senior pandits turned to signal that the ceremony was about to begin, and immediately they all fell silent.

The pandits resumed their invocations of the *shlokas*, the sacred verses, while Shiva and Daksha poured ceremonial ghee into the holy fire at regular intervals, all the while intoning, '*Swaha*.' In the pause between each *swaha* and the next, Shiva and Daksha talked softly about Sati; an objective observer would have found it difficult to decide who loved the princess more.

A little ghee spilled onto Daksha's hands, and as Shiva handed him a napkin to wipe it off, he noticed the chosen-tribe amulet on the emperor's arm. He stopped still, stunned, when he saw the animal represented there, but he didn't comment.

Daksha noticed Shiva's gaze. 'It was my father's choice, not mine,' he said with a warm smile, wiping the ghee off his hands. There was no embarrassment in his voice, and maybe just a hint of defiance in his eyes.

'I'm sorry, your Majesty,' said Shiva, a little embarrassed. 'I didn't mean to look – please accept my apologies.'

'Why should you apologise, my Lord?' asked Daksha. 'It's my chosen-tribe – I wear the symbol on my arm so that everyone can see it and classify me.'

'But you're much beyond your chosen-tribe – you're a far greater man than what that amulet suggests.'

'Indeed,' said Daksha, smiling. 'I really showed the old man, didn't I? The Neelkanth didn't choose to appear during his reign; he came in mine. The terrorists were not defeated during his reign – they were defeated in mine. And the Chandravanshis were not reformed during his reign. They will be reformed in mine.'

Shiva smiled cautiously; something about the conversation troubled him. He looked again at the amulet on Daksha's arm, which represented a humble goat, one of the lowest chosen-tribes amongst the Kshatriyas – in fact, some people considered the goat chosen-tribe to be so low that its wearer couldn't even be called a full Kshatriya.

Shiva was pondering these thoughts when he got the verbal cue from the pandit. Scooping some more ghee, he poured it into the sacred fire and chanted, '*Swaha!*'

At nightfall, in the privacy of their chambers, Shiva considered asking Sati about the relationship between Emperor Brahmanayak and his son, Daksha. His instincts told him that he would have to phrase his questions carefully.

'I've heard that Lord Brahmanayak was a truly great man. Your father must have learnt a lot from him?'

Sati stopped playing with Shiva's flowing locks. She took a deep breath. 'I don't know about that. Father and grandfather were very different characters. But Lord Bhrigu—'

The conversation was interrupted by a knocking at the door, and Taman, the doorkeeper, announced nervously, 'My Lord, Chief Scientist Brahaspatiji has requested an audience with you – he insists that he must meet with you tonight.'

Shiva was always happy to see Brahaspati, but before answering the doorkeeper, he looked at Sati. She smiled and nodded; she knew how important his relationship with Brahaspati was.

'Let him in, Taman,' he said, and got up to welcome his friend.

'My apologies for disturbing you so late,' Brahaspati started, but Shiva waved his apology away.

'You never need to apologise to me, my friend.'

'Namaste, Brahaspatiji,' said Sati, bending to touch the chief scientist's feet.

'*Akhand saubhagyavati bhav*,' said Brahaspati, blessing Sati with the traditional invocation: *May her husband always be alive and by her side.*

'So,' said Shiva, 'what's so important that you had to pull yourself out of bed so late at night?'

'Actually, I didn't get the chance to speak to you earlier.'

'I know,' said Shiva, smiling at Sati. 'Our days have been filled with one ceremony after another.'

'We Suryavanshis do so love our ceremonies,' he said sympathetically, 'but I have to leave for Mount Mandar tomorrow morning, and I really needed to speak to you before I go.'

'You're leaving now?' Shiva was surprised. 'You've survived six days of this — surely you can survive one more?'

'I'd love to stay, but there's an experiment that had already been scheduled – the preparations have been going on for months, and the Mesopotamian material required for it has already been prepared. We're going to test the stability of the *Somras* with lesser quantities of water and I need to be there to make sure the experiment starts correctly. Some of my other scientists will remain here to keep you company.'

'Right,' said Shiva sarcastically, 'because I do so enjoy their constant theorising about everything under the sun.'

Brahaspati laughed. 'I really do have to go, Shiva. I'm sorry.'

'No need to apologise, my friend,' said Shiva, smiling. 'Life is long and the road to Mount Mandar short. You're not going to get rid of me that easily.'

He stepped forward and hugged Shiva tightly, his eyes full of love for the man he'd come to consider his brother. Shiva was a little surprised – it was usually he who moved to embrace Brahaspati first, and the scientist tended to respond somewhat tentatively.

'My brother,' whispered Brahaspati.

'Ditto,' mumbled Shiva.

Stepping back slightly but still holding Shiva's arms, Brahaspati said, 'I'd go anywhere for you – even into *Patallok* if it would help you.'

'I'd never take you there, my friend,' Shiva said with a grin. He wasn't exactly keen himself on the idea of venturing into the land of the demons.

He smiled warmly and turned to Sati. 'Take care, my child. It's so good to see you finally get the life you deserve.'

'Thank you, Brahaspatiji,' Sati said, with a namaste.

Then the scientist added, 'I hope to see you soon, Shiva.'

'Count on it!' Shiva said with a grin.

CHAPTER 20

Attack on Mandar

'How are you, my friend?'

'What the hell am I doing here?' asked Shiva, startled as he found himself sitting in the Brahma temple in Meru. In front of him was the pandit he'd met during his first visit there, many months ago.

'You called me here,' said the pandit, smiling.

'But how did I get here?' asked Shiva, astounded, 'and when?'

'As soon as you went to sleep,' the pandit replied. 'This is a dream.'

'I'll be damned!'

'Why do you swear so much?' The pandit frowned.

'I only swear when the occasion demands,' said Shiva, grinning mischievously. 'And what's wrong with swearing, anyway?'

'I think it reflects poor manners – or reveals a slight deficiency in character.'

'On the contrary, I think it shows tremendous character. It shows you have the strength and passion to speak your mind.'

The pandit guffawed, shaking his head slightly.

'In any case,' continued Shiva, 'since you're here, why don't you tell me what your people are called? I was promised I'd be told the next time I met one of you.'

'But you haven't met one of us again – this is a dream,' said the pandit, smiling mysteriously. 'I can only tell you what you already know, or something that already exists in your consciousness that you haven't chosen to listen to yet.'

'So you're here to help me find out something I already know?'

'Yes,' said the pandit, his smile growing more enigmatic.

'So what are we supposed to talk about?'

'The colour of that leaf.' He beamed, pointing towards the many trees that could be seen through the temple's ostentatiously carved pillars.

'The colour of that leaf.' said Shiva, squinting.

'Yes.'

He frowned. 'Why in the name of the Holy Lake is the colour of that leaf important?'

'Often a good conversational journey to find knowledge makes attaining it that much more satisfying,' said the pandit. 'And more importantly, it helps you understand the context of the knowledge much more easily.'

'I'm not sure what you mean by "the context of the knowledge".'

'All knowledge has its context. Unless you know the context, you might not understand the point.'

'And I'll know all that by talking about the colour of that leaf, will I?'

'Yes.'

'By the Holy Lake, man,' groaned Shiva, 'let's talk about the leaf, then.'

The pandit laughed. 'So tell me – what colour is that leaf?'

'It's green.'

'Is it?'

'Isn't it?'

'Why do you think it looks green to you?'

'Because,' said Shiva, amused despite himself, 'it *is* green.'

'No, that's not what I'm getting at. Didn't you have a conversation with one of Brahaspati's scientists about how the eyes see?'

'Oh that, right,' said Shiva, slapping his forehead. 'Light falls on an object, and when it reflects back from that object into your eyes, you see that object.'

'Exactly! And you had another conversation with a different scientist about what normal white sunlight is made of.'

'Indeed – white light is nothing but the confluence of seven different colours – that's why the rainbow is made up of seven colours, since it's formed when raindrops disperse sunlight.'

'Correct! Now put these two theories together and answer my question. Why does that leaf look green to you?'

Shiva frowned as his mind worked the problem out. 'White

sunlight falls on that leaf, the leaf's physical properties are such that it *absorbs* the colours violet, indigo, blue, yellow, orange and red. It doesn't absorb the colour green, which is then reflected back to my eyes. Hence I see the leaf as green.'

'Exactly!' The pandit beamed again. 'So think about the colour of that leaf from the perspective of the leaf itself, the colours it absorbs and the one it rejects. Is its colour green? Or is it every single colour in the world *except* green?'

Shiva was stunned into silence by the simplicity of the pandit's statement.

'There are many realities,' continued the pandit, 'many versions of what may appear obvious. Something that seems to be the unshakeable truth in one context might look like the exact opposite in another. It's the context or perspective you're looking from that moulds which particular reality you see.'

Shiva focused on the leaf again. Its lustrous green colour shone brightly in the glorious sunlight.

'Are your eyes capable of seeing another reality?' asked the pandit.

Shiva continued to stare at the leaf as its appearance gradually altered. The colour seemed to be dissolving out of the leaf as its bright green hue gradually grew lighter and lighter, slowly reducing to a shade of grey. As he continued to stare, even the grey dissolved, until eventually the leaf was almost transparent, discernible only by its outline. Numerous curved lines of black and white appeared to move in and around the outline of the leaf, almost as if the leaf were nothing but a carrier used by the black and white curved lines as a temporary pause on their eternal journey.

It took Shiva some time to realise that the surrounding leaves had also been transformed into their outlines. As he shifted his gaze, he noticed that the entire tree had magically transformed into an outline, the black and white curved lines flowing in and out, easily and smoothly. He turned his head to take in the panorama. Every object, from the squirrels on the trees to the pillars of the temple, had been transformed into outlines of themselves, the same black and white curved lines streaming in and out of them.

Turning to the pandit to ask for an explanation, he was stunned to see that the priest himself was also transformed into an outline of his former self. Curved white lines flooded out of him with frightening intensity. Strangely, though, there were no black lines around him.

'What the—?'

Shiva's words were stopped by the outline of the pandit pointing back at him. 'Look at yourself, my *karmasaathi*,' he advised.

Shiva looked down. 'I'll be damned!' His body had also been transformed into a transparent outline, and torrents of black curved lines were gushing furiously into him. He looked at the lines closely and noticed that they weren't lines at all, but rather tiny jet-black waves, so minuscule that even from a slight distance they appeared to be lines. There wasn't a hint of the white waves close to Shiva's outlined body. 'What the hell is going on?'

'The white waves are positive energy and the black negative,' said the pandit's outline. 'They're both important, their balance crucial. If they fall out of sync, cataclysm will occur.'

Shiva looked up at the pandit, puzzled. 'So why is there no positive energy around me, and no negative energy around you?'

'Because we balance each other: the Vishnu's role is to transmit positive energy,' said the pandit, and Shiva saw the white lines pouring feverishly out of him appeared to flutter a little whenever he spoke. 'And the Mahadev's role is to absorb the negative. Search for it – search for negative energy and you'll fulfil your destiny as a Mahadev.'

'But I'm no Mahadev – my deeds don't qualify me for that title—'

'It doesn't work that way, my friend. You don't earn a title *after* you've done your deeds; you do your deeds because of and only after you believe that you already are the Mahadev. It doesn't matter what others think; it's about what you believe. Believe you're the Mahadev and you'll be one.'

Shiva frowned.

'Believe,' repeated the pandit.

BOOM!

A distant reverberation echoed through the temple's peaceful ambience and Shiva turned his eyes towards the horizon.

'That sounded like an explosion,' whispered the pandit's outline.

The distant, insistent voice of Sati came riding in. 'Shiva—'

BOOM!

Another explosion?

'Shiva—'

'I think your wife needs you, my friend.'

Shiva looked in astonishment at the outline of the pandit, unable to decipher where the sound came from.

'Maybe you should wake up,' advised the pandit's disembodied voice.

'Shiva!'

Shiva woke to find Sati staring at him with concern. He was still groggy after being yanked from such an outlandishly strange dream-state.

'*Shiva!*'

BOOM!

'What the hell was that?' cried Shiva, shaking the sleep from his head.

'Someone's using *daivi astras!*'

'What?'

'Divine weapons,' said Sati, clearly disturbed, 'but Lord Rudra destroyed them all – nobody has access to them any more!'

Shiva was completely alert now, his battle instincts primed. 'Sati, get your armour on and your weapons ready, right now.'

As Sati responded, Shiva slipped on his own armour, strapped his shield to his back and belted his sword at his waist. He slung his quiver smoothly over one shoulder and picked up his bow. Checking that Sati was also ready for battle, he kicked the door open to find Taman and eight other guards standing outside with their swords drawn, ready to defend their Neelkanth against any attack.

'My Lord, you should wait inside,' said Taman. 'We'll hold the attackers here.'

Shiva stared hard at Taman, frowning at the doorkeeper's well-intentioned but stupid words, and Taman immediately stepped aside. 'I'm sorry, my Lord; we'll follow you.'

Before Shiva could react, they heard footsteps rushing along the hallway. Shiva immediately drew his sword and strained his ears to assess the threat.

Four footsteps – just two men to attack a royal hallway? This doesn't make sense!

One pair of footsteps dragged slightly – clearly a large man using considerable willpower to make his feet move faster than his girth was comfortable with.

'Stand down, men,' ordered Shiva suddenly, 'they're friends.'

Seconds later, Nandi and Veerbhadra emerged around the corner, running hard, their swords at the ready.

'Are you all right, my Lord?' asked Nandi, admirably not out of breath.

'Yes, we're all safe – did you see the attackers?'

'No,' answered Veerbhadra, frowning. 'What the hell's going on?'

'I don't know,' said Shiva, 'but we're going to find out.'

'Where's Krittika?' asked Sati.

'Safe in her room,' Veerbhadra answered. 'She has five soldiers with her, and the door's barred from the inside.'

Satisfied that her maid was as safe as she could be, Sati turned to Shiva. 'So what now?'

'I want to check on the emperor first. Everybody pair up, and keep your shields at the ready for cover. Sati, you're at my side, Nandi in the middle, Taman, Veerbhadra at the rear. Don't light any torches. We know the way. Our enemies don't.'

The platoon moved with considerable speed and stealth, mindful of possible surprise attacks. Shiva was troubled by what he heard — or rather, what he *didn't* hear. Apart from the repeated explosions, there was absolutely no other sound from the palace: no screams of terror, no rush of panicked footsteps, no clash of steel: *nothing*. Either the terrorists had not yet begun their real attack, or Shiva was too late, and the attack was already over. Shiva frowned as a third alternative occurred to him. Maybe there were no terrorists in the palace itself; maybe the attack was being mounted from a distance, using the divine weapons Sati had mentioned.

When they reached Daksha's chambers, they found his guards at the door, tense and ready for battle.

'Where's the emperor?' asked Shiva.

'Inside, my Lord,' said the royal guard captain. 'Where are they, my Lord? We've been waiting for an attack since the first explosion.'

'I don't know, Captain,' replied Shiva. 'Stay here and block

the doorway. Taman, support the captain here with your men
– and everyone: remain alert.'

Shiva opened the emperor's door. 'Your Majesty?'

'My Lord? Is Sati all right?' asked Daksha.

'She is, your Majesty,' said Shiva as Sati, Nandi and
Veerbhadra followed him into the chamber. 'And the queen?'

'Shaken, but not too scared.'

'What's going on?' asked Shiva.

'I don't know,' replied Daksha. 'I suggest you and Sati stay
here for now until we find out.'

'Perhaps *you* should stay here, your Majesty,' countered
Shiva. 'We can't risk any harm coming to you. I'm going out
to help Parvateshwar – if this is a terrorist attack, we'll need
all the swords we have.'

'You don't have to go, my Lord. This is Devagiri – our
soldiers will slay any terrorists dim-witted enough to attack
our capital.'

Before Shiva could respond, there was a loud, insistent
knocking on the door.

'Your Majesty? Request permission to enter.'

Parvateshwar, thought Daksha. *Observing protocol even at a time
like this!*

'Come in,' growled Daksha, and as his general entered, he
let fly. 'How in Lord Indra's name can this be happening,
General? An attack on Devagiri? How dare they—?'

'Your Majesty,' Shiva intervened. Sati, Nandi and Veerbhadra
were present, and he couldn't allow Parvateshwar to be insulted

in front of them – especially not in front of Sati. 'Let's find out what's going on before we trouble ourselves with the why, shall we?'

'Devagiri is safe, your Majesty,' said Parvateshwar, glaring impatiently at his emperor. 'My scouts saw massive plumes of smoke coming from the direction of Mount Mandar – I believe that's what's under attack. I've already ordered my troops and the Arishtanemi to be ready to leave within the hour; I just need your approval to depart.'

'The explosions were in Mandar, *Pitratulya*?' asked Sati incredulously. 'How powerful were they to be heard in Devagiri?'

Parvateshwar looked gloomily at Sati, his silence conveying his deepest fears. He turned back to the emperor. 'Your Majesty?'

Daksha looked stunned into silence – or was that a frown darkening his eyes? Parvateshwar couldn't be sure in the dim light.

'Guards, light the torches,' he ordered. 'There's no attack on Devagiri!'

As the torches spread their radiance, Parvateshwar repeated, 'Do I have your permission to depart, your Majesty?'

Daksha nodded curtly, and as Parvateshwar turned to leave, he noticed Shiva's shocked expression. 'What's the matter, Shiva?' he asked quietly.

'Brahaspati left for Mount Mandar yesterday.'

'What?' He hadn't noticed the chief scientist's absence during the previous day's celebrations. 'Oh, Lord Agni—!'

Shiva turned slowly towards Sati, drawing strength from her presence.

'I'll find him, Shiva,' the general promised. 'I'm sure he's alive – I'll find him.'

'I'm coming with you,' Shiva announced.

'And so am I,' said Sati.

'What?' exclaimed Daksha, the light throwing his agonised expression into sharp relief. 'You don't need to go—'

Shiva frowned at Daksha. 'My apologies, your Majesty, but I must go. Brahaspati needs me.'

As Parvateshwar and Shiva turned to leave the royal chambers, Sati bent down to touch her father's feet, but Daksha was too dazed to bless her, and Sati didn't want to fall too far behind her husband. She quickly turned to touch her mother's feet.

'*Ayushman bhav*,' said Veerini.

Sati frowned at the odd blessing – *May you live long* – but she was going into battle; she wanted victory, not a long life! But there was no time to argue. Sati turned and raced after Shiva with Nandi and Veerbhadra at her heels.

CHAPTER 21

Preparation for War

The explosions stopped within the hour, and shortly there-after, Shiva, Parvateshwar, Sati, Nandi and Veerbhadra, accom-panied by a brigade of fifteen hundred cavalry, including the Arishtanemi, were on their way to Mount Mandar. Brahaspati's scientists joined the brigade, sick with worry over their leader's fate. They rode hard and covered the day-long journey in less than eight hours. The second *prahar* was almost at an end and the sun was directly overhead when the brigade turned the last corner, where the forest cover cleared, and they got their first glimpse of the mountain.

A furious cry arose from every throat as they saw the heart of their empire ruined almost beyond recognition. Mandar had been ruthlessly destroyed. A colossal crater stood where the mountain had been, as if a giant demon had struck his massive hands right inside the mountain and scooped out its core. The enormous buildings were in ruins, their remnants scattered across the plains below. The giant churners at the bottom of mountain were still functioning, their eerie sound a counterpoint to the macabre scene before them.

'Brahaspati—!' roared Shiva as he rode hard right into the heart of the mountain, where, miraculously, the pathway still survived.

'Wait, Shiva,' Parvateshwar cautioned him. 'It could be a trap.'

Shiva ignored him and continued to gallop along the pathway through the devastated heart of the mountain. Parvateshwar and Sati led the brigade behind him, trying to keep up with their Neelkanth. A horrific sight awaited them at the summit: in between the broken buildings, scorched and unrecognisable body parts were strewn everywhere, ripped to shreds by the succession of explosions. It would be impossible to identify the dead.

Shiva tumbled off his horse, his face devoid of the faintest trace of hope. Nobody could have survived such a lethal attack.

'Brahaspati . . .' he whispered.

— ⚹ ◍∪⚵✦ —

'How did the terrorists get their hands on the *daivi astras*?' Parvateshwar growled, the fire of vengeance blazing brightly within him.

The soldiers had been ordered to collect all the body parts and cremate them, to help the departed begin their onward journey. A manifest was being drawn up of the names of those believed dead, with Brahaspati, chief scientist of Meluha, Sarayupaari Brahmin, Swan chosen-tribe, the first name on the list. The others were mostly Arishtanemi who had been assigned the task of protecting Mandar. It was small consolation that the casualties were minimal, since most of the mountain's residents were in Devagiri for the Neelkanth's marriage. The list would be sent to the great ascetics in Kashmir, whose spiritual powers were considered second to none. If the ascetics could be cajoled into reciting prayers for these departed souls, there was a chance that their grisly deaths would not mar their subsequent births.

'The *Somras* could have caused this, General,' said Nachiket, one of Brahaspati's senior assistant scientists.

Shiva looked up suddenly on hearing Nachiket's words.

Sati sounded disbelieving as she asked, 'How could the *Somras* do this?'

'The *Somras* is very volatile during the manufacturing process,' Nachiket explained. 'It's kept stable by using copious quantities of water from the Saraswati. One of our main projects was to determine whether we could stabilise the *Somras* using less water – much less than we use at present.'

Shiva remembered Brahaspati talking about his new experiment and leaned over to listen intently to Nachiket.

'It was one of the dream projects—' Nachiket couldn't complete the statement. The thought that Brahaspati, the greatest scientist of his generation, the father-figure to all the learned men at Mount Mandar, was gone was too much for him to bear, and the intense pain he felt inside choked him. He stopped talking and shut his eyes, hoping that this terrible moment would pass.

At last, regaining some semblance of control over himself, he continued, 'It was one of Brahaspatiji's dream projects. He returned yesterday to supervise the experiment that was scheduled to begin today. He didn't want us to miss the last day of the celebrations, so he came alone.'

Parvateshwar was numb. 'You mean this could have been an accident?'

'Yes,' replied Nachiket, 'we all knew the experiment was risky. Maybe that's why Brahaspatiji decided to begin without us.'

The entire room was stunned into silence by this unexpected information. Nachiket retreated into his private hell and Parvateshwar gazed into the distance, shocked by the turn of events. Sati stared at Shiva, holding his hand, deeply worried about her husband's reaction to his friend's death. And to think, it might have been a senseless mishap . . .

— ⁑ ꙮ ꭲ ⚡ ☸ —

It was late into the first hour of the fourth *prahar* and the brigade had set up camp at the bottom of the ruined mountain. They would leave the next day, after all the ceremonies for the departed had been completed. Two riders had been despatched to Devagiri with the news about Mandar. Parvateshwar and Sati sat at the edge of the crater, whispering to each other. The drone of

Brahmin scientists reciting Sanskrit *shlokas* floated around them, creating an ethereal atmosphere of pathos. Nandi and Veerbhadra stood at attention a polite distance from Parvateshwar and Sati, watching Shiva, who was walking around the ruins of the Mandar buildings, lost in thought.

It was tearing him apart that he hadn't seen a single recognisable remnant of Brahaspati. Everybody in Mandar had been obliterated beyond recognition. Regardless, he desperately searched for some sign of his friend, something he could keep with him, something to soothe his tortured soul through the years of mourning ahead. He walked at a snail's pace, his eyes scanning the ground – when suddenly he caught sight of an object he recognised all too well.

He slowly bent down to pick it up: a leather bracelet, burned at the edges, its ties destroyed. The heat of the fiery explosions had scarred its brown colour black in most places, except at the centre where an embroidered design remained, astonishingly unblemished. Shiva studied it closely.

The Aum symbol glowed in the crimson light of the setting sun. At the meeting point of the top and bottom curves of the symbol were two serpent heads. The third curve, surging out to the right, also ended in a serpent's head, its forked tongue stuck out threateningly.

It was him! He killed Brahaspati!

Shiva swung around, staring at the scattered limbs not yet

consigned to a funeral pyre, hoping to find the owner of the bracelet, or some part of him – but he found nothing. Shiva screamed silently, a scream audible only to him and Brahaspati's wounded soul. He clutched the still-burning bracelet in his fist until it scorched his palm. Clasping it even more firmly, he swore a terrible vengeance: he vowed to bring upon the Naga a death that would scar him for his next seven births; that Naga and his entire evil army would be annihilated, piece by bloody piece.

'Shiva! Shiva!' The insistent call yanked him back to reality.

Sati was standing in front of him, gently touching his hand. Parvateshwar stood beside her, looking disturbed, and Nandi and Veerbhadra were on her other side.

'Let it go, Shiva,' said Sati gently.

Shiva continued to stare at her blankly.

'Let it go, Shiva,' repeated Sati softly. 'It's singeing your hand.'

Shiva opened his fingers to expose his palm and Nandi pulled the bracelet from his grasp – then screamed in surprised agony and dropped the bracelet as it scalded his hand. How had the Lord held it for so long?

Shiva immediately bent down and picked up the bracelet. Holding it carefully this time, he stared at the serpent Aum symbol dangling between his fingers. He turned to Parvateshwar. 'This was no accident,' he growled.

'Are you sure?' asked Sati.

Shiva held up the bracelet for Sati to see, with the serpent

Aum clearly in view, and she gasped as Parvateshwar, Nandi and Veerbhadra crowded in for a better look.

'The Naga,' Nandi whispered.

'The same bastard who attacked Sati in Meru,' growled Shiva. 'The same Naga who attacked us on our return from Mandar. It's the very same son of a bitch.'

'He'll pay for this, Shiva,' said Veerbhadra.

Turning to Parvateshwar, Shiva said, 'We ride to Devagiri tonight. We declare war.'

Parvateshwar nodded and headed off to round up his men.

$$- \lambda \, \text{ⓜ} \, \text{U} \, \text{ψ} \, \text{⊛} \, -$$

The Meluhan war council sat quietly, observing five minutes of silence in honour of the martyrs of Mount Mandar. General Parvateshwar and his twenty-five brigadiers sat to the right of Emperor Daksha. To Daksha's left sat the Neelkanth, the administrative Brahmins led by Prime Minister Kanakhala and the governors of the fifteen provinces.

'The council's decision is a given,' said Daksha, beginning the proceedings. 'The question is, when do we attack?'

'Realistically, we can be ready to march in a month, your Majesty,' said Parvateshwar. 'Unfortunately, as there are no roads between Meluha and Swadweep, our army will have to hack their way through dense forest, so even if we begin the march in a month, we won't be in Swadweep before three months from today. There's no time to waste.'

'Then let the preparations begin.'

'Your Majesty,' said Kanakhala, trying to balance the Kshatrya battle cry with a Brahmin voice of reason, 'might I suggest an alternative plan?'

'Like what?' Daksha looked surprised.

'Please don't get me wrong,' said Kanakhala. 'I understand our nation's rage over the atrocities at Mount Mandar — but we want vengeance against the perpetrators of the crime, not all of Swadweep. Could we try a scalpel before we bring out the mighty war sword?'

'The path you suggest is one of cowardice, Kanakhala,' said Parvateshwar scornfully.

'No, it isn't, General,' replied Kanakhala politely. 'I'm not suggesting that we sit like cowards and do nothing. I'm wondering whether there's a way for us to get our vengeance without sacrificing the lives of innocents.'

'My soldiers are willing to shed their blood for their country, Madam Prime Minister,' said Parvateshwar, his temper rising.

'I know they are,' said Kanakhala, maintaining her composure, 'and I know that you're also willing to shed your blood for Meluha alongside them. My suggestion is to send an emissary to Emperor Dilipa and ask him to surrender the terrorists who perpetrated this attack. If he refuses, then we will attack with all the might at our disposal.'

His eyes narrowed with impatience, Parvateshwar said, '*Ask* him? Why would he listen? For decades the Swadweepans have got away with their nefarious activities because they think we don't have the stomach for a fight. Taking this "scalpel approach" after an outrage like Mount Mandar will merely convince them that they can mount any attack at will and we won't respond.'

'I disagree,' said Kanakhala. 'They've mounted terrorist attacks because they're afraid to take us on in a direct fight – they're terrified that they won't be able to withstand our superior technology and war-machines. I'm trying to see things from Lord Shiva's perspective, and to take up the suggestion he made when he first came here. Can we try talking to them before we fight? A dialogue might offer them an opportunity to admit there are terrorists in their midst. If they hand them over, we may even find ways of coexisting.'

'I don't believe Shiva thinks like that any more,' said Parvateshwar, nodding towards the Neelkanth. 'He too wants vengeance.'

Shiva was sitting silently, his face expressionless. Only his eyes glowered with the terrible anger seething inside him.

'My Lord,' said Kanakhala, turning towards Shiva with her hands folded in a namaste. 'I hope that you at least understand what I'm trying to say. Even Brahaspati would have wanted us to avoid violence, if possible.'

The last sentence was like a torrential downpour on the fire raging in Shiva's heart and soul. He gazed deeply into Kanakhala's eyes before turning to Daksha. 'Your Majesty, perhaps Kanakhala's right. Maybe we can send an emissary to Swadweep to give them an opportunity to repent. If we can avoid killing innocents, only good will come from it. However,

I'd still recommend that we begin war preparations. We should be prepared for the possibility that the Chandravanshis may reject our offer.'

'The Mahadev has spoken,' said Daksha. 'I propose that this be the decision of the war council. All in favour, raise your hands.'

Every hand in the room shot up. The die had been cast. An attempt would be made for peace. If that failed, the Meluhans would go to war.

— ⁂ ◍Ʊ⚲ ⊛ —

'I've failed again, Bhadra,' cried Shiva. 'I can't protect *anyone*.' They were sitting together in a private section of Shiva's palace courtyard after Sati had begged Veerbhadra to try to draw her beloved out of his mourning. Shiva had retreated deep within himself, neither speaking nor crying, and she hoped her husband's childhood friend would succeed where she had failed.

'How can you blame yourself for this?' asked Veerbhadra, handing the chillum to his friend. 'How can this possibly be your fault?'

Shiva took a deep drag, but not even the marijuana coursing through his body could help. The pain was too intense. He snorted in disgust and threw the chillum away. He looked up to the sky and swore, 'I will avenge you, my brother, if it's the last thing I do. If I have to spend every moment of the rest of my life in pursuit of that goal, if I have to come back to this world again and again, I will avenge you!'

Veerbhadra glanced towards Sati, who was watching them from a distance. His worried expression matched hers. She stood and walked over to them, then sat next to Shiva and wrapped her arms around him tightly and drew his head until it was resting against her bosom, hoping to soothe her husband's tortured soul.

Shiva didn't raise his arms to return her embrace. He just sat motionless, barely even breathing.

'My Lord!' Brigadier Vraka snapped to attention at the Neelkanth's unexpected arrival, closely followed by the other twenty-four brigadiers in the war room.

Parvateshwar rose more slowly, and seeing the pain Shiva still carried over Brahaspati's grisly death, he spoke kindly, asking, 'How are you, Shiva?'

'I'm fine, thank you.'

'We were discussing battle plans.'

'I know. May I join you?'

'Of course,' he said, moving his chair to one side to make room at the table. 'The essential problem for us is the transport links between Meluha and Swadweep.'

'There aren't any, right?'

'Right,' said the general. 'The Chandravanshis pursued a "scorched-earth" policy after their last defeat at our hands a hundred years ago. They destroyed the entire infrastructure that existed between Meluha and Swadweep, then they depopulated their border cities and moved deeper into their land. Forests have grown where the cities and roads used to be, and no river flows from our territory to theirs. Basically, there's no way for us to transport our technologically superior war-machines to the borders of Swadweep.'

'So they've achieved their aim, then,' said Shiva. 'Your superiority is technology, while theirs is numbers. They've effectively neutralised your strength.'

'Exactly. And if our war-machines are taken out of the equation, our hundred-thousand-strong army may be swamped by their million soldiers.'

'They have a million-strong army?' asked Shiva, incredulous.

'Yes, my Lord,' said Vraka. 'We can't be absolutely sure, but that's our estimate. However, we also estimate that the regulars won't number more than a hundred thousand, while the rest will be part-timers – traders, artisans, farmers and the like – forcibly conscripted for use as cannon-fodder.'

'Disgusting,' said Parvateshwar. 'Their Kshatriyas have no honour, risking the lives of Shudras and Vaishyas like that.'

Shiva acknowledged Parvateshwar's comment, then suggested, 'Can't the war-machines be dismantled for transport and then reassembled in Swadweep?'

'That would work for some of them, but our most devastating machines – the ones that would give us the edge, like the long-range catapult – can't be assembled outside a factory.'

'What's your long-range catapult capable of?'

'It can hurl huge boulders and smouldering barrels over a

mile, potentially softening – perhaps even devastating – the enemy lines before our cavalry and infantry charge them. Basically, they do what elephants used to do.'

'Then why not use elephants instead this time?'

'They're unpredictable – no matter how long you train them, an army often loses control over them in the heat of battle. Elephants were the Swadweepans' downfall during our last war with them. We had great success with a very simple ploy,' Parvateshwar explained. 'We fired at the mahouts and generated tremendous noise with our war-drums, the Chandravanshi elephants panicked and ran into their own army, shattering their lines, especially the ones composed of irregulars. All we had to do then was charge in and finish the job.'

'So no elephants, then.'

'Definitely not,' said Parvateshwar firmly.

'So we need something portable that can be used to soften up their irregulars in order to negate their numerical superiority.' He stared out of the window, where the stiff morning breeze was fluttering the leaves of a tree outside. The leaves were green. Shiva stared harder. They remained green.

'I know what we can do,' said Shiva, suddenly fixing his intent gaze on Parvateshwar, his eyes bright. 'Why don't we use arrows?'

'Arrows?' The general sounded surprised; archery was the battle-art of the most elite Kshatriyas, used only for one-on-one duels between warriors of equal chosen-tribes. Archers earned huge respect for their rare skill, but they weren't decisive in battles; they had been effective in ancient times, when *daivi astras*, or divine weapons, were triggered by arrows. Once Lord Rudra had banned the *daivi astras*, the effectiveness of archery units in large-scale battles had reduced drastically.

'How can that reduce their numerical superiority, my Lord?' asked Vraka. 'Even the most skilled of archers will take at least five seconds to aim, fire and execute a kill; he will not be able to take out more than a dozen men a minute, and that's if every arrow is a hit. We have only one hundred gold-order Kshatriya archers – the rest can shoot, but their aim cannot be relied upon. So we will not be able to kill more than one thousand two hundred of our enemies per minute, and that's not enough, not against the Chandravanshis.'

'I'm not talking about using arrows for one-on-one shooting,' said Shiva. 'I'm talking about using them as a means of softening up the enemy, as weapons of mass destruction.' Ignoring the confused expressions around the table, Shiva continued, 'Let me explain. Suppose we create a corps of archers made up of the lower Kshatriya chosen-tribes.'

'But their aim wouldn't be good—' began Vraka.

'That doesn't matter. Let's say we have at least five thousand of those archers. Suppose we tell them to forget about aiming for a single target and train them just to get the range right. Suppose their job is simply to keep firing arrows in the general direction of the Chandravanshi army. If they don't have to aim accurately, they can fire a lot more quickly, maybe one arrow every two or three seconds.'

Parvateshwar's eyes narrowed as the brilliance of the idea sank in, but the rest of his brigadiers were still trying to get their heads around it.

'Think about it,' said Shiva, 'we'd have five thousand arrows raining down on the Chandravanshis every two seconds. Suppose we keep that up for ten minutes – an almost continuous shower of arrows – their irregulars would break formation and run, for sure. The arrows would have the same effect as the Chandravanshis' elephants in the last war!'

'That's brilliant,' cried Vraka.

Parvateshwar's keen military mind was already teeming with the possibilities. 'If the aim doesn't matter, we could train these archers to fire lying down – if they lay on their backs and put their feet on the limb of the bow, they could draw all the way up to their chins before releasing – as long as their feet are pointed in the right direction, the arrows will fly in the right direction—'

'That's inspired, Parvateshwar,' exclaimed Shiva. 'That way we can use bigger bows with a longer range.'

'And more substantial arrows, almost like small spears,' continued Parvateshwar, 'strong enough to penetrate even leather and thick wooden shields. Only the regular soldiers with metal shields would be safe from such an assault.'

'Do we have an answer to our problem, then?' asked Shiva.

'Yes, we do,' replied Parvateshwar with a grim smile. 'Vraka – create this corps. I want five thousand men ready within two weeks.'

'It will be done, my Lord,' said Vraka.

— ⟨symbols⟩ —

'What do you want to discuss, Shiva?' asked Parvateshwar as he entered the metallurgy factory with Brigadiers Vraka and Prasanjit, in response to Shiva's request to meet him there. Vraka had been reluctant to leave the archery corps he'd been training for the past week, but the hope of another brilliant idea from the Neelkanth piqued his interest.

He wasn't disappointed.

Shiva said, 'We're still going to need an equivalent of your stabbing ram to break their regulars. As long as they hold, our victory can't be guaranteed.'

'Right,' said Parvateshwar. 'We have to assume these soldiers will be disciplined enough to stay in formation despite the barrage of arrows.'

'Exactly,' said Shiva. 'We can't transport the ram, right?'

'No, my Lord,' said Vraka.

'How about trying to create a human ram?'

'An interesting notion,' said Parvateshwar slowly, listening intently.

'Say we form up the soldiers into a square, twenty men by twenty men. Each man will use his shield to cover the left half of his own body and the right half of the soldier to the left of him.'

The general's eyes gleamed. 'That formation will allow them

to push their spears between the shields.' 'Exactly,' replied Shiva. 'And the soldiers behind the front line will use their shields to cover themselves and the soldiers in front of them – like a tortoise's shell: the shields will hold off the enemy, but still allow our spears to cut into them.'

'And we put the strongest and most experienced soldiers at the front to make sure the tortoise is well led,' Prasanjit started, but the general shook his head.

'No, the most experienced men will be at the back and sides, to hold the square in case the younger soldiers panic,' said Parvateshwar. 'This entire formation only works if the team stays together.'

'Exactly,' said Shiva, smiling at Parvateshwar's quick grasp of his concept. 'And what if they carry one of these instead of their usual spears?'

Shiva raised the weapon he had designed, which the army's metallurgy team had quickly assembled: it had the same shaft as a spear, but the head had been broadened to accommodate two more spikes to the left and right of the main spike. Assaulting an enemy with this weapon would be like striking him with three spears simultaneously.

'Absolutely brilliant, Shiva,' marvelled Parvateshwar. 'What do you call it?'

'I call it a *trishul*.'

'Prasanjit, you're in charge of creating this corps. I want at least five tortoise formations ready by the time we march – I'll assign two thousand men to you immediately.'

'It will be done, my Lord,' said Prasanjit, saluting.

Parvateshwar gazed at Shiva with a new respect. His ideas were brilliant, and coming up with such innovative tactics despite his profound personal grief was a feat worthy of admiration. *Maybe what they say about Shiva is true after all*, he thought. *Maybe he is the man who'll finish Lord Ram's task.* He fervently hoped that Shiva would not prove him wrong.

— ⚛ ◍ ℧ ⚡ ◉ —

Shiva was sitting in the royal meeting room with Daksha and Parvateshwar at his side. Two legendary Arishtanemi brigadiers, Vidyunmali and Mayashrenik, were seated a short distance away.

In front of Shiva stood a muscular, once proud man, his hands clasped together in a namaste, pleading, 'Give me a chance, my Lord – if the law's been changed, then why can't we fight?'

The man, Drapaku, had been a brigadier in the Meluhan army before being declared a *vikarma* after the disease that blinded his father also killed his wife and unborn child.

'How's your father?' asked Shiva, remembering the blind old *vikarma* man at Kotdwaar who had blessed him.

'He's well, my Lord – and he'll disown me if I don't support you in this *dharmayudh*.'

Shiva smiled; he too believed this was a *dharmayudh*, a holy war. 'I understand, Drapaku, but who'll take care of him if something happens to you?'

'Meluha will take care of him, my Lord, but he'll die a

thousand deaths if I don't go into battle with you. What kind of a son would I be if I didn't fight for my father's honour? For my *country's* honour?'

Shiva could sense the others' discomfort with this conversation – and it hadn't escaped his notice that despite the repeal of the *vikarma* law, nobody had touched Drapaku since he entered.

'My Lord, we're heavily outnumbered by the Chandravanshis,' Drapaku said. 'We need every trained warrior we have. At least five thousand soldiers have been excluded because they've been declared *vikarma* – but I can bring them together. We're willing – and eager – to die for our country.'

'I don't want you to die for Meluha, brave Drapaku,' said Shiva, and Drapaku's face fell as he became convinced he'd be returning home to Kotdwaar in disgrace.

'I would like you to kill for Meluha,' Shiva said, and Drapaku looked up at him, hope sparking in his eyes.

'Raise the *Vikarma* Brigade, Drapaku,' Shiva ordered, knowing not everyone present would be comfortable with this decision.

But he was determined. This was the right move. It would send the right message. Meluha would fight as one.

— ⟶ 🜩 ◍ U ♀ ✵ ⟵ —

'How can we have *vikarmas* in our army? It's ridiculous!' said Vidyunmali angrily.

Vidyunmali and Mayashrenik were in their private gym, preparing for their regular sword-training session.

'Vidyu—' cajoled Mayashrenik.

'Don't "Vidyu" me, Maya. You know this is wrong!'

Mayashrenik just nodded and let his impetuous friend vent his frustration.

'How will I face my ancestors if I die in this battle?' Vidyunmali snarled. 'What will I answer if they ask me how I let a non-Kshatriya fight a battle that only we Kshatriyas should have fought? It is *our* duty to protect the weak – we are not supposed to use the weak to fight for us.'

'Vidyu, I don't think Drapaku is weak. Have you forgotten his valour in the previous Chandravanshi war?'

'He is a *vikarma – that* makes him weak!'

'Lord Shiva has ordered that there are no *vikarmas* any more,' Mayashrenik pointed out.

'I don't think the Neelkanth truly knows right from wrong—' Vidyunmali started, but his friend had had enough.

'Vidyu!' Mayashrenik shouted, and Vidyunmali's mouth dropped open in surprise at this uncharacteristic outburst.

'If the Neelkanth says it's *right*,' Mayashrenik said forcefully, 'then it *is* right!'

CHAPTER 22

Empire of Evil

'This is how we'll form up for the battle.' Parvateshwar showed Vraka the battle-plan: the men would be in a wide semicircle, like a bow, with the slower corps, including the tortoises, placed at the centre. The light infantry, the quicker units, would take the flanks, and the cavalry would be at both ends of the bow, ready to be quickly deployed wherever they were needed. The bow formation was ideal for a smaller army, providing flexibility without sacrificing strength.

'It's perfect, my Lord,' said Vraka. 'What does the Mahadev say?'

'Shiva thinks it suits our requirements perfectly.'

Vraka didn't like it when Parvateshwar referred to the Neelkanth by his name, but who was he to correct his general? Better to say nothing.

'I'll lead the left flank,' said Parvateshwar, 'and you'll take the right. I'll need your opinion on some things—'

'Me, my lord? But I thought the Mahadev would lead the other flank.'

'Shiva? No, I don't think he'll be fighting in this war, Vraka.'

Vraka's eyes widened in surprise, but he kept his thoughts to himself.

Parvateshwar clearly felt the need to explain, for he added, 'He's a good and capable man, no doubt, but the uppermost desire in his mind is retribution, not justice for Meluha. We'll help him wreak vengeance when we throw the guilty Naga at his feet. We can't expect him to risk his own life in a war just to find one Naga.'

Vraka kept his gaze downcast lest his eyes betray how strongly he disagreed with his general.

'To be fair,' Parvateshwar continued, 'we can't ask him to help us just because he has a blue throat. I respect him – a great deal – but I don't expect him to fight alongside us.'

Vraka met Parvateshwar's gaze briefly. Why was his general refusing to accept something that was so obvious to everyone else? Was his attachment to Lord Ram so great that he couldn't believe another saviour had arrived on earth to continue his work? Hadn't Lord Ram said that even he was replaceable, that only *dharma* is irreplaceable?

'He's also married now,' Parvateshwar added, 'and he's deeply in love – he won't risk Sati being bereaved again, and why should he? It would be unfair of us to demand this of him.'

Vraka didn't dare voice his opinion, but he couldn't stop

thinking it: *The Mahadev will fight for all of us, General. He will battle to protect us — because that is what Mahadevs do.*

Vraka was completely unaware that the same thoughts were echoing around Parvateshwar's mind; the general fervently hoped that he was wrong, and that Shiva would rise to be a Mahadev and lead them to victory against the Chandravanshis. But long years of bitter experience had taught him that while many men tried to rise to Lord Ram's level, none had ever succeeded. Parvateshwar had put his hopes on a few such men in his youth, and he had always been disillusioned at the end. He was simply preparing himself for disappointment, and he had no intention of being left without a back-up if Shiva refused to fight against the Chandravanshis.

— ⁂ ⓌU⚲ ☸ —

The war council sat silently while Daksha read the letter from Emperor Dilipa to himself. His reaction to what he was reading left no doubt about the message it contained.

He shut his eyes, his face contorted in rage, his fist clenched tight, then he handed the letter over to Kanakhala and sneered, 'Read it — read it out loud, so that the whole world may be sickened by the repugnance of the Chandravanshis.'

Kanakhala frowned slightly before taking the letter and reading it out loud. 'Emperor Daksha, Suryavanshi liege, protector of Meluha: please accept my deepest condolences for the dastardly attack on Mount Mandar. Such a senseless assault on peaceful Brahmins must be condemned in the strongest of terms. We are shocked that any citizen of India would stoop so low. It is, therefore, with surprise and sadness that I read your letter. I assure you that neither I nor anyone under my command had anything to do with this devious attack, and with regret, there is therefore nobody I can hand over to you. I hope you understand the sincerity of this letter, and that you will not make a hasty decision which may have regrettable consequences for you. I assure you of my empire's full support in the investigation of this outrage. Please do let us know how we can be of assistance in bringing the criminals to justice.'

Kanakhala took a deep breath to compose herself. Anger over the typical Chandravanshi double-talk was washing right through her, making her regret her earlier suggestion to seek a peaceful resolution to the conflict.

'It's signed personally by Emperor Dilipa,' she said.

'Not *Emperor* Dilipa,' growled Daksha, '*Terrorist* Dilipa of the Empire of Evil!'

Unanimous in their rage, the council members' voices united in a single word: 'War!'

Daksha glanced at Shiva, who scowled and nodded almost imperceptibly.

'War it is,' bellowed Daksha. 'We march in two weeks!'

The bracelet seemed to develop a life of its own. It had swelled to enormous proportions, dwarfing Shiva. Its edges were engulfed in gigantic flames. The three colossal serpents that formed the Aum symbol separated from each other and slithered towards him. The one in the centre nodded to the snake on its left and hissed, 'He got your brother.' Nodding to the snake on its right, it added, 'And he will soon get your wife.' Then the serpents to the left and right added their ominous hissing to their brother's.

Shiva pointed menacingly at the serpent on the right. 'You dare touch even a hair on her head and I will rip your soul out of—'

'As for me,' continued the serpent, not even acknowledging Shiva's threat, 'I'm saving myself. I'm saving myself for you.'

Shiva stared at the serpent with impotent rage.

'I *will* get you,' hissed the serpent as its mouth stretched wide, ready to swallow him whole.

Shiva's eyes flew open. He was sweating hard. He looked around, but couldn't see a thing – it was extraordinarily dark. He reached out for Sati, to check if she was safe, but she wasn't there. He was up in a flash, scanning the darkness as a chill constricted his heart, half-expecting to see the dream serpents transformed into reality.

'Shiva,' said Sati quietly.

He spun around to find her sitting on the edge of the bed, watching him. The tiny tent had been their travelling home for the past month as the Meluhan army marched towards Swadweep.

'What is it?' he asked, his eyes gradually adjusting to the dim light. He released his clenched fingers and slipped the offending bracelet back into his belt-pouch.

When did I take it out? he wondered.

Sati sighed. She'd been trying to talk to her husband for the past two weeks, ever since she'd been sure, but had never found an opportune moment. She almost managed to convince herself that this was minor news; that she should not trouble her husband with this, but it was too late now. He had to learn this from her and not somebody else. News like this did not stay secret in an army camp for long. 'I have something to tell you.'

'Yes?' said Shiva, though his dream still occupied most of his attention. 'What is it?'

'I don't think I'll be able to fight.'

'What? Why not?' Shiva was startled; it couldn't be cowardice because that word simply didn't exist in his wife's vocabulary. So why was she backing down now, when the army had already marched for nearly a month through the dense forests that separated Meluha from Swadweep? They were deep in enemy territory now, and there was no turning back. 'Sati, this isn't like you,' he started.

'Um, Shiva . . .' Sati was horribly embarrassed. Such discussions were always difficult for the rather prudish Suryavanshis. 'I – I have my reasons,' she tried.

'Reasons?' asked Shiva. 'What—?' Suddenly the reason smacked him like a silent thunderbolt and he cried, 'My God! Sati, are you sure?'

'Yes,' she said, blushing bashfully.

'By the Holy Lake! I'm going to be a father?'

Seeing the ecstasy on Shiva's face, Sati felt a pang of guilt that she hadn't told him sooner.

'Wow!' he whooped, thrilled, and whirled her around in his arms. 'This is the best news I've heard in a long, long time!'

Sati smiled warmly and rested her head on his strong shoulder.

'We'll name our daughter after the one who's comforted you during the last two months, while I've been of no help whatsoever,' said Shiva. 'We'll name her Krittika!'

Sati looked up in surprise. She hadn't thought it possible to love him even more – but apparently it was. She smiled. 'It could be a son, you know.'

'Nah,' he grinned, 'it will be a daughter – and I'll spoil her to high heavens!'

Sati laughed and Shiva joined in – his first spirited laugh in more than two months. He embraced Sati, feeling the negative energy dissipate from his being. 'I love you, Sati.'

'I love you, too,' she whispered.

– ⚚ 𝕎 ᚋ ⚛ –

Shiva raised the flap and left the tent where Sati was ensconced with Krittika and Ayurvati. A retinue of nurses had been tasked to attend to her every need – Shiva had been obsessive about the health of his unborn child, questioning Ayurvati incessantly about every aspect of Sati's wellbeing for the last two months of the march to Swadweep.

The valiant Suryavanshis had been travelling a far more

challenging path than they'd expected. The forest had reclaimed its original territory with alarming ferocity, and the army had fallen prey to wild animals and disease at every turn. They'd lost two thousand men so far, and not one of them to the enemy. After the endless exhausting weeks of hacking and marching, the scouts had finally managed to lead the Suryavanshis to the Chandravanshis.

The Chandravanshis were camped on the sweeping plain of Dharmakhet, a clever choice of ground. The vast plain gave the Chandravanshis plenty of room to manoeuvre their million-strong army, allowing the full weight of their numerical superiority to come into play. The Suryavanshi scouts had tried to lure the Chandravanshis into attacking on less advantageous ground, but the enemy had held firm.

In the end, the Suryavanshis set up their camp in an easily defensible valley close to Dharmakhet.

Shiva gazed up at the clear sky where a lone eagle circled the camp overhead. Five pigeons flew lower, unafraid of the eagle: a strange sign. His Guna shaman would probably have declared it a bad omen for battle, for the pigeons clearly had some advantage the eagle couldn't see.

Don't think about that nonsense!

Drawing the fresh morning air deep into his lungs, he headed towards Emperor Daksha's tent, and met Nandi walking towards him.

'I was just coming to fetch you, my Lord. The emperor requests your presence – there's been a troubling development.'

They hurried into Daksha's tastefully appointed royal tent to find the emperor and his general engrossed in intense discussion. Vraka and Mayashrenik sat at a distance, and Drapaku was seated a little further away still.

'This is a disaster,' groaned Daksha.

'Your Majesty?' asked Shiva.

'My Lord! I'm glad you're here. We face complete disaster!'

'Let's not panic, your Majesty,' said Shiva. Turning to Parvateshwar, he asked, 'So your suspicions were correct?'

'They were,' Parvateshwar replied gravely. 'The scouts returned a few minutes ago: there's a reason the Chandravanshis were refusing to mobilise – they've despatched a hundred thousand soldiers in a great arc around our position. They'll enter our valley by tonight and we'll be trapped between their main force ahead of us and another hundred thousand at our backs.'

'We can't fight on two fronts, my Lord,' cried Daksha. 'What shall we do?'

'Was it Veerbhadra's scouts who brought the news?' asked Shiva and when the general nodded, Nandi immediately rushed out and returned moments later with Veerbhadra.

'What route is the Chandravanshi detachment taking, Bhadra?' asked Shiva.

'They're approaching along the steep mountains on our eastern flank. I think they intend to enter our valley some twenty-five miles north of our position.'

'Did you take a cartographer with you, as General Parvateshwar ordered?'

'Yes,' said Veerbhadra as he moved to the centre table and unrolled a map on it. Shiva and Parvateshwar leaned across to follow Veerbhadra's finger as he traced the route he'd described.

Shiva's eyes widened as he noticed an ideal defensive position, a long way north of the Suryavanshi camp. He looked up to meet Parvateshwar's triumphant gaze. The same thought had occurred to the general.

'How many men do you think?' asked Shiva.

'Difficult to say; it'll be tough, but the pass looks defensible. It'll take a sizeable contingent, though – at least thirty thousand.'

'But we can't spare that many men – I'm quite sure the main Chandravanshi army will attack tomorrow as well, while our smaller force is divided.'

Parvateshwar nodded grimly. *We might just have to retreat*, he thought unhappily, *and attempt to manoeuvre into a more advantageous position.*

'I think five thousand men ought to do it, my Lords.'

No one had noticed Drapaku move to the table. He was examining the pass Shiva had just pointed out.

'See – here?' Shiva and Parvateshwar looked where he was pointing. 'The mountains constrict rapidly to this pass, which is probably no more than fifty yards across. It doesn't matter how big their army is – only a few hundred men can come through that pass at one time.'

'But with a hundred thousand men, they can launch one charge after another, practically continuously,' said Mayashrenik. 'And the mountains are so steep that our missiles will be useless. Victory is almost impossible.'

'It's not about victory,' said Drapaku. 'It's about holding them for a day so that our main army can fight.'

'I'll do it,' said Parvateshwar.

'No, General,' said Vraka, 'you must lead the main charge.'

Shiva looked up at Parvateshwar. *I need to be here as well*, he thought, then said out loud, 'I can't do it either.'

Parvateshwar stared at Shiva, disillusionment written across his face. Even though he had prepared his heart for disappointment, he'd hoped that Shiva would prove him wrong. But now it was clear that Shiva would be watching the battle from the viewing platform currently being constructed for Emperor Daksha.

'Give me the honour, my Lord,' said Drapaku.

'Drapaku . . .' whispered Mayashrenik, but he didn't need to finish the sentence. Everyone else had already reached the same conclusion.

With only five thousand soldiers, the battle against the Chandravanshi detachment at the northern pass was a suicide mission.

'Drapaku,' said Shiva, 'I don't know if—'

'It's my destiny, my Lord,' interrupted Drapaku. 'I'll hold them for one day – with Lord Indra's help, I'll even try for two. Get us victory by then.'

Daksha made his decision. 'Wonderful. Drapaku, make preparations to leave immediately.'

Drapaku saluted smartly and rushed out of the tent before any second thoughts could be voiced.

— ⚔ ◍∪⚕✸ —

In less than an hour the *Vikarma* Brigade was marching out of the camp. The sun was high in the sky and practically the entire camp was watching the soldiers begin their mission. Everyone knew the terrible odds the *vikarmas* were going to face, and that few – if any – of these men would be seen alive again. But the *Vikarma* Brigade marched to their fate without betraying the slightest hesitation or hint of fear. The camp looked on in silent awe, a single thought reverberating through every mind so loudly it could almost be heard: *How can the* vikarmas *be so magnificent? They're supposed to be* weak.

Drapaku led the brigade, his handsome face smeared with warpaint. Over his armour he wore a saffron *angvastram*, the colour of the Parmatma – the colour worn for the final journey. He didn't expect to return.

He stopped suddenly as Vidyunmali ran in front of him. Drapaku frowned, but before he could react, Vidyunmali had drawn his knife. Drapaku reached for his sword, but Vidyunmali was quicker. He sliced his own thumb across the blade and brought it up to Drapaku's forehead. In the tradition of the great brother-warriors of antiquity, Vidyunmali smeared his blood across Drapaku's brow, signifying that his blood would protect him.

'You're a better man than me, Drapaku,' Vidyunmali whispered.

Drapaku stood silent, astonished by Vidyunmali's uncharacteristic behaviour.

Raising his balled fist high, Vidyunmali roared, 'Give them hell, *vikarma*!'

'Give them hell, *vikarma*,' bellowed the Suryavanshis, over and over again.

Drapaku and his men looked around the camp, absorbing the respect denied to them for so long – too long.

'Give them hell, *vikarma*!'

Drapaku saluted, then turned and resumed his march before his emotions spoiled the moment.

His soldiers followed to the constant chorus: 'Give them hell, *vikarma*!'

— ⁂ ⁂ —

And hell was exactly what the *Vikarma* Brigade gave the unsuspecting Chandravanshi detachment when they reached the northern pass. The battle was long and brutal, but the *vikarmas* fought like demons and held the enemy back throughout the night, buying precious time for the main Suryavanshi army.

The new day dawned bright and uncharacteristically warm for the time of year, and Shiva greeted it, prepared for war.

Sati stood resplendent, looping the *aarti thali*, the fire-ritual plate, in small circles around Shiva's face. After seven turns, she stopped winding, dipped her thumb in vermilion pigment and smeared it on Shiva's forehead. 'Come back victorious or don't come back at all.'

Shiva raised one eyebrow and grimaced. 'What kind of a send-off is that?'

'What? No, it's just—' stammered Sati.

'I know, I know.' Shiva smiled reassuringly as he embraced Sati. 'It's the traditional Suryavanshi send-off before a war, right?'

She looked up at him, her eyes moist. Her love for Shiva was overcoming decades of Suryavanshi training, and she was gradually becoming accustomed to letting him see her true feelings. 'Just come back safe and sound.'

'I will, my love,' whispered Shiva. 'You won't get rid of me that easily.'

Sati smiled weakly. 'I'll be waiting.' She stood on her toes and kissed Shiva lightly. He kissed her back and then turned away quickly before his heart could overwhelm his head with second thoughts. Lifting the tent flap, he walked out into the morning's heat and light. He looked up at the skies for omens in the clouds. There were none.

Thank the Holy Lake for that, at least.

The dry winter breeze carried the distant droning of Sanskrit *shlokas*, accompanied by the smooth, rhythmic pulse of war-drums. Shiva had thought this particular Suryavanshi custom odd at first, but conceded that maybe there was something to the Brahmin 'Call for Indra and Agni' after all. The drums and *shlokas* blended together somehow to rouse a fierce warrior spirit in whoever heard them, and the tempo would quicken as the battle began.

Eager to begin the fray, Shiva turned and strode towards Daksha's tent.

'Greetings, your Majesty,' said Shiva as he entered the royal tent, where Parvateshwar was explaining the battle-plan to the emperor. 'Namaste, Parvateshwar.'

Parvateshwar smiled and folded his hands, returning the greeting.

'What news of Drapaku and his men, General?' asked Shiva. 'The last despatch I heard is at least three hours old.'

'The *vikarma* battle is still on and Drapaku still leads them,' replied Parvateshwar. 'He's bought us invaluable time. May Lord Ram bless him.'

'May Lord Ram bless him indeed,' he echoed. 'He just has to hold on till the end of this day.'

'My Lord,' said Daksha, hands in a formal namaste, head bowed, 'it's an auspicious beginning – we'll have a good day, don't you think?'

'The news of Drapaku is very welcome,' replied Shiva, 'but perhaps we'll be better placed to answer that question in the fourth *prahar*, your Majesty.'

'I'm sure the answer will be the same: by the fourth *prahar* today, Emperor Dilipa will be standing in front of us in chains, waiting for justice to be done.'

'Careful, your Majesty,' said Shiva, with a smile to soften

his warning, 'let's not tempt fate. We still have to win the war.'

'With the Neelkanth on our side we just need to attack – victory is guaranteed.' The emperor sounded ebullient.

'I think more than a blue throat will be required to beat the Chandravanshis,' said Shiva. 'We shouldn't underestimate our enemy.'

'I'm not, but I won't make the mistake of underestimating you, either.'

Shiva gave up. He'd learned some time ago that it was impossible to win a debate against Daksha's unquestioning conviction.

'Perhaps I should take my leave, your Majesty,' said Parvateshwar. 'The time has come. With your permission?'

'Of course, Parvateshwar. *Vijayibhav,*' said Daksha, then, turning to Shiva, he continued, 'My Lord, they've built a viewing platform for us up on the hill behind the camp.'

'A viewing platform?' echoed Shiva, perplexed.

'Yes – we'll have the best view of the battle from there, plus it's the best place from which to direct the troops.'

Shiva's eyes widened in surprise. 'Your Majesty, my place is with the soldiers, on the battlefield.'

Parvateshwar stopped in his tracks, startled and delighted at having been proved wrong.

'My Lord, this is a job for butchers, not the Neelkanth.' Daksha sounded concerned. 'You don't need to sully your hands with Chandravanshi blood. Parvateshwar will arrest that Naga and throw him at your feet – then you can exact such a terrible retribution on him that his entire tribe will dread your justice for aeons.'

'This isn't about *my* revenge, your Majesty. It's about the vengeance of Meluha. It would be petty of me to think that an entire war is being fought just for my sake. This is a war between good and evil, a battle in which everyone has to choose a side and fight for it to their final breath. There are no bystanders in a *dharmayudh* – it's a *holy war*.'

Parvateshwar watched Shiva intently, his eyes blazing with admiration. Shiva was quoting Lord Ram's words: *There are no bystanders in a* dharmayudh.

'My Lord, we can't afford to risk your life,' Daksha pleaded. 'You're too important – I'm sure we can win this war without taking that gamble. Your presence has inspired us – there are many willing to shed their blood for you.'

'If they're willing to shed their blood for me, then I must be willing to shed my blood for them.'

Parvateshwar's heart was swamped by the greatest joy an accomplished Suryavanshi could feel: the joy of finally finding a man worth following, a man who was truly inspirational – a man who deserved to be spoken of in the same breath as Lord Ram himself.

Worried, Daksha came closer to Shiva. He realised that if he really wanted to persuade the Neelkanth out of this fool-hardiness, he'd have to speak his mind. He whispered softly, 'My Lord, you're my daughter's husband. If something happens to you, she'll have been bereaved twice in one life-time. I can't let that happen to her.'

'That's not going to happen, your Majesty,' whispered Shiva.

'In any case, Sati would die a thousand deaths if she saw her husband stay away from a *dharmayudh*. She'd lose respect for me – and rightly so. If she weren't pregnant, she'd be fighting alongside me, shoulder to shoulder. You know that.'

Daksha stared disconsolately at Shiva, troubled and apprehensive.

Shiva smiled reassuringly. 'Everything's going to be fine, your Majesty.'

'And what if it's not?'

'Then remember that whatever happens, it's for a good cause. And Sati will be proud of me, whether I live or die.'

Daksha continued to stare at Shiva, his face a portrait of agonised distress.

'Forgive me, but I must go,' said Shiva with a formal namaste, turning to leave.

Parvateshwar, as if commanded by some higher power, followed Shiva distractedly.

As Shiva strode briskly out of the tent towards his horse, he heard Parvateshwar's booming voice. 'My Lord!'

He continued walking.

'My Lord!' bellowed Parvateshwar again, more insistently this time.

Shiva stopped abruptly and turned, a surprised frown on his face. 'I'm sorry, Parvateshwar – I thought you were calling out to the emperor.'

'No, my Lord,' said Parvateshwar, catching up with Shiva, 'It's you I'm calling.'

His frown deeper, Shiva asked, 'What's the matter, brave General?'

Parvateshwar drew himself to rigid military attention. He kept a polite distance from Shiva – he could not stand on the hallowed ground that cradled the Mahadev. As if in a daze, he slowly curled his fist and brought it up to his chest, then bowed low, completing the formal Meluhan salute, lower than he had ever bowed before a living man – as low as he bowed before Lord Ram's idol during his regular morning prayers.

Shiva continued to stare at Parvateshwar, his expression an odd mixture of surprise and embarrassment. He respected Parvateshwar far too much to be comfortable with such open idolisation.

Drawing himself upright but with his head still bowed, Parvateshwar whispered, 'I'll be honoured to shed my blood with you, my Lord.' Raising his head, he repeated, 'Honoured.'

Shiva smiled and touched Parvateshwar's arm. 'Well, if our plans are good, my friend, hopefully we won't have to shed too much of it!'

CHAPTER 23

Dharmayudh, the Holy War

The Suryavanshis were deployed in a bow-like formation, strong yet flexible. The brand-new tortoise regiments were positioned at the centre, flanked by light infantry, which was bordered in turn by cavalry. This was almost exactly according to the battle plan they had made earlier. Heavy rain during the night had led to the decision to abandon the chariots — they couldn't risk the wheels getting bogged down in the mud and breaking the formation. Hidden from view behind the Suryavanshi infantry were the new archer regiments, lying on skilfully designed backrests. Just as Shiva and Parvateshwar had envisioned, the supine archers braced the extra-large bows with their feet, which allowed the strings to be drawn up to their chins to release hefty arrows almost the size of small spears.

The Chandravanshis were positioned in a more standard offensive formation that played to their numerical strength.

A full legion of infantry – fifty squads of five thousand soldiers each – were deployed in a straight line that stretched as far as the eye could see, with three more such legions positioned behind the first. This formation offered tremendous strength and solidity for a direct assault against a numerically inferior enemy, but it had the disadvantage of being somewhat rigid. Spaces between the squads would allow the cavalry to charge through if required. On seeing the Suryavanshi formation, the Chandravanshi cavalry had been moved from the rear to the flanks to match their opponents. The Chandravanshi general was clearly well versed in the ancient traditions of pitched battle, and the formation he'd selected would have been the perfect offensive against an enemy also employing standard tactics. But he was up against a Tibetan tribal chief whose innovations had transformed the usual Suryavanshi plan of attack.

As Shiva rode towards the hillock at the edge of the main battlefield, the Brahmins picked up the tempo of their *shlokas* and the war-drums pumped the energy level ever higher. Despite being vastly outnumbered, the Suryavanshis had buried their fear deep within and they faced their enemy with straight backs and heads held high.

Suddenly the war-cries of the brigades' clan-gods rent the air.

'*Indra dev ki jai!*'

'*Agni dev ki jai!*'

'*Jai Shakti devi ki!*'

'*Varun dev ki jai!*'

'*Jai Pawan dev ki!*'

And then the soldiers saw a magnificent white steed canter in over the hillock carrying a handsome, muscular figure, and every voice united in a thunderous roar that pierced the sky, a battle-cry loud enough to draw the attention of the gods in their cloud palaces to the events unfolding below. The Neelkanth raised his hand in acknowledgement as General Parvateshwar, Nandi and Veerbhadra rode up to join him.

Vraka was off his horse in a flash as Shiva approached. Parvateshwar dismounted equally rapidly and was standing next to Vraka before Shiva could reach him.

'With your leave, the Lord will lead the right flank, Brigadier,' said Parvateshwar.

'It'll be my honour to fight under his command, General,' said a beaming Vraka. Dropping to one knee, he drew his field commander's baton from his belt and raised his hand high to hand over the charge to Shiva.

Jumping down from his horse, Shiva smiled ruefully and said, 'You people really will have to stop doing this kind of thing – you're embarrassing me!' Pulling Vraka to his feet, Shiva embraced him tightly. 'I'm your friend, not your Lord, Vraka.'

The brigadier stepped back quickly, startled by the gush of positive energy flowing from Shiva. He mumbled, 'Yes, my Lord.'

Shaking his head, Shiva gently took the baton from Vraka's

extended hand and raised it high for the entire Suryavanshi army to see.

An ear-splitting cry ripped through the ranks: 'Mahadev! Mahadev! Mahadev!'

Shiva vaulted back onto his horse in one smooth movement. Holding the baton high, he rode up and down the line as the Suryavanshi roar grew louder and louder.

'Mahadev!'

'Mahadev!'

'Mahadev!'

'Suryavanshis,' bellowed Shiva. 'Meluhans! Hear me!'

The army quickly quietened down to listen to their living god.

'Who is a Mahadev?' roared Shiva, and to a man, they listened in rapt attention, hanging on his every word.

'Is he one who sits idly by, looking on while ordinary men do *his* job for him? No!'

Some soldiers were mouthing inaudible prayers.

'Is he one who lazily bestows his blessings while others do the fighting? Does he stand nonchalantly by and count the dead while the living sacrifice themselves to destroy evil? No!'

Now you could have heard a pin drop as the Suryavanshis absorbed their Neelkanth's message.

'A man *becomes* a Mahadev only when he fights for good. A Mahadev isn't born from his mother's womb. He's forged in the heat of battle, when he wages a war to destroy evil!'

The army stood hushed, flooded with Shiva's positive energy.

'I am a Mahadev,' bellowed Shiva.

The Suryavanshis let loose a resounding triumphant roar. They were led by the Mahadev, the God of Gods. The Chandravanshis didn't stand a chance.

'But I am not the only one!'

A shocked silence descended on the Suryavanshis. What did the Mahadev mean? Did the Chandravanshis have one, too?

'I am not the only one,' Shiva repeated. 'I see a hundred thousand Mahadevs in front of me! I see a hundred thousand men willing to fight on the side of good! I see a hundred thousand men willing to battle evil! I see a hundred thousand men capable of *destroying* evil!'

The stunned Suryavanshis gaped at their Neelkanth as his words filled their minds with a question they dared not ask: *Are we gods?*

Shiva had the answer: '*Har Ek Hai Mahadev!*'

The Meluhans stood there, astounded. *Every single one a Mahadev?*

'*Har Har Mahadev*,' bellowed Shiva.

The Meluhans took up his cry and roared, 'All of us are Mahadevs!' Pure primal energy coursed through every Suryavanshi's veins. They were gods! It didn't matter that the Chandravanshis outnumbered them ten to one. Even if the evil Chandravanshis outnumbered them a hundred to one, victory was assured. They were gods!

'*Har Har Mahadev*,' cried the Suryavanshi army.

'*Har Har Mahadev*,' yelled Shiva. 'All of us are gods – gods on a mission!'

Drawing his sword, he pulled on the reins and his horse reared on its hind legs with a ferocious neigh, then pirouetted smartly to face the Chandravanshis. Shiva pointed his sword at his enemies. 'Gods on a mission to destroy evil!'

The Suryavanshis echoed their Lord's triumphant cry: '*Har Har Mahadev!*'

Victory would be theirs. '*Har Har Mahadev!*'

Evil's long reign of terror would end today. '*Har Har Mahadev!*'

As the army roared like the gods they were, Shiva rode towards a beaming Parvateshwar, who was flanked by Nandi, Veerbhadra and Vraka.

'Nice speech,' said Veerbhadra, grinning from ear to ear.

Shiva winked at his old friend as he turned his horse towards Parvateshwar. 'General, I think it's time we started our own rainfall.'

'Yes, my Lord.' Turning his horse smartly around, Parvateshwar gave the orders to his flag-bearer. 'The archers!'

The flag-bearer raised the coded flag – vicious black lightning on a red ground – and flag-bearers along the lines repeated the message through the ranks in a blood-red wave. The Suryavanshi infantry immediately crouched down and Shiva and his companions dismounted rapidly, pulling their horses down to their knees.

And then the arrows flew in a deadly downpour.

The archers had been positioned in a semicircular formation to cover as wide a swathe of the Chandravanshi army as possible. The sky turned black as five thousand archers rained death on the Chandravanshis. The hapless Swadweepans were easy prey in their tight formations, and the spear-like arrows easily penetrated the leather and wood shields of the irregular Chandravanshi infantry. Only the regulars held metal shields. Within minutes, the ruthless hail of arrows raining down on the squads of the first legion began to take its toll and the Chandravanshi lines started to break. Terrified out of their wits by the massacre in their midst, the irregulars were the first to bolt, and soon chaos and confusion reigned in the legions behind them.

Parvateshwar turned towards Shiva. 'I think we should lengthen the range, my Lord.'

Shiva nodded his agreement and Parvateshwar signalled his flag-bearer to relay the message. The archers stopped shooting briefly and engaged the clever mechanisms in their backrests to rapidly raise the height of their feet to set a longer range. The next wave of arrows hit the Chandravanshis' second legion, and the combination of the retreating first legion and the hail of arrows created bedlam in the ranks.

Shiva noticed the Chandravanshi cavalry coming up into position. 'General, their cavalry's moving out to flank us and attack the archers. Our cavalry needs to meet them midfield.'

'Agreed, my Lord,' said Parvateshwar. 'I was expecting this move, so I positioned a block of Arishtanemi cavalry on each flank, led by Mayashrenik and Vidyunmali.'

'Perfect! But our cavalry mustn't move too far ahead or

our arrows will injure our own men. They will have to hold their position for at least another five minutes so our archers can finish their job.'

'Agreed.' Parvateshwar turned to his flag-bearer with detailed instructions and two couriers set off rapidly to the left and right. Within moments, the Arishtanemi thundered out to meet the Chandravanshi counter-attack.

Meanwhile, the disarray in the Chandravanshi second legion increased as the unrelenting rain of arrows pounded down on them. The Suryavanshi archers ignored their tiring limbs and bleeding hands, bravely continuing their unremitting assault, and soon the second legion's line started breaking as the Chandravanshis tried desperately to escape the ruthless carnage.

'Higher range, my Lord?' asked Parvateshwar, pre-empting Shiva's words, and he nodded in reply.

Meanwhile the Suryavanshi and Chandravanshi cavalries were engaged in fierce combat on the eastern and western ends of the battlefield. The Chandravanshis knew they had to break through – a few more minutes of the Suryavanshi archers' assault and the battle would be all but lost. They fought desperately, like wounded tigers. Swords cut through flesh and bone. Spears pierced body-armour. Soldiers with limbs hanging half-severed continued to battle away. Horses missing their riders attacked as if their own lives depended on it. The Chandravanshis were throwing all their might into breaking through the line protecting the Suryavanshi archers – but Mayashrenik and Vidyunmali were the fiercest brigadiers in the Meluhan army, and they and their men fought ferociously, holding the mammoth Chandravanshi force at bay.

The archers started their onslaught on the Chandravanshis' third legion. Vast numbers of their men were already dead, bleeding to death or deserting, but the remaining regulars grimly – courageously – held their positions. When their shields could no longer block the arrows, they used the bodies of their dead comrades. But they held the line.

'Do we stop now and charge, my Lord?' asked Parvateshwar.

'Not yet – I want the third legion devastated as well. A few more minutes should do it.'

'Yes, my Lord. I think half the archers should increase their range a bit more, to lay down fire on the weaker sections of the fourth legion. If their lines are broken too, confusion will engulf the heart of their troops.'

'Good thinking, Parvateshwar. See to it, please.'

Meanwhile, over on the western flank, the Chandravanshi cavalry, sensing the hopelessness of their charge, began to retreat. Some Arishtanemi riders moved to give chase, but Vidyunmali ordered them to hold their present positions, in case of counter-attack, and once their enemy had returned behind their remaining lines of infantry, Vidyunmali ordered his own cavalry to withdraw to their initial position on the flank of the bow formation.

The Chandravanshis facing Mayashrenik were made of sterner stuff, fighting on grimly, despite taking severe casualties; they refused to retreat, though Mayashrenik and his men battled fiercely, holding them at bay.

Suddenly, the hail of arrows stopped – the archers had been ordered to stand down – and the Chandravanshi brigadier immediately ordered his cavalry to retreat, now that their mission to stop the archers had been accomplished, with or without their intervention.

In turn, Mayashrenik quickly withdrew his troops to their earlier position to prepare for the main charge, which he knew was just a few moments away.

'General, shall we?' asked Shiva, nodding towards the left flank.

'Yes, my Lord,' replied Parvateshwar.

As Parvateshwar turned to mount his horse, Shiva called out to him, 'Race you to the last line of Chandravanshis!'

Parvateshwar raised his eyebrows in surprise, but smiling broadly, cried, 'I'll win that race, my Lord.'

'We'll see.' Shiva grinned, his eyes narrowed in playful challenge.

Parvateshwar rapidly mounted his horse and rode to his command on the left while Shiva, accompanied by Vraka, Nandi and Veerbhadra, rode to the right. In the centre, Prasanjit rallied his tortoise corps, ready for the attack.

'Meluhans,' roared Shiva, dismounting smoothly, 'your enemies lie in front of you, waiting to be slaughtered! It ends today! *Evil ends today!*'

'*Har Har Mahadev,*' bellowed the soldiers as the Meluhan

conch-shell announced the Suryavanshi attack, and with an ear-shattering yell, the infantry charged. The tortoise corps moved at their slow, unyielding pace towards the Chandravanshi centre, while the sides of the bow formation moved more quickly, the cavalry cantering along the flanks to protect the infantry from an enemy charge.

Meanwhile, the courageous remnants of the third and fourth Chandravanshi legions were rapidly re-forming their lines to face the Suryavanshi onslaught – but the mass of dead bodies, their fallen comrades, didn't allow them the space they needed to form their traditional *Chaturanga* formation, which would have allowed some lateral movement. And all too soon the Suryavanshis were upon them.

The battle was going almost exactly to plan for the Suryavanshis. The remaining enemy soldiers, trained and vicious regulars to a man, had managed to form a tight, slightly curved line – but the unstoppable tortoise corps tore ruthlessly into them, the shields providing protection against even the best Chandravanshi swordsmen while their *trishuls* ripped mercilessly through them. The Chandravanshis had only two choices: either fall to the *trishuls* or be pushed towards the flanks, where the Suryavanshi cavalry were rapidly bearing down hard on them. As the core of the Chandravanshi army finally broke under the unrelenting assault, the Suryavanshi flanks tore through their sides.

Shiva, leading his flank's ferocious charge, was decimating all in front of him. Noticing the enemy lines thinning unexpectedly, he allowed his fellow soldiers to charge ahead of him while he jumped high, using the shoulders of Nandi as leverage, to see what was happening – and was shocked to discover that a section of the Chandravanshi line opposing him was moving to attack the exposed flank of the tortoise corps, their right side, which could not be protected by shields. Someone in the Chandravanshi army was using his brains. If any of the tortoises broke, the Chandravanshis would swarm through the Suryavanshi centre in a tight line, to devastating effect.

'Meluhans,' roared Shiva, 'follow me!'

Shiva's flag-bearer raised his pennant and the men followed as the Neelkanth led the charge, this time into the flank of the Chandravanshi line bearing down on the tortoises. Caught in a pincer attack between the *trishuls* and the charge from Shiva's flank, the Chandravanshis' spirit finally broke.

The once mighty Chandravanshi army was now reduced to pockets of independent stragglers fighting valiantly for a losing cause. Shiva and Parvateshwar rallied their cohorts one last time to finish it once and for all. The Suryavanshi victory was absolute. The Chandravanshi army had been comprehensively routed.

CHAPTER 24

A Stunning Revelation

Sati rushed out of her tent, closely followed by Krittika and Ayurvati, who called, 'Slow down, Sati! In your condition—'

Sati turned her head and grinned back at Ayurvati, but she didn't reduce her pace as she sprinted to the royal tent where Shiva and Parvateshwar had retired after the declaration of victory. Nandi and Veerbhadra stood guard at the entrance. They moved aside to let Sati in, but barred Ayurvati and Krittika.

'I'm sorry, Lady Ayurvati,' said Nandi apologetically, his head bowed. 'I have strict instructions not to let anybody in.'

'Why?' asked Ayurvati, surprised.

'I don't know, my Lady. I am very sorry.'

'I understand,' said Ayurvati. 'You're only doing your job.'

Veerbhadra looked at Krittika. 'I'm sorry, darling.'

'Please don't call me that in public,' whispered Krittika, embarrassed.

Meanwhile Sati had pulled the curtain aside and entered the tent.

'I don't know, my Lord,' said Parvateshwar. 'It doesn't make sense.'

Sati was surprised to hear Parvateshwar calling Shiva 'my Lord', but her joy at seeing her husband safe brushed every other thought aside. 'Shiva!'

'Sati?' mumbled Shiva, turning towards her.

Sati froze. There was no smile of greeting when his eyes met hers, no flush of victory on his face. He hadn't even allowed his wounds to be dressed. 'What's wrong?' she asked.

Shiva stared at her, a deeply worrying expression on his face.

She glanced at Parvateshwar, who met her gaze for an instant with an obviously forced smile – the smile he usually wore when he was trying to shield her from some bad news. 'What is it, *Pitratulya*?'

He looked at Shiva, who spoke at last. 'Something about this war is troubling us.'

'What could possibly trouble you?' she asked, surprised. 'You've led the Suryavanshis to their greatest victory of all time – this defeat of the Chandravanshis is even more comprehensive than my grandfather's achievement. You should be proud!'

'I didn't see any Nagas with the Chandravanshis,' said Shiva.

'The Nagas weren't there?' asked Sati, frowning. 'That doesn't make sense.'

'No, it doesn't,' replied Shiva, his eyes shadowed with fore-boding. 'If they're true allies of the Chandravanshis, they'd have fought alongside them – their skills would have been invaluable on the battlefield. But where were they?'

'Maybe they've fallen out with each other,' suggested Sati.

'I don't think so,' said Parvateshwar. 'This battle was trig-gered by their joint attack on Mandar – why would they not be here for it?'

'Shiva, I'm sure you'll figure it out,' said Sati. 'Don't trouble yourself too much.'

'Dammit, Sati,' he yelled, 'I'm worried precisely because I *can't* figure it out!'

Stunned by his uncharacteristic vehemence, Sati stepped back. He wasn't like this.

Shiva realised instantly what he'd done and immediately reached out his bloodied hand. 'I'm sorry, Sati. It's just that I—'

The conversation was interrupted as Daksha, accompanied by an aide, raised the curtain and swaggered into the tent.

'My Lord,' cried Daksha as he embraced Shiva.

Shiva flinched – his wounds hurt – and Daksha immedi-ately stepped back.

'I'm so sorry, my Lord,' said the emperor. Turning to his aide, he asked, 'Why is Ayurvati outside? Bring her in at once – let her tend to the Lord's wounds.'

'No – wait,' said Shiva, raising a hand to stop the aide. 'There'll be plenty of time to dress our wounds later, and right now we have more pressing business.' He turned to Daksha. 'Your Majesty, I need to tell you—'

'My Lord, if you'll allow me to speak first,' said Daksha, as enthusiastic as a little boy who had just been given a long-denied sweet. 'I want to thank you for everything you've done for me — for Meluha. With your help we've achieved something even my father couldn't: this is an absolute victory!'

Shiva and Parvateshwar glanced briefly at each other before Daksha demanded their attention again.

'Emperor Dilipa is being brought here even as we speak,' he said.

'What?' asked Parvateshwar, taken aback. 'But we only just despatched our soldiers to the enemy camp. They can't possibly have arrested him so soon.'

'But I sent my personal guards much earlier,' said Daksha. 'We could tell from the viewing platform that the Chandravanshis had already lost by the time you began the third charge — the benefit of the perspective you get from a distance. I was worried that Dilipa might escape, like the coward he is, so I sent my personal guards to arrest him.'

'But, your Majesty,' said Parvateshwar, 'shouldn't we discuss the terms of surrender before we bring him in? What terms are we going to offer?'

'Offer?' cried Daksha, his eyes ablaze with the euphoria of triumph, 'we don't need to *offer* him anything – not after such a decisive rout – Dilipa's being brought here as a common criminal. Nevertheless, we'll show him how merciful Meluha

can be. We'll make him such an offer that his next seven generations will be singing our praises!'

Before a surprised Shiva could ask exactly what the emperor
had in mind, the royal guard's crier announced Emperor Dilipa's
arrival. He was accompanied by his son, Crown Prince
Bhagirath.

'Just a minute, Kaustav,' said Daksha as he rushed around
the tent, making sure everything was arranged exactly as he
wanted it. He sat down on a chair placed in the centre of the
space and asked Shiva to sit to his right. As Shiva sat, Sati
turned to leave the tent, but Shiva reached for her hand.
Turning, she saw his need and positioned herself on a chair
behind her husband. Parvateshwar sat to the emperor's left.

Daksha then called out loudly, 'Let him in.'

Shiva was interested to see the face of evil. Despite his
misgivings about the absence of the Nagas, he genuinely
believed he had fought a righteous war on the right side.
Seeing the defeated face of the evil Chandravanshi king would
complete the victory.

Dilipa entered, and Shiva straightened in surprise. Dilipa
was not at all as he'd expected. He looked like an old man –
a rare sight in Meluha due to the *Somras* – but despite his age,
he had a rakishly handsome bearing. He was of medium height,
with dark skin and a slightly muscular build. His clothes were
radically different from the sober Meluhan attire; in his bright
pink *dhoti*, a gleaming violet *angvastram* and a profusion of
gold jewellery he looked like something of a dandy. His face

had the crow's feet of a life lived well. A trimmed salt-and-pepper beard, accompanied by thick white hair under his extravagant crown, completed the effetely intellectual look.

'Where's Crown Prince Bhagirath?' asked Daksha.

'He can be a bit . . . hot-headed,' said Dilipa, 'so I've asked him to wait outside for now.' He looked only at Daksha, refusing to acknowledge the presence of the others in the tent. 'Don't you Meluhans have the courtesy to offer a seat to your guests?'

'You're not a guest, Emperor Dilipa,' said Daksha. 'You're a prisoner.'

'Yes, yes, I know – can't you take a joke?' asked Dilipa superciliously. 'So what do you people want this time?'

Daksha stared at Dilipa quizzically, a little taken aback by his unexpectedly blasé attitude.

'You stole the Yamuna's waters a hundred years ago,' continued Dilipa. 'What else do you want?'

Surprised, Shiva turned towards Daksha.

'We didn't steal the Yamuna's waters,' yelled Daksha angrily. 'They were ours and we took them back!'

'Oh, whatever,' said Dilipa with a dismissive wave of his hand. 'What are your demands this time?'

Shiva was astonished at how the conversation was going. They'd just defeated this evil man – he should be contrite, repentant, not condescending and self-righteous.

Daksha gazed at Dilipa with wide eyes and a kindly smile. 'I have no demands. I want to give you something.'

Dilipa raised his eyebrows warily. '*Give* us something?'

'Yes – I intend to give you the benefit of our way of life.'

Dilipa continued to stare at Daksha with suspicion.

'We're going to elevate you to our superior way of life,' continued Daksha; from the sound of his voice he was marvelling at his own generosity. 'We're going to reform you.'

'*Reform* us?' said Dilipa, barely suppressing a snigger.

'Yes. My general, Parvateshwar, will run your empire from now on as viceroy of Swadweep, although you'll continue to be the titular head of state. Parvateshwar will ensure that your corrupt people are re-educated in the Meluhan way of life. We'll live together as brothers from now on.'

Stunned, Parvateshwar turned towards Daksha – he hadn't expected to be despatched to Swadweep.

Dilipa appeared to be having great difficulty controlling his laughter. 'You actually think your strait-laced men can run Swadweep? My people are mercurial – they won't listen to your moralising!'

'Oh, but they will,' sneered Daksha. 'They'll listen to everything we have to say – you don't know where the actual voice will be coming from.'

'Do enlighten me.'

Daksha motioned towards Shiva and said, 'Look who sits with us.'

Dilipa barely glanced at Shiva. He asked incredulously, 'Who's he? What in Lord Indra's name is so special about him?'

Shiva squirmed, feeling increasingly uncomfortable.

Daksha raised his voice a little, his tone becoming ever more strident. 'Look at his throat, O king of the Chandravanshis.'

Dilipa flicked his arrogant gaze towards Shiva again. Despite the dried blood and gore, his blue throat blazed. Dilipa's haughty smile disappeared as his mouth fell open. He tried to speak, but was at a loss for words.

'Yes, O corrupt Chandravanshi,' scoffed Daksha. 'We have the Neelkanth.'

Dilipa had the dazed look of a child brutally knifed by his beloved father, and Shiva's apprehension increased. His heart was troubled. This was not the way this meeting was supposed to go.

Daksha continued his hectoring. 'The Neelkanth has sworn to destroy the evil Chandravanshi way of life. You *have* to listen to him.'

A bewildered Dilipa stared at Shiva for what felt like an eternity. At long last he recovered enough to softly whisper, 'Whatever you say.'

Before Daksha could bluster further, Dilipa turned and staggered towards the tent curtain. At the exit, he looked at Shiva once again. Shiva could have sworn he could see tears in those proud eyes.

As soon as Dilipa left the tent, Daksha got up and hugged Shiva, gently this time, so as not to hurt the Neelkanth further. 'My Lord, did you see the look on his face? It was precious!' Turning towards Parvateshwar, he continued, 'Parvateshwar,

Dilipa is broken. You'll have no trouble controlling the Swadweepans and bringing them around to our way of life. We'll go down in history as the men who found a permanent solution to this problem!'

Shiva wasn't listening. His troubled heart was desperately searching for answers. How could a struggle that had appeared so righteous just a few hours back now suddenly appear wrong? He turned towards Sati, forlorn.

She gently touched his shoulder.

'What are you thinking, my Lord?' asked Daksha, intruding on Shiva's troubled thoughts.

Shiva shook his head, at a loss for words.

'I asked if you'd like to travel to Ayodhya in Dilipa's carriage,' said Daksha. 'You deserve the honour, my Lord – you've led us to this glorious victory.'

Shiva had lost all interest in the conversation and couldn't summon the energy to reply. He just nodded distractedly.

'Wonderful,' said Daksha, oblivious to Shiva's unease. 'I'll make all the arrangements.' Turning to his aide, he continued, 'Send Ayurvati in immediately to dress the Lord's wounds. We must be on our way to take control of Ayodhya by tomorrow morning before chaos reigns in the aftermath of Dilipa's defeat.'

With a namaste towards Shiva, Daksha turned to leave. 'Parvateshwar, aren't you coming?'

Parvateshwar was gazing at Shiva, his face creased with concern.

'Parvateshwar?' repeated Daksha, his tone a little sharper.

Glancing rapidly at Sati, Parvateshwar turned to follow his emperor. Sati stood and moved to kneel in front of Shiva, holding his face gently. Shiva's eyes suddenly drooped with the heavy weight of exhaustion.

Ayurvati ducked her head around the curtain. 'How are you, my Lord?'

Shiva looked up, his eyes half-shut as he felt himself slipping into a strange sleep. Suddenly he yelled, 'Nandi!' and the captain came rushing in.

'Nandi, can you find me a cravat?'

'A cravat, my Lord?' asked Nandi. 'Why?'

'Because I need one,' shouted Shiva.

Nandi, stunned by the vehemence, hurried out immediately to do Shiva's bidding. Sati and Ayurvati looked at Shiva in surprise, but before they could say anything, he suddenly collapsed, unconscious.

— ✸ ◍ ∪ ⵌ ⊕ —

He was running hard, the menacing forest closing in on him. He was desperate to get beyond the trees before their ravenous claws could slice into him. Suddenly, a loud, insistent cry pierced the silence.

'Help! Please help!'

He stopped. No, he wouldn't run away this time. He would fight that monster. He was the Mahadev. It was his duty. Shiva turned around slowly, his sword drawn, his shield held high.

'*Jai Shri Ram*,' he yelled as he raced back to the clearing. The bushy thorns slashed his legs. Bleeding and terrified, he ran hard.

I will reach her in time.

I won't fail her again.

My blood will wash away my sin.

He sprang through the last clump of shrubs into the clearing, ignoring the thorns greedily cutting at his flesh, his shield held defensively, his sword gripped low to retaliate. But nobody attacked. A strange laughter finally broke his concentration and he slowly lowered his shield.

'Oh Lord,' he shrieked in agony.

The woman lay stricken on the ground, a short sword buried in her heart. The little boy stood at her side, stunned, his hand bloodied from the struggle of his kill. The hairy monster sat on the rocky ledge, pointing at the little boy. *Laughing*.

'No!' screamed Shiva as he jerked himself awake.

'What's happened, Shiva?' asked Sati, darting to hold his hand.

Shiva looked around the room, startled. Worried, Parvateshwar and Ayurvati got up too.

'Shiva, it's all right. It's all right,' whispered Sati, gently running her hand along Shiva's face.

'You were poisoned, my Lord,' said Ayurvati. 'We think some of the Chandravanshi soldiers may have had poisoned weapons – many others have been affected.'

Shiva slowly regained his composure and made to rise from his bed. Sati tried to help him up, but he insisted on doing it himself. His throat felt excruciatingly parched. He stumbled over to the ewer, reached over and gulped down some water. 'I feel like I've been asleep for hours,' he said, finally noticing the lamps and the dark sky beyond the tent flap.

'You have,' said Ayurvati. 'Close to thirty-six hours.'

'Thirty-six hours?' As he collapsed onto a comfortable chair he noticed a forbidding figure sitting at the back of the tent, his right eye covered with a bandage, his left arm, from which his hand had been amputated, in a sling. 'Drapaku?'

'Yes, my Lord,' said Drapaku as he tried to rise and salute.

'My God, Drapaku – it's so good to see you. Please sit down!'

'It's heavenly to see you, my Lord,'

'How was your battle?'

'I lost too many men, my Lord – almost half of them – and this hand and eye,' he whispered, 'but by your grace, we held them until the main battle was won.'

'It wasn't my grace, my friend. It was your bravery,' said Shiva. 'I'm so proud of you all.'

'Thank you, my Lord.'

Sati stood next to her husband, gently caressing his hair. 'Are you sure you want to sit, Shiva? You can lie down for a while longer, if you like.'

'I've slouched around enough, Sati,' said Shiva with a weak smile.

Ayurvati was relieved to see that. 'Well, the poison certainly hasn't affected your sense of humour, my Lord.'

'Really? Is it still that bad?' said Shiva, grinning now.

Parvateshwar, Drapaku and Ayurvati laughed weakly at his joke, but Sati didn't join them. She was watching Shiva intently. He was trying too hard, trying to get others to focus on something other than himself. Had this last dream been so much worse than the others?

'Where is his Majesty?' asked Shiva.

'Father left for Ayodhya this morning,' said Sati.

'My Lord,' said Parvateshwar, 'the emperor thought it unwise to leave Swadweep without a sovereign for too long, considering the circumstances. He decided to march the Suryavanshi army off immediately, with Emperor Dilipa as his prisoner, to consolidate the Suryavanshi victory and show the Swadweepans who's in charge here now.'

'So we're not going to Ayodhya?'

'We will, my Lord,' said Ayurvati, 'but in a few days, when you're strong enough.'

'Some twelve thousand of our soldiers remain with us,' said Parvateshwar. 'His Majesty also insisted that Emperor Dilipa leave behind one of his family members as a hostage to ensure that no Swadweepans are tempted to attack our much smaller force.'

'So who has Emperor Dilipa left with us?'

'His daughter,' said Parvateshwar, 'Princess Anandmayi.'

Ayurvati smiled, shaking her head slightly.

'What are you smiling at?' asked Shiva.

Ayurvati looked sheepishly at Parvateshwar and then grinned at Sati. Parvateshwar glared back at Ayurvati.

'What's happened?' asked Shiva again.

'Nothing important, my Lord,' said Parvateshwar, looking strangely embarrassed. 'It's just that she's quite a handful.'

'I'll be sure to keep out of her way, then,' said Shiva, smiling.

— ⁂ ⊙U⊕ ⊛ —

'So this route appears to make the most sense,' said Parvateshwar, pointing at the map.

Five more days had passed, and Shiva and the other poisoned soldiers had finally recovered enough to travel.

'I think you're right,' said Shiva, his mind wandering back to the meeting with the Emperor of Swadweep.

No point thinking about Dilipa. I'm sure he was acting during the meeting. The Chandravanshis are evil, capable of any deception. Our war was righteous.

'We leave for Ayodhya tomorrow morning, my Lord,' said Parvateshwar. Turning to Sati, he added, 'You can finally see Lord Ram's birthplace, my child.'

'Indeed, *Pitratulya*,' replied Sati, 'although these evil people may have destroyed his temple in their hatred.'

A loud commotion outside interrupted their conversation, and Parvateshwar asked Nandi, 'What's going on out there?'

'Princess Anandmayi is here, my lord,' said Nandi from the other side of the curtain. 'She has some demands, but we can't fulfil them. She insists on meeting with you, General.'

'Please tell her Highness to wait in her tent,' growled Parvateshwar. 'I'll be over in a few minutes.'

'I won't wait, General,' screamed a strong yet feminine voice from beyond the curtain.

At Shiva's signal Parvateshwar, sighing, said, 'Nandi, Veerbhadra, bring her in – but check her first for weapons.'

In a few moments, Princess Anandmayi stormed into Shiva's tent, flanked by Nandi and Veerbhadra. Shiva raised an eyebrow at her appearance. She was taller than her father, and quite distractingly beautiful. A deep walnut-coloured complexion enhanced a bountifully voluptuous body. Darkly seductive doe eyes complemented a perpetual pout that was both sensual and intimidating. She was provocatively clothed, her *dhoti* tied scandalously low at the waist and tightly hugging her curvaceous hips before ending well above her knees. It was barely longer than the loincloths Meluhan men wore during their ceremonial baths. Her blouse was similar to the cloth piece Meluhan women wore, but it had been cut low to emphasise the shape of her ample breasts, affording a full view of her generous cleavage. She stood with her hips tilted to one side, exuding raw passion.

'You really think I can hide any weapons in this?' she said sarcastically, pointing at her skimpy garments.

Nandi and Sati glared at her in annoyance, while Shiva and Veerbhadra shared a surprised grin.

'How are you doing, General Parvateshwar?' asked

Anandmayi, flashing him a smile while scanning him from head to toe, her eyebrows raised lasciviously.

Shiva couldn't help smiling as he saw Parvateshwar blush slightly.

'What do you desire, Princess?' barked Parvateshwar. 'We're in the middle of an important meeting.'

'Will you really give me what I desire, General?' said Anandmayi seductively.

Parvateshwar's blush deepened. 'Princess, we've no time for nonsensical talk!'

'Ah, that's most unfortunate. Then perhaps you can find me some milk and rose petals in this sorry little camp of yours.'

Parvateshwar turned towards Nandi in surprise, and the Captain cried, 'My lord, she doesn't want just a glass, but fifty pints of milk – we can't spare that much from our rations.'

'You're going to drink fifty pints of milk?' said Parvateshwar, his eyes wide in astonishment.

'I need it for my beauty bath, General,' she glowered. 'You're going to drag us on a long march tomorrow – I can't go unprepared.'

'I'll try—' began Parvateshwar.

'Don't *try*, General. *Do it*.'

Shiva couldn't control himself any longer and burst out laughing.

'What the hell are you laughing at?' Anandmayi turned to glare at Shiva.

'You'll speak to the Lord with respect, Princess,' snapped Parvateshwar.

'The *Lord*?' Anandmayi's penetrating gaze swept contemptuously over Shiva. 'So he's the one in charge? The one Daksha was allegedly showing off? What did you say that troubled my father so much that he won't talk to anyone? You don't look that threatening to me.'

'Speak with care, Princess,' advised Parvateshwar fiercely. 'You don't know who you're addressing.'

Shiva signalled for Parvateshwar to calm down, but Anandmayi was the one who required soothing.

'Whoever you are, you'll all be smashed when our Lord descends to Swadweep to destroy the evil of your kind.'

What?

'Get her out of here, Nandi,' said Parvateshwar.

'No, wait,' said Shiva. 'Anandmayi, what do you mean, "when our Lord descends to Swadweep to destroy the evil of your kind"?'

'Why should I answer you, *Parvateshwar's Lord?*'

The general moved rapidly, drawing his sword and holding the point close to Anandmayi's neck. 'When the Lord asks something, you will answer!'

'Do you always move that fast?' asked Anandmayi, her eyebrows raised saucily. 'Or can you take it slow sometimes?'

Bringing his sword-point even closer to her throat, Parvateshwar repeated, 'Answer the Lord, Princess.'

Shaking her head, Anandmayi turned towards Shiva. 'We're

waiting for our Lord, who will come to Swadweep and destroy the evil Suryavanshis.'

Deep worry-lines began to crease Shiva's handsome face. 'And who is your Lord?'

'I don't know. He hasn't shown himself yet.'

Shiva's heart sank with an unfathomable foreboding. He was profoundly afraid to ask his next question, but something inside told him that he had to ask it. 'How will you know he's your Lord?'

'Why are you so interested in this?'

'I need to know!'

Anandmayi frowned at Shiva as if he were mad. 'He won't be from the Sapt Sindhu, neither a Suryavanshi nor a Chandravanshi, but when he comes, he'll fight on our side.'

Shiva's inner voice whispered miserably that there was more to come. Clutching the armrests of his chair, he asked, 'And?'

'And,' continued Anandmayi, 'his throat will turn blue when he drinks the *Somras*.'

An audible gasp escaped Shiva as his body stiffened and the world seemed to spin. Anandmayi frowned, even more confused by the strange conversation.

Parvateshwar glowered fiercely at Anandmayi. 'You're lying, woman – admit it, you're lying!'

'Why would I—?'

Anandmayi stopped mid-sentence as she noticed Shiva's cravat-covered throat. The arrogance suddenly vanished from her face and she found her knees buckling under her. Pointing weakly, she asked, 'Why is your throat covered?'

'Take her out, Nandi,' ordered Parvateshwar.

'Who are you?' shouted Anandmayi.

Nandi and Veerbhadra tried to drag Anandmayi out, but she struggled against them with surprising strength. 'Show me your throat!' she screamed.

Grabbing her arms, Veerbhadra began to haul her backwards, but she kicked him in the groin and wrenched herself from his grasp as he fell back in pain. She faced Shiva once again. 'Who the hell *are* you?'

Shiva stared down at the table, unable to find the strength even to look at Anandmayi. He gripped his chair's armrests tightly. It felt like the only stable thing in a world spinning desperately out of control.

Veerbhadra staggered to his feet and grabbed Anandmayi's arms again while Nandi tried to subdue her with an arm around her neck. Anandmayi bit Nandi's arm brutally, and as Nandi, howling, pulled his arm away, she screamed again, 'Answer me, dammit! Who *are* you?'

Shiva met Anandmayi's tormented eyes for the briefest of moments. The pain that filled them lashed his very soul, and flames of agony burned his conscience.

Anandmayi suddenly stopped struggling. The misery in her eyes would have stunned the bravest of Meluhan soldiers. In a broken voice, she whispered, 'You're supposed to be on our side . . .'

All fight gone from her, she allowed Nandi and Veerbhadra to drag her from the tent.

Parvateshwar kept his eyes downcast. He dared not look at Shiva. He was a good Suryavanshi – he wouldn't humiliate his Lord by looking at him at his weakest moment. Sati, however, refused to leave her husband to suffer alone. She came to his side and gently caressed his face.

Shiva looked up, his eyes devastated with tears of sorrow. 'What have I done?'

Sati held Shiva tightly, pressing his throbbing head against her bosom. There was nothing she could say to alleviate the pain. All she could do was hold him.

Shiva's agonised whisper suffused the tent with his soul-deep grief. 'What have I done?'

CHAPTER 25

Island of the Individual

It took Shiva's entourage three weeks to reach the Swadweepan capital city of Ayodhya. A decrepit, winding road had eventually brought them to the Ganga, where they boarded boats and sailed that mighty and capricious river eastwards to meet the Sarayu River. Then they cruised north up the Sarayu to the city of Lord Ram's birth. It was a long, circuitous route, but the quickest, given the terrible condition of the roads in Swadweep, the 'island of the individual'.

The Meluhan soldiers' excitement was beyond compare – every Suryavanshi had heard the legends about Lord Ram's city, but no one had ever seen it. Ayodhya, literally 'the impregnable city', was built on the land first blessed by Lord Ram's sacred feet, and they expected to find a gleaming city the like of which they had never seen, an oasis of order and harmony amid the devastation the Chandravanshis had wreaked on the landscape.

They were sorely disappointed. Ayodhya turned out to be nothing like Devagiri.

At first glance, it promised much. The outer walls were thick and looked formidable, and unlike the sober grey Meluhan cities, Ayodhya's exterior had been extravagantly daubed with all the colours in God's universe, with every other brick painted a pristine white, the royal colour of the Chandravanshis. Pink and blue banners festooned the city's towers, permanent fixtures adorning the city rather than decorations for a special occasion.

The road ran parallel with the fort wall before curving sharply towards the main entrance, to prevent elephants and battering rams from getting a straight run at the mighty doors if the city were attacked. At the top of the main gates, a wonderfully ornate, horizontal crescent moon had been sculpted into the wall, below which the Chandravanshi motto was inscribed: *Shringar. Saundarya. Swatantrata — Passion. Beauty. Freedom.*

Within the outer walls, the city itself was something of a shock for the order-loving Meluhans. Krittika described the city's organisation best as 'functioning pandemonium'. Unlike Meluhan cities, Ayodhya was not built on a platform — if the Sarayu River ever flooded like the temperamental Indus did, the city would be inundated. The numerous interior fort walls, built in seven concentric circles, were surprisingly thick and sturdy, but it didn't take a general's strategic eye to see that these concentric walls hadn't been planned by a military mastermind. Rather they'd been added one after another in a haphazard manner as the city burst its seams and extended beyond the previous perimeter. Consequently there were many weak points along each wall that an enemy laying siege could easily exploit. Perhaps that was why the Chandravanshis preferred to fight their wars on far-away battlegrounds rather than trying to defend their city.

The infrastructure was a sorry indictment of the Chandravanshi penchant for debate over action. The roads were no better than dirt tracks, with one notable exception – the neatly paved and strikingly smooth Rajpath, the 'royal road', which led straight through the city from the outer wall to the opulent royal palace. All in all, the streets of Ayodhya were a far cry from the exceptionally well-planned, rigorously sign-posted, smoothly paved and tediously standardised roads of Meluhan cities.

Throughout the city, public areas of open ground had become giant slums where illegal immigrants simply pitched their tents, and the already narrow roads had been further constricted by the encroachment of the cloth tents of the homeless. Constant tension simmered between the richer home-owning class and the poor landless who lived in the slums. The emperor had legalised all encroachments established before a certain date, which meant that the inhabitants of those particular slums couldn't be removed unless the government provided alternative accommodation for them. Unfortunately the Chandravanshi government was so inefficient that not even one new house had been built for slum-dwellers in the last twelve years, and there was talk of legalising slums constructed after the original cut-off point. The encroachments, the bad roads and the poor construction combined to give the impression of a city in a state of terminal decline.

The Meluhans were outraged. What had these people done to Lord Ram's great city – or had it always been like this? Was that why Lord Ram had crossed the Sarayu River to establish his capital in far-away Devagiri, on the banks of the Saraswati?

Yet as the initial shock at the ugliness and frenzied disorder wore off, the Meluhans began to find a strange and unexpected charm in the city's constant chaos. Every Ayodhyan house was unique, unlike those in Meluhan cities where even royal palaces were built to a standard design. The Swadweepans, unencumbered by strict rules and building codes, created houses that were expressions of passion and elegance. Some structures were so grand that the engineering talent required to create them was beyond the Meluhans' imagination. The Meluhan concept of restraint meant nothing to the Swadweepans. Everything was painted in bright colours – from orange buildings to parrot-green ceilings to shocking-pink windows.

Civic-minded rich Swadweepans had created grand public gardens, temples, theatres and libraries, naming them after their family members since they had received no government assistance to build them. The Meluhans were awed by the grandeur of these structures, despite finding it strange that public buildings were named after private families. Ayodhya was a vibrant city which both disgusted and fascinated the Meluhans with its juxtaposition of exquisite beauty and poverty-stricken ugliness.

Chandravanshi dress reflected their way of life. The women wore skimpy clothes, brazen and confident in their sexuality, and the men were as fashion-conscious as their women – though Meluhans would call them dandies. The Swadweepans conducted their personal relationships as flamboyantly as they dressed, loudly expressing every emotion from passionate love to intense hatred, and everything in between. Moderation was a word that simply didn't exist in the Ayodhyan's dictionary.

It was unsurprising, perhaps, that the mercurial and emotionally charged rabble of Ayodhya scoffed at Daksha's proclaimed intention to 'reform' them. The Meluhan emperor entered a sullen city, its populace quietly lining the Rajpath and refusing to welcome the conquering force. Daksha was genuinely astonished by this reception – he had honestly expected the city's residents to welcome him with showers of flowers for finally freeing them from their evil rulers. He put their coldness down to the malign influence of the Chandravanshi royalty.

Shiva arrived a week later, and he was under no such illusions. The quiet reception he received was a vast improvement on some of the possibilities he'd anticipated. He'd expected to be attacked and vilified for not standing up for the Swadweepans, who apparently also believed in the prophecy of the Neelkanth; he thought he'd be greeted with hatred for choosing what they would consider the wrong side.

But although he wasn't as convinced as he had been that the

Chandravanshis were the evil creatures the Suryavanshis had made them out to be he was not quite ready to classify the Suryavanshis as the 'wrong side' either. Until now, he'd found the Meluhans almost without exception to be honest, decent, law-abiding people who could invariably be trusted. Shiva was deeply confused about his karma and his future course of action, and found himself sorely missing Brahaspati's keen wit and advice.

His thoughts weighing heavy on him, Shiva quickly disembarked from the curtained cart and turned towards the Chandravanshi palace. For a moment, he was startled by the grandeur of Dilipa's abode, but he quickly gathered his wits, reached for Sati's hand and began climbing the hundred steps leading up to the main palace platform. Parvateshwar trudged slowly behind them. Glancing behind them, Shiva saw Anandmayi quietly ascending the steps a little way beyond the general. She hadn't spoken to Shiva since that terrible encounter when she'd realised who he was. Her face was devoid of any expression, her eyes set on her father who was waiting at the top of the steps for Shiva and his entourage.

'Who the hell is that man?' asked an incredulous Swadweepan carpenter, held back at the edge of the palace courtyard by Chandravanshi soldiers. 'And why are our emperor and the sincere madman waiting for him on the royal platform – and in full imperial regalia, at that?'

'Sincere madman?' asked his friend.

'Oh, haven't you heard? It's the new nickname for that fool Daksha!'

The friend burst out laughing.

'Shush,' hissed an old man standing next to them. 'Don't you young people have any sense? Ayodhya's being humiliated and all you can do is crack jokes! Shame on you.'

Shiva finally reached the royal platform, where Daksha bent low with a namaste. Shiva smiled weakly and returned the greeting.

Dilipa, his eyes moist, also bent low towards Shiva. In a soft whisper, he said, 'I'm not evil, my Lord. We're *not* evil.'

'What was that?' asked Daksha, straining to hear Dilipa's whispered words.

Shiva's choked throat refused to utter a sound. Not hearing anything from Dilipa either, Daksha shook his head and said, 'My Lord, perhaps this is an opportune time to introduce you to the people of Ayodhya. I'm sure they'll mend their evil ways once they know that the Neelkanth has come to their rescue.'

Seeing her husband's anguish, Sati answered for him. 'Father, Shiva's very tired – it's been a long journey. May he rest for a little while?'

'Oh – yes, of course,' mumbled Daksha apologetically. Turning to Shiva, he said, 'I'm sorry, my Lord. Sometimes my enthusiasm gets the better of me. Why don't you rest today? We can introduce you at court tomorrow.'

Shiva briefly met Dilipa's eyes, but unable to bear his tormented gaze any longer, he looked beyond the Chandra-vanshi emperor towards the other members of his court standing at the back of the entrance platform. With the exception of the emperor's daughter, they looked as confused as the

Chandravanshis in the city below. Shiva realised that no one at court but Dilipa and Anandmayi knew his true identity – not even Dilipa's son, Bhagirath. Dilipa hadn't told a soul. Clearly, neither had Daksha, who was probably hoping to stage a grand unveiling in the presence of Shiva himself.

'My Lord.'

'Yes, Parvateshwar,' Shiva replied, his voice barely audible.

'Now that the ceremonial march is done, I'll lead the army outside the city to the camp that his Majesty Daksha's troops have already set up. I'll be back at your service within two hours.'

Shiva nodded faintly in response and watched the general trudge back down the long stairway.

Shiva had not spoken a word since their arrival in Ayodhya some hours ago other than to acknowledge the general. Now he stood quietly at the window of his chamber, staring out at the city as the afternoon sun shone down in its dazzling glory. Sati sat silently at his side, holding his hand, summoning up all the energy she had and passing it to him. Shiva's attention was focused on a grand structure right in the heart of the city that appeared to be built of white marble. For some unfathomable reason, looking at it soothed his soul. Built on the highest point in the city atop a gently sloping hill, it was clearly visible from every part of Ayodhya. Shiva wondered what made the building so important that it, not the royal palace, occupied the highest point in the city.

A loud, insistent knocking disturbed his thoughts.

'Who is it?' growled Parvateshwar, rising from his chair at the back of the chamber.

'My Lord,' came Nandi's muffled voice, 'it's Princess Anandmayi.'

Parvateshwar groaned softly before turning towards Shiva. The Neelkanth nodded.

'Let her in, Nandi,' ordered Parvateshwar.

Anandmayi entered, her smiling demeanour startling Parvateshwar, who frowned in suspicious surprise. 'How may I help you, your Highness?'

'I've told you so many times how you can help me, Parvateshwar,' teased Anandmayi. 'Perhaps if you listened to my answer rather than repeating the question again and again, we might actually get somewhere.'

Parvateshwar's reaction was a combination of embarrassment and anger.

Shiva smiled feebly, for the first time in three weeks. He was cheered a little by the fact that Anandmayi appeared to have returned to her original self.

Anandmayi turned towards Shiva with a low bow. 'The truth of the situation has just dawned on me, my Lord. I apologise for my sullenness earlier, but I was deeply troubled at the time. I thought there could only be two explanations for you being on the Suryavanshis' side: either we're evil, or you're not who we think you are and the prophecy is false. Accepting either of these explanations would destroy my soul.'

Shiva was listening attentively. He nodded for her to continue.

'But just now I realised that the prophecy isn't false,' she continued, 'and we're obviously not evil. The truth is that you're too naïve – you've been misled by the evil Suryavanshis. I'll set the record straight by showing you the goodness of our path.'

'We're *not* evil,' glowered Parvateshwar.

'Parvateshwar,' said Anandmayi with a sigh, 'I've told you before – there are much better uses for that lovely mouth of yours than talking. You shouldn't waste your breath unnecessarily.'

'Enough of your impudence, woman,' cried Parvateshwar. 'You think *we're* evil? Have you seen the way you treat your own people? Hungry eyes have followed every step of our journey. Children lie abandoned on the side of potholed highways. Desperate old women beg for alms throughout your "impregnable city", while the Swadweepan rich lead more opulent lives than a Meluhan emperor. We have a perfect society in Meluha. Perhaps the Lord is right and you're not utterly evil, but you certainly don't know how to take care of your people. Come to Meluha to see how citizens should be treated. All your lives will improve under our way of governance.'

'We're not perfect, I agree,' she argued, 'and there are many things our empire could do better – but at least we give our people freedom. They're not forced to follow some stupid laws mandated by an out-of-touch elite.'

'And you give them freedom to do what? Loot, steal, beg, kill?'

'There's no point arguing with you about our culture. Your puny mind won't be able to understand the benefits of our way of doing things.'

'I don't want to! It disgusts me to see how this empire has been managed. You have no morality, no control, no laws – it's no wonder you've contaminated yourselves by allying with the Nagas, by fighting like cowardly terrorists rather than brave warriors. You may not be evil, but your deeds certainly are!'

'Nagas? What *are* you wittering about? Do you really think us mad enough to ally with the Nagas and pollute our souls for the next seven lives? And *terrorism*? We've *never* resorted to terrorism – we've strained against our natural instincts to avoid a war with your cursed people for the last hundred years. We retreated from the border provinces and cut all ties with you. We've even learned to live with the reduced flow of the Ganga since you stole the Yamuna from us. My father told you that we had nothing to do with the attack on Mount Mandar, but you didn't believe him. And why would you? You needed an excuse to attack us again!'

'Don't lie to me,' snarled Parvateshwar, 'at least not in front of the Mahadev. Chandravanshi terrorists have been found with the Nagas.'

'My father told you that nobody under our control had anything to do with the attack on Mandar. We have *nothing* to do with the Nagas. It's possible that some Chandravanshis, just like some

Suryavanshis, could have helped the terrorists – if you'd worked with us, we might even have tracked down the criminals!'

'What rubbish is this? No Suryavanshi would ally with those monsters. And you'll have to answer for any Chandravanshis who assisted the terrorists – Swadweep is under your control, and you're responsible for the actions of all its citizens.'

'If you'd maintained diplomatic relations with Swadweep, you'd know that we're a confederacy, not an authoritarian regime. My father Dilipa is the ruler of Ayodhya, but he is just a figurehead for the other kingdoms of Swadweep. The other kings within Swadweep pay Ayodhya tribute for protection during war, but beyond that they have the freedom to run their kingdoms any way they choose.'

'So you're saying the Emperor of Swadweep doesn't run his own empire?'

'Please stop this,' begged Shiva. The argument reflected the debate raging in his own mind and he didn't want to be troubled by any more questions for which he had no answers – at least, not yet.

Parvateshwar and Anandmayi immediately fell silent.

Turning slowly towards the window again, Shiva asked, 'What's that building, Anandmayi?'

'That, my Lord,' said Anandmayi, smiling smugly at being spoken to first, 'is the Ramjanmabhoomi Temple, built at the site of Lord Ram's birthplace.'

'You built a temple to Lord Ram?' asked Parvateshwar, startled. 'But he was a Suryavanshi – your sworn enemy.'

'*We* didn't build the temple,' said Anandmayi, rolling her eyes in exasperation, 'but we have refurbished and maintained it lovingly. And what makes you think Lord Ram was our sworn enemy? He may have been tricked into following a different path, but he did a lot of good for the Chandravanshis as well. He's respected as a god in Ayodhya.'

Parvateshwar's eyes widened in shock. 'But he swore to destroy the Chandravanshis—'

'If he'd truly vowed to destroy us, we wouldn't exist today, would we? He left us unharmed because he believed we were good, and that our way of life deserved to survive.'

Deeply troubled, Parvateshwar finally ran out of arguments and fell silent.

'Do you know Lord Ram's full ceremonial name?' asked Anandmayi, pressing home her advantage.

'Of course I do,' scoffed Parvateshwar. 'Lord Ram, Suryavanshi Kshatriya of the Ikshvaku Clan, son of Dashrath and Kaushalya, husband of Sita, honoured and respected with the title of the seventh Vishnu.'

'Perfect,' said Anandmayi, beaming, 'except for one minor mistake. You missed out one small word, General. You missed the word *Chandra*. His full name was Lord Ram *Chandra*.'

Parvateshwar frowned and opened his mouth to argue, but Anandmayi continued before he could find any words: 'Yes, General, his name meant "the face of the moon". He was more Chandravanshi than you know.'

'This is typical Chandravanshi double-talk,' argued

Parvateshwar, finally gathering his wits. 'You're lost in words and names rather than deeds. Lord Ram said that only a person's karma determines his identity. The fact that his name had the word moon in it means nothing. His deeds were worthy of the sun – he was a Suryavanshi, through and through.'

'Why couldn't he have been both Suryavanshi and Chandravanshi?'

'What nonsense is that? It's not possible – it's contradictory.'

'It appears impossible to you only because your puny mind can't understand it. Contradictions are a part of nature.'

'No, they're not. The universe can't accept paradoxes. For something to be true, the opposite must be false. One scabbard can have only one sword!'

'Only if the scabbard is small. Are you saying that Lord Ram wasn't big enough to have two identities?'

'You're just playing with words now,' growled Parvateshwar, glaring angrily at Anandmayi.

Shiva had stopped listening. He turned towards the window – towards the temple. He could feel it in every cell of his body. He could feel it in his soul. He could hear the soft whisper of his inner voice.

Lord Ram will help you. He will guide you. He will soothe you. Go to him.

— 🜁 ⊙U✚⊗ —

In the third hour of the third *prahar*, Shiva stole into the chaotic Ayodhya streets by himself. He was on his way to meet Lord

Ram. Sati hadn't offered to accompany him – she knew he needed to be alone. Wearing a cravat and a loose shawl to protect him from curious eyes, and carrying his sword and shield, just in case, Shiva ambled along, taking in the strange sights and smells of the Chandravanshi capital. Nobody recognised him, and he liked it that way.

The Ayodhyans appeared to live their lives without the slightest hint of self-control. Loud, emotional voices assaulted Shiva's ears like a hideous orchestra trying to overpower his senses. The common people either laughed as if they'd just gulped down an entire bottle of wine, or fought as if their lives depended on it. Shiva was pushed and shoved on several occasions by people rushing around, hurling obscenities and calling him blind. Manic shoppers bargaining with agitated stallholders at the bazaar looked as if they would come to blows over ridiculously small amounts of money. But the harried negotiation wasn't about the cash itself; it was about the honour of striking a good bargain.

Shiva noticed a large number of couples crowded into a small garden on the side of the road, doing unspeakable things to each other with brazen disregard for the presence of voyeuristic eyes on the street or in the park itself – and he also noticed with surprise that the eyes staring from the street were not judgemental, but excited; a glaring contrast with the Meluhans, who wouldn't even embrace each other in public.

Shiva suddenly started in surprise as he felt a hand brush lightly against his buttock. He spun around to see a young woman grin back at him and wink. Before he could react, he spotted a much older woman, walking right behind her, and thinking she must be the younger woman's mother, he decided to let the indiscretion pass for fear of causing any embarrassment. As he turned, however, he felt a hand on his buttock again, this time more insistent and aggressive, and this time when he turned back, he was shocked to find it was the older woman smiling sensuously at him. Flabbergasted, he hurried down the road, escaping the bazaar before any more passes could shatter his composure completely.

As he approached the towering Ramjanmabhoomi Temple, the incessant jangle of Ayodhya faded significantly. This was a quiet residential area of the city – probably for the rich, judging by the exquisite mansions lining the wide avenues. The main road curved gently up the hill to his destination, caressing its sides in a sensuous arc. This was probably the only road in Ayodhya besides the Rajpath not pitted with potholes. Magnificent gulmohur trees flanked the road, their dazzling orange leaves lighting the path for the weary and the lost: the path leading towards answers. The path to Lord Ram.

Shiva closed his eyes and took a deep breath as anxiety gnawed at his heart. What would he find there? Peace? Answers? Would he, as he fervently hoped, learn that he'd done some good, good that wasn't visible to him right now? Or would he find out that he'd made a terrible mistake and thousands had died a senseless death as a result? Shiva opened his eyes slowly, steeled himself and began walking, softly repeating the name of the Lord.

Ram. Ram. Ram. Ram.

At a bend in the road, Shiva came across an old, shrivelled man sitting on the pavement who looked as if he hadn't eaten in weeks. A wound on his ankle had festered due to humidity and neglect, and his only clothing was a torn jute sack hung from his shoulders and tied haphazardly at his waist with a frayed hemp rope. His sinewy right hand scratched vigorously at his head, disturbing the lice, while in his weak left hand he precariously balanced a banana leaf topped with a piece of bread and gruel. The Meluhans wouldn't feed such awful fare to their animals, let alone a starving, homeless human being.

Intense anger surged through Shiva. This old man was begging – no, *suffering* – at the doors of Lord Ram's abode and nobody seemed to care. What kind of government would treat its people like this? In Meluha, government programmes ensured that there was enough food for everyone and that nobody was homeless. This old man would have been spared this humiliation if he lived in Devagiri!

Shiva's anger was suddenly washed away in a flood of positive energy as he realised that he'd found his answer. Parvateshwar was right: the Chandravanshis might not be evil, but they certainly led a wretched existence. The Suryavanshi system would improve their lives dramatically, and Parvateshwar would bring abundance and prosperity to this devastated land by honing the moribund Chandravanshi administration. Some good *would* come from this war. Perhaps he'd not made such a terrible mistake after all. He thanked Lord Ram for this insight.

But even this small consolation offered only a momentary respite for his troubled heart and soul. The old beggar noticed Shiva staring at him, and his haggard cheeks sprang to life with a smile in response to Shiva's sympathetic expression. But it wasn't the pained smile of a broken man begging for alms that Shiva had expected. It was the warm, welcoming smile of a man at peace with himself. Shiva wasn't remotely prepared for that.

The old man smiled even more warmly while raising his weak hand with great effort. 'Would you like some food, my son?'

Shiva stared at him speechlessly, utterly humbled by the mighty heart of the wretched man he'd thought was deserving of his pity and kindness.

Seeing Shiva gaping, the old man repeated, 'Would you like to eat with me, son? There's enough for two.'

Overwhelmed, Shiva still couldn't find the strength to speak. There wasn't enough food on the banana leaf for one person, so why was this man offering to share what little food he had? It didn't make sense.

Thinking Shiva might be hard of hearing, the old man spoke a little louder. 'My son, sit with me. Eat.'

Shiva pulled himself together sufficiently to shake his head slightly. 'No, thank you, sir.'

The old man's face fell immediately. 'This is good food,' he said, his eyes showing the hurt he felt. 'I wouldn't offer it to you otherwise.'

Shiva realised with horror that he'd insulted the old man's pride by treating him like a beggar. 'No, no, that's not what I meant – I know it's good food. It's just that I—'

'Then sit with me, my son,' interrupted the old man, grinning warmly once more and patting the pavement beside him.

Shiva nodded and sat down, and the old man placed the banana leaf on the ground between them. Shiva stared at the bread and watery gruel that moments ago he'd deemed unfit for human consumption. The old man looked up at Shiva, his half-blind eyes full of an inexplicable joy. 'Eat.'

Shiva picked up a small morsel of the bread, dipped it into the gruel and put it in his mouth. It slipped into his stomach easily enough, but it weighed heavily on his soul. He could feel his self-righteousness being squeezed out of him by the poor old man's generosity.

'Come on, my son. If you're going to eat so little, how will you maintain your big muscular body?'

Shiva glanced up at the old man; his shrunken arms were smaller in circumference than Shiva's wrists. The old man was taking ridiculously small bites, while moving larger portions of the bread towards Shiva. Shiva dropped his gaze, his heart sinking deeper as tears rose in his eyes. He quickly ate the portion the old man offered. The food was gone in no time.

Freedom: freedom for the wretched also to have dignity. Meluha's system of governance doesn't allow its citizens that.

'Are you full now, my son?'

Shiva nodded slowly, still not daring to look into the old man's eyes.

'Good. Now go – it's a long walk to the temple.'

Shiva finally looked up, bewildered by the beggar's astounding generosity. The old man's sunken cheeks broadened with an affectionate smile. He was on the verge of starvation, yet he'd given practically all his food to a stranger. Shiva cursed his own heart for the blasphemy he'd committed: the blasphemy of thinking he could actually 'save' such a man. Shiva found himself bending forward, obeying the volition of a greater power. He extended his arms and touched the old man's feet.

The old man raised his good hand and touched Shiva's head tenderly, blessing him. 'May you find what you're looking for, my son.'

Shiva stood, his heart heavy with guilt, his throat choked with bitter remorse, his leaden soul's self-righteousness crushed by the old man's munificence. He had his answer: he'd made a terrible mistake. These people weren't evil.

CHAPTER 26

The Question of Questions

The road leading to the Ramjanmabhoomi Temple hugged the gently sloping hill, ending its journey at the entrance to Lord Ram's abode. The hilltop afforded a breathtaking view of the city below, but Shiva didn't see it. Nor did he notice the magnificent construction of the gigantic temple – poetry in white marble, crafted by the gods' own architect – or the gorgeously landscaped gardens surrounding it. A grand staircase leading up to the main temple platform somehow managed to be both awe-inspiring and inviting. Colossal ornate reliefs in sober blue and grey marble had been engraved on the platform itself, while elegantly carved pillars supported an elaborate yet tasteful ceiling of blue marble. Lord Ram's favourite time of day was the morning, and accordingly a fresco of the morning sky adorned the entire ceiling. Above, the temple spire shot upwards to a height of almost three hundred feet, like a giant namaste to the gods. The Swadweepans, to their credit, hadn't imposed their own garish sensibilities on the temple, and its restrained beauty was entirely in keeping with Lord Ram's rather more sober taste.

But Shiva noticed none of this. Nor did he wonder at the intricately carved statues in the inner sanctum. Lord Ram's idol was placed in the centre, surrounded by his beloveds. To the right was his loving wife Sita, and to the left his devoted brother Lakshman. At their feet, on his knees, was Lord Ram's most fervent and favourite disciple, Hanuman, of the Vayuputra tribe, 'the sons of the wind god'.

Shiva couldn't find the strength to meet Lord Ram's eyes, fearing the verdict he would receive. He crouched behind a pillar, resting against it, grieving. At last his intense feelings of guilt overwhelmed him and the tears he'd long been holding back flowed, flooding from his eyes as though a dam had burst. Biting into his balled fist, overcome by remorse, he curled his legs up against his chest and rested his head on his knees.

Drowning in his sorrow, Shiva didn't feel the compassionate hand on his shoulder at first. Getting no reaction, the hand gently squeezed his shoulder. Shiva recognised the touch, but he kept his head bowed. He didn't want to appear weak, to be seen with tears in his eyes. The gentle hand, old and worn with age, withdrew quietly and its owner stepped away a short distance to wait patiently until Shiva had composed himself. When the time was right, the old man came forward and sat down in front of him.

Sombrely, Shiva offered a formal namaste to the pandit, who

looked almost exactly like the pandits Shiva had met at the Brahma temple at Meru and the Mohan temple at Mohan Jo Daro. He sported the familiar flowing white beard and mane of white hair. Like the other pandits he wore a saffron *dhoti* and *angvastram*, and his wizened face bore the same calm, welcoming smile. The only significant difference was this pandit's ample girth.

'Is it really so bad?' he asked, his eyes narrowed and his head tilted slightly in a typically Indian expression of empathy.

Shiva shut his eyes and lowered his head again. The pandit waited patiently for his reply. 'You don't know what I've done—'

'I do.'

Shiva looked up at the pandit, his eyes full of surprise and shame.

'I know what you've done, O Neelkanth,' said the pandit, 'and I ask again, is it really so bad?'

'Don't call me the Neelkanth,' he snapped, glaring at the pandit. 'I don't deserve the title. I have the blood of thousands on my hands.'

'Many more than thousands have died,' said the pandit, 'probably hundreds of thousands. But do you really think they'd still be alive if you hadn't been around? Is the blood really on your hands?'

'Of course it is! It was my stupidity that led to this war. I had no idea what I was doing. I wasn't worthy of the responsibility thrust upon me and hundreds of thousands have perished as a result!' He curled his fist and pounded his forehead, desperately trying to soothe the throbbing heat on his brow.

The pandit stared in mild surprise at the deep red blotch on Shiva's forehead, right between his eyes. It wasn't the colour of a blood clot but a much deeper hue, almost black. The pandit controlled his surprise and remained silent. Now wasn't the right time to comment on it.

'And it's all because of me,' moaned Shiva, his eyes moistening again. 'It's all my fault.'

'Soldiers are Kshatriyas, my friend,' said the pandit, a picture of calm. 'Nobody forces them to die. They choose their path knowing the risks *and* the potential glory that come with that choice. The Neelkanth isn't the kind of person on whom responsibility can be thrust against his will. You *chose* this. You were *born* for it.'

Shiva's startled eyes met the pandit's, silently asking, *I was born for it?*

The pandit ignored the question in Shiva's eyes. 'Everything happens for a reason. If you're going through this turmoil, there's a divine plan behind it.'

'What divine reason can there possibly be for so many deaths?'

'The destruction of evil? Wouldn't you say that's a very important reason?'

'But I didn't destroy evil,' yelled Shiva. 'These people aren't evil – *they're just different*. Being different isn't evil.'

The pandit's lips curled into his typically enigmatic smile. 'Exactly. They're not evil, they're just different. You've come to that realisation very quickly, my friend – a lot sooner than the previous Mahadev.'

For a moment Shiva was perplexed by the pandit's words, then he said, 'Lord Rudra?'

'Yes, Lord Rudra.'

'But he did destroy evil – he destroyed the *Asuras*.'

'And who said the *Asuras* were evil?'

'I read it—' Shiva stopped mid-sentence. He finally understood.

'Yes,' said the smiling pandit, 'now you understand. Just as the Suryavanshis and the Chandravanshis see each other as evil, so did the *Devas* and the *Asuras*. If you read a book written by the *Devas*, how do you think the *Asuras* are going to be portrayed?'

'So they were similar to today's Suryavanshis and Chandravanshis?'

'More alike than you can imagine. Just like the Chandravanshis and the Suryavanshis, the *Devas* and the *Asuras* represented two balancing life-forces – a duality.'

'What do you mean by "duality"?'

'Duality is one of the many perspectives of the universe, like light and dark; or positive energy and negative energy. One of the dualities is the masculine and the feminine: the *Asuras*, like the Suryavanshis, are the masculine; the *Devas* and the Chandravanshis are the feminine. The names change, but the life-forces they embody remain the same. They will always exist. There's no way that either can be destroyed – if they are, the universe will implode.'

'And each sees their fight with the other as the eternal struggle between good and evil?'

'Exactly.' The pandit beamed, pleased that he had grasped such difficult concepts even though he was so obviously distressed. 'But they haven't been fighting all the time – there have been long periods of cooperation as well. However, in times of strife, which usually arise when there is evil at work in the world, they find it easiest to blame their troubles on each other. In this way, a difference of opinion between two dissimilar ways of life becomes portrayed as a fight between good and evil. Just because the Chandravanshis are different from the Suryavanshis doesn't mean that they're evil. Why do you think the Neelkanth has to be an outsider?'

'So that he wouldn't be biased towards any one point of view,' said Shiva as a veil lifted from his eyes.

'Exactly: the Neelkanth has to be above all this, devoid of any bias.'

'But I *wasn't* beyond bias – I was convinced that the Chandravanshis are evil. Maybe Anandmayi's right to say I'm naïve and easily misled.'

'Don't be so hard on yourself, my friend. You couldn't drop from the sky knowing everything, could you? You had to enter from one side or the other, and you couldn't help but be influenced by their viewpoint. You've realised your error early; Lord Rudra didn't see his until it was almost too late – he nearly destroyed the *Asuras* completely before he grasped the simple fact that they weren't evil, just different.'

'*Nearly* destroyed them? You mean some *Asuras* still exist?'

The pandit smiled mysteriously. 'That's a conversation for another time, my friend. The point you need to understand is that you're not the first Mahadev to be misled, and you won't be the last. Imagine how guilty Lord Rudra must have felt.'

Shiva kept quiet, his eyes downcast. The knowledge that Lord Rudra felt the same guilt as he did didn't reduce the shame that racked his soul.

The pandit continued, 'You made the best decision you could under the circumstances. I know this will be cold comfort, but it's not easy to be the Neelkanth. You'll have to bear the burden of this guilt – I know what kind of person you are, and it *will* be a heavy burden. Your challenge is not to find a way to ignore the guilt or the pain, but to stay true to your karma, to your duty, *in spite of* the pain. That's the fate and the duty of a Mahadev.'

'But how am I to destroy evil if I don't even know what evil is?'

'Who said your job is to destroy evil?'

Shiva glared at the pandit. He hated the irritating word-games they all seemed to love.

Glimpsing the anger in Shiva's eyes, the pandit clarified immediately, 'Evil's strength is overestimated, my friend – it's not so difficult to annihilate. All it takes is for a few good men to decide that they will fight it. Practically every time evil has raised its ugly head, it's met the same fate: it's been destroyed.'

'Then why am I required?'

'You're required to fulfil the most crucial task of all: to answer the most important question.'

'And what would that be?'

'*What* is evil?'

'*What is evil?*'

'Yes. Men have fought many wars,' said the pandit, 'and they'll fight many more in the future – that's the way of the world. Only a Mahadev can convert one of those wars into a battle between good and evil. Only a Mahadev can recognise evil and lead men against it, before evil grows strong enough to extinguish all life.'

'But how do I recognise evil?'

'I can't help you there, my friend; I'm not the Mahadev. You must find your own answer to that question. But you have the heart and the mind to succeed. Keep them open and evil will appear before you.'

'Evil will *appear*?'

'Indeed,' the pandit explained, 'evil has a relationship with you – it'll come to you. You have to keep your mind and your heart open so that you recognise it when it appears. I've only one suggestion: don't be hasty in trying to recognise evil. Wait for it. It *will* come to you.'

Shiva frowned and looked down, trying to absorb the strange conversation. He finally turned towards Lord Ram's idol, seeking some direction. Instead of the judgemental eyes he expected, he saw a warm, encouraging smile.

'Your journey isn't over, my friend – it's only just begun. You have to keep walking, otherwise evil will triumph.'

Shiva's tears dried up. His burden wasn't any lighter, but now he felt strong enough to carry it. He knew he had to keep walking to the very end. He looked up at the pandit and smiled weakly. 'Who are you?'

The pandit smiled. 'I know you've been promised the answer to that question, and a vow by one of us is honoured by all. I won't break it. We are the Vasudevs.' He held up a hand and answered Shiva's inevitable question before he could ask it. 'Each Vishnu leaves behind a tribe entrusted with two missions. The first is to help the next Mahadev, if and when he comes. The second is that one of us will become the next Vishnu, whenever we are required to do so. The seventh Vishnu, Lord Ram, entrusted this task to his faithful lieutenant, Lord Vasudev, and we are his followers. We are the tribe of Vasudev.'

Shiva stared at the pandit as he absorbed the implications of this information. He frowned as one consequence suddenly occurred to him. 'Did the Mahadevs also leave some tribes behind? Did Lord Rudra?'

The pandit smiled, pleased by Shiva's intelligence. His brother pandit at Mohan Jo Daro was correct: *this man is truly capable of being a Mahadev.*

'Lord Rudra did indeed leave behind a tribe – the tribe of Vayuputra.'

The name sounded oddly familiar to Shiva, but before he

could ask another question, the pandit placed his hand on Shiva's shoulder.

'Leave that for another time, my friend. I think we've spoken enough for today. Go home. You need your good wife's comforting embrace. Tomorrow is another day, and your mission can wait until then. For now, go home.'

Shiva smiled — an enigmatic smile, out of character with his usual simple Tibetan ways. But he'd become an Indian now. He leaned forward to touch the pandit's feet and the pandit placed his hand on Shiva's head to bless him, quietly chanting, '*Vijayibhav. Jai Guru Vishwamitra. Jai Guru Vashishta.*'

Shiva accepted the blessings with grace, then got up and walked towards the temple steps. At the edge of the platform, he turned around to look at the pandit once again. He was on his haunches, touching his head reverentially to the ground where Shiva had just been sitting. Shiva smiled and shook his head slightly. He looked beyond the pandit and gazed intently at the idol of Lord Ram. He put his hands together in a namaste and paid his respects to the Lord.

My burden isn't any lighter, but I feel strong enough to bear it, he thought.

He turned and started descending the long stairway.

He was surprised to find Sati in the courtyard below, leaning against the statue of an *apsara* in the middle of the square. He smiled. There was nobody in the world he would rather have seen at that moment.

Walking towards her, he said teasingly, 'Are you always going to follow me around?'

'I know when you need to be alone,' said Sati, smiling, 'and when you need me.'

Suddenly Shiva froze as he glimpsed a robe flapping behind the trees, a short distance from Sati. The light evening breeze had given away the skulking man's position. Sati followed Shiva's gaze and turned around to see a robed figure wearing a *Holi* masquerade mask emerge from behind the trees.

It's him!

Shiva's heart was suddenly racing. He was still a considerable distance away from Sati, and the Naga was too close for comfort. The three stood rooted, assessing the situation, each evaluating the options. Sati moved first. Shifting quickly, she pulled a knife from the sheath at her waist and flung it at the Naga. The Naga barely stirred, but the knife just missed him and slammed hard into the tree behind him, sinking hilt-deep into the wood.

Shiva moved his hand slowly towards his sword.

The Naga reached behind him and yanked the knife out of the tree – but instead of throwing it at Sati or Shiva, he tied it tightly to his right wrist with a cloth band. Then he began to move, and quickly.

'Sati!' screamed Shiva as he drew his sword and started sprinting towards his wife, pulling his shield in place as he ran.

. . . To be continued in *The Secret of the Nagas*

Glossary

Agni   God of fire

Agnipariksha   Trial by fire

angvastram   Cloth for draping over the shoulders

Arishtanemi   Elite Meluhan soldiers

Asura   Demon

Ayurvedic   Derived from Ayurved, an ancient Indian form of medicine

Ayushman bhav   May you live long

Chandravanshi   Descendants of the moon

Chaturanga   Ancient Indian game which was the basis of the modern game of chess

chillum   Clay pipe, usually used to smoke marijuana

choti   Braid, knotted tuft of hair at the crown of the head

Construction of royal court platform   The description here of the court platform is a possible explanation for the mysterious multiple-column buildings made of brick discovered at Indus Valley sites, usually next to the public baths, which many historians suppose could have been granaries

daivi astra   *Daivi* = divine; *astra* = weapon. A term used in ancient Hindu epics to describe weapons of mass destruction

Deva   God

dharma   Literally translates as 'religion'. But in traditional Hindu custom it means far more than that. The word encompasses holy, right, knowledge, right living, tradition and the natural order of the universe and duty. Essentially, *dharma* refers to everything that can be classified as 'good' in the universe

dharmayudh   Holy war

dhobi   Washerman

dhoti   Piece of material tied around the waist and covering most of the leg

divyadrishti   Divine sight

dumru   A small, hand-held percussion instrument

Guruji   Guru = Teacher; ji = a term of respect, added to a name or title

gurukul   The family of the Guru or the teacher. In ancient times, also used to denote 'school'

Har Har Mahadev!   The rallying cry of all of Lord Shiva's devotees. I believe it means 'All of us are Mahadevs'

Hariyupa   This city is presently known as Harappa. A note on the cities of Meluha (or, as we call it, the Indus Valley civilisation): historians and researchers have consistently marvelled at the fixation that the Indus Valley civilisation seemed to have for water and hygiene. In fact, historian M. Jansen used the term *wasserluxus* (water splendour) to describe their magnificent obsession with the physical and symbolic aspects of water, a term Gregory Possehl builds upon in his brilliant book, *The Indus Civilisation – A Contemporary Perspective*. In *The Immortals of Meluha*, the obsession with water is shown to arise from its properties for cleansing toxic sweat and urine, the release of which invariably followed the consumption of *Somras*. Historians have also marvelled at the sophisticated standardisation in the Indus Valley civilisation. One of the examples of this is their bricks, which across the entire civilisation, seem to have similar proportions and specifications

Holi   Festival of colours

Indra   The god of the sky and believed to be King of the gods

Jai Guru Vishwamitra   Glory to the teacher Vishwamitra

Jai Guru Vashishta Glory to the teacher Vashishta. Only two Suryavanshis had the privilege of having both Guru Vashishta and Guru Vishwamitra as their teachers, namely Lord Ram and Lord Lakshman

Jai Shri Ram Glory to Lord Ram

janau A ceremonial thread tied from the shoulders, across the torso; one of the symbols of knowledge in ancient India. Later, it was corrupted to become a caste symbol to denote those born as Brahmins as opposed to those achieving knowledge through their efforts

karma Duty and deeds; also, the sum of a person's actions in this and previous births, believed to affect his or her future fate

karmasaathi Fellow traveller in karma or duty

kathak Type of traditional Indian dance

kulhads Mud cups

Mahadev *Maha* = great, *Dev* = god. Hence Mahadev means the greatest god or the God of Gods. I believe that there were many 'destroyers of evil', a few of whom were so great that they would be called 'Mahadev'. Amongst the Mahadevs were Lord Rudra and Lord Shiva

Manu Those interested in the historical validity of the South Indian origin theory of Manu should read Graham Hancock's path-breaking book, *Underworld*.

mausi Mother's sister, considered almost equivalent to a mother

Mehragarh Modern archaeologists believe that Mehragarh is the original site of the Indus Valley civilisation. Mehragarh represents a sudden burst of civilised living, without archaeological evidence of a gradual progression to it. Hence, those who established Mehragarh were either immigrants or refugees

Meluha The land of pure life, the land ruled by the Suryavanshi kings; the area we in the modern world situate the Indus Valley civilization

Nagas Serpent people

namaste An ancient Indian greeting. Spoken with the open palms of both hands joined together. Three words combined: *Namah*, *Astu* and *Te* – meaning 'I bow to you'. 'Namaste' can be used as both 'Hello' and 'Goodbye'

nirvana   Enlightenment; freedom from the cycle of rebirths

oxygen/anti-oxidants theory   Modern research backs this. Interested readers can peruse the article 'A Radical Proposal' by Kathryn Brown in *Scientific American*, vol. 282, no. 6, (June 2000)

pandit   Priest

Parmatma   The ultimate soul, or the sum of all souls. The Almighty

Patallok   The Underworld

Pawan dev   God of the winds

Pitratulya   A man who is 'like a father'

prahar   Four slots of six hours each into which the day was divided by the ancient Hindus; the first *prahar* began at midnight

puja   Prayer

rajat   Silver

Ram Chandra   *Ram* = face; *chandra* = moon. Hence Ram Chandra is 'Face of the Moon'

Ram Rajya   The rule of Ram

Rangbhoomi   Literally, the ground of colour; in ancient times, stadia where sports performances and public functions would be carried out

rangolis   Traditional geometric designs made with coloured powders or flowers as a sign of welcome

Rishi   Man of knowledge

sanyas   Mendicants, often in seclusion, having renounced materialism and worldly pleasures in pursuit of godhood. In ancient India, householders of advanced age, having fulfilled their worldly responsibilities, often sought Sanyas

Sapt Sindhu   Land of the seven rivers – Indus, Saraswati, Yamuna, Ganga, Sarayu, Brahmaputra and Narmada. Sapt Sindhu was the ancient name of North India

Saptrishi   One of the 'Group of Seven *Rishis*'

Saptrishi Uttradhikaris   Successors of the Saptrishis

Shakti devi   Mother Goddess; also, goddess of power and energy

shamiana   Canopy

shloka   Couplet

Shri   Polite term of address, as in 'Shri Jhooleshwarji'; and *Jai Shri Ram!*', 'Glory to Lord Ram'

Shudhikaran   Purification ceremony

Somras   Drink of the gods

Sutlej   River known as the Dhrishadvati in ancient times. Many believe that the Sutlej was the main Saraswati river and when Yamuna, its tributary, merged into it, it became the mighty river of yore

svarna   Gold

Swadweep   The 'island of the individual'. This is the land ruled by the Chandravanshi kings

Swaha   Legend has it that Lord Agni's wife is named Swaha. Hence it pleases Lord Agni, the god of fire, if a disciple takes his wife's name while worshipping the sacred fire. Another interpretation of *swaha* is that it means 'offering of self'

tamra   Bronze

thali   Plate

varjish graha   Exercise hall

Varun   God of the water and the seas

Vijayibhav   May you be victorious

vikarma   Carrier of bad fate

Vishnu   The protector of the world and propagator of good. I believe that it is an ancient Hindu title for the greatest of leaders who would be remembered as the mightiest of gods

yagna   Sacrificial fire ceremony

Acknowledgements

They say that writing is a lonely profession. They lie. An outstanding group of people have come together to make this book possible, and I would like to thank them.

Preeti, my wife, a rare combination of beauty, brains and spirit, who assisted and advised me through all aspects of this book.

My family: Usha, Vinay, Bhavna, Himanshu, Meeta, Anish, Donetta, Ashish, Shernaz, Smita, Anuj, Ruta. A cabal of supremely positive individuals who encouraged, pushed and supported me through the long years of this project.

My UK publisher, Jo Fletcher, for believing in the story of a debut writer. I hope that I'm able to honour her trust.

My first publisher and agent, Anuj Bahri, for his absolute confidence in the Shiva Trilogy.

Rashmi Pusalkar, Sagar Pusalkar and Vikram Bawa for the exceptional cover.

You, the reader, for the leap of faith in picking up the book of a debut author.

And lastly, I believe that this story is a blessing to me from Lord Shiva. Humbled by this experience, I find myself a different man today, less cynical and more accepting of different world views. I was an atheist, but now I find beauty in all religions. Hence, most importantly, I would like to bow to Lord Shiva, for blessing me so abundantly, far beyond what I deserve.

Amish, 2008, 2012